KILLING THE BEASTS

KILLING THE BEASTS

Chris Simms

ISIS
LARGE PRINT
Oxford

First published in Great Britain 2005
by
Orion, an imprint of the Orion Publishing Group Ltd.

Published in Large Print 2006 by ISIS Publishing Ltd.,
7 Centremead, Osney Mead, Oxford OX2 0ES
by arrangement with
the Orion Publishing Group Ltd.

British Library Cataloguing in Publication Data
Simms, Chris
    Killing the beasts. – Large print ed.
    1. Serial murder investigation – England –
    Manchester – Fiction
    2. Police – England – Manchester – Fiction
    3. Advertising executives – England –
    Manchester – Fiction
    4. Detective and mystery stories
    5. Large type books
    I. Title
    823.9'2 [F]

ISBN 0–7531–7481–2 (hb)
ISBN 0–7531–7482–0 (pb)

Printed and bound in Great Britain by
T. J. International Ltd., Padstow, Cornwall

Once again, to Chops

My thanks to Nessy

"... the cracked mind of the schizophrenic may let in light which does not enter the intact minds of many sane people ..."

R.D. Laing, 1927–1989

You live, you consume, you die.

Acknowledgements

This novel would never have seen the light of day without the faith shown by Gregory & Company and the expertise of Jane Wood at Orion. Huge thanks must also go to, in no order of preference:

Dr Allan Jamieson for providing me with so much information on forensics and toxicology

Aidan O'Rourke, whose photographs of Manchester allowed me to describe so much of the city during the Commonwealth Games

Simon Roberts for showing me around a Vutek 5300

Paul Rourke for explaining the outdoor advertising market to me

Dr Ian Collyer for describing the process of suffocation

Claire and Paul for letting me look at their holiday snaps from the Seychelles!

Prologue

Leaning forward on the sofa, she gratefully accepted the stick of gum, unwrapped it and then folded it into her mouth. "Thanks," she said breathlessly, looking expectantly at her visitor and eagerly chewing.

"My pleasure," came the reply from the smartly dressed man sitting opposite her. They continued looking at each other for a moment longer. "Now, if you could just get . . ."

"Oh God, yes, sorry! It's upstairs." She jumped to her feet. "I'm all excited. Sorry."

He smiled. "No problem."

She almost skipped across the room, then ran up the stairs. While she was gone the man stood up, walked over to her living room window and checked the street outside. By the time she returned he was sitting down once again.

"Here," she said, handing him a small booklet.

"Great." He looked up at her with a slightly embarrassed expression. "Do you mind if I have a cup of tea before we get started?"

"Oh!" She jumped up again, her dressing gown falling slightly open to reveal a flash of upper thigh. "I'm so rude. Sorry. Milk? Sugar?"

"Milk and two sugars, thanks."

Flustered, she paced quickly down the short corridor to the kitchen, bare feet slapping against the lino as she crossed the room. She plucked two mugs from the dirty crockery piled up in the sink and quickly washed them out. As she waited for the kettle to boil she jigged from foot to foot, occasionally taking a deep breath and running her hands through her spiky blonde hair.

A few minutes later she walked back in, a red flush now evident on her throat and cheeks. "Here you go." She placed a mug decorated with a cartoon snail on the low table in front of the man's knees. Now furiously chewing on the gum, she went to sit down again but, on impulse, veered towards the hi-fi system in the corner and turned up the music.

"God, I feel like I could dance," she said urgently, blowing her breath out and running her fingers through her hair once again. "Is it hot in here? Are you hot?"

The man looked around the room as if heat was a visible thing. "No," he replied with a little shake of his head.

"I feel hot," she said, placing her mug on the table, then waving one hand a little too energetically at her cheek and pulling distractedly at the neck of her dressing gown. The man kept his head lowered, pretending to search for a pen in his jacket pocket.

The girl went to sit down, stumbling against the leg of the coffee table. "Whoops!" she said with a strange giggle, though panic was beginning to show in her eyes. "I . . . I'm dizzy."

The room had begun to shift in and out of focus and her breath wouldn't come properly. She leaned forward and tried to steady herself by putting one hand on the arm of the sofa.

The man watched impassively.

Now visibly distressed, she attempted a half turn to sit down, but her coordination was going and she missed the sofa, crashing onto the carpet. As she lay on her back, her eyes rolled up into her head and then closed completely.

The man calmly got to his feet and put his briefcase on the table. After entering the combination for the lock, he opened it up and removed a long pair of stainless steel pincers from inside.

CHAPTER
ONE

30 October 2002

Jon Spicer was driving back to the station when he heard the Community Support Officer's call for help on his police radio. The CSO said he was outside a house in which a corpse had just been discovered. He said the dead girl's mother was still inside, refusing to leave her daughter's body. He went on to explain to the operator that his patrol partner was in the kitchen, trying to comfort her. His voice was high and panicky.

When the address in Berrybridge Road was read out Jon realized he was just a few streets away. Telling the operator he would attend the scene, Jon turned off the main road, cut down a side street and pulled up outside the house.

As he got out of his car and straightened his tie, the sight of a very young and nervous-looking officer confronted him. The officer was trying to reason with an irate woman, who stood with one hand rocking a buggy, stout legs planted firmly apart. As the officer repeated that she wasn't allowed past, the red-faced toddler in the buggy leaned back, shut its eyes and started to bawl.

"You can't stop me getting in my own sodding house," the woman said, holding another chocolate button in front of the angry infant's face. "The kid wants his lunch — you can hear, can't you?" In an attempt to keep the cold autumnal breeze off him, she began tucking the tattered blanket around his legs, "It's all right, Liam."

Crafty little shit, thought Jon Spicer, noticing how he immediately stopped crying when the button appeared. If his eyes were shut in genuine distress, he wouldn't have known the button was there. Jon had accepted long ago that deviousness was as much a part of human make-up as kindness or joy. What always amazed him was how early people appeared to learn the process of manipulation.

"Sorry madam, we won't be much longer," Jon intervened, a placatory tone in his voice. Hoping that, if he and Alice had the baby they were trying for, it didn't turn out like that one, he guided the CSO out of earshot. "Hello. My name's Jon Spicer."

The young officer glanced at Jon's warrant card, saw his rank, and replied, "CSO Whyte and I'm glad to see you, sir."

"You said on the radio that you heard wailing noises from inside the house. Then what?"

He took out his notebook as if in court. "Yes, that was at 9.55 a.m. We proceeded up the driveway to the front door, which we found to be ajar. On receiving no response from the person in distress within the property, we proceeded inside and found a middle-aged woman sitting on the floor of the living room hugging a deceased woman of around twenty. My patrol partner, CSO Payne, entered the room and crouched down to

6

check for a pulse. At that point she noticed thick white matter at the back of the deceased woman's mouth." He looked up and breaking from his notes, said, "It was hanging open you see, though I didn't catch sight of it myself. When we separated the mother from the body, the dead girl's head lay back on the carpet and I couldn't see in."

Jon nodded. "So you called for assistance. And no one has been in there except you and your patrol partner?"

"Yes, that's correct, sir."

"And this woman has confirmed the deceased is her daughter and that her daughter lives in the house?"

"Yes."

"And no one else lives there?"

"That's correct."

"OK, good work. Well done."

A smile broke out momentarily across the young man's face. Then, remembering the gravity of the situation, he reorganized his features into an expression of appropriate seriousness.

The toddler started its bawling once again. His mum gave in and shoved the entire packet of chocolate buttons into his hands. The crying immediately stopped and Jon thought: another victory to the little people. "So, we've just got to keep Lucifer and his mum, Mrs Beelzebub, at bay for a bit longer," he murmured, turning back to the woman.

"OK madam. I'm afraid, because you share a driveway with your neighbour's house — and she's died in what could be suspicious circumstances — I'm having to declare the driveway and front gardens a designated crime scene. Have you a friend you could stay with just while we search this area in front of the house?"

"Pissing hell," said the woman, pulling a mobile from the pocket of her padded jacket and dialling a number. "Janine? It's me, Sue. That little blonde ravehead next door won't be keeping me awake with any more loud music. She's turned up dead and the police won't let me up the driveway and into my own frigging house. Can I come round for a cuppa and to give our Liam his lunch? Cheers."

"Thanks very much, madam," Jon said, making a mental note of the ravehead description. "If I can have your number we'll call as soon as access is possible."

He jotted it down and she trundled moodily off up the road, the buggy's wheels picking up bits of sodden brown leaves littering the street.

"Right," said Jon, looking at the house. "Have you checked the rest of the property?"

"No," said CSO Whyte, looking alarmed that he'd failed in his duty.

"That's fine," said Jon. But, having been caught by surprise on a recent murder investigation when the offender had still been hiding in the upstairs of the house, Jon was taking no chances. "What's your patrol partner's name again?"

"CSO Margaret Payne. She's comforting the girl's mother in the kitchen."

Jon trod carefully across the patchy lawn, eyes on the driveway for any suspicious objects. When he reached the front doorstep he called over his shoulder, "CSO Whyte, only people with direct permission from me are allowed past, understood?"

"Yes sir," he replied, checking down the street as if there was a danger of being charged by a curious crowd.

Pushing from his mind the information he had been given by the officer, Jon turned his attention to the front door. He saw that there were no signs of a forced entry. He stepped into the hallway, keeping his feet as close to the skirting board as possible. Immediately he was struck by an odd smell — sharp and slightly fruity. For some reason he was reminded of DIY superstores. As he made his way along the hall he examined the carpet for anything unusual. Reaching the doorway to the front room he glanced in. The body of a young white female with bleached spiky hair lay partially on its side by the coffee table. Her pale pink dressing gown was crumpled up around her legs and had partly fallen open at the front, revealing her left breast. He didn't know if it was the lack of obvious injuries, but she didn't look like she was dead. Unconscious perhaps, but not dead.

He carried on into the kitchen where CSO Payne was sitting, holding the mother's hand across the table. Aware that a six-foot-four stranger with a beaten-up face suddenly stepping into the room could prove unsettling for both women, Jon gently coughed before quietly announcing, "Hello, my name is Jon Spicer. I'm a detective with Greater Manchester Police."

The woman lowered a damp handkerchief and looked up at him. Her face had that emptiness which shock and grief instils, but her eyes were alert. He felt them flickering over his face, settling for a second on the lump in the bridge of his nose, which had been broken in a rugby match.

"Could I ask your name, please?" he continued.

"Diane Mather," she whispered, reaching out and taking a sip of tea from a mug with a snail on it.

"OK Diane," said Jon, walking round the table and checking the back door. A bolt was slid across the top and a key was in the lock. "Has anyone touched this door?" he asked them both.

CSO Payne answered no and he looked at Diane, who also shook her head.

"And have you been in any other parts of the house apart from the hallway, here and the front room?"

"No." Now she was watching him a little more closely.

Jon walked from the kitchen. Carefully he climbed the stairs, pausing when his head was level with the landing to check where the doors were. The first led into a little bathroom: no one behind the shower curtain. The next was the spare room, only just big enough for a clothes horse that was adorned with vest tops, socks and knickers. The final room was the main bedroom, fairly tidy except for the middle drawer of the chest in the corner. It hung half open, and a few photo albums and booklets lay haphazardly on the corner of the bed, as if dumped there in a hurry. Jon checked under the bed and in the wardrobe. Satisfied no one else was in the house, he walked over to the bedside table and looked in the ashtray. Amongst the Marlboro Light cigarette butts were a few crumpled bits of foil, dried brown crusts on one side. A plastic tube lay next to the small alarm clock.

Jon shook his head. From his earliest days as a uniformed officer, he had watched as more and more drugs crept into Manchester. Now, along with the alcohol riots on Friday and Saturday nights, they were dealing with the devastating effects that crack, heroin, speed and God knew what else were having on people's lives.

At the window he looked down to the road below and saw the CSOs' supervisor had arrived. He went back down the stairs and headed outside.

"Sergeant Evans," the older man said, shaking Jon's hand over the police tape now cordoning off the driveway and front garden.

"DI Spicer, MISU. I was just passing when I heard the radio call."

The sergeant nodded. "So, we have a body inside?"

"Yup," Jon replied. "Apparently her throat is blocked with a load of white stuff." Jon looked at CSO Whyte. "Could it not have been saliva? An allergic reaction or something?"

The officer looked at him as if he had asked a rhetorical question and was about to supply the answer.

Sergeant Evans then dropped a question into the silence. "When CSO Payne checked for a pulse, did she say how cold the body felt?"

CSO Whyte thought for a second. "No. She was trying to get the mother away from the body when she spotted the white stuff . . ." Abruptly, he stopped talking.

"What?" Jon prompted.

The officer stumbled slightly with his words. "She didn't actually check for a pulse. But the mum — she kept on saying, 'She's dead. She's dead.' So we just sort of assumed —"

"Jesus Christ," said Jon. He went to his car, grabbed a pair of latex gloves from inside and hurried back into the house. In the hallway he spotted a pile of women's magazines by the telephone. One by one he laid them across the living room floor, creating a series of stepping stones that enabled him to get to the girl without treading on the carpet.

As he got closer to her, he noticed that the strange smell was getting stronger. As he'd noted before, the dressing gown was crumpled, but he couldn't tell whether she had been assaulted, dragged there or the disturbance to her clothing was from where her mother had been hugging her.

He crouched down and checked for a pulse. The skin was cold to the touch. He let out a sigh, then examined the rest of her more closely.

No defence wounds to her forearms or hands, no obvious sign of any injury at all. He leaned in for a closer look at her fingers. Apart from being bluish in colour, the nails were fine — no debris under them or damage caused by a struggle.

Next he looked at her face. Her eyes were shut, a few small red dots around them. Mouth slightly open, lips also a faint blue. No blood, saliva or vomit on her lips. No bruising to her throat. Getting up he made his way back across the magazines and into the kitchen. "CSO Payne," he said, pointing to her utility belt, "could I borrow your torch please?"

In the front room he switched it on and directed the beam into the girl's mouth. Peering in, he saw the back of her throat was completely clogged with something white and viscous. The substance had completely blocked her airways. Death by suffocation? Some sort of lung purge or bizarre vomit?

He bent forward so his head was just above the carpet. Holding the torch to one side he swept the beam backwards and forwards across the floor, looking to see if the light picked out any tiny fragments lying on the carpet. Nothing apart from fragments of cigarette ash and an old chewing gum wrapper. Standing up, he noted the bin in the corner was full of crushed cans, empty cigarette packets, bits of cigarette paper and other pieces of rubbish. Next to it were a couple of empty three-litre cider bottles.

Back in the kitchen he sat down and quietly asked the mother, "Do you know what time it was when you discovered your daughter?"

"About quarter to ten," she replied shakily, stubbing a cigarette out in the full ashtray.

"And you found her in the front room?"

She nodded once.

"On the floor?"

"Yes, lying on her back with her arms out by her sides."

"How did you get into the house?"

"I have a key. We were going shopping together in town."

"Was the door locked when you arrived?"

Another nod.

Keeping eye contact, Jon continued, "OK, Mrs Mather, it's best you go now and let us take over. Margaret here will accompany you down to the station. We'll need to take a statement. Is that OK with you?"

"Yes." Then she whispered beseechingly, "What happened to my little girl?"

"We'll find out, Mrs Mather. We'll find out," Jon said, a note of firmness now in his voice.

As they stood CSO Payne asked, "Can we call anyone to meet you at the station?"

She shook her head and Jon wondered if it was an unwillingness to share with anyone else what had happened to her daughter.

He led the way back towards the front door, CSO Payne with her arm round the mother's shoulder. He paused in the doorway to the living room, subtly trying to discourage any further contact. "We'll be as fast as we can, Mrs Mather. You'll have your daughter back as quickly as possible." No mention of the coming autopsy, the gutting of her corpse, the sifting-through of her stomach contents.

At the front step he instructed CSO Payne to keep to the grass. Once the two women were back on the street

14

he called out to the young policewoman, "Oh, your torch. I've left it in the kitchen."

She walked back across the grass and into the house. Jon was waiting for her. "Did you touch anything in here?" he asked, handing it back to her.

"I don't think so. We got the mum out of the front room as quickly as we could. I brought her in here and made her a cup of tea . . ." She pointed to the draining board at the side of the sink.

Jon saw that she wasn't pointing at the sink full of dirty cups and glasses. "Where did you find the mug?"

"Just there sir, washed up on the draining board. Next to that other one."

"Washed up? You mean still wet?"

"Yes, I dried it with the tea towel."

Jon ran his fingers through his cropped brown hair in a gesture of disappointment. "Go on."

Aware that she was now being questioned, the officer went on more carefully. "She smoked three or four cigarettes. Stubbed them out in the ashtray on the table."

"Yeah, they were Lambert & Butler." Jon looked into the ashtray and said almost to himself, "The daughter smoked Marlboro Lights, I think. There's Silk Cut and Benson & Hedges in there, too." The urge to light up suddenly hit him. He turned away from the ashtray and its stale smell that should have been so unpleasant. "OK, get her to the station; we'll need her fingerprints, a DNA swab and samples from her clothes. Her fibres will be all over the body."

"So it's definitely suspicious then, sir?" She sounded thrilled. "I thought she might have had a heart attack or something."

"Don't get too excited — you're in for a bollocking from your sergeant out there. You forgot to check for a pulse. But yeah, I'd say it looks dodgy. The neighbour described her as a ravehead and there are signs of her smoking heroin in the bedroom. And whatever that stuff is blocking her throat, it doesn't look or smell like puke to me."

As soon as he was alone, Jon went back into the kitchen. Balanced on top of the soiled glasses and cups in the sink was a bowl and spoon, fragments of bran flakes clinging to the surfaces. If the cups and glasses were left over from the night before, and the bowl was from breakfast, why were there just two freshly washed up cups on the draining board? Had someone else been here that morning? Someone she had offered to make a drink for?

He pulled his phone out and called his base. "Detective Chief Inspector McCloughlin, please. It's Detective Inspector Spicer."

After a few moments his senior officer came on the line. "DI Spicer, I hear you were the first plain clothes officer at the scene of a suspicious death. What have you got?"

"Young female, appears to have choked to death on something. We'll need a post-mortem to ascertain what. My guess is that, if we have a killer, he came in and went out by the front door. It appears the person was let in, so she probably knew them. There's certainly no signs of forced entry or any kind of struggle."

"So you don't think the case will turn into a runner?"

"I doubt it. My guess is it will be the usual — a friend or family member. I think it should be fairly clear-cut."

"Right, how do you want to play it?"

"Well, until we've established cause of death, there's no point panicking and calling the whole circus out. We need to photograph her and get a pathologist down to pronounce her, so we can get the body to Tameside General for an autopsy. The scene is preserved here, so I'll call in a crime scene manager to make sure it stays that way. Then, if cause of death turns out to be suspicious, we can start worrying about calling in a SOCOs and the full forensics rigmarole."

"Sounds like a good way of playing it. Which other cases are you working on?"

"My main one is the gang hooking car keys through people's letterboxes."

"Operation Fisherman?" asked McCloughlin. "How many officers are assigned to it?"

"Seven, including me."

There was a pause as McCloughlin mentally divided up manpower and caseloads.

Jon knew his senior officer was deciding whether to move him to the murder investigation. Before he could decide, Jon said, "I'd really like to remain on Operation Fisherman, if only in a minor role, while this murder investigation is ongoing."

"Your partner's still off with his back problem, isn't he?"

"Yeah," Jon replied.

"Listen. It's time you led a murder investigation yourself. This one seems like it should be quite straightforward. I think it'll be a good one for you to cut your teeth on."

"You're making me Senior Investigating Officer?"

"You've got it. Just keep me up to speed on everything."

"And Operation Fisherman?"

"They can do without you while you get this one wrapped up."

A mixture of excitement and disappointment ran through him. The gang stealing high-performance cars had taken up so much of his time over the last few months, but now he had his own murder case. "Will do, boss," Jon replied.

Next he called his base. "Hello, Detective Inspector Jon Spicer here. We need a pathologist, a photographer and a CSM at Fifteen Berrybridge Road, Hyde. Who's available for scene management?"

"Nikki Kingston is on duty," said the duty officer.

Jon immediately smiled — the case had just become a whole lot more attractive. "Send her down please," said Jon, flipping his phone shut and popping a stick of chewing gum in his mouth.

The pathologist and photographer arrived less than fifteen minutes later. While they were still clambering into their white suits, Nikki's car pulled up. She climbed out and went straight round to the boot, opened it up and put on a large red and black jacket that looked like it had been designed for scaling Everest in. As she walked over, the bulky garment only emphasized how petite she was and Jon found himself wanting to scoop her up and hug her.

Looking Jon up and down she said, "You not freezing your nuts off in that suit?"

Jon grinned. "Good to see you, Nikki."

She was already looking at the house. "So come on then: scores on the doors, please."

"OK, the two CSOs over there are passing the house on a foot patrol when they hear a commotion inside. They go in to find what turns out to be the victim's mother in the front room hugging the body. One officer retires immediately to call for supervision; the other officer manages to get the mum away from the daughter and into the kitchen. I arrive, check over the rest of the property . . ."

Nikki interrupted, "So you've been round the rest of the house?"

Jon nodded.

"OK," said Nikki. "I'll probably need a scraping from your suit for fibre analysis at some point."

"No problem," Jon replied. "On realizing the body hadn't been checked for a pulse, I re-entered the house and, using a load of magazines for footplates, got to the body. Obviously she was dead."

Nikki raised her eyebrows. "Magazines for footplates? Nice bit of improvisation."

Jon smiled briefly. "One other thing. There's a cup on the draining board next to the sink and another on the kitchen table with a kiddy-style picture of a snail on it. They're worth bagging up as potential evidence — someone was drinking out of them recently. Problem is the CSO made a brew for the mum in the one with the snail on the side."

Nikki shook her head. "We'll be lucky to get anything off that."

At that moment the ambulance pulled up, so Jon moved his car to allow it to reverse into the mouth of the driveway.

The pathologist and photographer approached the house, pausing on the front doorstep to put on white overshoes, caps and face masks. Laying rubber footplates out before him, the pathologist led the way inside. Almost immediately the front room was filled by white flashes as the photographer went about his work. Ten minutes later the pathologist reappeared in the doorway and beckoned the ambulance men in with the stretcher. Stepping carefully on the footplates, they disappeared into the property.

Nikki and Jon moved round the side of the vehicle, out of sight of the small crowd of onlookers who had now gathered.

"How's giving up going then?" asked Nikki, still looking towards the house.

He thrust his hands into his pockets as if to stop them scrabbling around for a cigarette. "Doesn't get much easier. I haven't had one since before the Commonwealth Games though."

"That's bloody good. How long is that — three months or so?"

"Yeah, about that. Did you find it a nightmare for this long?"

"Did? Still do. Though on fewer and fewer occasions. Pubs are the place to avoid for me. That and meetings about the divorce with my solicitor."

"Your ex is still acting the prick then?"

"Oh yes, he's really honing that skill of his nowadays."

Jon's lips tightened in sympathy and he said, "Well, just thank God no kids are involved I suppose."

Nikki let out an incredulous laugh. "There's no way that's ever going to happen. I've seen too many friends go on Prozac immediately after they give birth. Motherhood? No bloody thank you. Anyway." She clapped her hands together softly to end that part of the conversation. "You're still using chewing gum. Is that to fight your cigarette cravings or to make sure your breath smells sweet for me?" Impishly, she glanced up at him.

Enjoying the game, Jon caught her eye then looked skywards, only to see Alice's face in the clouds above him. Quickly he looked down and said with a smile, "In your dreams, Nikki — you know I'm way out of your league."

"Cheeky bastard," she laughed, and went to jab him in the ribs.

Jon caught her fist just as the ambulance men reappeared with the body, the pathologist following along behind. Clicking instantly back into professional mode, Nikki pulled her hand free and walked back round the ambulance. Once the body was safely inside, she got the ambulance men to sign their names in the log book for people who had entered the crime scene. Meanwhile Jon had stepped over to the pathologist. "Any ideas?"

He pulled off his face mask and started removing the white shoe covers. "Well, I'd say death occurred due to suffocation. All the signs are there: bluish lips, ears and nails, petechiae — burst capillaries around the eyes and on the eyeballs themselves."

"And the white stuff blocking her airway?"

"It's not any sort of secretion I've seen. I'd say she's had the stuff pumped down her throat somehow, but until I've seen in her lungs and stomach, I can't say for sure."

"Can you start the autopsy?"

"Yes, that's fine. Of course, I'll hand over to the home office pathologist as soon as I can confirm it wasn't natural causes."

"OK — can one of you call me as soon as you know?" said Jon, handing him a card.

He turned to Nikki. "I need to get away and interview the mum. Can we completely seal the house until the autopsy result is confirmed? If it's suspicious you can arrange for forensics to come over."

In a voice kept low so none of the onlookers could hear, she said, "Tighter than a camel's arse in a sandstorm."

Jon winked in reply and walked over to his car.

After a bit of persuasion Mrs Mather had accepted the fact that her fingerprints, a swab from the inside of her cheek for DNA testing and combings from her clothes for fibre analysis were needed. After that, she answered Jon's questions about her daughter, Polly.

Twenty-two years old, single, keen on music and clubbing, worked in the Virgin Megastore on Market Street. As was often the case with people hovering at the edge of an industry, she had ambitions for a more central role. In Polly's case she was lead vocalist of a band, The Soup.

The beer cans and full ashtrays in Polly's front room were the result of the band having been round at her house the night before. Because he had recently been her daughter's boyfriend, Mrs Mather had a phone number for the band's bass player, Phil Wainwright. She asserted that the split had been amicable — the result of Polly wanting to travel round the world while he wanted to concentrate on gigging and trying to find a record deal.

Shortly after Jon had arranged for a patrol car to take her home, his mobile went. It was the home office pathologist. The autopsy had been handed over to him because there were only small amounts of the white substance in the oesophagus and trachea, and none in the lungs or stomach. This meant it had definitely been introduced from the outside, probably while she was still alive. What was confusing the pathologist was how it could have got there. He explained to Jon that, for the cough reflex not to function, a person would have to be in a coma or under very heavy sedation. In his opinion this was the case — the substance had formed a neat plug at the back of the girl's throat with almost no evidence of her choking and spluttering. Therefore, with the victim unconscious at the time of the substance being introduced, a third party had to be involved.

"So we'll need a toxicology report then?"

"Yes. If she was subdued with a hospital anaesthetic — propofol or maybe sodium thiopentone — it should be present in her blood in the form of metabolites, but I haven't found any marks so far to suggest she's been injected. Of course, in order to find evidence of narcotics, a full toxicology analysis will be needed. We haven't got the necessary facilities here."

"Right — can you prepare a blood sample for me? I'll get it sent down to the forensic science lab at Chepstow."

Next he called DCI McCloughlin. "Boss? It looks like murder."

"OK, open an incident room. Ring round and see which stations have any rooms available and I'll start getting a team together for you."

"Will do."

After finding a room at the divisional headquarters in Ashton, Jon decided to give Phil Wainwright a ring. As soon as the phone was answered Jon could hear loud talking and music in the background. A second later a gruff voice said, "Hello?" It was spoken loudly, as if the person was anticipating not being able to hear very well.

"Is that Phil Wainwright?"

"Yeah! Who's this?"

"Detective Inspector Jon Spicer, Greater Manchester Police."

"Oh, hang on." The voice disappeared and Jon could hear only background noise until a door shutting caused it to suddenly grow fainter. "Sorry, you caught me behind the bar. This is about Polly?"

Emotion made the last syllable wobble and Jon thought, he knows already. "Yes."

"I thought it would be. Her mum rang me an hour or so ago. You're going to question me, aren't you?"

"Not formally, no. But I need to talk with everyone who was at her house last night. Where are you now, Phil?"

"Peveril of the Peak. I'm a barman here."

"Nice boozer. Any chance of chatting to you?"

"Well, the evening rush hasn't started yet, if you can get over here."

"I'll see you in a bit."

It was dusk as he crossed over the junction for the M60 ring road, a steady stream of cars gliding by beneath him. Following the signs for Aldwinian's Rugby Club, he entered Droylsden. The perfectly straight road stretched far off into the distance, regularly interspersed by traffic lights shining red, amber or green. Flanking each side of the road was an endless terrace of the chunky red-bricked houses with grey lintels that made up so much of Manchester's Victorian estates.

Abruptly the built-up area came to an end and he emerged into the open space of Sportscity, Manchester City Football Club's new stadium dominating the facilities around it. Then he was past and the road dipped, only to start rising upwards to dark mills that loomed forlorn and empty, brickwork crumbling and broken windows gaping in silent howls. Reaching the crest of the slope he could see beyond them to where the lights of the city centre twinkled, Portland Tower and the CIS building clearly visible. Jon felt an itch of adrenaline as he looked at the city and contemplated all that was happening in its depths.

Dating from the mid 1800s and one of Manchester city centre's proper pubs, Peveril of the Peak was a strangely shaped wedge of a building. Clad in green glazed bricks and tucked away on a little triangular concrete island, it was closed in on all sides by towering office buildings and apartment blocks. Jon parked by some recently completed flats and slipped through the side door of the pub. The bar was in the centre, various rooms leading off to the sides. He looked round the smoke-filled interior, surprised by the lack of people: his mobile phone had made it sound like the place was packed. Instead just a few students and real-ale types were dotted about. Jon glanced over the three bar staff, eyes settling on a youngish man with about four days' stubble. He was dragging nervously on a cigarette and wearing a T-shirt from a Radiohead concert.

"Phil Wainwright?"

"Yeah," he replied, grinding the cigarette out with a bit too much urgency. "Fancy a drink? The Summer Lightning is a great pint." His finger pointed to the tap marked "Guest Beer".

26

"Tempting, but no thanks," said Jon. "Is there a quiet room we could . . .?"

Phil lifted up a section of the wooden counter and stepped into the customers' side of the pub. "This room's empty."

They sat down on some ancient and battered chairs, the upholstery rubbed smooth through years of use. He pulled another cigarette out of a packet of Silk Cut and offered one to Jon.

Another show of hospitality. Another attempt to break down the occasion's formality. Slightly irritated, Jon waved it away and took out his notebook.

"So, how are you feeling?"

Flicking a lighter, Phil dragged hard on the cigarette. "Pretty numb, actually." Smoke crept from his lips by the second word.

Jon's eyes strayed to the tip of the lit cigarette and he reached into his pocket for a fresh stick of gum. "Giving up," he explained, unwrapping it and regretting the fact he had allowed Phil an angle into him as a person, not a police officer. Before the insight could be seized upon Jon continued, "Now, you were round at Polly's last night? What time did everyone leave?"

"Just before midnight."

Noting this down, Jon continued, "And was anyone else there apart from the members of your band?"

"No, just us."

"Did anyone stay the night?"

"No, we all left together. Ade walked back with Deggs — they share a flat. I went about halfway and turned off to go to my own place."

"How did Polly seem to you last night?"

"Fine." He paused and frowned. "Although she's been up to something lately. She's had the odd call on her mobile that she's been really shifty about."

Jon kept quiet to tease another comment out of him.

"Walking off to have conversations — it was really annoying. I assumed she had started seeing someone else."

The silence began to stretch out as Phil examined the tip of his cigarette, so Jon said, "She was due to be going out today with her mum to do a bit of shopping."

"Yeah, she was looking forward to it. In fact, she hoofed us all out before midnight so she wouldn't be too rough this morning."

"Did she mention that she was expecting any visitors before her mum?"

"No."

"OK, what are Ade's and Deggs' full names?"

"Adrian Reeves and Simon Deggerton."

"Telephone numbers and addresses?"

Phil pulled out a mobile and started pressing buttons. As he did so Jon suddenly dropped in, "Why did you and Polly split up?" watching closely for the reaction.

Phil's finger hovered for a moment over a button as he lost his train of thought. "Erm, we'd just drifted apart. God, that sounds a cliché, but we had. She was saving up to go backpacking round the world. I wasn't into it."

"That's bad news I presume — to lose your lead vocalist?"

He looked up, a slightly wounded expression on his face. "Yeah, but what could we do? It was her decision. You want those numbers?"

Jon noted them down and then drove back to Ashton police station. He removed his box from the car boot and headed up to the incident room on the top floor of the building — the usual soulless set-up of empty desks, blank monitors and silent phones. Putting the box on a corner desk, he got out his paper management system, desk tidy, stapler, hole punch and calculator then sat back in his chair and blew out a long breath.

The place would be a hive of activity first thing the next morning: office manager, receiver, allocator, indexer, typist, all arranging their stuff on the desks; plants and other personal effects appearing, the outside enquiry team milling around, waiting to be briefed. And him, in charge of it all.

He booted up the computer, entered his name and password, then went on to HOLMES — the Home Office Large Major Enquiry System. The computer package was based on strictly designated roles and procedures in order that every large enquiry progressed in an ordered manner. It was established directly in the wake of the chaotic hunt for the Yorkshire Ripper, when it was discovered that he had been questioned on various occasions, but the paper reports had never been cross-matched.

Jon studied the search indexes, deciding whether to concentrate on any to steer the investigation in a particular direction. With the information he had at this stage, he decided the usual ones would suffice —

family, friends, house by house enquiries and victim profile. He then created an additional one marked "Narcotics/sedatives".

On impulse he went on to the Police National Computer's database and typed in all three band members' names.

Nothing showed up for Adrian Reeves or Simon Deggerton, but after he typed in Phil Wainwright the computer pinged up a result: two cautions for possession of cannabis, the second one accompanied by an order to attend a drugs rehabilitation course.

It was almost nine thirty by the time he got home. The front door clicked shut behind him, provoking the usual Pavlovian reaction from the kitchen. Paws scrabbled excitedly on the lino floor and an instant later the crumpled face of his boxer dog appeared round the corner, eyebrows hopefully raised.

Jon slapped his hands against his thighs and crouched down. "Come here, you stupid boy!"

The dog let out a snort of delight through its squashed nose and bounded towards the front door. Jon caught it by its front legs and twisted it onto the faded carpet. Grabbing it by its jowls, he planted a big kiss on its grinning mouth, then released the animal and stood up. Instantly it regained its feet, stumpy tail wagging so violently its entire back half shook.

By now Alice was standing in the doorway to the telly room, arms folded and a smile on her face. "Nice to see you getting your priorities right," she said, nodding down at the dog. "You're late back — you've missed rugby training again."

Jon let his shoulders drop. "New case," he said, walking towards his partner and bending forward to kiss her.

"Not after you've just snogged that ugly hound," she said, raising her arms and shying away from his puckered lips. "Go and wash your mouth out first."

"Did you hear that, Punch?" he asked the dog, feigning outrage. "You're ugly and Daddy gets no kiss!"

From the corner of his eye he saw that she had lowered her arms. Suddenly he dipped to the side, then straightened his legs so his face burrowed upward to her throat.

Instinctively she pressed her chin down to her sternum to protect her windpipe. Giggling through clenched teeth, she said in a contracted voice, "Get off!" A foot snaked round the back of his right ankle.

Not fully aware whether it was a playfight or not, Punch had started up a half-anxious, half-delighted barking. Jon felt Alice's forearm forcing its way across his chest, and realized she was manoeuvring towards one of her tae kwon do throws. He broke the embrace, stepping away from her and laughing breathlessly. "I'll have none of your martial arts high jinks in my house."

Her feet now planted firmly apart, Alice flexed her knees and held up the back of one hand to Jon. The tips of her fingers flexed inwards once and she whispered with Hollywood menace, "Come and try it, motherfucker."

His eyes flicked over her combat stance and he took another step back, realizing that he'd think twice about taking on someone like that in a real life situation. "Later," he smiled, then looked towards the kitchen door and sniffed, signalling that the fooling around was over. "Something smells good."

"Shepherd's pie," Alice answered, relaxing her posture. "With salad in the fridge."

"Ah, nice one, Ali," Jon answered with genuine appreciation. "Do you mind if I go for a quick r — u — n first?" Having missed rugby training, he was twitching for some exercise.

"Course not; I ate mine hours ago."

Jon looked down at the dog. "Fancy a run?"

At the word "run" the dog let out a moan of delight and padded towards the front door, eyes fixed on his lead hanging from the coat peg.

"How was your day?" he asked as he began climbing the stairs. "Tell me as I'm getting changed."

"I was late for work again. The stupid train into Piccadilly was cancelled." She followed him up to the spare room, stepping over the weights stacked on the floor and sitting down on the gym bench in the corner. Jon was standing at an open wicker unit, pulling his running gear from the assorted items of sports kit piled up on its shelves. Quickly he removed his shoes and socks, hung up his suit and returned his tie to a coat hanger that had another half dozen threaded through it.

As he began unbuttoning his shirt, Alice said, while innocently examining the nails on one hand, "Actually Melvyn introduced a new beauty regime to the salon today."

Clocking her tone, Jon replied guardedly, "Go on, what's he up to now?"

He dropped his boxer shorts to the floor and bent forward to pick up the neoprene cycling shorts he wore under his cut-off tracksuit bottoms when running. He glanced up and caught her looking meaningfully at his arse.

"It's waxing for men. 'Backs, cracks and sacks', Melvyn's calling it."

Jon digested the information for a second, then looked at her. "You're not ripping the hair off other men's bollocks?"

She gave him a provocative little grin.

"Oh, sweet mother of God, tell me it isn't true," he groaned, holding his head in his hands and pretending to cry. "If this gets out I'm a dead man." He looked at her again for confirmation that she was having him on.

Alice held his glance for a second longer, then suddenly smiled. "Why, got a problem with that?"

"Backs I can understand. Cracks maybe at a push — but sacks? Oh, Jesus."

"Don't worry. It's going to be Melvyn's special treatment; he's already drooling at the prospect." She grimaced. "Can you imagine it? First booking on a Monday morning, pulling some bloke's knackers to the side and . . ." She yanked sharply at the air while making a ripping noise at the back of her throat.

"Don't," Jon winced. "It's making me feel ill. What is the world coming to? Backs, cracks and bloody sacks." He shook his head in disbelief.

"You'd be surprised at the demand for it. And not just gay guys, as you're probably imagining. Besides, you've never objected to me doing other women's bikini lines."

"Well, that's different, isn't it?" answered Jon, voice suddenly brighter. "Why, any recent ones to tell me about?"

"Sad," she replied, as Jon pulled on a running top with reflective panels at the front and back. Downstairs he clicked the lead on his dog's collar.

"Punch, if you ever catch her creeping up behind you with a waxy strip in her hands, run for the bloody hills."

He could still hear her laughing as he slammed the door shut.

The cold night air hit him as he ran along Shawbrook Road to Heaton Moor Golf Course. After cutting on to the grass, he kept to the perimeter, making his way round to the playing fields of Heaton School where he could do some sprints up and down the dark and empty football pitches. Rounding the corner of the school buildings, he saw a group of young lads sitting on a low brick wall, the scent of spliff hanging in the air. Having chosen to ignore them, Jon was jogging past when one of them let out a low wolf whistle. A burst of raucous laughter broke out. Jon carried on and another cocky voice said, "I hate fucking boxer dogs."

Jon slowed up, turned round and jogged back, Punch's claws tick-tacking on the concrete as they approached. Jon surveyed them for a second, then narrowed his eyes and lowered his voice to a whisper.

"My dog don't like people laughing. He gets the crazy idea you're laughing at him. Now, if you apologise like I know you're going to, I might convince him that you really didn't mean it."

From the blank silence he knew they didn't have a clue what he was on about — and certainly no idea which film he was quoting from. "I thought you lot looked too thick to be anywhere near a school."

Now aware he was having a go at them, they looked uncertainly at each other, wondering who would be first to speak. Jon switched to bullshit mode. "I'm doing two circuits of these fields. Next time I pass this point I'll have my warrant card on me. If you're still here, I'll lift you."

"You a policeman?" one asked, eyes now wide.

"That's right. And I've got better things to be doing with my free time than nicking little twats like you. But I will, if you make me."

They started getting to their feet, joint now hidden up a coat sleeve. Without another word Jon turned away and resumed his run.

Back home, he showered and pulled on an old rugby shirt and tracksuit bottoms. After retrieving his supper from the oven, he sat down on the sofa. Punch was already stretched out in front of the gas fire, one brown eye tracking Jon's every move.

"What's this?" he asked, looking at the telly.

"I don't know," Alice answered sleepily, moving across the sofa to rest her head on his leg. Holding the plate below his chin to stop any bits falling into her hair, he began shovelling great forkfuls of food into his mouth.

After a few seconds he felt her jaw moving as she began to chew. He glanced at the table. Next to a jar of folic acid pills was an open packet of nicotine gum. "You fighting an urge?" he asked quietly.

"Mmmmm," she replied without moving. "It came on just after you went out. First one since lunch, though."

"That's great; well done babe," he answered, thinking how close he'd come to sneaking a cigarette earlier that day. "By the way, this new case I'm on . . . it's a murder investigation and McCloughlin's made me SIO."

Alice sat up. "That's brilliant! Why didn't you tell me before?"

Jon scratched his head. "I was mulling it over, I suppose."

"Why? Surely you think it's good news?"

He gave a half smile. "It is and it isn't. It means I'm being taken off the car thief case."

"Jon!" said Alice, holding both palms up as if weighing two objects. "A gang of scrotes nicking cars." She lowered one hand a couple of inches. "And SIO on a murder case." She dropped her other hand so it banged against the sofa. "Come on."

Jon nodded. "I know."

She settled back into the crook of his arm, head against his chest. "That's the problem with you. You get your teeth into something and you can't let it go. What's this new case, then?"

Jon leaned over the arm of the sofa and placed the empty plate on the floor. He noticed a strand of saliva set off on a vertical journey from Punch's lower lip and make it to the carpet without breaking. "A young woman, twenty-two, lived over in Hyde. Someone choked her to death."

"That's so sad," Alice murmured. Jon knew she'd be curious to learn more, but she understood that he hated bringing the details of his cases into their home. "By the way, I heard a bit of gossip in the salon today. That guy you used to play rugby with for Stockport. Married a blonde girl called Charlotte."

"Tom Benwell?"

"That's him. Have you seen him recently?"

"No. I had two tickets for us to see the rugby sevens at the Commonwealth Games. But he didn't show up. I ended up giving it to a Kiwi then had to sit next to him and watch as his team demolished everyone."

"That was three months ago, Jon," said Alice, cutting in as he was about to start giving a blow-by-blow account of each match.

"Yeah, you're right." He realized how time had flown by. "But I tried ringing his mobile a few times. There was never any answer and eventually the line went dead. He must have changed networks."

"Well, one of the ladies who comes in to get her legs waxed trains at the same gym as that little bimbo he married. She thought Charlotte had walked out on him. Something about him losing his job."

"Really?"

"Apparently he turned up at the gym searching for her one time. She said he looked a complete wreck."

"Fuck," said Jon, feeling guilty. "We went for a beer once and he told me how he was getting out of the rat race. Said he was selling up and moving to Cornwall, starting a beach cafe or something. I just assumed he'd done it and would ring me when he got the chance."

"I think you should at least go round and see him, especially after what happened a few years ago."

"What?" said Jon.

"What," repeated Alice, rolling her eyes. "When he got ill, remember? Missed half the season at Stockport?"

Jon frowned. "That was just some stress thing, wasn't it?"

Alice shook her head. "Men. What is it with your inability to discuss health problems? According to the gossiping girlfriends at the rugby club, he had a complete breakdown — ended up on the psychiatric wing at Stepping Hill Hospital for two months."

"Really? He never told me it was that bad."

"Did you ever ask him?"

"No."

"Exactly," said Alice, point made.

Jon sat staring at the TV screen, but uneasiness was now nagging at the back of his mind. He unwrapped his arm from Alice's shoulders.

"What are you doing?" she asked.

"Calling him."

He got up and retrieved his mobile from the hall. He dialled Tom's mobile but got the same continuous tone as the last time he'd tried. Scrolling to his phonebook's next entry, he rang Tom's home number. The line was also dead. "Sounds like both numbers have been disconnected. When did that customer say she'd seen him?"

"About a month ago, I think."

Worried now, Jon shoved the mobile into his trouser pocket and began pacing back and forth. Punch raised his eyebrows to watch him. "I'll pop round to his house. It's only five minutes in the car," Jon announced, looking at Alice for confirmation.

She glanced at the clock on the video. "At ten forty?"

"I won't start hammering at his door. Just check the house over, see if it's up for sale or if any lights are on."

Jon pulled out of his side street. Soon he crossed Kingsway, a main road leading into the city centre, and headed towards Didsbury. A few turns later and he was on Moorfield Road. He pulled up outside number sixteen and looked at the house. It was dark and deserted, every light turned off.

He got out of the car and glanced around for an estate agent's sign telling him the property was up for sale. Nothing. Walking up the driveway, he noted the absence of any vehicle, then crouched down at the front door. As he lifted the flap of the letterbox up, he prepared himself for the buzz of flies and stench of rotting flesh. Pitch blackness greeted him, the temperature inside the house no warmer than the night air outside.

He walked across the lawn to the front window. The main curtains weren't drawn and a chink in the net curtains allowed a strip of light from the street into the room beyond. He saw bare floorboards and no sign of any furniture.

After plunging his hands into his pockets, he walked back down the drive. With each step the sense of being watched grew stronger. At the end of the drive he swivelled round, eyes going straight to the first-floor windows. For an instant he thought something pale shifted behind a dark pane of glass. But focusing on the window, all he could see was dim light from the street lamps reflected there.

Turning the mobile over and over in his pocket, Jon's mind went back to the start of the summer.

CHAPTER
TWO

May 2002

Jon's mobile began to vibrate on the hard surface of his desk, angrily buzzing as if a giant wasp was trapped inside.

He dragged his eyes away from the latest statement. It was the usual story. The owner of the Porsche had gone to bed, enjoyed a good night's sleep, got up, had breakfast, gone to pick up the car keys from their customary place on the hallway table and discovered they weren't there. After searching his coat, briefcase and the kitchen, he presumed he had somehow left them in the car. He unlocked the front door and found his driveway was empty.

That was the sixteenth this month in the south Manchester area. Somewhere a load of thieving little scumbags were getting very wealthy.

He picked up his phone. "Jon Spicer here."

"Jon, it's Tom Benwell. Are you OK to talk?"

"Tom! Yeah, I'm just finishing off some paperwork. As usual. How are you?"

"Good. A bit busy preparing for the Games, but can't complain. How's things? Caught any bad guys lately?"

"Oh, you know. As fast as we catch them the courts let them out. Still, it keeps me busy."

Tom chuckled. "Listen, I've got tickets for the Cheshire Sevens this Sunday at Sale. Seats in the corporate box, free beer and sandwiches. You up for it?"

"Mate, you've just made typing out this witness statement far more enjoyable. What time?"

"Eleven fifteen at the main gates, if you like."

"OK, I'll see you there. Thanks for the offer."

Sunday morning and Jon joined a throng of people moving through the narrow residential roads towards Sale Rugby Club's ground. He caught snatches of the conversations going on around him, mostly about whether Sale would move into Manchester City's old stadium when the football club took over the Commonwealth Games stadium once the competition ended.

As the flow of people carried him towards the entrance, his eyes were drawn to the man casually leaning against one of the gateposts. Stepping across to him, Jon smiled. "Thanks for the invite, mate. How are you?"

He looked down a good five inches into the other man's face and noticed the dark smudges under his friend's eyes.

Tom Benwell smiled crookedly and said, "Hey — you know. Surviving. You're looking horribly fit as usual. Do you coppers do anything else but work out in the gym?"

"That and the odd crossword sat at our desks. How about you? Still having to take clients out to all the best restaurants round town?"

Tom accepted the riposte with a grin. "Yeah, that and swanning around in my company car."

"What are you driving nowadays?"

"Audi TT."

Jon shook his head. "Nice." Then the thought struck him. "Don't leave the keys on that table in your front hall. I'm working on a case at the moment where some little scrotes are hooking them through letterboxes and nicking the car."

"Seriously? What with? A fishing rod?"

"Lengths of garden cane with a hook on the end. A couple have been left in people's front gardens. Thing is, some insurers are claiming that, because the car has been opened up and driven off with the keys, they don't have to pay out. And high-performance vehicles like yours are what they're going for."

"So there are even more luxury cars on housing estates round Liverpool then?" said Tom in a Scouse accent.

Jon laughed. "No, we reckon these are being shipped straight out of the country. Probably ending up in Eastern Europe."

"Cheers for the advice." Tom showed his company's season ticket to an attendant and led the way to the corporate hospitality suite. "When was the last time we saw each other? Was it that European cup match back in February?"

"God, you're right. How crap is that? Alice still hasn't met . . ." John faltered, ". . . your wife."

"Charlotte, you dim twat," Tom answered for him.

Jon rolled his eyes in agreement. "How's married life going, then?"

"Fine. Expensive, but fine," answered Tom.

"Expensive? You haven't got a kid on the way, have you?"

Tom glanced over his shoulder, a strange expression on his face. "Not that I know of. I'm talking about Charlotte. She blows money like nobody's business." He patted his Timberland jacket. "You don't think I'd pick something like this, do you?"

Jon eyed the expensive-looking item, then glanced at the sleeve of his own battered leather jacket, which he'd found in a stall that smelt of joss sticks in Affleck's Palace years ago.

Tom had met Charlotte only the previous year and, much to everyone's surprise, they had flown out to Barbados and got married within weeks. Jon decided to put the subject on hold, at least until they'd had a few beers.

By now they were at the door to the hospitality suite. Tom showed their pass to another attendant and then stepped back. "After you, mate."

Jon bounded up the stairs two at a time. He looked back at the top only to see Tom halfway up. By the time he caught up, he was puffing slightly.

"Jesus, are you trying to make me feel unfit? This is the most exercise I've done for months."

Playfully Jon cuffed him on the back of the head. "You should never have given up playing. Fly halves like you don't need to make tackles — us flankers do all that kind of stuff for you."

"You're saying you used to do all my tackling?" said Tom. "As far as I can remember, you were too busy trying to get the opposition's fly half stretchered off to be doing any of my tackling."

Jon grinned. "Well, you fly halves. Serves you right for prancing round the pitch doing your poncey little side steps and shimmies."

There was an awkward pause and Jon cursed himself. He should have remembered how sensitive Tom could be.

Regret hung on Tom's face. "Not with the hours I work," he murmured. "Don't tell me — you're carrying on playing for Cheadle Ironsides next season?"

"Hope so," answered Jon, now anxious not to make his friend feel bad. "It's nowhere near the standard we used to play at for Stockport, but I turn out when I can."

"For which team, you old bastard?" Voice now brighter. "The veterans? When do you get to wear those purple 'don't tackle me' shorts?" Tom shoved his mate aside with a smile.

Relieved Tom hadn't taken the comment to heart, Jon hissed, "Piss off," and kicked at Tom's heels as they headed for the bar.

The sevens tournament was played in the spirit of the season's final event. Looking down at the teams warming up on the touchlines, it was obvious plenty of players were still nursing hangovers from the previous night. When one threw up before running on to the pitch the crowd cheered with delight. During the matches themselves, all the teams avoided playing safe and kicking — instead the ball was run from everywhere with outrageously long passes and overly complicated moves being attempted. The play was great to watch, but the teams soon tired, even with each match only lasting fifteen minutes.

At one point a slimly built back tried to sell an unconvincing dummy to a forward running on a defensive angle across the pitch. The forward didn't buy it, aiming his charge at the ball carrier and not the man he was apparently passing to. The forward's shoulder caught the back full in the kidneys, doubling him over before sending him crashing to the turf.

A collective "Oooohhhh" rose up from the crowd and Tom swivelled in his seat to punch Jon delightedly on the shoulder. "Straight out of 'Spicer the Slicer's' tackling manual!" he said. "What a hit!"

Aware of several other spectators glancing over at Tom's comment, Jon modestly kept looking down at the match below. But the mention of his nickname when playing for Stockport hadn't gone unnoticed. Sure enough an elderly man wearing a tie approached.

"Jon Spicer? Rupert Horsely."

Jon looked up, taking in the posh accent and Manchester Rugby Football Club badge on the man's blazer. With the faintest reluctance, he stood up to shake hands. "Good to meet you."

"Still playing, Jon?" the man asked in a blustery sort of way, a pint of bitter held against his paunch.

Jon rubbed the back of his neck with one hand. "Yeah, but just socially nowadays. Cheadle Ironsides."

"Open side flanker?"

Jon nodded.

"First team?"

"Yup."

The man stroked his moustache for a moment, then looked down at Tom. "Saw this man taking apart more than a few players when he ran out for Stockport. Finest number seven outside the professional code I've ever seen play."

Jon cringed as Tom raised his eyebrows to indicate he was impressed.

As the man turned away to rejoin his friends, he placed a hand on Jon's shoulder and murmured, "You could have gone all the way in my opinion."

He walked off without waiting for a reply and Jon sat back down awkwardly. Once the man was safely out of earshot, Tom leaned to one side and whispered from the corner of his mouth. "I like that! Doesn't even bloody remember seeing me play. The old fart."

As the afternoon wore on they kept up a disjointed conversation between bursts of action on the pitch. Once the final had been battled out by a pair of very weary teams, several pints had gone down and Jon could feel Tom relaxing.

"How's life in . . . what's the bit you're in again?" asked Tom.

"MISU. Major Incident Support Unit. Hard work and the hours can be shocking when we get a new case, but it couldn't be better, cheers."

"When did you switch to them? Two months ago?"

"Nearly four."

"God, that's gone fast. But you still count as a CID officer?"

"Yeah, it's a bit of a nightmare set-up. Basically, I work for Trafford division CID, but when a major incident occurs — usually a murder — I can be seconded into MISU to investigate it. All the CID divisions round Manchester contribute officers into MISU as and when they're needed. It's decided by some sort of extraction formula, but all the divisions moan about its fairness."

"Don't tell me — they're paying a firm of consultants to come up with a better system?"

"No, we're just ripping off how they do it down in London."

"Which is?"

"AMIT. Stands for Area Major Incident Unit, I think. A permanent collection of officers who are there solely to investigate big crimes. Except we won't call ours AMIT. Probably be FMIT — Force Major Incident Unit."

Tom laughed. "And I thought Manchester's advertising agencies' names were bad. JWT, BDH, MKP, MAP — I always get them mixed up. So you'll apply for this FMIT when it starts up?"

"Definitely. All the top people and all the best cases. It'll be tough getting in, though."

"Not like MISU, where you get dumped with looking for car thieves?"

"Hey," Jon answered, holding a forefinger up. "Don't knock that case; they're stealing dozens of vehicles each month. Whoever is in that gang is making a lot of money. But that's just a single investigation. We have more than one to work on at a time."

"So what else?"

Jon searched his mind for a case that he could talk about. "Remember that woman who was found under the viaduct near Stockport last year?"

Tom nodded. "Some barmaid who'd taken a battering?"

"That's the one. Her killer's just gone down for life and the team I was on caught him. Well, us and forensics."

Tom stayed silent, looking expectantly at his friend.

"She had a particular type of gravel embedded in her face. Turned out to be part of a very small batch used to landscape a park in north Manchester. We searched the bushes around it and retrieved the brick she'd been bludgeoned with. Forensics got a DNA sample from some skin caught on a jagged bit at the unbloodied end. It matched a sample already on the national database. We lifted him — the landlord — from his pub about three hours later. His car had fibres and blood in the boot. He'd battered her in the park, then driven her across town and dumped her."

"Nice one," said Tom, visibly impressed.

"So how's work for you?"

Tom grimaced slightly and looked out of the window. "It's all right. Pays a shedload but, to be honest, I'm getting a bit sick of it."

"Why's that?" asked Jon, leaning forward.

Tom glanced at him before looking back out of the window. "I don't know. Arse-kissing clients the whole time doesn't get any easier. Trying to get enthusiastic about their posters and promotions. You work in the industry a while and you begin to realize that all advertising campaigns are based on the same things."

"Such as?"

Tom let out his breath as if bored. "Yeah. Greed, sloth, envy, pride . . . I forget the rest."

Jon was surprised. "Those are the motives for most crimes. I hadn't realized they're the basis for most advertising too."

"Not most — all. Take credit cards; that's greed. The ads are always along the lines of 'Why wait? Get what you want right now with this card.' No mention about how you'll pay for it further down the line. Cars? That depends on the angle they work. Usually it's pride: 'Drive this and people will admire you.' It's all about achieving the same at the end of the day — feeding the machine."

Jon continued looking at him, unsure of what he meant.

"The economy," Tom explained. "People have to keep buying products. That's how it works. You can't have people keeping stuff or getting it repaired. You use it for a bit, then chuck it away and buy something new. That's what advertising is there to do: create demand, encourage you to keep on buying. Otherwise the whole capitalist machine would grind to a halt."

"You think too deeply to be working in that industry."

Suddenly Tom's eyes lit up. "Want to know what I'm really thinking about?"

"Go on."

"Getting out of it. It's all just a bit of a daydream at the moment, but I'm looking at buying a little business down in Cornwall. A cafe or some kind of shop."

"Could you afford it?"

"Almost. If we sold my place in Didsbury and then added the company bonus I'm due, we could just about afford to buy a smaller place to live in and use the leftovers to purchase the business."

"Bloody hell," said Jon. "I thought you loved city life."

Tom tapped his fingers against his pint glass. "More and more I'm happy just staying in. The odd meal out, yeah. But the clubs and bars . . ." He smiled briefly and leaned forward as if divulging a secret. "I'm just feeling past it, mate. How old are you now?"

"Thirty-three."

"A year older than me — you do nearly qualify for the veterans!"

Jon laughed. "I know what you mean. Apart from our local pub, me and Alice hardly go out. The last time we stumbled into a club it was full of teenagers. Or at least it seemed like it to me. But what about Charlotte? I thought she was a nightclubbing fiend."

Tom nodded. "She's full into it, just like I was at twenty-two. I daren't tell her that I'd prefer to stay in most nights and watch telly."

Jon had hardly met his friend's wife, so he decided to ask a little more. "Is she working at the moment?"

From the slight pursing of Tom's lips before he spoke, Jon guessed this was a bone of contention between them.

"She sometimes talks about going on a course at college, but I think she just likes floating around, doing her tennis and keep-fit stuff at the leisure centre. She certainly never wants to work as a receptionist again."

Jon turned the information over in his head. Tom's choice in women always seemed based purely on looks, but there was no doubt Charlotte possessed a very shrewd side. The first time he'd met her, Jon had walked away from the occasion with one expression lodged firmly in his head: gold digger. He had given it about two months before Tom dumped her for someone else. So when Tom had rung to say they had got married on the spur of the moment in Barbados, Jon was amazed. There was no doubt in his mind that she had engineered it: there hadn't even been a stag night.

"Is it all right with you that she doesn't work?" Jon asked.

From countless police interviews, Jon could sense when someone wasn't being honest. Now he couldn't help applying this ability to his old team mate.

"Yeah, of course it is," said Tom, brushing a knuckle across the tip of his nose. "It's quite nice being the main earner, having her waiting for me when I get in from work." Then, changing the subject, he said, "What about you and Alice? How long have you been together now? It must be time for marriage and a sprog soon."

"Eleven years. And yes, it looks like that's on the cards."

"Shit! You mean you're getting married? Or is she pregnant? Or both?" Tom pulled out a packet of cigarettes and offered one to Jon.

"No thanks — that's part of the deal. No marriage yet, but we're giving up smoking and starting to try for a kid. A general clean-living caper." He looked down at his pint and tilted it reflectively to the side. "Apart from the odd ale, of course."

"Jesus," said Tom, lighting up. "Feel ready for all that stuff, then?"

Jon took a long sip from his pint. He would have given a totally honest answer if he hadn't felt that Tom was holding back on his own description of married life. He would have admitted the whole prospect terrified him, admitted that he feared his entire life was about to be ruined. He might even have admitted that now he couldn't help looking at Nikki Kingston, the crime scene manager he casually flirted with, as a potential escape route if he turned out to be as big a failure at fatherhood as he feared. Instead he said, "Ready as you can ever be, I suppose. It's about time. Alice is thirty two now and you know women — they start getting very aware of their biological clocks after thirty. You've got eight years to go with Charlotte."

"Yeah," Tom faintly replied. Jon got the feeling it was a source of regret for his friend.

"Anyway," said Jon, draining the last of his pint. "What are we doing? Staying here for another or calling it a day?"

Tom looked down at the pitch. Most of the crowd had now gone and a group of kids tussled over a rugby ball beneath one set of posts while a couple of groundsmen trod back dislodged lumps of turf at the halfway line, their shadows stretching far out across the grass. "Come on. Let's get a cab into town."

"Yeah, why not?" Jon felt a sudden warm surge of pleasure at the prospect of a lazy Sunday evening spent getting drunk. He caved in to it and picked up his friend's pack of Silk Cut. "Don't bloody tell Alice," he mumbled, a cigarette bobbing between his lips.

Tom laughed and offered him a light.

Evening sun flooded through the windscreen as they waited for the lights to change. Drumming his fingers on his knee, Jon squinted up at the twenty-two-storey office block on his right. Its entire side had been coated in a vivid yellow and almost 250 feet above, three painted figures — one red, one blue, one green — stood with arms raised in triumph. Below them classically styled, twenty-foot-high lettering proudly proclaimed, "Manchester 2002. The XVII Commonwealth Games."

Jon's eyes slid halfway down the building to the enormous digital readout mounted on its side. The orange number glowing from the screen had dropped again.

"Eighty-one days to go. Can you believe it?" he said, looking up the four lanes of Portland Street towards Piccadilly Gardens. Suspended from each lamppost along the length of the street were vertical banners. Orange, purple, lime or turquoise, each one had the same three triumphant figures at the top and the words, "The XVII Commonwealth Games" stretching below. They lent the street a celebratory air, the kind Jon imagined ancient Rome enjoyed prior to an event in the Colosseum. "So come on then, talk me through what you actually do to deserve your flash car and big house in Didsbury."

"Loads, actually," Tom told him pompously. "Big, big, high-powered stuff. Very complicated for the lay person to understand." He grinned, dropping the act. "Just sales, really. Ringing people up and persuading them to part with some cash. Only this time round I'm usually offering people money to take my product."

In explanation, he swivelled round and pointed to the intersection behind them, "See that derelict martial arts centre at the corner of Princess Street? I've just persuaded the owner to take a big payment from Cusson's so they can wrap it in a giant advertisement for their soap. That site is a monster — it'll probably need eighteen drops of material stitched together to cover it. Did you know Cusson's have also just confirmed their contribution to the sponsorship pot? It's now got over forty million in it."

By now they were parallel with the Commonwealth Games visitor centre. Located in a recently built office, its plate glass windows were blanked out with poorly arranged sheets of white paper. Through the gaps, workmen could be seen hurriedly constructing the shop's interior.

Nodding towards it, the taxi driver joined in. "I was driving one of the guys on the council's organizing committee the other day. He told me what the sales projections are for that outlet and the one at Sportcity once the Games start. What do you reckon, mate? How much merchandise are they planning to flog?"

Tom thought for a few moments. "I don't know, twenty grand's-worth a day?"

The driver gave a little whistle and pointed a forefinger up at the ceiling of the car. "Fifteen grand an hour. Fifteen thousand pounds each bloody hour. I tell you, there are fortunes to be made once this thing gets going. Absolute fortunes."

Slowly the cab eased out of the block-shaped shadow cast by the seventies-style Piccadilly Hotel. As they passed over a set of tram rails, the space on their left opened up into the newly revamped Piccadilly Gardens. Jon thought back to when the area was nothing more than a sunken collection of flowerbeds that seemed to suck in rubbish and debris like a drain attracts water. When lunch hour arrived office workers, desperate for any sort of green surroundings in the city centre, used to make do with the patchy grass slopes. He reflected on how much time he'd spent as a fresh-faced constable moving on the bickering huddles of drunks from the lacerated benches that bordered the gardens. The statues that interspersed the area had greened over with age. Pigeons would nestle on Queen Victoria's head, staining her hair white with their shit.

Now, after a ten-million-pound facelift, the area was almost ready to reopen. Behind ten-feet-high perimeter panels displaying colourful snapshots of central Manchester, the sunken gardens had been filled in, the all-day drinkers moved on and the pigeons made perchless while the statues were taken away for cleaning. Expanses of freshly laid turf and multitudes of designer benches awaited the rush. At the far end, in front of the Burger King, clusters of newly planted saplings stood in a sea of pristine pavement. Square after square of Spanish limestone and slabs of grey York stone silently waited their first footfalls.

The car had now reached the turning for London Road, which led down to Piccadilly station, gateway to Manchester's city centre. Again the workmen had been busy, altering the road layout to incorporate a raised concrete area dotted with trees down its middle.

Tom pointed to a partially converted building on their left. "That is going to be a Rossetti hotel. The scaffolding won't be down before the Games start, so I rang them and asked if they'd be interested in a nice building wrap to hide all their builders' hairy arses. Nastro Azzurro rang last week looking for a site, so I paired them up. You know how Italians like doing business with each other — the Godfather and all that."

"And how much money are they paying for it?" asked Jon, examining the mass of scaffolding.

"Thousands."

"And what sort of commission do you get on the deal?"

"Thousands," repeated Tom, unable to help smiling.

Jon sat back in his seat and blew out his cheeks.

At the junction to the half-built station concourse Tom asked, "You really want to drink in the Bull's Head?" He looked down the road to the pub.

"Yeah," answered Jon. "Why?"

Tom laughed. "Nothing. It's just that we come all the way into town — Castlefield, Deansgate Locks, the Northern Quarter — and you choose an old boozer behind the station."

Jon shrugged. "I told you. Give me somewhere with decent beer, music that lets you talk and enough seats. It's not like we're out trying to pull, are we?"

Tom nodded. "Tell you what, let's have a look at my office first. It's only round the corner in Ardwick." He leaned forward to address the driver. "That all right, mate?"

"You're the boss," he replied. "What's the address?"

"Seven, Ardwick Crescent."

The car carried on through the lights, past the redeveloped rear of the station with its new taxi rank. Within seconds, they'd pulled up outside what had once been a cramped terrace of residential housing.

Above the front door of the house before them was a sign reading, "It's A Wrap". The office was two old houses turned into one, the narrow alley between them sealed off with plated glass which arched backwards to form a curved atrium between the two buildings.

"This is where it all happens," said Tom, looking up at the building and seeing the windows lit up on the first floor. "I don't believe it; Creepy George is in."

They flicked the driver a fiver each and climbed out. "Who's Creepy George?"

Tom shook his head. "Don't ask. Hopefully someone's just left the lights on and he's not there at all."

He pulled out his keys and opened up the heavily reinforced front door. When the alarm didn't start up with its warning beeps Tom said over his shoulder, "He's here."

Jon followed him into a foyer that continued the theme of a modern office carved from an industrial town house. The walls were stripped back to the brickwork and an old mangle stood in the corner. Hessian sacks with the word "cotton" were piled to the side of the brushed stainless steel desk.

Tom opened a side door that led into the main boardroom. He pulled open the pale yellow Smeg fridge in the corner, took out two bottles of Becks, popped the caps on the wall-mounted opener and handed one to Jon.

"You can just help yourself?" said Jon, surprised.

"As long as you don't take the piss."

Jon stepped into the room, opened up the fridge and saw it was stacked full of bottles. "Bloody hell! Why am I in the public sector? We even have to pay for our coffee and tea."

Tom laughed. "Come on, I'll show you my office."

They proceeded through an archway that led into the flagstone alley. Beneath the protective glass panels, two giant rubber plants thrived. Stepping through into the adjoining building, Tom pointed towards a door marked "Head Honcho". He raised his hand to his forehead and made a dickhead gesture, then began climbing up the circular iron staircase that curled up to the first floor where former bedrooms had been knocked through to form a single, open-plan office. Inside five workstations had been crammed in for the account handlers. The corner alcove was entirely taken up by a fortress of monitors and computer equipment.

Tom stepped through the doorway and was about to wave a hand at his desk when a flurry of activity started up. Visible behind the barricade of equipment in the corner was a mass of black hair. Creepy George. Their sudden appearance had obviously taken him by surprise and he was scrabbling to close down whatever he had been viewing on his monitor.

"Evening, George. Keeping busy?" Tom asked, not stepping any closer to his colleague's work area.

"Mmm, yes. I . . ." Slowly Creepy George rose to his feet, the bushy hair connecting with an equally dense pair of sideburns. Framed in it all was a pair of wire-rimmed glasses with particularly thick lenses. His eyes flashed darkly. "Just tidying up some old files on the main server." He reached for the front pocket of his thick khaki shirt and pulled out a Phillips screwdriver. Pointing it at the semi-disembowelled hard drive on his desk, wires and circuit boards exposed for everyone to see, he added, "I need to fix Tris's machine before Monday, too."

He still hadn't looked at Jon.

"Oh right," said Tom. "Well, we're only popping in so my friend here can have a look round. Jon, this is George."

"Hi," said Jon, stepping forwards and holding a hand out over the monitors separating George from the rest of the room. A pair of magnified eyes blinked once, almost black irises giving him the stare of a corpse. Then a clammy palm was pressed briefly against Jon's hand, fingers barely flexing before contact was broken.

To Jon's surprise, a feeling that bordered on revulsion suddenly reared up inside him, instinctive and instantaneous.

Ten minutes later they were settling into two leather chairs in the snug surroundings of the Bull's Head. An early Van Morrison track was playing quietly from invisible speakers as Jon gulped a mouthful of beer and said, "What's the score with that bloke in your office?"

"Creepy George?" said Tom, shrugging his shoulders. "He was at the company long before I joined. One of those people who melt into the background whenever the occasional job has to be cut. I'm not really sure what his exact role is — I've heard him described as office manager; he's responsible for the computer system and in charge of getting the photocopiers and colour printers up and running again when they get jammed or run out of toner. Aside from that, he backs up all the files at the end of the day, orders new pieces of kit and upgrades equipment when it's needed. He chooses to work really strange hours — comes in late morning then works through far into the evenings, totally alone. If he's ever at his desk first thing in the morning, he's been there all night. Doing exactly what, I've no idea. No one has ever seen him eat anything other than family-size bags of Minstrels and he only drinks some type of purple squash from a bottle he brings in with him each day."

"Well," said Jon. "He wasn't tidying up old computer files when we walked in on him. He couldn't get rid of whatever was on his computer screen fast enough."

"That's the copper in you," said Tom. "I hadn't noticed. He was probably about to beat off to some teenage sex site."

Or worse, Jon almost replied.

Another pint later and Jon felt he could ask Tom about Charlotte again. "So come on, mate. Cards on the table. How are you really finding married life?"

"What do you mean?" Tom answered, a tiny note of defensiveness in his voice.

Jon decided to lay out an admission of his own and see what it prompted. "To be honest, the whole marriage thing makes me shit my pants."

"What? But you're as good as married already! You've been with Alice for donkey's years."

"Yeah, I know." He looked at Tom's wedding band. "But it's the formality of it all. I don't know, it makes me feel claustrophobic."

"It doesn't change a thing, mate. I tell you what should make you feel really trapped — your shared mortgage with her. That's harder to get out of than any marriage."

Jon smiled wryly in agreement. "Until you have kids. Then you're really tied down."

Again Tom sounded surprised. "You're not a hundred per cent, then?"

Jon looked up at the ceiling and kicked his legs straight under the table. "I don't know. It's the biggest step you can take. I just reckon I'll be crap at family stuff. I avoid holding babies like the plague." He raised a large hand and stared at it, the knuckles peppered with scars and cuts from rugby studs. "Tiny little things, just keeping you awake for months on end. I'd probably hate it. And there's my job — the hours I work. Nights and all that. It would really screw things up."

"I'd love to start a family."

Now Jon was stunned. "You're serious?"

Tom's eyes dropped to his drink and when he spoke there was a melancholy note in his voice. "Absolutely. Something's kind of shifted in me lately. It's all part of this plan to get out of the city and move to Cornwall."

"You're getting broody."

Tom smiled regretfully. "I am. I admit it. But it's the last thing that Charlotte wants."

Jon plucked a cigarette from Tom's pack and leaned forward a fraction. "You've discussed it?" He touched a flame to its tip, listening to the tiny crackles as he took a deep drag.

Tom shook his head. "There's no need to. It couldn't be more obvious."

"You know, when you two got married, it took me totally by surprise."

Tom looked up. "I know what you're thinking. Tom the shag monster."

Jon laughed.

"But I tell you, the first time I saw her in the ad agency where she was the receptionist . . . fuck, my mouth filled up with saliva. I couldn't get my eyes off her body." He stared into space. "I went through the entire meeting on autopilot. As soon as it ended I was at the reception desk making up some bollocks reason to use their fax machine. Honestly Jon, if you gave me nude photos of every female film star and said put together your perfect woman, I couldn't do better than Charlotte."

"And had you actually spoken to her by the time you'd decided that?"

Tom didn't even register the joke, and Jon groaned inwardly at how precarious the basis of their relationship must be. But then Nikki Kingston's face appeared in his mind. "I know what you mean when the sight of someone just makes you go . . ." he snapped his fingers. "There's this woman I work with sometimes. A crime scene manager. We flirt around a bit, but more and more I'm . . ." He shook his head.

Tom tapped a finger on the table. "Don't even go there, Jon. What you've got with Alice — don't risk that for a quick shove." He swept up their empties and returned a minute later with two fresh pints. "You know what I really miss about rugby?" he announced, sitting down.

64

Jon acknowledged the switch in conversation by sitting up and grinding out his cigarette.

"The pain."

Jon took a long sip and placed his pint on the table. "Go on," he said.

Tom slid a cigarette from the pack, picked up the lighter and put both elbows on the table. "Thing is, the way the world has got today, it's too easy to forget what it's really like to be alive. You get up, go to work, sit at a desk, go home, sit down and watch TV, go to bed. Maybe you visit a gym once or twice a week. Our lives are so cocooned and predictable. I look at people and think we've become so safe, we're all half asleep. Trudging around our daily business, living in our artificial environment. Know what I mean?" he concluded, lighting up.

Jon remained silent for a second. "That's what I like about getting pissed with you," he suddenly said, affection flooding his voice. "Football? Women? Films? Yeah, they're worth covering. But you always drop in some big psychological point."

Tom grinned at him. "But you still play," he said. "When I think of the adrenaline surge I used to get on the pitch . . . At the time you don't realize how immune you are to the knocks, the impacts, getting stamped all over in a ruck. You get so into the match you don't feel it until afterwards. And that pain is a reminder that you've been out there, that you're actually alive. If I went out and played tomorrow, the first tackle would have me hobbling. I've gone soft. And this life I lead has made me that way."

Jon nodded. "But you're talking about *our* lives which, comparatively speaking, are very safe and comfortable. Some parts of Manchester I work in — the run-down areas, the parts where people are trying to sell stuff like curtain rails in their local newsagent's window for two quid. Cushion covers. Old plates. Knives and forks. And those are the people trying to get by honestly. Then there's the scum and what they'll do for cash. Plenty of people experience pain in their daily lives thanks to them. Plenty of people are made aware that they're alive and reminded how shit being alive can be, thanks to them. It's a different world to ours and believe me, you don't want your world coming into contact with the one those scum live in."

Tom breathed deeply. "Yeah, I suppose you're right." He glanced at his empty glass. "Anyway, get them in."

The next morning Tom found himself looking up at the massive yellow side of Portland Tower once again. Only this time he was a passenger in his boss's car.

Despite the exhaust fumes drifting through his open window, Ian took a satisfied breath in. "Can you smell it in the air?" he said, waiting for Tom to ask him what he meant. Dutifully Tom turned his head and raised an eyebrow in question. "Money, my friend. Filthy fucking money!" He growled with delight and pounded the heels of his hands on the top of the wheel, making the steering column judder.

The traffic began moving forward and he casually pressed "play" on the dashboard CD. Though the action appeared to be spontaneous, Tom suspected it was a pre-planned move. Sure enough Wagner's "Ride of the Valkyries" started and his boss looked to the side. "Don't you just love the smell of money in the mornings!"

Tom knew that barking out a GI-style "Yo!" in reply would be the appropriate answer, but it was too early in the day to start putting on an act, papering over his true emotions with a veneer of enthusiasm. Instead all he could bring himself to do was smile, then sip at the small hole in the lid of his Starbucks coffee cup.

They battled their way to the top of Portland Street, then turned left into the traffic jam leading down to Piccadilly station. As they crawled along, Ian said, "We need to get on to the owners of that derelict building on Great Ancoats Street, the big white one with the bushes growing out of its gutters."

"Will do," answered Tom, taking the lid off his cup, swirling round the dregs and draining the last of his latte. Fraction by fraction he succeeded in arousing something that resembled a professional interest, and as he did so his feelings of self-loss increased. He knew by the time they reached the office, the real Tom Benwell would have been fully replaced by a serious and eager executive for yet another day.

At last the car made it onto the emptier road beyond the lights, Tom glancing wistfully at the Bull's Head as they drove past. Soon they had parked outside It's A Wrap.

The driver's door of the Porsche Boxter swung open and Ian hauled his bulk onto the pavement. Holding his empty coffee cup, Tom climbed out, raised his arms above his head and gave his far thinner frame a good stretch. Then he followed his boss through the front door.

The woman behind the stainless steel desk said chirpily, "Good morning," and lifted up two piles of post.

"Morning Sarah," replied Ian. Tom greeted her with a smile and nod of his head. They took their post and crossed the flagstone alleyway into the other half of the office. Ian walked towards the door marked "Head Honcho" while Tom, with a heavy heart, started climbing the iron staircase to his office.

"So if you find out who owns that derelict building that would be great," called out Ian as he opened his door.

Tom leaned over the stair railing, careful to sound keen, but not sycophantic. "No problem — it will be perfect for any one of our sponsors."

"Good work," answered Ian, disappearing into his office.

Tom continued up to the top of the metal steps. As he stepped into the room, Creepy George was just sinking down behind his monitors and their eyes met for an instant. Waving hello to his more friendly colleagues, Tom lobbed his empty cup into the bin by his desk and heard the empty Becks bottles from the evening before clink together. Next he dropped his post into his tray, sat down and turned his computer on in one fluid motion.

Safely out of sight behind his monitor, he dropped his cheerful expression like a piece of litter. Raising a hand to his head he gripped his temples, head still pounding from last night. He'd got in at about ten o'clock, nicely drunk from the beer session with Jon. But then Charlotte had wanted to go out. A dab of speed later and he was up for it too, joining the other clubbers desperately in denial that the weekend was over. They hadn't got in until after two.

Hung over on a Monday morning. Not good at any age, much less at thirty-two, he thought while shifting round the contents of his top drawer looking for some paracetamol. And he had to get his Audi back from the garage and put a halt to these Monday morning drive-ins with his boss. What a way to start the week! No easing into the day with some Zero7 or Cafe Del Mar album gently washing over you. Instead it was stop-start all the way along Oxford Road with a continual stream of enthusiastic business talk battering his ear. Then a quick diversion through the city centre to check on the abandoned properties and half-finished developments that needed screening off for the Commonwealth Games.

He went to "Favourites" on his screen and scrolled down to an entry that simply read "Cornwall". He clicked on it and the view from the web cam overlooking Fistral Bay filled his screen. The golden sand was almost deserted. There were just a couple of people walking their dogs, waves breaking nicely about forty metres out and the bobbing heads of half a dozen surfers visible in the swell beyond.

Tom's shoulders sagged a little more and he let disillusionment flood his head like a wave rushing into a rock pool. Shutting his eyes, he imagined the life he was yearning for more and more. Striding along the beach at dawn with a Border collie or perhaps a long-haired Alsatian at his side, sucking in the clean air, feeling the sea spume fleck his face with microscopic drops, skin growing tight as the salt water dried.

He let the image hang in his head, savouring it like the delicious instant before a long-awaited sneeze.

Then a phone rang from the next workstation and the reality of his surroundings returned. With an effort he pushed the listless feelings back down and opened his eyes. The view of the beach still filled his screen. He stared at it for a second longer, then closed it down and reached for his post.

After shuffling paper round for as long as he could, he turned his attention to tracking down the owner of the derelict building on Great Ancoats Street. He could remember it used to have a religious message across its front, something about miracles happening every day. Obviously not where paying the rent on the building was concerned, he thought. A phone call to the Land Registry revealed that the Christian Mission had sold it on to a businessman, a Mr K Galwi. He dialled the man's phone number but got a "number no longer available" message.

Tom clicked on Directory Enquiries and typed in the surname and initial. Forty-eight hits came up for the Greater Manchester area. He printed the list off, grabbed three cans of full-fat Coke from the fridge in the kitchen, then returned to his desk and picked up the phone. A succession of bewildered-sounding old ladies with broken English, dead phone lines and answer machines greeted most of his calls.

By 12.30 he'd had enough. His headache had been washed away and his sugar levels restored by the Coke, but now he was starving. Standing up, he glanced round the room, noticing how flat the atmosphere was. Everyone's head was bowed as they settled down for another week on the meaningless hamster wheel that was work. Knowing that it was weak of him to keep relying on his company credit card to bolster morale, he stood up and asked the room if anyone wanted a sandwich from town — he was doing a run to First Taste.

As he expected, there was a flurry of activity, Ges being the first to order. While he went through his routine of being undecided about what to choose, his free hand had crept across his desk and on to his considerable paunch. Tom scribbled down, "Ges — Indian starter selection with chutneys, club sandwich, dessert (strawberry cheesecake)."

"Oh, I don't know," said Ges. "The Indian starter selection with chutneys and a club sandwich, I suppose."

Tom pretended to write it down, then Ges added, almost as an afterthought, "And the lemon and lime cheesecake."

Tom crossed out "strawberry" and scrawled "L&L" above it. "Gemma?"

A girl of about twenty-three with wiry ginger hair glanced round her screen. "Smoked salmon with low fat cream cheese on brown, thanks." Due to get married at the end of the summer, she had been slimming mercilessly for months.

Tom looked towards a blonde woman at the next workstation to Gemma's as she struggled over the unfamiliar menu. "Julie, a jellied eel?" Sent up from the London office as temporary help in the run up to the Commonwealth Games, Julie's southern accent and feisty attitude had been a welcome jolt to the office. Tom had noticed Creepy George staring at her on several occasions.

"I'll go for the Thai ginger chicken on whole grain and a bag of those salt'n'vinegar organic crisps, cheers."

"Ed?"

When getting his Coke earlier on, Tom had seen Ed's sandwiches in the fridge. He knew his colleague would now have been thrown into confusion. Were the sandwiches going to be on the company or should he eat his own and save some money?

Tom put him out of his misery. "Don't worry. I'll get them on expenses. We're way over target this month."

They all smiled while Ed looked relieved and said, "Beef with horseradish on a white roll, please."

Even though he knew the offer would be refused, Tom called over to the corner out of politeness. "George?"

The mass of black hair rose slowly from behind the barricade. "No, thanks." He lowered himself back into his seat.

"OK," said Tom, sitting back down and pressing a speed-dial button on his phone. He read out the sandwich order and said he'd be over in about twenty minutes. Down in reception he grabbed the keys for the pool car and set off back towards the centre of town.

Three quarters of an hour later he walked back into the office, unzipped the cooler bag, put the tray on the table in the middle of the room and popped the lid. "Lunch," he announced, grabbing his All Day Breakfast baguette and bag of crisps.

Creepy George manoeuvred the digital camera into the small gap between two of his monitors. A cable ran from the back of the camera into the Apple Mac on his right. The monitor's screen filled with the view of his colleagues crowding round the table. George tilted the camera up slightly, then focused in on Julie's face. No one heard the faint click as he took a picture.

George disconnected the camera, placed it in his top drawer and turned his eyes to the image captured on his screen. Her mouth was open, eyes half closed in mid-blink. The tip of his tongue flicked across his upper lip — her expression was far better than he dared hope for.

Closing in, he used Photoshop to cut round the edge of her face and neck, then dropped her decapitated head on to his desktop and dragged the rest of her body into the trash bin on the corner of his screen. Next he brought up the image he'd downloaded from comatosex.com the afternoon before. The woman lay on the flowery carpet of some anonymous living room, the edge of a faux-velvet settee encroaching in the top right-hand corner of the photo. Face slack, she lay with arms and legs akimbo, like a corpse photographed on the street of some war-ravaged city.

Clicking on Julie's forehead, he dragged her face over the unconscious woman's. George's expression darkened with frustration; the scale was out and the lighting and backgrounds didn't match. It would take hours of manipulation on the Apple Mac to make the image even remotely convincing. Sighing, he saved it into his special file that needed a codeword before it would open. Once everyone else had gone home he would retrieve it and begin his work.

CHAPTER
THREE

May 2002

The following Monday Tom got the call from head office in London. With all the rush of chasing business before the Games began, he'd failed to notice how much Ian was away from the office. Now it turned out his meetings were with a prospective employer — "The Giant Poster People", their biggest competitor. The conflict of interest meant Ian had to leave It's A Wrap immediately.

The director from the London office asked him to pop down to Ian's office and make sure that he wasn't in. Shocked, Tom did as he was told. It was obvious Ian had been in over the weekend; all of his personal effects had disappeared, even down to the "Head Honcho" placard from the door. Tom went over to the filing cabinets. The keys were all in the locks. He pulled drawers open and looked over the clients' files inside. They all seemed in order. He sat down at Ian's bare desk and had a quick peek in the drawers: a couple of biros and Post-it pads. He'd even taken hole punches, staplers and the big calculator with built-in clock and alarm. Tom picked up the phone and let the London office know that Ian was well and truly gone.

Next he was put through to the IT department and asked to turn on his former boss's PC. Once it was booted up, the person at the other end of the phone gave him Ian's logging on details, Tom wincing as he had to type the word "WINNER" into the password field. He was asked if the computer's desktop appeared especially empty, as if things had been deleted. Tom thought that nothing looked amiss. An inner box then appeared on the screen, asking him if he would let jim.morrel@itsawrap.info remotely access the computer. The person asked him to click on the "Yes" button and as soon as he did the cursor began to move of its own accord with bewildering speed. The IT specialist shot through Ian's directory, opening up files and asking Tom if everything appeared in order. As far as he could tell, it seemed to be. The cursor carried on its quest, taking Tom deep into the machine's hard drive, rummaging through deleted files while the voice in the phone's earpiece supplied an emotionless commentary. The only stuff Ian had wiped was of a personal nature — emails to his wife, downloads from BBC Sport on anything to do with Chelsea football club and bookings for hotels round Manchester with lastminute.com.

Finally the voice said nothing to do with any clients appeared to have been deleted, though an unusually large number of files had been accessed over the course of the previous week. He was passed back to one of the directors. After a bit of a talk that included the phrases "rudderless ship", "crucial period", "man with local expertise" and "exceeding targets", Tom was offered Ian's old job.

Sitting back, he stalled for time. He would have to talk it through with his wife, Tom replied. Launching into a few plans Charlotte knew nothing about, Tom explained they were thinking of starting a family, possibly moving house. Finally he added that he had a week's holiday booked, starting from that Thursday.

With a soothing tone to his voice, the director said he fully understood. He appreciated that stepping into Ian's shoes in the circumstances was a "big ask" but, he added, it would be a move accompanied by a "commensurate pay rise and profit-related bonus".

Knowing the extra money would bring the move to Cornwall within his reach, Tom thanked him for his offer and requested a little time to come back with an answer. The director instantly agreed, adding, with a hint of regret in his voice, that he would need an answer in twenty-four hours.

Pushing his front door shut behind him eight hours later, he flung the keys to his Audi TT on the hallway table. "Honey, I'm home," he called out in a fake American accent, placing his briefcase on the oak plank floor and shrugging off his Paul Smith suit jacket.

"In here," called a voice off to his side. Passing the doorways leading into the living room and dining room, he paused to glance in the mirror on the wall at the end of the corridor. Then he stepped into the kitchen, poured a glass of red wine from a newly opened bottle and sauntered back into the front room. His wife was sitting on the leather sofa, long legs curled up under her and strands of blonde hair swirling over the cushions behind her head. Spread out on the coffee table before her was a mess of holiday brochures: Greek Villas, Tapestry Travel, Ionian Idylls. None looked remotely mass market.

Slumping down next to her, Tom cocked his head to the side. "Snaff, snaff, snaff, what have we here then?" he announced in a creaky voice, but their age difference meant his Professor Yaffle impersonation was lost on her.

She folded open the brochure across her lap and looked at him with heavily lidded eyes. "Darling, it's got to be Greece; look at these properties. Private beaches, their own olive groves, pools. This one even has a rooftop garden and barbecue area."

Tom smiled, wondering how to start telling Charlotte about his day. After the conversation with the director in London, Tom had logged on to the Cornwall tourism web site, clicking through the "businesses for sale" section. The small cafe on Harbour Road overlooking Towan Beach was still for sale. It was going for a London price, but then so would his house in Didsbury if he sold it.

Tom knew he was at a crossroads in his life: either pack in his job now and avoid the stress of the coming months, or see it through until after the Games and reap the financial rewards. The part of him that always sought compromise was already urging him to put off the move to Cornwall for a while longer. The only question nagging at the back of his mind was whether he could cope with all the added responsibility of taking over Ian's job.

"So, you like the idea of your own private beach, then?" he asked, the Cornish coastline in his mind's eye.

Charlotte smiled at him. "Well, it would beat the sunbeds at the gym."

Tom took a breath. "Ian's left. Buggered off to our biggest competitor. Really left us in the shit. I got a call from one of the directors down at the London office."

Charlotte raised herself up, turning to face her husband, her mind working through the implications. "And?"

"Well," said Tom, feeling like he was blundering into a pool of quicksand. "They were sounding me out about taking over. But," he carried on swiftly, before she could interrupt again, "it's going to be mayhem in there over the next few weeks." Voice trailing off weakly, already knowing how things would turn out.

Sure enough, Charlotte leaned towards him and took his hand in both of hers. "They've offered you Ian's job?" she said slowly.

"Yes."

She screeched with delight and flung herself on to him. The wine in his hand came dangerously close to sloshing over the carpet and he had to lean forward to quickly place it on the table.

"Oh Tom, Tom, Tom. I'm so proud of you," she said, face pressed against his chest. Slowly he was forced backwards by her weight until he was lying diagonally across the sofa.

The decision had been made. Tom told himself that, as long as he packed the job in once the Games were over, he could get through it.

Having pinned him beneath her, Charlotte raised her chin, wisps of fine hair hanging over her face, a wild and mischievous look in her eyes. "They'll have to up your pay bigtime," she said, grinning.

Tom nodded, thinking of the work and pressure.

"And didn't Ian drive a bright yellow Porsche Boxter?"

He nodded again, knowing everything would be resting on his shoulders.

A strangled "Yes!" escaped her lips and she banged her fists up and down on his sternum. He felt like a heart-attack victim.

"Bollocks to Greece. I know where we deserve to go!" she squealed. She launched herself off him and ran across the room towards the computer in the corner. "I'll check for flights now. Oh, I can't believe this!"

From his ungainly position on the sofa Tom watched as his wife pushed the chair towards the terminal. Her tight buttocks quivered under white cotton tracksuit trousers with each step and his chest clenched with desire. Twenty-two and she hasn't got a clue, he thought with a smile.

Later that night, as they lay naked and asleep, an empty bottle of champagne and a mirror speckled with dots of white on their bedside table, a dark-blue Ford passed their driveway and pulled up in a space under the trees further down the street. The passenger door clicked quietly open and a man got out, straggly ginger hair briefly lit by the car's inner light. Treading carefully, he walked back up the road and turned confidently through Tom's open gates.

The metallic grey paint of the Audi TT reflected back with a liquid shine what little moonlight was breaking through the cloud layer above. The man's eyes lingered on its shimmering form as he passed the vehicle. Cutting across the small patch of grass at the side of the garage, he stepped noiselessly up to Tom's front door and crouched down.

With the tiniest of creaks, the letterbox slowly opened and a second later a thin torch beam probed the dark hallway. The spot of bright light slid across the floor, crept up a wooden leg and then eased on to the surface of the small table just inside the front door. A polished coconut shell full of loose change. A mobile phone. A packet of extra strong mints. A tube of lipstick. A couple of unopened letters. And a set of car keys.

Next the man hung a square of felt-like material through the letterbox. The flap lowered, then opened again as a garden cane with a hook on the end was fed through, the quivering length of wood extending out into the darkness like the tremulous tendril of a plant seeking sunlight. The hooked tip finally made it to the end of the table but stopped short of the keyring itself. The man strained against the other side of the door, trying to increase the reach of his implement by a few millimetres, but it was no good. He drew the length of metal and flap of material back through the letterbox and the circle of light moved to the edge of the table, jumping suddenly to the far wall and briefly dazzling him as the beam was reflected back by a mirror. The torch clicked off and the letterbox was lowered back down.

The man walked back down the driveway, the forefinger of one gloved hand lightly tracing the length of the vehicle as he did so.

Back in the car the driver looked at him. "Hey Sly, not like you to come back empty-handed."

Sly shot him a sour look. "I'll get them next time," he murmured.

They drove on towards Altrincham, coming off the M56 at junction six, moving along Altrincham Road and ignoring the first houses they passed: the driveways were too long and the gates too high. Instead they headed towards the centre of the village, searching for houses that directly bordered the road with driveways only fractionally longer than the cars parked on them. Soon after passing the fire station they spotted a black BMW A5 parked outside a 1930s semi-detached house. The men glanced at each other and the driver pulled over in the first available space.

Sly got out and went to the house, automatically noting the absence of a burglar alarm. Seconds later the letterbox was pushed open and the torch shone through the gap. Immediately it revealed an art deco lamp on a small shelf just inside the doorway. Holding up the globe-shaped lampshade was a coppery green female nude and from the outstretched fingers of her free hand hung a set of car keys.

"Bingo," he whispered, hanging his flap of thick material through the letterbox. Next he fed the garden cane through, angling the hook at the end upwards towards the lamp. Breathing in deeply, he made an effort to steady his hand, then, focusing on the keyring itself, he expertly threaded the hook through it. Gripping the implement as tightly as he could, he joggled the thin length of wood up and down until the keys were dislodged from the statue's fingers. Their weight transferred to the hook and the cane bent slightly, but he was ready for that. He slid everything out, the keys brushing silently against the flap of soft material.

He turned the torch off, placed it at his feet, then grasped the set of keys and slipped them off the end of the garden cane. After extracting the flap of cloth, he turned his attention to his prize. On the fob was a photo of a young boy, the sort given to grandparents. The key to the BMW was obvious enough, as was the key to the front door itself. Thinking about the lamp in the hallway, he walked to the end of the drive and held up a thumb. The Ford's engine started up and the car pulled quietly away.

Knowing he wasn't meant to take anything else from the houses, he returned to the front door and slid the key into the lock. The door opened with hardly a sound. Stepping into the hall, he looked at the collection of photos of the same young boy crowding the little windowsill to the side of the door. Definitely a grandparent's house, he decided. Reaching round the back of the lamp, he found its cord with his fingers and traced it back to the plug in the wall. Just as he pulled it out he heard a footstep on the landing above. He froze, head bowed. A faint pull of breath came from the top of the stairs. Perhaps it was the absence of a male voice telling him to get out, but he somehow knew that it was a woman. All the advantage was his. She was up there, disoriented with sleep, in her nightclothes, probably alone and without a phone.

He pulled a Stanley knife from his coat pocket, held it against one of the photos and slowly dragged it down the glass. A thin rasping noise filled the silent house.

He heard a sharper intake of breath and then a wavering voice said, "Leave this house immediately. I'm calling the police."

From the dark hallway below her Sly leered, "And how will you do that, Grandma? You won't be able to speak if I come up there and kill you."

She let out a gasp of fright and he heard bare feet running away from the top of the stairs. A door slammed shut and a key turned in a lock.

He climbed halfway up the stairs and announced in a menacingly low voice, "If this key doesn't work for that Beemer out there, I'm coming back inside for you."

Then, laughing to himself, he slid the blade back into the stubby handle and returned the knife to his pocket. After wrapping the cord round the figure, he walked calmly from the house, held the key fob towards the vehicle and pressed the button. The vehicle's security system beeped as all the doors simultaneously unlocked. Minutes later he was driving back towards the motorway, heading towards the Russian's garage on the industrial estate in Belle Vue. After the car had been dropped off, its registration plates would be changed and documents prepared for the agent to ship it out to the Russian's contacts in Moscow.

CHAPTER
FOUR

May 2002

At times the sky merged seamlessly with the ocean below and it felt like they'd been hanging in a bubble of blue for hours. Looking up, the only thing Tom could find to provide a reference point against the all-enveloping colour was the sun stabbing down above him.

Eventually the angle of their approach changed and, as their descent began, he was able to look through the tiny Perspex window and watch the shadow of the plane racing over the surface of the motionless sea. Soon the pilot announced that the Seychelles were now visible to those on the right-hand side of the aircraft. Charlotte immediately leaned across him for a look as Tom said with a note of apprehension, "Well, let's make the most of this. It's the last time I'll be coming up for air until August."

After clearing the tiny customs hall at Victoria International airport on Mahé, they transferred to a worryingly small eight seater Air Seychelles plane for their onward flight to Praslin Island. They touched down minutes later on a small runway constructed of crudely interlocking slabs of white concrete. Standing next to the plane, waiting for their luggage to be unloaded as if from a bus, Tom could feel powerful waves of heat bouncing up from the ground: it felt like someone was holding a hairdryer under his chin. Once their bags had been placed on a small cart, they were led across to the low building by the edge of the runway. Standing inside the open doorway was a slightly built man in a light cotton suit.

"Mr and Mrs Benwell, I am Daniel Gedeon from Coco de Mer Resort. Welcome to Praslin."

They shook hands, walked through the small terminal building and out onto the road. An old Mercedes taxi stood waiting for them, its boot already open. The porter from the airport placed their luggage inside and they were just about to climb into the back when Tom spotted the ox standing on the other side of the road. Across its neck was a roughly hewn yolk, carved from bulky sections of timber. Attached to the other end was a cart with two rows of sideways-facing seats under a pale blue canopy.

"Daniel," said Tom. "Can we go in that instead?"

Daniel looked confused. "It will take you twenty minutes to get to the resort in that."

Tom shrugged. "We're on holiday. Who cares about time?"

He winked at Charlotte, who giggled and said, "You're bloody mad."

Daniel smiled. "I'll go ahead with your baggage." He strode across the road and spoke quietly with the driver in a language that resembled French then handed over some crumpled rupee notes. "OK, I will see you at the resort. Enjoy your ride."

The driver goaded the beast into a slow amble, while Tom and Charlotte sat back on the wooden seats to enjoy the scenery. Passing a cluster of palm trees, Charlotte squeaked with disgust: hanging from their lower fronds was a mass of interlocking webs. Dotted around were hand-sized spiders, swaying gently in the breeze.

"Oh, how gross. Do you reckon those things are poisonous?"

Tom leaned forward, tapped the driver on the shoulder and pointed to the webs. "Dangereuse?"

"Non," the man said with a languid shake of his head. "Ils peuvent piquer," he jabbed at the back of his hand to indicate it being stung, "comme un abeille."

"OK, merci," Tom replied, sitting back. "They can sting like a bee."

At the resort Daniel led them across the lawns to a bungalow, which lay behind a straggly cluster of palm trees, the veranda leading directly down on to the thick white sand of the beach.

"Oh my God," whispered Charlotte. As soon as Daniel had gone they tore open their suitcases and yanked out swimming costumes. Charlotte darted into the bedroom while Tom just stripped off where he stood. Seconds later, Charlotte re-emerged in a bright orange, low-cut number. Tom eyed the perfect profile of her breasts as she raced for the door, then raised his eyes upwards in thanks that she was his. He pulled on his swimming shorts, pausing for a moment at the desk and checking the wall behind for an extra phone socket for his laptop's modem. Then he too ran from the bungalow. The sand was bleached white and so powdery it squeaked every time his feet connected with it. Charlotte was standing motionless in the shallows, the water boiling around her knees as the recently collapsed wave was sucked back out to sea in a mass of hissing bubbles. He drew level with her and wordlessly she pointed across the water.

Over a backdrop of purple islands rising from the horizon, a distant flock of seabirds was crossing the sky. The slow flap of their wings caused shimmering sunlight to glance off their white underfeathers, making them glint and flash like a shoal of fish in a hazy sea.

"It's so beautiful," she murmured dreamily, as he curled an arm around her waist.

Half an hour later, dripping wet from their swim, they staggered across the sand, hanging on to each other, bouts of breathless laughter making them unsteady on their feet. Back in the bungalow, neither said a word. Instead they made straight for the bedroom, leaving damp, sandy footprints on the tiled floor behind them.

Shrugging the shoulder straps of her swimming costume off, Charlotte unrolled it down to her waist and lay back on the white sheets. Tom gazed down for an instant before climbing on to the bed. Staying on his knees, he leaned over her, swept wet tendrils of hair to the side and began kissing her damp neck. The draft from the ceiling fan above made him aware of the droplets of seawater still clinging to his back as he brushed his lips across her breasts, tasting the salt water on her skin, licking where it had pooled in the hollow of her navel, working his way further downwards before slipping her swimming costume off completely.

The next morning they were just finishing off two tropical fruit salads in the huge timber-framed resort restaurant when Daniel wandered over and asked if they would like to book a "Discover Scuba-diving" course.

"The Seychelles have some of the finest reefs in the world," he proudly announced. "I can recommend it as the thing to do during your stay. Our diving instructor, Sean, is from Cairns in Australia. He says what we have here is equal to anything you'll see on the Great Barrier Reef."

Tom looked at Charlotte uncertainly — he'd never so much as snorkelled before.

"Can we?" she asked.

Tom sat back. "Why not?"

"Excellent. I will let Sean know," replied Daniel. "When would you like to start?"

"Let's not rush anything. Tomorrow, after lunch?" said Tom.

After breakfast the next day Tom said with a sigh, "Well, I suppose I'd better check back with the office and make sure everything hasn't collapsed." They walked back to the bungalow and he plugged in the laptop and modem. Once the machine had booted up he tried to go online, but a window soon informed him that it could not make a connection. "Shit!" swore Tom as the screen popped up for the second time.

"What's wrong?" Charlotte called through from the kitchen.

"No bloody internet connection." Angrily Tom unplugged the laptop and put it back in the carry case. "It'd better not be something wrong with the computer."

In the resort's office he was able to link up to the internet without problems. "So it's the socket in the bungalow," said Tom. "Can you get it fixed immediately?"

Daniel made a call, spoke briefly in the French dialect before looking mildly sheepish. "An engineer can come out from Mahé in two days' time," he told Tom.

"Can we move bungalows, then? I stipulated that office facilities were essential when I made my booking." Tom was irritated at how, even in such idyllic surroundings, his businesslike tone had reappeared so easily.

Daniel's embarrassment deepened. "Your bungalow was a last-minute cancellation. All the others have been booked for months. But we can clear a desk for you here — you can make use of all our facilities until the problem is resolved."

Tom looked around the cramped room, catching the eye of the receptionist, who looked like her entire future happiness depended on him saying yes. "OK, it will have to do."

Eagerly they cleared the desk in the corner and he sat down. As soon as he connected to his mailbox a message marked "Urgent" appeared at the top. "Lorzo's gone into receivership. Please call asap. Ges."

Tom stared at the screen, totally stunned. The printers were their sole supplier of building wrap posters and were midway through at least half a dozen jobs. He couldn't believe they'd gone bust.

"Everything OK?" asked Daniel, nodding his head as if that could influence the answer.

Tom looked up at him. "I'll need to make a phone call. Could I have some privacy, please?"

Daniel waved the girl from the room and closed the door behind him.

"Ges, tell me that's a joke," said Tom into his mobile, knowing it wasn't.

At the other end of the line Ges said, "Sorry, Tom. We heard yesterday. Anthony's buggered off back to Italy. His son's left here to pick up the pieces."

"How could they go belly up? They were raking it in from our business alone, surely?"

"Everything was leased. They were so heavily into the bank you wouldn't believe it. You know how costs have come down now everything's gone digital; they were doing our stuff for next to no profit. Anyway, they missed too many payments and the bean counters decided enough was enough."

"I don't believe it. Erection dates are due for at least three of those fucking building wraps. Email me the contracts. I'll have to see how much liability rests with us if we miss the deadlines."

Tom opened the top drawer of the desk, vainly hoping a packet of paracetamol might be inside.

When Charlotte knocked on the door at 2.30 Tom had to blink several times to adjust from the view on his laptop screen to his real-life surroundings.

"Tom, you've been in here for hours! It's our diving lesson now. Do you need some lunch first?"

Tom nearly burst out in hysterical laughter; his appetite had completely vanished. Instead he looked at his watch, deciding that nothing major was likely to occur in the next couple of hours. "No," he said, attempting a smile. "Let's go for it." Plugging his mobile into the charger, he locked down his laptop and stood up.

"Problems in the office?" asked Charlotte breezily as they walked across the foyer.

"Yeah, a few hiccups."

As they approached the small hut by the swimming pool they could see a figure lounging in a hammock off to the side, one brown leg dangling above the grass. As they got nearer the well-toned torso of a young man, face hidden beneath a straw hat, was revealed to them.

"Are you Sean?" asked Charlotte.

The hat was removed and a handsome face appeared, all sparkling blue eyes and white teeth. Sean eased himself from the hammock and held out a hand. "Charlotte and Tom, yeah?" he asked in an easygoing Australian accent.

"That's us," answered Charlotte, smiling.

"Cool," he said, looking up at the sky. "I thought we could cover the theory bit today — about two hours' worth — and do the pool bit tomorrow. Sound good?"

Thinking that he had to get back to events in Manchester, Tom quickly agreed, "Yes, that's fine." Hearing his own uptight tone, he looked at Charlotte and added more gently, "No point in rushing anything, is there?"

Charlotte shrugged her shoulders in passive agreement.

"No worries," answered Sean. "Let's sit in the shade out here. I'll get the flipcharts. You guys want a Coke or anything?"

The theory consisted of going over the basics of how the equipment worked, including the instruments on the tank and the rubber mouthpiece, known as the regulator. Finally he explained how an actual dive was conducted, pointing out that he would be divemaster and they would be each other's dive buddy. Tom found his attention kept wandering back to the office as he ran over in his mind how they would reschedule their printing jobs now Lorzo's had ceased trading.

The end of the afternoon and early evening was spent exchanging emails and the odd phone call with Ges and the London office. It was 10p.m. in the Seychelles and 6p.m. in England when Tom finally conceded they would have to call it a day and resume tomorrow.

In their bungalow he threw off his shirt and lay back on the bed, mind still racing. A light caress took him by surprise and he looked down to see Charlotte's fingers drawing a lazy circle across his stomach. Instead of instant stirrings of desire, all he felt was irritation at her touch. He turned away and, as her hand fell on to the mattress, he mumbled that the flight had finally caught up with him.

The phone began to blast out tinny music. Sly paused, the carapace of a live cricket held between one finger and thumb. At the bottom of the vivarium the tarantula's eight eyes fixed on the waving legs of the insect above and its own legs shuffled slightly in readiness for the coming meal.

When Sly saw whose name was glowing on the display screen, he dropped the cricket to its death, slid the hood back over the vivarium and picked up the phone.

"Hey Dan, where are yous?" Manchester accent almost pushing the words through his nose.

"Outside the building, man. You ready?"

He looked round the interior of his brand new Urban Living flat, eyes settling on the ornately carved wooden box sitting on the arm of the reclining chair that was positioned directly in front of the widescreen TV. "Fancy coming in for a smoke or a toot before we get started?"

"Nah, man, it'll be light in a few more hours. Let's get going."

Sly sighed and looked at his watch. "OK." Crouching down, he watched with pride as the spider crept stealthily towards the chirruping cricket, bunched legs rising and lowering as if controlled by a puppeteer's strings. Grinning, he stood up and put on a Helly Hansen jacket, then positioned a Burberry baseball cap over his ginger hair. After grabbing his little kit off the peg in the hall, he opened up the industrial-style metal door and stepped out onto the decking that bordered the feng shui courtyard shared by the flats in the renovated mill.

He glanced up at the sound of footsteps. Making their way towards him were his immediate neighbours. On seeing him, their conversation had instantly dried up.

He looked the woman up and down, sucked his teeth and raised a forefinger. "Now I don't want you two coming back from your clubbing and rousing the rest of us with your boom boom music." He smiled, knowing the reverse was usually the case. Avoiding eye contact, the couple huddled at their front door while the husband tried to get the key in the lock.

Laughing quietly to himself, Sly jumped down on to the freshly raked white gravel making up the Zen part of the courtyard and strode across its middle, his trainers crunching out a trail of footprints behind him. He could feel the couple's eyes burning into his back and he imagined how pissed off they must be — over a hundred grand for a one-bedroom city-centre flat and they end up with a gangster like him for a neighbour. Fuck 'em.

Beyond the front gate of the building, Dan's Ford idled on the street outside. Sly pressed the unlock button on the side panel and the gate slid slowly back into the wall. Stepping through, he crossed the pavement and leaned down to the driver's window.

"Dan, my man," he said, letting a touch of Jamaican patois creep into his accent.

The black face smiled up at him and they pressed their knuckles together for an instant. "Sly. Ready to roll?"

He nodded in reply, walked round the vehicle and slid into the front passenger seat.

"I thought we'd take a little drive out Wilmslow and Alderley Edge way," Dan said. "Our friends are still looking for BMW A5s, preferably black. Plenty of folks out there need them for getting over those nasty bumps in the Marks and Spencer's car park at Handforth Dean."

Sly laughed, "Yeah — or maybe we should find a footballer's house. Half those wankers playing at Old Trafford turn up in them on match days."

The car pulled away.

"They still after Audi TTs?" Sly asked.

"Always."

"Let's go via Didsbury, then. I want to check on that house from a couple of weeks ago — I've got a longer garden cane to play around with this time."

Jon Spicer's radio finally came to life. "Unit one here, we have a scrote alert. Blue Ford Mondeo turning into School Lane, two male occupants, passenger wearing a baseball cap."

Jon was sitting in the passenger seat of an unmarked Golf VR6. He'd been scanning the deserted Didsbury Street while listening for any sort of contact on the police radio for almost four hours.

Parked at strategic positions in the area were three other unmarked cars, each one waiting to catch a glimpse of the gang taking high-performance vehicles in the south Manchester area.

Jon looked up. They were parked at the intersection of Atwood Road and Catterick Road, six streets away from School Lane.

The voice on the radio continued, "Unit three, if he continues along School Lane you should see him on your right any second."

"Unit three here; I'm looking," Jon replied, leaning forward in his seat, eyes fixed on the stretch of road leading down to School Lane. Twenty seconds passed and no car crossed the intersection. "Nothing has shown, Boss," he announced.

"OK, units two and four, anything?"

Both cars answered negative.

"Unit three, have a little scout around. There's not many side roads he could have turned down."

Next to him, Sergeant James Turner of the Tactical Vehicle Crime Unit took the last sip from a can of Tango, crumpled it and dropped it into the small box on the floor behind the driver's seat that served as their makeshift bin. He started up the engine and turned right on to Catterick Road, then on to School Lane itself.

He cruised to the end of Ladybrooke Road and was slowly turning around when unit one came over the radio. "We have a member of the public reporting a prowler on Moorfield Road. Some guy fiddling at the letterbox of number sixteen."

Jon flicked on the interior light to look down at his blown-up page of the A to Z. "That's the next street," he said, thinking the address somehow rang a bell. Turner accelerated back up to School Lane and turned right. As they were about to enter the junction for Moorfield Road, a dark blue Ford crossed the road in front of them and Jon caught a glimpse of the driver. "The Ford has just crossed in front of us, going into Parrs Wood Road. One occupant only." He craned his head to the left. "Registration Alpha 478 . . . I've lost the rest. Shall we go after him?"

"Negative," answered unit one. "We'll intercept him. Get to number sixteen and see what's happening."

They had got halfway along the street, trying in vain to spot a number on any of the dark houses, when a car reversed sharply out of a driveway ahead. It quickly swung around, headlights sweeping across the front of Jon's vehicle, making his pupils contract so quickly his eyeballs hurt.

"Is it him?" Turner said.

By now they were level with the car. Jon looked to his right, saw the silhouette of the driver, a baseball cap on his head. He realized it was an Audi TT, and everything suddenly clicked. They were at Tom Benwell's house. "Yeah, it's him! Turn around!"

Turner yanked the car sharply across the road and executed the fastest three-point turn Jon had ever experienced. As he was thrown back and forth against the seat belt, Jon said, "Unit three here; we're following an Audi TT. It's turning left, left, left on to School Lane, repeat School Lane."

Keeping in second gear, Turner floored the Golf and it accelerated up to forty in seconds. He shot out of the junction with School Lane, skidding slightly as the car veered to the left. Thirty metres in front the Audi suddenly bolted forward like a spooked animal.

The radio blared, "Unit four here; we're at the junction of School Lane and Wilmslow Road. I'm parking sideways across the street."

"Unit three here," said Jon. "He knows we're after him."

A couple of seconds later unit four responded. "I can see his headlights approaching! Come to Daddy you little bastard."

The Audi showed no signs of slowing down. It raced past La Tasca's then, at the last second, cut up a tiny alleyway, joining Wilmslow Road metres away from unit two.

"Shit!" came the shout from the side-parked vehicle.

Turner mirrored the Audi's manoeuvre, bouncing out on to the main road. "He's turned right, right, right on to Wilmslow Road, repeat Wilmslow Road," announced Jon.

"Unit one here; no sign of the Ford. For God's sake maintain visual contact with the Audi. I've requested helicopter assistance for you!"

Turner raced along the high street, the trendy shops and bars thinning out as they left the village. "He's heading for Kingsway and the motorway junction. We don't want him to make that — if he gets back onto home ground he can lose us in some maze of a housing estate," Turner said.

Jon nodded, eyeing the road as it opened up in front. They were now doing almost eighty, whipping past a church on their left. Suddenly the Audi began losing speed.

"What the hell is he doing?" asked Jon, unable to understand why the car should be suddenly slowing up.

Turner was laughing. "He can't find a gear, the prick."

They had nearly caught up with him when the driver finally got the car in gear. But his speed had been lost. He turned sharply to the left, cutting between two traffic islands and into a narrow lane running alongside a huge cream-coloured pub.

"What the . . .?" said Turner, screeching to a halt and spinning the wheel around.

"Oh, superb," said Jon, slapping his free hand on the dashboard. "It's a dead end. Just leads towards Didsbury Toc H's pitches. Beyond that is the River Mersey." He lifted the handset to his lips. "Suspect has turned right, right, right on to . . ." he looked up at the side of the pub as they entered the lane, ". . . Stenner Lane, repeat Stenner Lane. It's dead end. Where's the helicopter? He's likely to be on foot soon."

"About five minutes away," answered unit one.

The Golf clattered along the uneven surface, its lowered suspension making every bump jar through the seats. Up ahead the red taillights of the Audi jerked up and down as the car also struggled over the cobbles. Suddenly the trees seemed to close in as a gate reared up from the darkness. Unable to stop, the car crunched into the thick gatepost at its side. The driver jumped from the car.

Thirty metres behind, Jon watched it all happen in the glare of the Golf's headlights. "Suspect on foot, heading along the lane past Didsbury Toc H Rugby Club and towards the River Mersey."

Before they had come to a halt, Jon's door was open and he was clear of the vehicle. Vaulting the gate, he began sprinting along the footpath, sets of white rugby posts just visible through the screen of trees to his right. He heard the sound of feet on wooden steps, reached them seconds later and bounded up. He was on a footpath. To his right he could just make out the dark figure running away, rasping breath clearly audible in the still night. He knew that up ahead a footbridge led over the Mersey to the next stage of the Trans-Pennine Way, a walk connecting Liverpool on the west coast and Hull on the east. "I hope you enjoy running," Jon shouted out, resuming the chase. "You're on a pathway that's over three hundred and fifty kilometres long."

Now gasping for air, it was the last thing Sly needed to hear. Worse, the pig who had shouted it didn't even sound out of breath. Emerging from the darkness in front was a bridge. He ran halfway out over the river and looked back. The dark figure was racing towards him. It looked like the huge bastard would never slow down, never give up. Sly's bottom lip began to go as a wave of self-pity welled up: he was going to be caught. He looked at the inky blackness below, climbed up on to the waist-high metal railings and leaped out into space.

★   ★   ★

Jon heard the splash and looked up. The silhouette had vanished from the bridge ahead. He got to the end of it, straining to hear anything. Silence except for the sound of the river gliding quickly past. He stepped back and went to jump down the grassy bank to the water's edge. The dark green cast-iron post caught him full on the left kneecap and before he knew what had happened, he was lying with his face pressed into thick grass that reeked of dog's piss. He had been kicked in the kneecap during rugby matches and knew that it was the next worst thing to being booted in the testicles. All he could do was lie still, clutch the sides of the joint in both hands and wait for the agony to pass. The searing pain didn't dissipate outwards or convert to a gentle throb — instead it remained concentrated in the bone itself, losing strength with the speed an oven cools down. Several minutes later he was able to hobble to his feet, just as he heard the thrum of the approaching helicopter. He realized his radio was in the car.

Tom was working in Daniel's office when his mobile rang. He glanced down at the phone's display and picked it up. "Jon, how are you?"

"Fine Tom, cheers. Are you at work?"

"You could say that. I'm in the Seychelles, but believe me, it's no holiday. There's been a disaster at work."

"Oh," said Jon. "I'm afraid I'm not ringing with good news either."

"Go on. It can't get any worse."

"Your Audi was taken off your driveway last night. I actually chased the guy. He crashed your car into a gatepost and, I hate to say, escaped. The car's pretty much screwed. It's in the police compound now, being dusted for prints."

Tom let out a long sigh. "They didn't do the house too, did they?"

"No," said Jon. "Just hooked the keys through the letterbox."

Tom groaned. "And you bloody warned me."

Jon said nothing.

"Oh well," Tom continued. "Cheers for letting me know. Look, I'd better go — there's all sorts going on."

"OK mate, phone me for the number of the police compound when you get back."

Two thirty arrived and with it Charlotte rapping on the door. Tom had spent the morning writing to his clients with the nearest deadlines, explaining their problems with the printers. He'd been able to speak with Ges at one o'clock, only to learn that the other two companies in the Manchester area with printers capable of producing building wraps were booked out for weeks with council-paid banners for the Games.

"OK, OK," he answered irritably. "Just shutting down."

She came in and looked at the untouched sandwiches a staff member had brought into him an hour earlier. "You've missed lunch again?"

"What? Oh yeah, I'm not hungry. It's this heat," he said, even though the room was air-conditioned.

At the pool they stripped down to their swimsuits and climbed in the shallow end. "Right," said Sean. "Tom, let's get yours on first." He hoisted the single tank on to Tom's back and then pointed out how to tighten the straps. Turning to Charlotte he did the same for her. Tom noticed him gently reposition her shoulder straps, letting his hand brush against the outside of her breast as he did so. She glanced up, but Sean's eyes were hidden behind his mirror shades.

Once his own gear was on, Sean said, "So, the way the regulator works is simple. You put the entire thing inside your lips and up against your teeth. When you want air you bite down on it and breathe in slowly. Of course, opening up your lungs goes completely against your instincts once your head is underwater, so take your time."

Looking suspiciously at the black mouthpiece, Tom sniffed it then slipped it into his mouth. Immediately he found the size of it intrusive, the rubbery surface nauseating. It felt similar to the type of gum shield rugby players wore. He could never face using one of those during his playing career. Slowly he tried to bite down on the inner part, but the sensation was unpleasant — like chewing on especially tough gristle. His tongue made contact with it and he realized that it tasted the same as it smelled. Suddenly the presence of it under his lips and against his teeth was too much. He began to retch and pulled it out.

"Made you feel sick, yeah?" asked Sean.

"Yes." Tom wiped his lips, looking at the glistening object.

"Don't worry mate, plenty of people spit their dummy out to begin with. Just try again; there's no rush."

Tom looked at him, wondering if the reference to dummies was part of some diving lingo or an attempt to belittle him. Gingerly he tested the mouthpiece in his hand, feeling its pliability and imagining all the other mouths it had been in before, picturing their saliva coating its surface, particles of food catching in its crevices. Meanwhile Charlotte, used to snorkelling, had sunk slowly below the surface. Aware of Sean watching him, Tom tried again. But as soon his lips stretched round the rubbery object, the retching returned, this time with some burning liquid at the back of his throat. He had to swallow quickly before its acrid taste flooded his entire mouth. "I can't do it. I'll puke."

Sean waded slightly closer to him. "It's called a gag reaction. Plenty of people experience it. You want to give it another try?"

Tom looked down at the sun-dappled form of his wife beneath the water. Every so often a stream of bubbles rose to the surface. "Can she continue the course without me? You know . . . the buddy system you described."

Sean flicked a strand of sun-bleached hair from his face. "I can buddy for her; that's not a problem."

No, thought Tom, I bet it isn't. But he couldn't insert that disgusting thing in his mouth again. Old memories began to stir, ones he tried to suppress: the days of struggling with physics and chemistry, lying awake in the early hours of the morning wracked with worry. The dream still recurred now whenever he was under pressure: him looking at the timetable in the corridor at school and realizing there was an exam that afternoon for which he had completely forgotten to revise. The dread sense of impending, and completely unavoidable, failure.

Full of trepidation, he raised the mouthpiece to his lips once again. Immediately his stomach constricted and, as he felt the bile rising at the back of his throat, his mouth formed into an "o" in readiness to vomit. He dropped the regulator into the water. Attached to his tank by a long black tube, it snaked lazily off to the side.

Not looking at Sean, Tom moved over towards his wife, bent down and held a hand beneath the water to touch her. She got to her feet, breaking out into the air, water cascading off her. Plucking the regulator from her mouth, she swept back her streaming hair. "Everything OK?"

Tom tried to mask his sense of humiliation with humour. "It's bizarre, but I can't do it, babe. There's something about the rubberiness of the regulator. All slippery and bouncing off my teeth." He shuddered in disgust. "It makes me want to puke more than a shot of tequila. Listen, Sean here can buddy you, so carry on without me. I need to try and sort out this work stuff anyway."

Charlotte placed a hand on his arm, "Are you sure? You really can't stand the feel of it in your mouth?"

"No." He shook his head, grinning. "But hey — the only fish I like to see come served with a lemon wedge. You enjoy yourself." Before she could object further he began shrugging off the canister.

After a quick shower Tom hurried back over to the hotel's office, head bowed as he picked over the problem. He realized he was now barely noticing the beautiful scenery around him.

By the end of the afternoon they had located a printer in London who could, for a price, print two of the building wraps over that weekend. Once they'd negotiated a price for transporting the wraps and the printer crew up to Manchester to actually hang the things, that was two of the four jobs with the most imminent deadlines taken care of. Next Ges suggested looking for printers in Europe or even North America.

"Jesus," answered Tom. "But what about the logistics? And do we know if they even use the same Vector and In Position software as us?"

"Well, unless you can come up with anything else, I suppose we're going to have to find out," Ges answered, now sounding as stressed as Tom felt.

That evening, as they ate red snapper cooked on a barbecue by the side of the main pool, Charlotte asked if everything had been sorted out yet.

"We're getting there, babe," he replied. "Two of the most urgent jobs are sorted, and we're now trying to find another printer for the remaining two. Problem is, we're talking twelve-floor-high images here, and that takes a specialist . . ."

Seeing her eyes beginning to wander, he cut off his reply, claiming he'd had enough of work. Instead he asked her how the diving was going.

Immediately Charlotte perked up. Taking a large gulp from the ice-cold bottle of Seybrew, she began telling him how great it had been gliding along the bottom of the pool, listening to the rumble of bubbles as they flooded over her ears. Even as Tom sat back, content just to watch his wife describe something that so obviously delighted her, office issues were pinging up in his head like emails arriving on a computer.

After a few more beers they ambled back along the softly lit path to their bungalow. Inside the air conditioning was gently humming and Charlotte headed straight for the bedroom. Tom paused at the desk in the dining room and sat down to write out some reminders for himself the next day. A few minutes later Charlotte called out, "Are you coming to bed?"

"Yeah, in a second," Tom replied. But the stress he was under had obliterated any desire for sex and he knew he was deliberately delaying. Anxiety flickered in his stomach. The thought of slipping into bed next to her had only ever created a primal urge welling up inside him. Until now. He leaned forward and pressed his forehead against the desk in frustration. What was happening to him? By the time he wandered through to the bedroom his wife was already asleep.

While Sean took Charlotte out on her first open-water dive the next day, Tom carried out a fruitless search for a printer who could help them. "What about America? What's the score over there?" Tom asked Ges.

"I've got an email back from a firm in San Francisco. They do wraps for a lot of film promotions round Hollywood. It looks promising — I'll forward it on to you. Thing is, with the time differences, they're opening up just as we're going home: and I've got to take my mum to hospital this evening."

Tom didn't hesitate. "Put everything on email, I'll contact them myself. So when can I ring them?"

There was silence as Ges worked out the time difference. "Nine in the morning for them is nine in the evening for you."

Great, thought Tom; there goes my night with Charlotte. "OK, I'll call them as soon as they open. How's other stuff? Have we signed up any more merchandise promotions?"

"Julie's chasing Kellogg's. Oh, and there's something come through for Ian from X-treme, a chewing gum company. They're doing a special limited edition flavour for the Games. Free samples with a handout for a holiday competition at Piccadilly station. I'll put it in the crate on your desk."

"Crate?"

"Yeah. Your inbox isn't big enough."

Tom tried to laugh.

Charlotte got back after lunch, ecstatic about the dive. "It was like being in a big aquarium, Tom. All those fish you see in pet shops — striped ones, luminous blue ones, they're all out there. Shoals of them. And there were Moray eels, poking their heads out of crevices in the coral, doing a weird opening and shutting thing with their lower jaw. Like that politician off the telly. You know, Gordon someone."

Only hearing her last comment, Tom turned away from the sea and looked at her. "Gordon Brown?"

"Yeah, that's him."

"What's he got to do with your dive?"

"Nothing. It's the Moray . . ." her enthusiasm abruptly vanished. "Oh, never mind, you've obviously got more important things on your mind. Office stuff, by any chance?"

Tom chose to ignore the mocking tone of her voice. "We need to speak to a printer in San Francisco. Thing is, they only open when it's nighttime here, so we need to eat early this evening. I have to get on to them as soon as possible."

"Fine," said Charlotte, picking up a magazine and walking off towards a sun lounger on the deserted beach.

Tom called the San Francisco printer the moment it reached nine. A receptionist dealt with him at first, before putting him through to the voicemail of the new business director. Reluctantly Tom left a message, then sat by the phone listening to guests come and go in the foyer outside. Just before midnight his mobile went and he eagerly picked it up.

"Tom Benwell? Al Nevitt here. I understand you got some urgent business to discuss. How can I help you?"

Tom sat back in the seat, relieved to be speaking with someone who sounded so friendly. Al worked quickly and efficiently, reporting back within the hour that, with payment in advance, they could take care of both jobs within days.

Tom held up a fist in silent triumph — at last the worst of their disaster was over. He put the phone down and wandered out into the reception. The area was lit by a small lamp behind the desk and another in the corner. A couple of moths were buzzing lazily around them, watched hungrily by a smattering of geckos on the walls. The elderly night porter was sitting behind the desk, a book open on his lap. Looking at the clock, Tom was surprised to see it was the early hours of the morning. He stepped round to the customer's side of the desk, a smile on his face. Lifting an imaginary bottle to his lips, Tom said, "A beer, please?"

"Biere?" the man replied. "Oui." He unlocked the fridge to his right and took out a bottle of Seybrew then prised off the lid with the opener mounted on the wall.

"Merci," answered Tom, before giving his bungalow number and walking through the open doors and into a night lit so brightly by the moon that he cast a dark shadow across the silvery lawn. He sat down on the grass, rotating his shoulders to ease the ache in his neck. Then, almost reverently, he shut his eyes and raised the chilled bottle to his lips. As he tilted his head back, he wished every sip could taste as magical as the first.

Opening his eyes, he saw the night sky above him shimmering with an immense spray of stars. They twinkled with such intensity it seemed strange to Tom they weren't making any noise. Instead the canopy just hung there, incredibly vibrant yet utterly quiet.

112

He lay back and stared upwards, making out layer upon layer of stars, misty washes of faint ones lying behind brighter clusters, mind-numbing distances between them. He had never, apart from a few vague memories of childhood camping holidays, seen a sky like it. A sense of profoundness filled him and he felt on the verge of some revelation: as if the heavens themselves were about to speak. But the sky just carried on sparkling, as it had done since the dawn of time and as it would do for long after he was reduced to mere particles of dust.

After a while he began to try and spot which clusters of stars might form signs of the zodiac or other constellations he had heard about. Thinking back to those camping holidays he recalled that the only thing he could ever spot was the saucepan-shaped grouping of seven stars known as The Plough.

After shuffling round through three hundred and sixty degrees he eventually located it. The constellation was much lower in the sky than he expected and standing on its end. Of course, thought Tom, reasoning that being far nearer to the equator must have a bearing on the constellation's relative position in the sky. He began walking across the lawn, taking a shortcut through the palm trees for his bungalow. As he stepped between the first two trunks a web enveloped his head. It felt strong enough to trap a large bird. He stopped in his tracks, realizing that the owner of the structure couldn't be far away. Carefully he stepped backwards, relieved to feel the sticky strands slowly springing away from his face. Only when he was fully clear did he dare to look up, slowly making out the spider's black silhouette hanging like a bad omen against the glittering sky.

Sucking his teeth, Sly leaned forward in the chair in front of his widescreen TV. "Seriously, they were trying to ram me off the fucking road. One of those big Range Rovers you see on the motorways. Souped to fuck because it caught me in no time."

Dan nodded away.

"So this pig is trying to slam me into the wall all the way along Wilmslow Road. We get to a sharp bend and I see that they've only got a stinger set up ahead. Two vans, filth everywhere. I take the gap between these two traffic islands at sixty, car nearly flips, just get it under control and shoot down the side of this pub. Now I'm on a little narrow road, dark as fuck. It's only a dead fucking end. This Range Rover is still coming at me, so I smash the Audi into a post, jump out, flick him a V and sprint off down the path. End up on the banks of this river, lungs bursting, this pig still after me. Like being chased by the fucking Terminator. I run halfway over the bridge, climb up and shout at him, 'Fuck you and fuck your mum.' Then I jumped." He sat back and crossed his arms.

"Nah," said Dan. "That's how you got away? You jumped in the river?"

Sly nodded. "I knew he didn't have the bottle to go after me. And I had my Helly Hansen on. It trapped the air like a life jacket. I just bobbed off down the river."

"Where the fuck to?"

"Dunno. I floated for a while watching the cop-copter flying around with its searchlight on in totally the wrong place. Climbed out after a bit, walked over a few fields to this estate, wired a shitty old Astra and drove home."

Dan held up a fist and they pressed their knuckles together. "Safe, man. They're gonna love hearing that one in the Athenaeum."

The prospect of making an impression with Manchester City's firm thrilled Sly. "So what's on the list tonight?"

"Mercs," Dan answered, getting up.

They had got out on to the Mancunian Way when Sly said, "Let's go back to Didsbury. I want to check on that Audi address again. If his insurance company are any good he might already have a replacement one."

Dan kept looking at the road in front. "You sure after last time?"

Sly nodded, enjoying the feeling of recklessness. "The pigs won't still be there. Besides which, the Audi guy owes me."

"How?"

"I had to chuck my Rockports away after that swim. That guy is going to pay for them with his car."

"You developing a vendetta against this guy? Remember Sly, this is business."

Sly just chuckled.

As the car passed in front of Tom Benwell's house both men saw the driveway was empty.

"No one home," Dan stated, starting to accelerate away.

Sly held up a hand. "Pull in. It could be in his garage."

"Since when did we start breaking into garages?"

"Since tonight. Now fucking pull in."

Sly walked up the driveway and round the side of the garage. Cupping a hand over the end of the torch, he turned it on and held it against the window, but a tarpaulin or something similar was shoved up against the glass, obstructing his view in. Sly's eyes narrowed with irritation as he went round to the front of the garage and examined the lock. Nothing a decent screwdriver wouldn't take care of, he thought.

CHAPTER
FIVE

31 October 2002

Jon's mind drifted back to the previous night, when he had stood on Tom's empty driveway. He still couldn't believe that several months had passed since Tom's Audi had reversed out of the same driveway and he'd chased it through Didsbury. The fact that the little shit had escaped him still caused an angry throbbing in Jon's head. He knew that he shouldn't dwell on his failure, but he had been so close to catching the thief. So close.

He sighed, thinking about the Sunday evening when they'd called in at Tom's office and disturbed the shifty-looking bloke with the thick glasses. Creepy George. He decided to drive back to the office later and see if the man knew what was going on.

A sudden gust whipped raindrops against the incident room's window and Jon blinked at the noise, his reverie broken. It was his least favourite time of year — the remnants of autumn still littered the city and the clean, hard cold of winter hadn't yet set in.

Turning round, he stepped out from behind his desk and said, "Outside Enquiry Team. Door to door enquiries for the street. Anyone unusual seen entering or leaving the victim's house that morning, any strange cars parked on the road. You know the score. I'll take the neighbour — the one who shares a driveway with the victim's house. She mentioned some stuff to me yesterday, so I'll follow it up."

He glanced at a notebook before continuing. "We also need to statement her friends and associates. With the exception of the three other band members, we'll hold off taking fingerprints and DNA swabs, unless forensics come up with something specific. First thing is to interview and eliminate the other three band members. Probable scenario here is that the victim willingly let her killer into the house, so it seems she knew him. All the band members were at her house that evening — in fact they were the last people to see her alive. According to Phil Wainwright, they all left together. What we need to ascertain is this: did any of them return to her house later? Either Phil, her ex, or maybe one of the other two if she had something going on the side with them. One other thing Phil Wainwright mentioned was that Polly had been receiving the occasional call on her mobile which she was being very secretive about." He turned to the office manager. "Have we got her phone records yet?"

"Arriving today, Boss."

It was going to take a while to get used to being called that. "Right, any thoughts or questions so far?"

There were plenty of frowns from members of the Outside Enquiry Team as everyone looked at their notes. Finally a young officer spoke up. "Who was she going to go travelling with? A woman in her early twenties — she probably wasn't setting off on her own."

"Good point. Everyone put that question down on the list. Right, back here for four thirty."

He shut his notebook so the pages slapped together and everyone jumped to their feet.

Heather Rayne tied back her hair in a loose ponytail and began wiping down the beech worktops in her kitchen. The IT training sessions she ran for Kellogg's in Manchester didn't start until late morning on a Thursday so she liked to use the couple of free hours to give her house a quick clean.

As she opened the microwave up and began scrubbing away at the spatters of dried baked bean sauce on its sides, she considered her next Cancer Relief marathon. It wasn't due for another two months and her training regime was going very well. Now the evenings were darker she had to rely on the treadmills at the gym; but when there weren't any other people waiting for the machine, she could happily notch up twenty kilometres.

Mopping the kitchen floor, a thought suddenly occurred to her. She could use her Thursday mornings to get in a decent road run. But that, she reflected, would mean doing all her cleaning in the evenings. Heather didn't like upsets in her weekly routine. When they had moved the meetings in her local Conservative club to a Thursday it had really irritated her; not least because it meant recording ER and watching it on a Sunday instead.

Now in her bedroom she gathered up the assortment of shoes scattered in the corner. All but her knee-high leather boots went on the rack under the window. The boots were carried over to the wardrobe and placed inside, beneath the black PVC costume hanging there. She wiped a smear of dried saliva from its hem, smiling at the memories of when she had last worn it and looking forward to the next time it would make an appearance.

She glanced at her watch as if the wait shouldn't be a long one, and the chimes of her front door bell rang out.

Opening up, she looked at the suited man standing there. He moved the briefcase to his other hand and said, "Miss Rayne?"

At Berrybridge Road, Jon parked in the space nearest to number fifteen. Avoiding the puddles of rain dotting the driveway, he noticed the crime scene tape had been repositioned so that the neighbour had full access to her front door. Parked across the driveway with its front bumper pressed up against the tape was a Subaru Impreza.

Jon knocked on the front door and a man with a shaved head and shiny black leather jacket answered. He took one glance at Jon and shouted back into the house, "Sue, it's for you."

The man stepped past without a word and Jon could smell his furtiveness. The woman appeared in the doorway, arms folded.

Jon opened with a smile. "I hope it wasn't too much trouble yesterday."

"No," she conceded reluctantly.

"Could I ask you a few questions about your neighbour — Polly Mather?"

"I knew this would happen," she complained, stepping backwards to let him in.

The layout of the house was the mirror image of Polly's. In the kitchen piles of baby clothes were stacked on the table and an ironing board was set up in the corner. She motioned for him to sit.

Getting out his notebook, Jon looked at a pair of pixie-sized socks. "How old's little Liam?"

Guessing correctly that his interest was feigned, she answered abruptly. "Year and a bit. Can we get this done? He's due awake in another half hour. I haven't even started this bastard pile." She placed a T-shirt on the ironing board, picked up the iron and pressed it with a hiss into the material.

Jon dropped his grin, knowing she would see that as fake too. "OK, how was Polly as a neighbour?"

"Bloody noisy. Too much music. Late at night, in the mornings — didn't matter when. But I suppose it doesn't, when you're on stuff."

"Stuff?"

"I don't know. Pills and that, I should think."

"What makes you say that?"

"Well, look at her for a start. No one arrives home in the early hours and keeps going through 'til morning if they're not."

"She'd do this on her own?"

"I wish. She'd bring back all sorts. Those band members, clubber types like her. All sorts. She must have bloody handed out invites round town."

Jon groaned inwardly. The investigation looked like it might run and run after all. "How about the day before yesterday? It appears she'd had a few round that evening."

"That wasn't too bad. They kept the music down. I heard the front door shut at around midnight. The ones she was in the band with."

"You saw them leave?"

"No — heard them. Liam woke up wanting a bottle. His room overlooks the street." Another hiss as she ran the iron over a tiny sweatshirt.

"How many voices did you hear?"

"Three, maybe four. More than two, anyway."

"How about the next morning? Did you see or hear anyone leave her house?"

"No."

"When I was here, you were just getting back from somewhere. What time had you gone out?"

"About nine. I needed a couple of things from the corner shop."

"Pass anyone on the street you've not seen before?"

She gave the question a moment's consideration. "No."

"OK, thanks for your time." He stood up. "Oh, one last thing. Who was that leaving when I arrived just now?"

Her face became even more guarded. "Why?"

"Just squaring off our records."

"Liam's dad. He'd just popped round."

"He doesn't live here?"

"Not with Liam up half the night he doesn't."

Jon imagined the shrill cries of a baby cutting into his sleep in the early hours of the morning. As if on cue a bawling started upstairs.

"Shit!" She looked at the mound of unfinished ironing.

"Right, I'll be out of your hair then," replied Jon, wanting to get away before she fetched the screaming baby. Once out of the door, he scooted round to his car, retrieved a flask from the boot and went over to the crime scene caravan now parked on the kerb outside Polly's side of the house.

"Morning, Nikki. Coffee?"

"Oh, you beauty," she answered, taking the flask and pouring out a cup. "So what's shown up?"

"I was hoping you'd tell me. What time did the dodgy dad show up this morning?" He nodded towards Polly's neighbour.

"What — him with the penis-extension car?"

"That's him."

"He was here overnight. At least, he showed up mid-evening yesterday and the car was still in the same place this morning. The uniform on the door will know."

Jon shook his head. "Sad — the mum just tried to claim she lives on her own. You'd think she'd realize I'm not arsed about her scamming housing benefit payments. It's a bloody murder investigation, after all."

"Speaking of which . . . forensics have been in this morning," Nikki replied. "The SOCO found this on the victim's bed during his initial look around. It seems

Polly wasn't only earning cash in the Virgin Megastore."

She held up an evidence bag. Inside was a booklet-style photo album, just large enough to hold a single photograph on each page. With some trouble she managed to open the booklet up inside the bag, revealing two shots of Polly on her bed. In one she wore a nurse's uniform. In the other she was naked, the curtains drawn behind her, camera flash caught in the bedside mirror. The lighting was harsh and flat, giving the picture the cold and clinical feel of a gynaecological study.

Jon grimaced. "I've seen more artistic shots in the Readers' Wives section of a bog mag."

"Bog mag?" asked Nikki.

Jon let out a self-conscious cough. "Well, that's where they get read a lot: in toilets."

"You blokes," said Nikki, half amused and half disapproving. "This was at the back of the album."

She held up another bag inside which was a page from a contacts magazine. Printed on cheap paper-stock, the page was divided into a load of boxes, the text and photo inside each one slightly blurred. Looking more closely, Jon saw adverts for amateur glamour models, charges ranging from £60 to £120 per private photo session. Turning to Polly's details in his notebook, he checked her mobile number against the ones in the adverts. He quickly found a match.

"So what do you reckon? Was she in debt? Trying to pay it off by doing this sort of stuff?" asked Nikki.

"More like saving up, I think," answered Jon. "She was planning to bugger off on a backpacking trip round the world for a year. Shall I take them back to the incident room?"

"So long as you sign for them." Nikki held out her log book. "And no stopping off in the bogs en route," she added, with a quick glance at his crotch.

He wasn't sure whether to laugh or be embarrassed, but that was what he liked about Nikki: such foul things from such a sweet face.

Back at the incident room he handed in the evidence bags to the exhibits officer and sat down. "Anything in yet?" he called over to the office manager.

The other man walked over, several pieces of paper in his hand. "Nothing significant from the drains or the dustbins in the immediate area. Her bank records are due any time now and these are her mobile phone records — incoming and outgoing calls. Most caller numbers are registered, with the exception of three pay-as-you-go mobiles. Who they belong to is, as you know, anybody's guess."

"Could belong to some very interesting characters," remarked Jon.

Just before lunch the forensics lab in Chepstow called with the initial report on Polly's blood sample.

"What's showing up?" said Jon, grabbing a pen and hunching over his desk.

"It might be easier to approach this from the stance of what isn't," replied the man at the other end of the line. "Gas chromatography gave me a graph with enough peaks in it to put the Himalayas to shame. We've got all the usual suspects in there — cannabis, heroin, speed, alcohol and ecstasy."

"In what sort of amounts? Enough to render her unconscious?"

"Could be. It depends on her tolerance. Was she a frequent user?"

"Seems like she was no stranger to it."

"Well, I'd say the levels weren't enough to prove fatal. But I got an interesting blip on the graph, just above the background reading. It doesn't match any profile for the types of drugs we routinely test for, so I'll need to separate the ions in the mass spectrometer if you want to know what it is. The pH reading is acidic, so it could be some type of tricyclic antidepressant or something derived from ecstasy. Whatever it is, your run of the mill narcotic it is not. Want me to go ahead?"

Jon thought about the budget he had to play around with. Delaying a decision he said, "How about the sample from her throat?"

"Haven't had a chance to look yet. It's set in the test tube, though."

"How do you mean?"

"Become firmer, like jelly does in the fridge." There was a pause. "Come to think of it, perhaps her residual body temperature was keeping it gel at the time of collection. Odd stuff, whatever it is."

Jon came to a decision. The nude photos had given him a very promising line of enquiry. "OK, hold off on the mass spectrometer test for the moment, cheers. And please —"

The man interrupted him. "Call you as soon as I know anything more. Don't worry."

The Outside Enquiry Team began to filter back after four. By half past the briefing area of the incident room was full as the process began of entering completed actions on to HOLMES and trawling over the day's findings. No residents on the street had noticed anyone unusual hanging around and no one had observed anyone leaving number fifteen that morning.

The other two members of the band had been interviewed but, because they were both single, neither had any bed-partner to vouch for the fact they didn't return to Polly's flat later that night. The same applied to Phil Wainwright.

"Right," Jon announced. "We've had the toxicology report back. Like we thought, she was pumped full of all sorts, heroin and ecstasy included. The neighbour tells me that she would hold impromptu parties after the nightclubs had shut. She said that she used to see all sorts coming and going. I want to know where she was getting her drugs from. Someone go back to Phil Wainwright and lean on him. He's got priors for possession and he was obviously close to her."

Next Jon retrieved the evidence bags from the exhibits room and showed them to the team. "Any possible significance?" he asked the room in general.

"Could her ex — this Phil Wainwright — have found out and lost it?" someone asked.

"Possibly," nodded Jon. "Of course, she'll have had some pretty freaky people calling after she placed an ad in one of those magazines. And there are three unregistered numbers from her phone records." He looked at his watch. "People will be getting back from work soon. Let's get back over to Berrybridge Road and press on with the door to doors. We'll start working the contacts magazine angle tomorrow."

At 8.15 Jon phoned home. "Hi Al, it's me."

"Hello to the SIO. How's it going?"

Jon sighed. "Coming along, I think. There's some promising stuff to follow up so I'll be a while longer."

He hated being trapped in the office for too many nights on the trot, not least because it forced him into eating grease-laden take-away food.

"I've bunged a stew together. It's in the slow cooker. There's enough for a couple of nights . . ." She left the comment open-ended.

"That sounds great, but I'll have to save it for tomorrow. The team is phoning out for some pizza."

"That's fine," said Alice. "It'll keep."

With the issue of food sorted, Jon sat back. "How was your day?"

Alice gave a two-note hum. "OK. Not too busy. Melvyn's 'Backs, Cracks and Sacks' is going a storm. Word's out by the looks of it."

"I'll try and put that image out of my mind."

"Oh yeah, Ellie rang," Alice said. "She wanted to know if we're on for going to Edale this Sunday. We

128

could walk up to Kinder Scout and then head back down to the Nag's Head Inn for a late lunch."

Jon remembered that his little sister had just been dumped by her boyfriend. "How is she?"

"Putting on a brave face, I think. She's started to make an effort to get out of her flat more often, starting salsa lessons at Havana's in Manchester. I recommended that; you get some really fit men turning up."

"Why not bring her down to the rugby club?"

"What, and have that crowd of grunts you play with crowding round her, pints of bitter drooling down their chins?"

Jon pictured the club after most matches: a couple of dozen blokes milling around on a beer-soaked floor, each one recounting his version of how the match had turned out. He loved it, but not many women seemed to. "Yeah, you're right. But salsa? Won't it be full of sweaty Latino types?"

"Exactly," said Alice. "In fact, I might go along too."

Jon smiled. "That sounds like a good idea — Edale, I mean."

"Good," Alice replied. "I already said we'd go."

"I'm briefing the team in at eight thirty tomorrow and not due to see McCloughlin until eleven thirty. We could meet in town just after nine. You're not doing the morning at the salon, are you?"

Alice sounded surprised. "No, I'm due in after lunch."

"How about it then?"

"Yeah, sounds lovely. Jon," she said suddenly, "have you spoken to Tom yet?"

"Oh shit, I meant to visit his office today. I totally forgot." He glanced at his watch. "I'll drive round on my way home. There's a guy there who usually works late at night. He should be able to fill me in."

The traffic was almost nonexistent by the time he got away. Ten minutes later he hit the junction with Great Ancoats Street, then cut right into Ardwick. As he drove slowly along Ardwick Crescent the narrow strip of park was in darkness to his left. The glow of the petrol station across the road revealed the forms of two men as they lurked in the shadows beneath the trees. But unless they started mugging someone, he couldn't be bothered.

Instead he looked to his right, getting a glimpse through the open doors of The Church and seeing it packed with drinkers. Thursday night. In these parts the weekend kicked off tonight and kept going until Monday.

Getting to number seven he looked across the street, then climbed out of the car, confused. The office door was blocked up with a sheet of heavy-duty chipboard that had already been covered in a mishmash of graffiti. He walked over, eyes on the most legible line of writing.

There's nothing smart to dying, read the fat felt tip.

Below it a thinner scrawl replied, *Piss off and do it then.*

Looking between the bars in front of the windows, Jon could see a mound of post on the reception floor. He walked to the glass panels screening off the alleyway between the two houses: the pair of rubber plants stood tall and brittle, their leaves yellow and curled to parchment. Glancing up he saw the remains of an estate agent's sign hanging by a couple of nails, most of it torn off.

As Jon walked slowly back to his car, he thought back to the summer, analysing his last encounters with Tom, probing for any clues in what he'd said and how he'd appeared. There was no doubt he was sick of Manchester when he got back from the Seychelles.

CHAPTER
SIX

June 2002

"Hi, Jon Spicer here."

"Jon, it's Tom."

"Hello mate, nice end to your holiday?"

"Not really. I spent the whole time bathing my brain in low-level radiation from my mobile phone."

Jon held his own mobile a little further from his ear. "So when did you get in?"

"Yesterday, just after lunch. Listen, what's the score with my car?"

His friend's abruptness put Jon on edge. "It's at a secure compound just outside Stockport. You'll need to sign some forms and they'll release it. You've got some ID on you?"

"Yeah, and a spare key. Is it driveable?"

"No," said Jon, wincing with guilt. "But various towing companies hang around the place like vultures. Tick the boxes on the forms and it'll get taken back to the Audi garage your company hired it from. Let the insurance company take care of it from there."

"OK, what's the address? I'll get a cab over."

Jon couldn't help feeling responsible for the situation. "I'll pick you up. Where are you?"

"On the train, just getting into Manchester."

"All right, I'll be there in ten. Meet outside the Bull's Head?"

Tom had picked up a slight suntan during his time away, but the strain on his face cancelled out any healthy appearance. He settled into Jon's passenger seat with a preoccupied look.

"So where were you staying out there?" asked Jon, trying to find something about the holiday that might raise a smile.

"Some sort of hut on the beach," said Tom. "It was meant to have an internet connection, but that was bullshit. I spent most days shut away in the manager's office, hunched over my laptop."

It was obvious the holiday wasn't a good choice of conversation. Seeing how wound up Tom seemed, Jon hoped he wouldn't ask to see the state of his car.

"So, the wrap that's just gone up on the big building on Great Ancoats Street: one of yours?"

"Yeah." He seemed to get a bit of satisfaction from that.

"You must be creaming in the cash."

Tom grinned. "Should be the mother of all bonuses when it comes through."

When they reached the side street leading to the car compound Jon said, "Right, this place is a bit grim. Let's do the paperwork and get out as fast as possible."

Tom regarded the poles at each corner of the yard. At the top of each were CCTV cameras and arc lamps in wire mesh cages. The front gates were made from twelve-foot-high sheets of grey metal. At the top of each was a spiked fence entwined with razor wire.

"Jesus, it's like Fort Knox."

"We use it for storing a lot of vehicles recovered from crime scenes. Joyriders, ramraiders, that sort of thing. Obviously we don't want the bad guys getting in to destroy any evidence they might have left behind."

They walked up a concrete ramp and into a featureless waiting room with a security hatch in the opposite wall. On the counter was a buzzer with a sign taped in front of it: Ring ONCE and wait.

Jon pressed the button as Tom looked round the room. Car crime prevention posters and insurance notices provided the only reading. A bald man eventually peered through the small window.

"Hello there, Ernie. I've got the owner of the Audi TT from a few nights ago. Can we get the release forms signed?"

He vanished and reappeared a few moments later. A few sheets of paper were slid underneath the protective glass.

Jon picked them up and turned straight to the last page. "Here, here and here."

Tom got a pen from his pocket. "Can I have a look at it?"

Jon's heart sank. "The Audi? I should think so. Ernie, can we have a quick look?"

"Sure." The man shrugged, buzzing them through the inner door. He led them into the courtyard, blue boiler suit rasping with each step.

Dotted around the place was a sad collection of wrecks, some burnt out, some with signs slapped on the windscreens that read, "Please do not touch. Police aware of this vehicle."

"In the corner." Ernie pointed matter of factly and walked away.

As they made their way over Jon began to provide a nervous explanation. "As I said, the little bastard was going too fast. He went full into a gatepost, then jumped out and legged it . . . I'm sorry."

Tom crossed his arms and looked at the car's stoved-in front end. "Well, I see what you mean about not driving it." He stepped closer. "What's all the sooty stuff around the doors?"

"Ninhydrin powder — for fingerprinting. We've lifted plenty from inside. Same as the prints on quite a few people's letterboxes. When we get this little shit in court he's going to cop some grief."

Tom was leaning forwards and looking through the passenger window. "Hey, I can see my Café del Mar CDs in the glove compartment."

As he reached for the door handle, Jon grabbed his wrist. "Wait a second. I don't know if the guys have checked underneath."

"Checked for what?"

"Razor blades. Some joyriders glue them there for a joke. I don't think this guy has because he's probably selling the cars on. But better safe than sorry." He ran a key under the metal flap, then eased the door open. "Also needles. They jab them into the seats from underneath. So when you sit down . . ." He poked a forefinger at the back of his leg.

Tom was looking shocked. "Seriously?"

"Yup. I said, these people are from a different world. Sometimes I think it would be easier just to herd them up and fire them into outer space." Carefully he reached in and took Tom's CDs out. "Anything else?"

Tom looked in. "No. That's it."

Jon pushed the door shut with his foot. "Hopefully your insurance company won't take long getting you a replacement."

Tom shook his head. "It's sorted already. My boss left and I got his Porsche Boxter as part of the promotion."

"What, you're the MD now?"

Tom nodded.

"Congratulations, mate. How does it feel to be in charge?"

Tom shook hands unenthusiastically. "Like a ton of shit is on my shoulders."

As the waiting room door banged shut behind them Jon said, "I'll drive you back to the office."

"Are you sure? Don't you have a load of work on yourself?"

Jon shrugged. "Nothing urgent." He unlocked the car and they got in. "Besides, it's the least I can do."

The anger in Tom's voice caught him by surprise. "For fuck's sake Jon, will you stop being so apologetic about all this? You've been hovering around, fretting like an old woman. It wasn't your fault and it wasn't even my car."

"The person who nicked your car got away from me. It pisses me off."

Tom sighed as he pulled the seat belt across his chest. "You can't approach your job like you approach rugby matches, making it your mission to hunt down and take out the playmaker in the opposite team."

Jon was silent as they headed back towards Manchester, his grip tight on the steering wheel. Finally he spoke. "Cheers for reducing my rugby skills down to those of a hatchet man."

"Well, like it or not, that was your primary role at Stockport. And you were the best at it by a long way. But this isn't the same. There are no touchlines to confine this gang. Unless you count the whole of Manchester as your playing area."

"I do," answered Jon. "And there's no full-time whistle either."

Tom laughed. "God, I'm glad you work for the police. Just remember though, this gang are breaking the law by nicking cars. They're not trying to get at you personally."

Jon's grip on the steering wheel hadn't relaxed. "When you spend so long after them, only to be flailing at shadows half the time, it gets pretty fucking annoying." He started bringing his fingertips down on the steering wheel, making a sound like a horse galloping. "Work. What a pain in the arse it can be."

The comment seemed to make Tom wither in his seat. "I know. I've just had the company lawyers on to me about authorizing a cheque to this firm in the States. We paid them up front to print us two building wraps."

"And?"

"They're worried that's the last we'll see of the money."

CHAPTER
SEVEN

June 2002

"So you're saying we can't do a single thing?" Tom pinched the bridge of his nose with a forefinger and thumb, eyes shut.

The company lawyer on the other end of the phone replied, "From a practical point of view, I'm afraid so. It will cost us far more in legal fees and associated costs. As I said —"

"OK, OK," Tom interrupted. "No need to go over it all again. If you could put it in writing though, thanks."

"You'll have something by tomorrow."

Tom replaced the receiver, shaking his head. The news had probably screwed up a chunk of his bonus. Choosing to ignore the piles of paper on the desk in front of him, he got up, walked out of his boss's old office and climbed the circular stairs.

"You won't believe this," he announced to the room in general, then looked towards Ges. Heads appeared round the other monitors, all eyes on him.

"That company over in San Francisco? We're writing the money off."

Ges let out a low whistle. "How come?"

"Any legal action would have to take place in the States, paid for by us. The costs are just too prohibitive."

"But surely it's fraud. Can't the American authorities do anything about it?" asked Ed.

Suddenly Julie jumped to her feet and everyone looked in her direction. London accent made stronger by the outrage in her voice, she began speaking. "Same thing happened to a mate of my dad's! He ran a cosmetics company, joined forces with a similar outfit on the West Coast of America to market his product over there. They asked if he could set up a joint bank account to make everything easier. He kept on paying more and more money in to cover what they said were production costs. All the while they were draining every penny, telling him profits would start clocking up soon. But this is the critical bit. If the rip-off is under a certain amount — a million dollars or something — it's not a federal offence. You have to pay to prosecute the case yourself, and do it in their courts over there. There was no way he could afford it. He had to walk away."

The room was silent for a few seconds before Ges spoke. "Well thank God it looks like that printer in Dublin can pick up the pieces."

"We hope," said Tom, sitting down at his desk. Looking around he realized that he'd left the file he needed downstairs — it was becoming ever more unrealistic trying to avoid moving in to his old boss's office. But in his mind he still didn't regard himself as the new managing director, even with the keys to the Porsche Boxter in his jacket.

"I need to head back downstairs to chase up Manchester Airport for some bridge banners. Anyone fancy hitting the pub at lunch?"

Julie, Ges and Ed agreed. Gemma made noises about needing to pop out and see a florist about the wedding. Creepy George kept silent behind his screen of monitors.

Downstairs Tom opened up the cabinet Manchester Airport's file should have been in.

Like so many of the others, it had been mixed up. Cursing that nothing was going right, Tom started rifling through the stacks of documents on the desk. Rather than find the missing paperwork, he discovered a load of invoices that needed sorting out. With a sigh of frustration, he scooped the lot up and placed them in his briefcase for looking at once he got home.

Tom called up to Ges's phone. "You lot ready?"

"Yeah," he replied. "We're coming straight down."

As they headed for the stairs, Creepy George stood up. "Erm, Julie. Could I keep you for a minute?"

Ges looked at his slightly blushing face and wondered what he was up to.

"I'll catch you guys up," said Julie.

George unlocked the cabinet behind his desk and got out a roll of pale blue material. "Could I just take your photo for the Manchester staff page of the company website?"

The snap he'd got of her a few weeks ago wasn't good enough, the match with the woman's torso making her look like some sort of female Frankenstein's monster.

"Can't you transfer my photo from the London page?"

"I'm having trouble accessing it. Dreamweaver is playing up." He reckoned a reference to something technical would seal his case. "It will be easier to just take another."

"Oh, OK," she answered, automatically adjusting her hair.

George pinned the material up on the wall in the corner and wheeled a chair in front of it. Then he took a digital camera and tripod out of the cabinet. "If you take a seat, I'll be two seconds."

She perched stiffly on the chair, hands in her lap, knees pressed tightly together. George examined a light meter in his hand and then looked at her through the viewfinder, zooming in on her face. "OK, the flash will go off, so just keep your eyes shut for the test shot."

Julie raised her chin a fraction and closed her eyes. There was a light click as the photo was taken.

"That's great," said George. "Now one with your eyes open and a nice smile."

She did as he asked and he took another photo. "Perfect," he said, straightening up. "I won't keep you any longer."

"Cheers," said Julie, hurrying from the room.

George watched her nervous exit with some concern: he wanted her to feel relaxed in his company. As soon as she set off down the stairs, he hurried round to the Apple Mac on his desk. He plugged in the digital camera and transferred the two shots to the desktop. He'd put the one with her eyes open on the company website later. Now he clicked on the other image. Her eyes were closed. She looked defenceless, helpless. As he stared at her face, he thought about the two of them alone, lying next to each other. He imagined whispering how beautiful she was, caressing her cheek, sweeping stray strands away from her face. Then, with a thumb, lifting her eyelid to check she was completely unconscious.

The door to The Church creaked open and they pushed their way into the dimly lit interior. The pool table was free, so Ges flicked Ed a quid coin. "Rack them up and I'll get the drinks in."

"Don't worry, Ges, I'll take care of it," said Tom, holding up his company credit card.

"You sure?" asked Ges uncertainly. "We're not exactly clients."

Tom shrugged. "So? What are you having?"

"I like your management style. Pint of lager, cheers."

"Ed?" Tom called over to the younger man as the balls were released into the end of the table with a sound like distant thunder.

"Same as Ges, thanks."

Tom turned to the barman. "And a large glass of white wine for me." He was just placing the drinks on the table when Julie walked in. He waved at her. "Julie? It's on the company."

She grinned. "Vodka and Coke, thanks."

"What did Creepy George want?" Ges asked her.

Involuntarily, she shivered, causing Tom and Ges to laugh. "My photo for the Manchester staff page of the company web site."

"Oh yeah?" said Tom. "I bet he's in the toilets with it right now."

"Oh don't!" she cried. "I can just imagine him and all . . . not that I want to." She picked up her drink and went over to the pool table.

"So what can we do about that twat Ian?" asked Ges, elbows on the bar and head slightly bowed so he didn't bang it on the glasses hanging down from the rack above.

Tom's face soured. "I suppose we have to hope he hasn't actually removed stuff. If he's just fucked the filing system up we should be able to sort it out again, given time. I imagine that's what he's done; that way we can't prove it was him. If stuff has actually gone missing, I imagine we could look at taking legal action. Jim Morrel, the IT guy down in the London office, is trawling the computer system checking through all the files there. I should think he'll find deleted or sabotaged electronic files quicker than we'll find paper ones up here."

"Jesus." Ges picked up his pint and took a sip. "It's just one thing after another."

"Tell me about it," said Tom. "Anyway — let's not talk office; it's doing my head in. I'm taking a leak. You lot can decide on who plays with who." He pushed through the double set of doors leading into the toilets and walked across to the stainless steel urinal running the length of the far wall. Undoing his fly, he looked down. Nestled among the yellow squares of soap, he saw lump after lump of spat-out chewing gum. The urinal's flush started up and a fine spray of water began hissing down, droplets gathering in the dimpled and creased surfaces of the discarded gum. Staring at their rubbery surfaces, he was reminded of the little droplets of water in the folds and crevices of the regulator in the swimming pool on the Seychelles. Once again, he could taste the rubber and feel the sensation as it entered his mouth, pushing up under his lips.

Suddenly his stomach churned and he let out a little retch. He turned round, walked across the narrow room to a cubicle and emptied his bladder into a toilet.

CHAPTER
EIGHT

June 2002

"This is asking for trouble," said Dan uneasily as he turned into Moorfield Road.

"Chill," answered Sly. "We're just looking."

Outside Tom Benwell's house, Sly clicked his tongue in appreciation. "Our man is moving up in the world. Porsche Boxter. I'll settle for that."

The car pulled over and Sly got out and made his way quietly up to Tom's front door. Once again the letterbox was pushed open and the torch probed the interior of the hall, moving slowly over the small table, searching for the keys. Unable to see them, Sly hoped the bastard hadn't started taking more care where he left them. Before standing back up he whispered through the letterbox, "You'll leave them out one of these nights."

At the roundabout off junction six, Dan looked at Sly. "Which way, Altrincham or Wilmslow?"

"Let's do Wilmslow," announced Sly and the car took the first exit. The road was single lane until it reached the tunnel going under the end of Manchester airport's runway. Dual lanes opened up and Dan increased speed, following a Hackney cab ferrying a passenger from a late-night arrival. As they entered the tunnel they were plunged into a world of orange provided by the continuous bank of bulbs running along both edges of the ceiling. Sly watched the multiple reflections racing along the sides of the taxi like a display on a fruit machine. Then they were out the other side, following the winding road in darkness until the street lights at the edge of Wilmslow began.

The streets had a village-like feel to them — pretty terraces of houses, erratic and jumbled, roads leading to little triangles of grass or narrow junctions. Clogging the pavements and driveways all around were the latest models of expensive cars.

Soon they reached a house at the end of a slender street. Beneath a cherry tree in the front garden gleamed a Mercedes. The gates at the end of the short drive were open.

"Try this one?" asked Dan, parking up.

"OK." Sly jumped out and pushed the door quietly shut. A quick look through the letterbox revealed a table with a set of keys almost within touching distance. He hooked them out in a couple of seconds, then waved Dan off. But when he pressed the key fob, the lights that flashed belonged to a Renault on the road in front of the house.

"Bollocks," said Sly, eyes on the silver Mercedes. He examined the other keys, saw the one for the front door and let himself in. Fresh flowers in the hallway, a red umbrella standing in a pot by the front door. He shone the torch at the coat rack — no man's jacket in sight. A good search of the lady's coat hanging there revealed no keys so, taking his Stanley knife out, he climbed the stairs. First bedroom had breathing, the other two were silent. He stepped into the occupied room and turned the torch on to her face. She blinked a couple of times, then raised herself up on one elbow, letting out a low moan of fear.

He stood over her, relishing the sense of power, wondering whether to yank the duvet off. "The keys to the Mercedes. Now."

She started shaking violently, silent tears streaming down her cheeks. No reply.

He took the Stanley knife out of his pocket and held it in front of her face. The triangular blade eased out of the stubby handle with a series of clicks.

Still no reply.

Sly leaned forward and realized her eyes were tightly shut. She was trying to pretend it was all a bad dream. He slapped her hard across the face, sent her banging against the headboard. "The Mercedes, bitch."

She heard that and pointed to the bedside cabinet.

He crouched down, opened the door and pulled out her handbag. Purse with a wodge of tenners. Mobile phone. Mercedes keys. He pocketed the lot and looked at her again. If she wasn't such an ugly munter he would have considered it. Instead he picked up the phone on the bedside cabinet and cut the wire with his knife. "Stay in your bed for the next half hour. My mates are parked outside to make sure you do."

He walked out of the room, trying not to laugh.

CHAPTER
NINE

June 2002

As Tom walked towards his front door, he held a hand up to shoulder height and pressed the key fob. Behind him the Porsche replied with three pips, the hazard lights flashing with each one.

As he pushed open the front door, it caught on something just inside the hallway and he had to step through a narrow gap to get in. Looking down, he saw piles of Habitat bags strewn across the floor, a couple of Diesel ones hung over the banisters. A musty smell of cigarettes hung in the air and then he noticed a trail of dusty footprints running up the stairs. "Charlotte!" he called out.

"In here!" she answered from the front room.

Wearily, he pushed the door shut with one heel and dropped his briefcase next to the shopping bags. In the front room he found her standing in a little vest top and shorts, ironing the collar of a white shirt.

"What's all that mess in the hallway?"

"If you're talking about the Habitat bags, it's stuff for the bathroom."

"And all those footprints?"

She draped the shirt on the end of the ironing board and grabbed his hand. "Come on, I'll show you."

Following the trail of plaster dust, they went up the stairs and along to the door leading into the bathroom. "Where's the fucking bath?" he asked, surveying a room stripped of all its appliances, workmen's tools littering the floor. The smell of cigarettes was much stronger.

His wife sat down on a stack of floor tiles, lifting up a Fired Earth brochure. "I told you — we're having this room redone. Ensuite? Knocking through in to our bedroom?"

Tom leaned against the door frame. "I don't remember you mentioning it."

Charlotte shook her head and turned back to the brochure. "It's been on the calendar ever since we got back from the Seychelles. You just never listen to me."

Deciding whether to escalate things into another argument, Tom said, "What are those tiles you're sitting on?"

Charlotte ran a hand over them, as if she could feel their quality through the layers of plastic wrapping. "Italian marble. They're absolutely gorgeous." She stood up. "We're having an oyster shell bath here." She made a lavish circular motion with both hands in the far corner. Swivelling on her heel she pointed to the wall where their sink used to be. A shorn-off pipe jutting through the floorboards was all that remained. "New sink here." She pointed to Tom's side. "Walk-in shower there; you know, those ones with the jets that nearly knock you over. And," she flicked her hand to the other corner, "toilet and bidet there."

"Bidet?" said Tom. "I don't think I've ever used one in my life. Except to clean that dog turd off my shoes that time in Paris."

"Very romantic," answered Charlotte, before raising a hand upwards. "Recessed halogen lights in the ceiling. That wall will be taken out so we can walk straight in from our room, and the door you're standing in will be closed up. We'll have one of those vertical radiators in its place."

"So how long are we going to be confined to the spare toilet and shower in the attic conversion?"

"They'll be about another eight days. I reckon less — you should have seen how fast they ripped everything out."

I bet, thought Tom. Probably sold it on to a reclaimer's yard already. Wrinkling his nose, Tom looked critically round the room, spotting the big ashtray from the dining room by a paint-splattered radio. It was brimming with the crumpled ends of roll-ups. Regarding the evidence of unfamiliar men in his house, Tom felt somehow that his territory had been violated. "Jesus, how many of them are on the job?"

"Four or five. I think another one joined them this afternoon."

Tom didn't want to know how much it was costing him. He stepped towards the ashtray. "Did you have to let them smoke in the house? The whole place stinks of those rancid roll-ups." He knew he was goading her.

"Oh stop bloody moaning, for God's sake," Charlotte replied, voice midway to anger. He had a bit of leeway yet.

Then he noticed the lumps of chewing gum amongst the butts. His attempt at winding her up was suddenly forgotten as he turned away in disgust. He waved a hand towards it. "For fuck's sake, that's a crystal ashtray. They've stuck their bloody chewing gum in it." He clamped a hand over his mouth.

That did it. Charlotte stepped up to him, one finger angrily jabbing the air. "Can't you be happy that I'm trying to improve our house? God, if it was left to you we'd still have exactly the same hallway carpets as when we moved in. And what is it with this aversion you've developed? Ever since the Seychelles, the slightest thing makes you start retching. You should see a bloody doctor," she snapped, striding angrily out of the room.

He walked after her. "Actually, it's just . . . just stuff that's been chewed, that's been in other people's mouths. I think . . ." He stopped speaking, realizing this revelation only opened him up further.

Sure enough, Charlotte paused in the doorway to their bedroom. "Do you realize how much of a freak that makes you sound?"

Tom knew he wasn't going to win this one. It was time to retreat. "Where are we going out?"

Charlotte's shoulders relaxed a little. "Our table at The Restaurant Bar and Grill is booked for eight thirty. Doors to Chilli Pete's open at ten, I think."

Tom glanced at his watch. That gave him forty-five minutes to get ready.

Then Charlotte added in a much sweeter voice, "Can you give that Brain a ring? See what he's got. I don't fancy any of that skaggy speed again."

There was the signal: if he rang Brain their tiff would be over. If getting more drugs would put her in a better mood, he was prepared to do it. It might even lead to other stuff later, he thought, trying to remember the last time they'd had sex. "Sure, we can call by on the way into town. I don't mind driving tonight."

Argument won, she blew a kiss over her shoulder and disappeared into the bedroom.

Downstairs, he switched on the computer. While it booted up, he gave Brain a ring.

"Hello." A voice box sounding like it had been rubbed with a cheese grater.

"Brain, it's Tom. Any chance of stopping by in about an hour?"

"Good timing Tom, shopping's just arrived."

"Excellent." Tom smiled. "See you in a bit."

He hung up and then went on to the internet. Clicking on the Cornwall Guide, he checked that the cafe on Harbour Road was still for sale. Finding that the little thumbnail photo and description of the property were still posted on the site, he directed a silent thank you to the heavens, then went upstairs to get changed.

Tom found a parking space on the street along from Chilli Pete's. Turning off the engine, he looked across

152

to his wife. Spread across her lap was a selection of pills and powders.

"E?" she said, holding up a pill.

"Don't mind if I do," he replied, popping it into his mouth and knocking it back with a swig of mineral water.

Charlotte took two and he passed the small plastic bottle to her. "Right, let's leave the coke for the weekend." She put the wrap of paper back in the glove compartment. "What was this stuff again? I can never understand his sandpaper voice." She held up a plastic sachet with a self-sealing top.

"He said it's something he brewed up himself. Like GBH, but it gives you a much cleaner lift. And a lot stronger, too. He said to just take a tiny dab."

"Sounds intriguing," Charlotte replied, slipping it into her push-up bra. "I might try a bit later."

Returning the rest of the ecstasy tablets to the glove compartment, they got out of the car and walked to the club's entrance. After a cursory search at the doors, they headed down the stairs and into a dimly lit lounge area. Huge brown leather sofas and armchairs were arranged in pods around low glass tables lit from below by single soft bulbs. Round the corner the dance floor pulsed with intricate laser effects as some sort of trance track slowly built up momentum.

"What are you having?" asked Tom as Charlotte nabbed a corner armchair.

"Just water," she replied, reaching for her cigarettes.

Tom made his way across the half-full lounge area to the bar and ordered a bottle of mineral water and a bottle of Tiger beer. Back at their seats he slumped down and lit a cigarette. Charlotte was leaning sideways in the seat, legs crossed just above the knee, one elbow on the wide handrest. With a cigarette held just in front of her lips, she surveyed the room, eagerly examining what everyone else was wearing.

After a while Tom began to sense waves of energy emanating from his chest. They spread to his arms and legs, infusing them with urgency. The music suddenly seemed to connect with him on a much deeper level. "You coming up yet?" he asked Charlotte, realizing that the question wasn't needed when he saw how fast her knees were jiggling.

She turned to him, eyes bright. "You dancing?" she said in a mock northern accent.

"Why, you asking?" Both of them laughed and jumped to their feet.

They stayed on the dance floor for almost an hour solid, just letting each successive song carry them along, swaying and grinding until a change of tempo or a burst of vocals lifted them up and set off another burst of energetic dancing. Eventually they took a break, breathlessly sharing a bottle of water at the side of the dance floor, Tom holding the cool plastic against his forehead before gulping down his half. Using his body as a shield, Charlotte slipped the plastic pouch from her bra and opened it up. "Fancy any?" she asked, glancing down at what was subtly cupped in her hand.

"No, cheers — I'll just see this E through," answered Tom, head nodding away.

Charlotte licked a finger then dipped it into the bag. It came out coated in a sherbet-like powder and she popped it into her mouth, washing it clean with her tongue. "Another for luck," she said with a mischievous smile, licking her finger and dipping it in again.

Back out on the dance floor the music was picking up, people were starting to shout in appreciation, glow sticks had started to appear and the mass of bodies moved with more purpose, the crowd sensing the next phase of music was going to build and build.

As usual Charlotte had quickly manoeuvred her way into the middle of the dance floor. Her hair was tied back in a long ponytail and as her body pulsed back and forth she started sweeping her head from side to side, the blonde mane flicking against those around her, causing several people to turn and watch. Tom was just clicking into his usual routine — hovering slightly to her side, just close enough to let the other men in the vicinity know they were together — when Charlotte lurched against him.

Instinctively he grabbed her waist to steady her, but next thing her legs folded and she crashed to the floor. Those in the immediate vicinity stepped back, but other people, unable to see that someone was down, carried on dancing, bumping into the stationary people. Moving quickly before someone fell over her, Tom hooked his hands under her armpits and hauled her upright. Someone helped him to carry her off the dance floor and place her in a chair at the back of the lounge area.

"She's out of it!" the guy shouted. "What's she taken?"

"Nothing much," Tom yelled back, wanting to get rid of him as soon as possible. "Just a vodka too many."

The man glanced at Tom, looking unconvinced. Then he turned back to Charlotte. "Can you hear me, love?" he asked her.

"I told you," said Tom impatiently. "She'll be all right."

"And who are you?" asked the man. "How do you know her?"

Tom held up his wedding ring, then grabbed Charlotte's hand and showed him the matching ring on her finger. "She's my wife, all right?" His voice was tight with irritation.

The man looked at their fingers and seemed reassured. "Listen mate, I'm not being funny, but you could have been anyone. You know, I was worried. All this stuff about date rape drugs. She's totally out of it, after all."

Tom could appreciate how dodgy the situation must have looked to a stranger. "No, you're all right mate, I see your point. But she's my wife. A bit of a headcase, but still my wife."

"OK. You sure you don't need help?"

"No, thanks anyway."

For some reason they shook hands and the man disappeared back towards the dance floor.

Tom looked back at his wife. Her whole body was limp, eyes shut. "Shit," he said, pulling her upright and having to grab her jaw to stop her head lolling forwards.

"Charlotte, can you hear me?" he shouted into her face. She appeared to be totally unconscious. He placed a hand against the left side of her chest — her heart was pounding, but not ridiculously so. Looking around, he saw a bottle of water on the table in front of them. Leaning her back in the seat, he reached out and grabbed it. Then, holding her head back, he tipped a little into her slightly open lips. She coughed but didn't come round. Beginning to panic now, he poured some into his hand and splashed it against her forehead. The water dripped down her face and neck, running into her raised cleavage. He poured more into the palm of his hand and splashed it into her hair, then raised the bottle and poured some directly on to her head. Her eyes stayed shut. Not caring if the bouncers saw, he got one arm under her legs, one round her back and lifted her out of the seat; they had to get to hospital. As he made his way between the armchairs and sofas several people nodded in his direction. A couple of blokes grinned and one called over, "She looks up for it!"

Then, as he neared the other side of the room, he felt her head begin to move. Away from the dance floor, the music was fractionally quieter. "Charlotte, can you hear me?"

She moaned and her eyelids began to move. He sat down in an armchair with her on his lap. Getting his face close to hers, he repeated her name. Bit by bit she came round until, after a few minutes, she half opened her eyes and mumbled, "Where are we?"

"You collapsed. Out on the dance floor."

She seemed to think about that for a few seconds, then her eyes slid shut. Just as he started to worry that she'd passed out again, she whispered, "Take me home."

After folding the duvet around her, he scraped up her damp dress and underwear. The little plastic sachet of powder fluttered to the floor. Picking it up, he walked downstairs and put the desk lamp on. Two teaspoons' worth of fine white powder formed a triangle in the corner, a couple of lumpy bits where Charlotte's damp fingertip had been.

He lifted the phone, knowing Brain rarely slept at night. "What the fuck was that powder?"

"Who's this?"

"Tom. I called in earlier tonight to pick up some shopping. You had a new . . . spice."

"Oh that," answered Brain and Tom could hear his grin. "Knockout, isn't it, my friend?"

"Knockout? You could fucking say. My missus is completely asleep upstairs."

"I told you — it's something new. I put it together using a recipe from the States." He put on a Mexican accent. "You only need a leetle beet, amigo. Es claro?"

"Yeah, you said," Tom felt slightly sheepish, realizing Brain had warned him. He thought about the two large dabs his wife had taken. "What is it?"

"I told you earlier. It's very popular with men who like their ladies a little more compliant, shall we say."

"You're talking about date rape?"

"Watch what you say over the phone. Those were your words, not mine."

Tom just had time to apologise before the line went dead. Hanging up, he looked at the little bag again, shook his head and tossed it on to the uppermost shelf above the computer, safely out of anyone's reach.

In the kitchen he opened up a beer and stepped through the French windows out on to the back patio. Hoping to try and spot The Plough once again, he looked up at the night sky. But all he could see was a greyish orange smear created by the massed lights of Manchester.

CHAPTER
TEN

June 2002

The sleek nose of the Virgin train eased slowly along before coming to a halt just in front of the buffer at the end of the platform.

As one, the train's doors fell outwards before sliding to the side. Watching from the barriers, Tom was returned for an instant to the Seychelles, disembarking from the plane into a holiday that never happened. Taking one last glance at the photos from his client's company web site, he started scanning faces. Soon he spotted them, briefcases and bags in hands.

Folding the printout into his jacket, Tom walked over. "James. Will. I'm Tom Benwell."

The taller, slightly balding man smiled and held out a hand. "Hello Tom, nice to put a face to your voice at last."

Tom shook hands and turned to the dark-haired man whose stare was a little too intense. Noticing his hands were still at his sides, Tom held out his own, wondering if it would be shaken. "Good to meet you, Will."

He grasped Tom's hand for an instant in a featherlike grip, then dropped his arm. "Likewise," he said with a guarded smile.

160

Tom nodded. "How was the trip up? You're actually a few minutes early."

"There you go — miracles happen. I must say, this station is immaculate." They all looked up at the gleaming new canopy of girders and plate glass arching over their heads.

"Yes," Tom replied. "The roof was replaced and the platforms revamped last year, I think. They're still working on the inner part of the station, but we're assured by countless notices it will be ready for the Games. Shall we?"

He held out a hand towards the doors leading into the main part of the station.

Inside, a corridor of blue hoardings led them towards the exit. From behind them came the sounds of drilling and hammering as dozens of workmen fought to beat the fast-approaching deadline.

Taking it all in, James said, "They'll really have this done in less than six weeks?"

In reply, Tom just raised his eyebrows as they made their way over the bare concrete floor. Out on the concourse the pedestrian walkway had been altered again to allow paving stones to be laid down.

"I'm parked just round the corner." Tom led them towards the main road.

"What's that going to be?" asked James, pointing up at a tall aluminium structure being erected at the end of the concourse.

"It's going to support the second largest LED screen in the UK. They'll use it for electronic advertisements and flashing up info on the Games."

The two visitors swapped a look that seemed to say, Why haven't we been offered space on it?

Tom spotted the exchange. "The contractors have run into funding problems — there's been no word on its completion date yet. My guess is it will still be half-built well after the Games have finished." He pointed to the line of trees stretching away up the middle of the road ahead, young leaves already covering their thin branches. "This road leads up to Piccadilly Gardens, kind of Manchester's equivalent to Trafalgar Square. Like the station, it's also been given a complete overhaul, along with much of the city centre in fact. I thought we could go back to the office for our meeting then head into town for lunch and I'll give you a guided tour."

Back at It's a Wrap they headed through the double doors and sat down at the long table. Laid out in the middle were the small folders he'd been preparing until 11.30 the night before.

"OK." Tom opened the folder before him. Below the first page's headline of "The Games Sponsors" was a mass of company logos including Manchester Airport, Microsoft, Cadbury's, Cussons, Asda, and Guardian Media Group plc. Tom began his presentation by reading out the caption at the bottom of the page. " 'The Commonwealth Games about to take place in Manchester has already attracted more sponsorship than any other individual sporting championship in the UK.' That, gentlemen, is a quote from Niels de Vos, commercial director of the Games, just last week. The

162

event has been the catalyst for an unprecedented level of development, one that has sparked a chain reaction across the city, resulting in an awe-inspiring collection of new buildings."

He turned the page, revealing a series of photographs and accompanying lines of text. "Manchester Art Gallery. Opened last month after a thirty-five-million-pound extension. Urbis, The Museum of the City, just opened at a cost of some thirty million. The Lowry Centre, opened April 2000 at a cost of sixty-five million. Chorlton Street Bus Station opened last month after a three million pound face lift. Piccadilly Gardens, opened last month after a ten million pound revamp. Piccadilly station, fully open next month after a fifty-five-million redevelopment. Imperial War Museum North, opening next month after thirty million pounds of investment. Essentially, Manchester has enjoyed two decades' worth of development in a twentieth of the time, and that list doesn't even touch on commercial ventures."

He turned to the next page.

"We have some of the most modern, exciting shopping developments in Europe. Aside from the mighty Trafford Centre, this city boasts a Selfridges, Europe's largest Marks & Spencer, The Great Northern Movie Megaplex, The Printworks and The Triangle, home to shops and restaurants such as Quicksilver, Muji, Jerry's Home Store, Zinc Bar and Grill, Wagamama . . ."

"Wagamama?" Will piped up. "I didn't know you had one of those up here. That's my favourite place to eat."

163

"Well," replied Tom, anxious to keep the momentum going, "let's eat there this lunchtime. Gentlemen, come the opening ceremony on the twenty-fifth of July, we expect more than one million visitors to be enjoying this city's unique atmosphere. And in the middle of all this celebration will be your building wrap."

"Would anyone like another Kirin?" asked Tom, as his clients picked out the last of their noodles from the giant bowls. Both men declined, so Tom discreetly asked for the bill. After everything was settled they climbed back up the stairs, emerging from Wagamama's subterranean floor on to the wide pavement.

"Right, if we wander past the new Marks & Spencer building, we'll get to the site of your building wrap in about ten minutes," Tom said.

They crossed the plaza, walking past the giant windmill-like structures with their slowly revolving sails outside the front of the store.

"All this seems new as well," remarked James, waving a hand at the plate glass and textured concrete surrounding them.

"It is — well, relatively at least," answered Tom. "This whole area had to be rebuilt after the IRA bomb went off in June '96." He pointed to an old-fashioned red postbox that stood somewhat inconspicuously in the modern city-centre street. "That was the only thing that remained standing in the immediate vicinity, so it was left as a sort of monument. We're actually standing at the bomb's epicentre, or what you'd call Ground Zero these days I suppose."

A short walk later, Tom pointed across the road at an old building that, like many others along the stretch of road, was clad in scaffolding. "There you go — Crossley House. Soon to be luxury flats but, for the next two months, the frame for Arturo Aftershave. Directly behind us, as you may already have smelled, is Chinatown itself — a magnet for diners each lunchtime and weekend. And of course Princess Street itself is one of the main roads shoppers and commuters take in and out of the city."

"Seems like a great site," answered James. "So where are we in relation to Piccadilly Gardens? I understand that will be quite a centre of activity during the Games."

"Absolutely," answered Tom. "If we turn left on to Portland Street, it's at the top of that."

Once on the main road the two visitors immediately looked up at the bright yellow side of Portland Tower. Will read out the lettering above the digital screen. "Counting down to Manchester 2002 Commonwealth Games." The screen now glowed with the number forty-one. "There's quite an atmosphere building up," he conceded.

Halfway up the road a white lorry with blacked-out windows pulled up at the lights beside them. In front of them a girl in a mini-skirt was waiting to cross the road and a load of banging started up inside the vehicle.

"It's a prison van, ferrying people from Strangeways to the courts over there," Tom explained, pointing vaguely ahead and to the right. The lights changed and the van pulled away. Written into the dirt on its rear doors were the words, "Crim Coach. Bad men insi-" The "d" and "e" of the last word had been wiped off by a handprint.

It was a side to the city Tom didn't want his guests to see. As if on cue, Will said, "Is there still a lot of deprivation in Manchester? Coming in on the train, outside of the pristine centre you're showing us around, there seemed to be a lot of run down and empty buildings. Ones with chimneys like in those Lowry paintings. They weren't being done up by any property developers."

Tom almost said that behind the nice building wraps, you're never far from dereliction in Manchester. Instead he parroted a politician's reply. "Well, the industrial parts of the city undeniably suffered as manufacturing died away. But things are looking up, thanks to over two billion pounds of government, council and EU money."

Will was looking unconvinced as they reached Piccadilly Gardens. Tom gestured around. "This was only opened four weeks ago. Once the Games start there'll be giant screens set up and carnival performers and street entertainers walking around. The side of Sunley Tower here," he directed a finger at a tall thin building overlooking the gardens, "will have a seventy-three-metre-tall image of an athlete hanging down it."

The two men looked around, James saying, "And if we get the weather, that fountain will prove a hit."

They watched as dozens of columns of water began emerging from the flat, round surface of what appeared

166

to be a large concrete disc laid over the lawns. Half a dozen soaking kids began screaming with delight.

A hit with whom? thought Tom, choosing not to tell his visitors that, before being revamped, the old Piccadilly Gardens had been listed as one of Europe's top five spots for picking up rent boys. Already complaints had been made to the police about older men loitering in the new gardens, watching children playing in the fountain.

Tom walked them over the lawns and on to the expanse of new paving interspersed with saplings and benches. "This area is already popular with workers at lunchtime."

James looked down. "It's lovely stone — swirling reds and greys. Such a shame about the gum."

"The gum?" Tom looked down at his feet.

"Those white blobs. It's chewing gum people have spat out. It's far worse round London. Mind you, these pavements are new. Give it a few weeks though . . ."

Tom looked with revulsion at the paving surrounding them. Dotted here and there was the occasional circular shape of greyish white. He'd always been vaguely aware of the strange markings on the pavements, but had never realized until now that it was discarded chewing gum. He felt saliva flood his mouth and the blood drain from his face.

To his side, Will said, "They spend a fortune trying to clear it up. I think they should ban it like they've done in Singapore."

Tom cleared his throat. "I imagine the council will keep close control. I know litter clearing is a massive priority with the number of visitors expected." He looked around and lifted his voice. "Shall we return to the office? I suppose it's time we got your bags and checked you in at your hotel."

James looked at his watch. "You're right. So you'll pick us up at around nine? We can't wait to try out Manchester's nightlife. Canal Street is where it all happens, isn't it?"

"Yeah, there are plenty of good bars there," answered Tom, wondering if they knew it was the gay village.

Back home he found a note in the kitchen. "At my evening aerobics class. See you later." He flipped the square of paper over and wrote. "Out with clients, back who-knows-when. See you in the morning." After heating up a meal for one, he showered and changed into a Ralph Lauren shirt and DKNY jeans then sat down to start signing off the internal expenditure for that week. Clicking open his briefcase, he stifled a yawn and began leafing through the pile of paper inside, looking for where he'd stashed the sheath of purchase orders.

His eyes caught on a fax at the bottom and before he'd even read the first line, his head was in his hands and he was whispering "Shit," over and over again. In a gesture that combined despair with defeat, he drew his fingertips down his cheeks, pulling the skin around his eyes down and exposing the red insides of his eyelids. Blinking several times he looked back down at the piece of paper, suddenly feeling very tired.

It was a reminder from Centri-Media telling him that, if he didn't immediately confirm their slot at Piccadilly Station for the X-treme chewing gum promotion, it would be offered to another company. He remembered shoving the papers in his briefcase before a pub lunch with his colleagues days ago. He hadn't looked at them since. Tom's eyes crept over the page to the date of the fax: it had been sent ten days ago.

The energy seeped out of him and he sat back in the seat. He felt like he was sinking. As fast as he cleared jobs, more were piling up. The only thing to keep the pressure from totally stifling him was the thought of resigning in just a few weeks' time. He imagined the bonus that he was due — the key to his move to Cornwall. The clock in the corner of his computer screen told him it was almost time to go out and meet his clients, but all he wanted to do was slump in front of the TV or, better still, go straight to bed and catch up on his sleep.

He stood up, raised a hand to his jaw and began massaging it, wondering what to do. There was nothing he could do but forget about the missed promotion until the morning and go and pick up his clients. Fatigue seemed to have suddenly rooted him to the spot. He reached up to the top shelf and felt around with his fingertips until he located the little plastic bag.

Brain's words came back to him: "Just a leetle beet, amigo." He licked the very tip of one finger and lightly dabbed the powder. It clung to the moist skin like a dusting of mould. Licking it off he rubbed his tongue on the roof of his mouth savouring for an instant the faintly sharp taste. Then it was gone, diluted by his saliva. He swallowed and put the sachet back on the shelf.

By the time his taxi dropped him off at the Malmaison a new lease of life was flowing through him. On the way he'd chatted animatedly with the cab driver about the forthcoming Games, the driver joking that if tourists wanted to walk through the likes of Beswick to get to Sportcity, the police had better form a corridor of officers the entire way or there would be the biggest mugging spree the city had ever seen.

Tom found himself laughing as he walked through the smoked glass doors into the hotel lobby. Will and James were waiting for him in the bar so he sat down, took out his company credit card and enthusiastically said, "Another drink before we hit Canal Street?"

Five bars later and Tom was fairly certain his clients were gay. What had clinched it was Will's reaction on seeing the defaced CANAL STREET sign. Someone had scratched off the first letter of each word, causing Will to burst out laughing at the words "ANAL TREET".

As ten o'clock approached James said, "A friend of mine recommended a club called Cruise — is it near here?"

"Yeah," nodded Tom. "Just over there. You want to go now?"

"Sounds good," replied James.

They cut round the back of Bar Med, walking along the side of a deserted NCP car park towards the brightly lit rainbow banner hanging above the doors to Cruise. As they neared the club they could hear music thumping. Groups of immaculately dressed men were moving inside, the light colours of their clothes contrasting with the black suits of the bouncers. Stepping into the pool of light shining down from the lamps above the door, Tom saw that the pavement in front of the entrance was covered in a cluster of pale chewing gum circles. As he watched, a man approaching the open doorway paused to pick a piece of gum from his mouth and flick it away. Tom watched it land and then roll a few inches before sticking fast to the stone surface, glistening slightly in the bright light. Imagining the warm, slippery sensation of it in his mouth, his stomach contracted. To make it to the doors, he would have to cross the marbled patch of pavement.

"I'm sorry guys — I . . ." He struggled for an excuse. "I really need to call it a night."

He looked at their confused faces.

"You don't want to go in?" asked James, frowning.

"Is that all right? It's just suddenly caught up on me." He reached into his pocket. "Here, you two go for it. Have a good time." He held out a fan of ten-pound notes.

"Tom." Will stepped towards him with a patronizing smile. "We're not a couple, you know. You won't be playing gooseberry while we snog on the dance floor."

"No, it's not that. Loads of my friends are gay." He couldn't believe he'd just come out with that. "As I said, I'm just knackered. Here — please take it; it's all on expenses."

He held out the money but James waved it away. "Not if you're not coming in with us. We'll pay our own way, thanks."

"OK." Tom knew he was breaking the cardinal rule of client entertainment by not being the last to bed. "What time shall I pick you up tomorrow?"

"Ten?" said James, already moving away from him.

Unable to step any closer to the gum-spattered area in front of the doors, Tom could only stand where he was and weakly call out, "Have a great time!"

CHAPTER
ELEVEN

1 November 2002

Jon shifted the shopping bag to his other hand and looked at his watch. "I'm not going to make this. McCloughlin wants to see me at 11.30. If I walk with you back to Piccadilly station, you can get the train home and I'll get a cab over to the nick. Is that all right?"

Alice linked her arm through his. "Two whole hours of shopping; I should count my lucky stars I've had you this long." She looked up into his face. "You're going to be buried in this new investigation, aren't you?"

Jon looked away, eyes on the passing traffic. "Not necessarily. There are some promising leads."

Alice squeezed his arm. "Jon Spicer, the only time you agree to go shopping with me is when you're trying to atone in advance for something."

Jon thought about the coming weekend. He'd already made himself unavailable for Cheadle Ironside's match on Saturday, receiving a load of grief from the coach when he did. He was fairly certain their plans to go walking in the Peak District with his sister on Sunday were going to fall by the wayside too. "OK, yeah. You might be having Sunday lunch at the Nag's Head Inn without me."

She pressed her head against his upper arm. "There'll be other weekends when we can do that."

He put his arm around her and hugged her close, thankful as always for how understanding she was. But a small part of him quietly whispered, Will she be this reasonable if there's a baby in the house?

Jon stared down at his feet. "I'm going to miss Ellie again. I was looking forward to seeing her."

"What about if we invite her round tonight? She hates being stuck in on her own on a Friday. I'll get a video and stuff."

"Nice thinking. I'll try and get away at a decent time." He pulled his mobile out and dialled. "Ellie, it's me, Jon. How are you doing?"

He could detect the forced cheer in her voice as she claimed that she was fine.

"Listen," Jon continued. "I'm caught up in this new investigation, so probably can't make Edale with you and Alice this Sunday."

"Oh," she said, voice now small.

Jon continued quickly, "What are you doing tonight?"

There was silence as Alice waved at him vigorously. "Just ask her!" she silently mouthed.

Realizing his question had put her on the spot, Jon said, "How about coming round to ours? Alice will get a video and curry so we can just take it easy."

Ellie pretended to think about it for a second. "Yeah, that sounds great. Cheers."

"OK," said Jon, winking at Alice. "By the way, I'm going to be flitting round the city centre. You want me to get you anything from that delicatessen you like? Some of that Aussie chocolate — what's it called, Violet Crumble?"

There was a smile in her voice as she said, "No, you're all right. But thanks for the offer."

Mary Walters smoothed her bedcovers down and straightened up. One by one, she picked up the soft toys from the bedside table and placed them carefully on her pillow. The routine was a daily one, largest bears at the back, leaning against the headboard, smaller ones at the front, leaning against their larger companions. Sometimes she would swap the smaller toys round a bit, just to give each one a front-row view of her bedroom.

Satisfied with her arrangement, she turned her back on their collection of sweet faces. In the hallway she went through her coupons and vouchers, deciding that she would visit Netto later to cash in her discounts on Robinson's Barley Water; even though the sunny weather was long over, the taste would remind her of the summer. She thanked the Lord for little pleasures like that.

Now in her front room, she peeked out of the window at the yard behind her flat, face squirming with distaste at what she might see. But, to her relief, no used condoms were stretched out on the asphalt like huge albino slugs. Her sign had really worked and she thanked the Lord again.

At the table she sat down, knowing there were a couple of hours before her friend Emma arrived. She began sorting through the notices for the forthcoming play at Sunday school. Noah's Ark. It never failed to get the children excited, all the pairs of lovely animals trooping on to the cardboard ship, blue sheets ready in the wings for when the flood waters began to rise.

She glanced at her watch and, as if on cue, the doorbell rang. Mary looked round the curtain and saw a man standing on the top step. He was wearing a suit and holding a briefcase. He looked just like one of the men she went knocking on doors with, handing out the Lord's magazines. As she opened her front door to him, he smiled and said, "Miss Mary Walters?"

Jon and Alice continued their walk up Portland Street. As they drew level with the Yates's Wine Lodge, Jon said, "Let's cut round by the law courts — it'll save us a few minutes."

He moved the shopping bag back to his other hand, examining the ruts the thin plastic handles had gouged in his fingers, flexing them back and forth to help get the blood flowing again.

"No pain, no gain," Alice joked. "It'll be worth it, you'll see."

Jon looked into the bag at the juicer box inside. "It had better, the amount it cost."

"You just wait — I've found this excellent recipe book. With the amount of healthy drinks we'll be having, there'll be no colds in our house this Christmas."

"No, just mounds of fruit pulp!"

"There's even suggestions for juice drinks to combat cravings. Ginger, aniseed or wheat grass can all help, apparently."

An image of Alice as some modern-day witch dropping God-knows-what into the top of the appliance appeared in his mind. "Hubble bubble," he murmured to himself as they got to the corner of the law courts.

Jon looked at the derelict building opposite, The Department of Employment. There's got to be some sort of irony in that, he thought, scrutinizing the court entrance as the last of another bunch of shaven-headed scrotes in shell suits shuffled inside for their hearing.

They crossed the tram tracks curving away to Piccadilly station and Alice began examining the fly sheets that had been pasted on to the chipboards nailed over the ground-floor windows of the empty building. The council had been round making half-hearted attempts at peeling them away, but had only succeeded in ripping off the top layers and revealing what had been taking place on the music scene several months before.

"Heathen Chemistry by Oasis," said Alice. "That bombed."

"Kylie Minogue's Fever Tour, the little minx," said Jon looking at another. Alice punched him on the arm as he continued, "David Bowie at the Move festival; we really should have got tickets for that."

"Yeah," answered Alice, a nostalgic look on her face. "The Thin White Duke — that brings back memories." She snaked both arms round Jon's waist and pressed her body against his. "In fact, one of our first ever snogs was to "Ashes to Ashes". Do you remember? Outside the scout hut disco?"

Jon smiled with the memory.

"How about it? Just for old time's sake," she asked mischievously.

Jon looked around, seeing other bag-laden shoppers making their way back towards the station. "Here? Now?"

She pouted with mock petulance. "You never kiss me in public any more." She dropped her arms and walked away.

They carried on, walking past the top of Canal Street and then along the side of the Malmaison hotel, crossing over London Road at the big set of traffic lights. The station's gently sloping approach road had only been properly completed in the weeks after the Commonwealth Games had finished — an attendant permanently stationed in a little hut at the junction prevented cars from trying to drive up what was now a road reserved for buses and British Transport Police vehicles. They slipped between the bollards placed across it, stepped on to the pavement and made their way up to the main entrance.

In the tunnel below the station a tram slid to a halt and Sly stepped out on to the platform. He followed the other passengers up the stairs and then on to the shiny escalator, emerging in the main station area.

Looking around, he saw that the interior had been carefully designed to make it hard for beggars to find places to sit. Shame, he thought, thinking about the money he used to make around the old station.

Without consciously doing it, he began to scan the people around him, automatically looking for anyone not guarding their bags properly.

Jon and Alice were standing at the departures board, trying to work out when the next train to Heaton Chapel was. Finally the display changed. "Ten minutes," Jon announced.

"Great. Listen, I've got to have a wee; the toilets are over in the far corner now, I think. Wait here with the shopping."

"Go on then," said Jon, putting the bag down.

Alice followed the curved wall around, reached the toilets and found her way barred by a turnstile. Placing her handbag on the barrier, she rummaged inside for change, but could only find two ten-pence pieces. "Excuse me?" she asked a lady coming out, "Do you have a twenty-pence piece I could swap for two tens?"

Sly saw the fit-looking blonde woman place her bag on the barrier, then turn her back on it as she tried to get change. His reaction was as automatic as that of a spider seeing a fly land on its web. He strode over, one hand darting out and snatching it in an instant. As he went past he moved it round his side, then held it close to his stomach, out of her sight as he sauntered away.

Jon was watching the giant screen flashing up the day's headlines. The bulletin came to an end and he glanced down to see a weaselfaced man with wiry ginger hair walking towards him. Just before he looked back up at the screen he half noticed a brown leather bag in the other man's hands. It seemed odd that a man should be carrying a handbag, but his attention was on the trailer for some new series starting on Channel Four.

A minute later Alice appeared at his side, visibly upset.

"What's up?" He held a hand towards her.

She stopped short of his reach and banged a fist angrily against her thigh. "Oh Jon, I'm such a stupid arse. I've just had my bag snatched. I was trying to . . ."

Jon remembered the ginger-haired man. He thought that he'd looked dodgy, but now he realized the bag held against his stomach was Alice's.

Without saying a word he spun round and ran back towards the sliding doors at the station's entrance, taking in the number of people around, already knowing the chances of spotting him were slim. There was no sign of him. Looking to his right, he saw a passage leading into a car park — no way of telling which way the man had gone.

"Shit!" He strode angrily back into the station. A policeman was standing next to Alice and Jon walked up to them. "No sign of the little shit," he said.

"This, by the way, is my partner," Alice told the uniformed officer.

He gave Jon a cursory nod and turned back to Alice, pen and notepad ready.

Jon looked round the station and saw the CCTV cameras positioned all around. Getting out his warrant card, he interrupted the officer. "Where's the control room? I got a glance of this guy — he has to be on film."

Seeing Jon's rank, the officer immediately turned his attention away from Alice. "This way, sir."

They followed him over to an anonymous-looking door marked "Private" and the officer punched in a code. Once inside they walked down a short corridor into a dark room lit by a stack of TV monitors. A man sat before them sipping a cup of coffee.

Taking his helmet off, the officer said, "Simon, DI Spicer. His partner just had her bag snatched from outside the toilets and DI Spicer might be able to provide an ID. Madam? You can use this phone to cancel your cards."

Jon crossed the room and, staring at the screens, sat down next to the man. Looking at the variety of views, he said, "Quite some system you get to play with here."

The man smiled. "Where were you when you saw him?"

"Under the departures board — he went right past me."

The man pulled his chair closer to the array of controls on the angled desk before him, punched a few buttons and turned on a screen to his right. "How long ago?"

"Four, five minutes, max."

The view from a camera directed at the area by the departures board came up with a date and time display in the right-hand corner. The tape rewound, and Jon watched as all three of them walked backwards into the picture. Next Jon reversed out of the shot, followed by the police officer. Alice stood on her own for a bit before Jon jumped backwards up to Alice's side then turned around. They talked for an instant before Alice backed off the screen. Jon now stood on his own looking upwards. A stream of people reversed past, before Jon suddenly said, "Stop!"

The image froze without a flicker or shake and Jon jabbed a finger at the monitor. "That's him."

"Here we go, the wonders of digital technology," said Simon, zooming in on the man. Alice's bag was just visible in his hands.

Simon leaned closer to the screen. "Well I never, it's the Ferret. Haven't seen him for many a month."

"The Ferret?" asked Jon. "You've got his details?"

Simon shook his head. "Unfortunately not. That's just my name for him. He's a nasty piece of work. Before the new station was built he used to tax the beggars for prime positions — by the entrance to the old Wimpy, next to the ticket office windows, those sorts of spots. The lowest of the low. Plus bag snatching — plenty of people could describe him, though we've never actually caught him in the act. But we didn't have this CCTV system then."

Jon stared at his image. "Can you send me a print of that?"

"You can have one right now." Simon pressed another button and the printer to his side began to whirr. "And I think I can go one better than that." He checked the time frame on the image of the Ferret then brought up the view from the camera trained on the entrance to the toilets. "He wouldn't still be snatching

182

bags if he had any idea of the power of this video system." He rewound to twenty seconds before the Ferret had passed Jon, pressed play and there was Alice, standing at the turnstiles, searching through her purse. She turned towards a lady, holding out a hand with two coins in it.

The Ferret entered the picture on her left, moving slightly quicker than the flow of people walking past. A hand shot out and Alice's handbag vanished.

"Gotcha!" Simon announced. "That's good enough for a prosecution. Now you just need to find the Ferret himself."

Half an hour later, Jon was staring at his boss's door, running through a quick mental check. Satisfied nothing so far in the investigation had been overlooked, he knocked twice.

"Come in," said the voice. Jon opened the door and stepped inside.

"Morning DI Spicer; it is still morning isn't it?" McCloughlin said, leaning forward to check the clock standing on the corner of his large desk. "Ah, yes it is."

Knowing this was McCloughlin's way of saying he was late, Jon replied, "Sorry about the delay, sir. My partner had her handbag snatched in town."

McCloughlin held his eyes for an instant, checking that it was a genuine excuse.

Jon took the chair opposite, file balanced on his lap. "Certainly feels later than 11.30 to me."

"Long day already?" McCloughlin said with some sympathy. "Come on then; what are the developments so far?"

Jon opened the file. "Well, not a major amount to be honest. We're just completing the Major Incident First Actions. The mother, Diane Mather, has filled us in on the basics of her daughter's life. Twenty-two years old, single, worked shifts in the Virgin Megastore on Market Street, vocalist in a band called The Soup — fairly well known locally. Few gigs in Band on the Wall and The Night and Day Cafe."

McCloughlin raised his eyebrows to indicate he had no idea what Jon was talking about. "Don't worry, it's my age. Carry on."

Jon gave a half smile. "Enjoyed clubbing, a regular out and about round town. Socialized mostly with the other band members and a few of the staff at Virgin, people she'd met on the club scene and old mates from college. Her neighbour described her as a bit of a ravehead, intimating that she used drugs. There was evidence of that in her house, too. Could be relevant."

McCloughlin nodded his agreement. "Which college did she go to?"

"Stockport. HND in Communications and Media."

His senior officer rolled his eyes. "What happened to courses where you actually learned something useful?"

Jon carried on. "Her mum insists, as they always do, that she didn't have an enemy in the world."

"Have you put together her movements during her last twenty-four hours?"

"Pretty much; she spent the evening at home with the other band members, and they all left her at about midnight."

"Boyfriend or recent ex?"

"Recent ex. Lead guitarist in the band. The other two band members concur it wasn't a nasty split. Can't have been too bad if they were still all doing their music together."

"So what are your first ideas?"

"Well, I think she knew her attacker. She certainly trusted him enough to let him into the flat. There's no sign of a forced entry and no sign of a violent struggle inside. But somehow she ended up dead, suffocated by a load of white gel in her throat. There are also questions about how she was subdued for the stuff to be introduced in the first place. Initial toxicology analysis has shown up quite a cocktail of drugs in her blood."

"Enough of anything to knock her out?"

"The toxicologist couldn't be sure."

"How about witnesses? Did no one see anyone enter her house?"

Jon shook his head. "Uniforms have questioned all the immediate neighbours and the OET has conducted door-to-door enquiries. Most people were out at work; the remainder didn't notice anyone coming or going."

McCloughlin tapped his fingers against the armrest of his chair.

"Other points of interest," Jon continued. "She was saving up for a round the world trip. The money is still in her bank account. Thirteen hundred and forty quid.

The drawers in her room had been disturbed and a few photo albums were on her bed when I checked upstairs. One contained various shots of her posing nude in her room. It seems she was charging for private glamour photo shoots. We're checking all numbers on her phone records."

"Well, that's got to be significant. Wasn't she found in her dressing gown?"

"Yes."

"Good. Looks like there are some promising avenues to follow up there."

Jon shifted in his seat.

"Something else on your mind?" McCloughlin asked.

Jon coughed. "You mentioned on the phone about taking me off Operation Fisherman so I could concentrate on this."

McCloughlin nodded. "And you're wondering if, seeing as this case has such solid-looking leads, you can keep an oar in Operation Fisherman?"

"Just pop my head in every now and again. Keep track of developments."

McCloughlin didn't look pleased. "This is your first murder case as SIO. Believe me, it will soak up attention levels you didn't know you had, however simple we think it appears. I don't want anything to distract you." He sat back in his seat and interlinked his fingers. "I pointed this out on your last assessment, Jon. You have a propensity to fixate on certain cases. You're not a Mountie, always getting your man. You're in the Greater Manchester Police and the modern system means you can be switched off cases as and when events demand. Get used to it."

Jon stared at the floor.

McCloughlin regarded him for a second longer. "Listen, once this case is cleared up, you can return to your place on Operation Fisherman. But remember, this one is . . ." The phone on his desk began to emit a pleasantly subdued beeping. Raising one finger, McCloughlin picked the receiver up. "Yes?" His eyes, previously on the pad of paper in front of him, suddenly lifted to Jon's face. "I understand. Give me the details again."

He scrawled them down on a memo pad and hung up. "Another body has been found. Mary Walters, twenty-three years old. Flat one, forty-six Lea Road, Whalley Range. The attending officer says her throat is blocked up by white stuff."

As they drove up Withington Road, Jon observed the cafe bars and stylish restaurants creeping outwards from Chorlton. "Jesus, this place has changed," he remarked.

McCloughlin didn't answer and Jon continued to stare out the window at a stretch of enormous houses flanking the road. Built for wealthy cotton merchants in the last century, all had long ago been divided into flats or converted into drab-looking guest houses with vacancy signs in the front windows. Now it seemed every other one was clad in property developer's scaffolding. Signs strapped to the metal poles announced who had laid claim to which building. A modern-day gold rush.

"I read somewhere this area's had the biggest jump in house prices for the whole of Manchester. Six years ago people couldn't sell their property around here for peanuts," Jon commented.

"Shit — another missed chance," McCloughlin said, whipping the car round into Lea Road. Five police cars and an ambulance were already parked haphazardly on the pavement in front of number forty-six, yellow crime scene tape shivering in the chill autumnal breeze. The house was similar to the massive ones on the main road, solid, chunky brickwork, large stone windowsills and a metal fire escape clinging to its side.

The two men cut through the crowd of curious onlookers and approached a uniformed officer holding a flip notebook. Flashing his warrant card, McCloughlin asked, "Who's in there?"

The officer glanced down at his pad. "Just the SOCO and the photographer at the moment, sir. The officers who first attended the scene are talking to CID over there." He pointed to a group of people gathered in the outer cordon.

"Is that who found her?" asked Jon, nodding discreetly at a heavily built girl sitting in the back of an ambulance, a paramedic comforting her.

"That's right," answered the officer. "Emma Newton."

"And it's the ground-floor flat?"

"Yes. It's got its own front door, round the back of the building."

188

McCloughlin pointed to the officer's pen. "OK, DI Spicer and DCI McCloughlin, MISU. We're going in." After introducing themselves to the other officers, they put on white scene-of-crime suits and overshoes, then passed into the inner cordon and walked down the driveway running along the side of the building. "That helps," remarked McCloughlin. "Private entry, no communal hallway."

They rounded the corner and found themselves in a large rear yard closed in by high walls. A rotting sofa lay next to a rusting car in the corner, front tyres missing. Large trees in the neighbouring gardens enclosed the area. A sign tacked to an overhanging tree read, "Smile! You're on CCTV."

They both turned round and started scanning the back of the building for cameras. "Perhaps it's sitting on one of the windowsills inside," said Jon, unable to spot it.

"Could be." They approached the short flight of steps leading up to the door of flat one. A little wind chime hung to the side of the door, the draft round the back of the building only strong enough to make the wooden tab at the end of the string twist slowly round and round.

Both men were now scanning the concrete steps, then the door itself.

"No forced entry," remarked Jon as McCloughlin pushed the door open with the end of a pen. "Hello? DCI McCloughlin and DI Spicer, MISU. Can we come in?"

A voice answered them from deeper inside the flat. "Keep to the footplates please, gentlemen." A tall man wearing a face mask stepped from one of the rooms.

As they approached him, Jon noticed a carefully arranged assortment of coupons cut from magazines on the little hallway table. Nearing the front room Jon said, "Same odour. Slightly fruity, chemical. Can you smell it?"

"Yeah, I thought someone had been painting," replied McCloughlin.

"So did I, in the first victim's flat. I think you'll find it gets a lot stronger the closer you get to her mouth."

Now in the dim front room itself, Jon looked down at the obese body of a young woman. Her arms were stretched out at right angles to her body, long strands of brown hair spread out to the side of her head, purple hairband keeping it off her face. Every so often the scene was lit by flashes from the photographer's camera as he snapped shots from every angle. She wore a knitted jumper with sheep on it, a thick corduroy skirt and beige tights. Sensible slip-on shoes.

"Very Mumsy," said McCloughlin.

Crouching down, they peered into her slightly open mouth.

The SOCO said, "The trees cut out a lot of the daylight. I haven't dusted the light switch yet. But here, use my torch."

Jon turned it on and held it centimetres from her lips. Just visible at the back of her mouth was a thick white substance. He played the beam over her hands, then the rest of her. "She's been dragged here. Jumper's tight over her shoulders, hair is pulled under her head and is lying off to one side." He directed the light at the corner of the rug nearest the door — it was slightly curled over.

"I'll go with that," answered McCloughlin.

"I think you'll find she may have collapsed in the bathroom," the SOCO stated.

They stepped back into the hallway. There were only three other doors to choose from: kitchen, bedroom, bathroom. Looking in the bathroom, they saw a sink that was partially full of water, a bottle of liquid soap lying half submerged inside. On the floor next to a neat arrangement of toilet rolls was a large clamshell holding several brightly coloured smaller shells in its concave surface. Several had spilled across the lino floor.

"So she went down in here. Struck or collapsed?"

They moved through into the kitchen and Jon immediately pointed to the draining board. "Two cups." Using the line of footplates, he approached the sink. "Recently washed up." He reached a hand round the back of the plastic kettle and held a knuckle against it. "Kettle's still faintly warm."

McCloughlin was looking at him quizzically.

"There were also two cups on the draining board at Polly Mather's flat," Jon continued. "If both victims made brews for someone just before they were killed, it could have been the same visitor."

"Go on."

"Well, this is just a starter for ten. The killer comes round, our victims let him in, make him a brew. They sit and chat. Then, somehow, each victim ends up collapsing and getting her throat filled with playdough or whatever it is. He rinses the cups out and leaves."

McCloughlin gazed up at the ceiling. "There are some pretty large gaps in that chain of events. But it would make sense that, if someone called round that she knew, she'd offer him a drink. But what happens after that?" He asked himself as much as Jon.

Next they walked down the short corridor and looked in the bedroom. A collection of teddy bears and other furry animals were carefully arranged at the top of a single bed. On the wall above it was a crucifix and on the bedside table a Bible.

"She must arrange them every morning," Jon murmured, looking at the soft toys. "That's very meticulous."

"Twenty-three years old, going on fifty," said McCloughlin behind him. "Childish, yet very methodical. The flat's spotless. Bible basher too. Ten quid says that bed's never seen any action."

Jon let out a snort of breath. "Not even debatable."

McCloughlin's chuckle was dry and emotionless. "Let's talk outside." At the bottom of the steps he said, "So, assuming that's the same stuff blocking her throat, we've got a second victim."

Jon nodded. "I don't like the look of this, Boss. Those two women couldn't inhabit more different worlds. A skinny ravehead with tattoos who works in a music shop and a fundo-freak with a weight problem who sleeps with half the cast of Disneyworld each night. I imagine that they're not the best of mates."

192

McCloughlin looked up. "It could work out to be great news. Let's assume those two girls' lives are as massively different as they appear to be. Their paths have crossed somewhere. They've been to the same place, met the same person or done the same thing at some point. If we can find out what that thing is, we're a huge step closer to catching whoever did this. So let's start cross-referencing every aspect of their lives. Who they know, where they've been, what they've done. The works."

Now there were two victims, Jon didn't know if he was still in charge of the investigation or not. He was just wondering how to ask the question when McCloughlin's mobile went.

He fumbled around trying to get his hand inside the scene-of-crime suit. "Yes?"

Once again his eyes wandered towards Jon as the information was relayed to him, but this time they showed genuine alarm. "OK, OK, yes. I understand." Finally he flipped the phone shut. "A third body has been found. Not four miles from here. Heather Rayne, thirty-two years old, IT trainer at Kellogg's, throat blocked with a white gel."

Jon could only manage a whispered, "Jesus."

McCloughlin was staring at the tarmac. "Right, this changes everything. I'm moving the incident room to Longsight. I'll need the facilities and extra space there. I'll talk to you later about moving your team over from Ashton. In the meantime, stay here and start asking questions. Begin with the girl who found her."

As McCloughlin started walking back across the yard, Jon said, "Boss? I wasn't sure about ordering a mass spectrometer analysis of the first victim's blood. Budgetary concerns . . ."

McCloughlin interrupted him. "Forget the budget on this; get it ordered." He disappeared round the corner.

CHAPTER
TWELVE

1 November 2002

Jon sat down on the footplate of the ambulance, making sure the level of his head was lower than hers, ensuring his presence was as unthreatening as possible. "Hello, my name's Jon Spicer from Greater Manchester Police. I understand that you discovered Mary?"

The girl raised her head, complete lack of make-up making the redness below her nostrils more apparent. She wore a sensible lilac-coloured overcoat, Marks & Spencer's probably, and her hair was held back by a band very similar to Mary's. Jon guessed they went to the same church.

"Yes I did," she whispered, dabbing a damp handkerchief at her nose.

"How did you know Mary?"

"We go to the same church, St Luke's on Alexandra Road. That was where we were going this morning. I call round for her."

Jon thought for a second. "So was her front door open? How did you get in?"

She fished in her pockets and produced a set of keys. "I let myself in. I have a key from when I looked after her cat, Mogwai. He died in the summer. She didn't answer the door, but I knew she was in. I'd spoken to her last thing yesterday night."

"Last thing? How do you mean, exactly?"

"We often ring each other before going to bed." She looked like she was about to start crying again.

"And she sounded normal?"

"Yes, we're preparing a play for the Sunday school class. She rang off saying she'd see me this morning."

"Was she expecting anyone else to be calling round last night?"

"I don't think so. Not at that time."

"A boyfriend?"

Emma's eyes widened in shock. "Oh no. She wasn't seeing anyone, I'm sure of that."

Jon noted her defensive, almost possessive tone. "Fair enough. One other thing. There's a sign round the back about a CCTV."

Her face reddened and she looked down at her hands.

"Is there a camera somewhere?"

Emma started fiddling with her hanky. "No. Mary put the sign up to stop the cars. Men would drive round the back with prostitutes. They'd leave soiled contraceptives behind. It went on all the time after it got dark."

Hiding his disappointment, Jon said, "OK Emma, when you feel ready, I'll get an officer to drive you to the station if that's all right. We'll need a statement."

The girl didn't object. Another car pulled up and two plain clothes officers got out.

Jon stood up. "Thanks for your help." Having recognized them as CID officers he had worked with once or twice before, Jon made a beeline for them. "All right boys? DI Spicer, MISU."

He saw recognition and then surprise play across their faces. Jon sensed slight resentment that he'd beaten them to the crime scene. "We got a call straight from the control room. This one matches another from two days ago."

"That girl over in Hyde?" asked one.

"Yup."

No one spoke and Jon could sense from their expressions that they were wondering if he was the SIO, not quite able to believe that he would have been handed such a major investigation so soon. He decided to leave them wondering. "I just need a word with the SOCO; see you in a bit." He walked back along the side of the house and called in through the back door. "Hello? DI Spicer again."

The SOCO reappeared in the hallway.

"Any chance of dusting the doorbell as a priority? Someone called round before her friend turned up."

Jon got in just before nine o'clock, Punch bounding down the corridor in delight at his arrival. As he tickled his dog's stomach, he could hear Alice and Ellie in the kitchen. The laughter in their voices made him smile.

"How's it going, girls?" He was careful to inject some life into his voice, even though he was completely exhausted.

They were laying out the cartons of curry on the table, a stack of naan breads to the side. "Good timing," said Alice as he kissed her on the cheek.

Ellie gave him a massive squeeze and opened up the fridge. "Does big bro want a Stella?"

Jon licked his lips. "You beauty."

She cracked two open and a can of diet Lilt for Alice.

"Any news on the handbag?" asked Jon, taking a swig.

"Nah," said Alice with a note of finality in her voice. "It's gone — probably at the bottom of a canal somewhere." She pointed with a fork at the cartons. "Prawn dopiaza, beef madras and vegetable korma."

As they were eating, Jon said to Ellie, "Have you seen the wrinklies lately?"

Ellie rolled her big brown eyes. "Mum's just enrolling on an evening class in picture framing at Ridge Danyers College. Before that they're going on a sailing holiday round the Greek islands. Dad's knees are giving him loads of grief now the weather's turning colder."

Their dad had worked all his life in the docks at Salford, unloading the cargoes that were carried up the Manchester Ship Canal on vessels from all over the world. During the early part of his career only low levels of mechanization existed and the years of toil had taken their toll.

Jon turned to Alice. "Our childhood holidays involved nothing more than trips to Southport, Formby or Blackpool. Oh yes, one year we travelled to Anglesey and that seemed adventurous. Now look at them. One

198

trip to Spain to celebrate the old man's retirement and they're addicted to as many foreign breaks as they can afford."

"Exactly," laughed Ellie. "I keep telling them to leave something for our inheritance."

Once the curry was finished Alice glanced at the clock on the wall. "Shit, it's nearly ten. We'd better get this video on."

After the lift of his first few sips, the beer had brought on a wave of tiredness. Now, with a stomach full of curry, Jon could feel sleep dragging him down. He got up to shake himself out of it. "What did you get?" he asked, pulling two more cans out of the fridge, hoping another might bring him back to life.

"*O Brother, Where Art Thou?*" answered Ellie, cramming the debris from the takeaway into the bin.

Nodding at her choice, he handed her a can and they went through into the TV room, turned the lights down and put the video on.

Twenty minutes later, Alice nudged Ellie and pointed over to Jon. He was fast asleep in the frayed old armchair, legs straight out, one hand curled round the can on his stomach, the other resting on the top of Punch's head.

Ellie reached over and plucked the beer from his fingers. "Poor old codger."

Alice laughed quietly as she reached towards the table. Spread out on it was a variety of different chewing gums.

"Got enough flavours there?" Ellie asked as Alice selected a cinnamon one.

"Anything's better than the nicotine type. Taste like some sort of mouthwash gone wrong. Help yourself, by the way."

Ellie started sifting through them, "Still finding giving up hard then?"

Alice blew her cheeks out. "Those first few cigarettes you sneak on the way back from school? It was so exciting, but if I'd known what a nightmare it would turn out to be . . ." She looked across at Jon. "I'll never touch one again though, I can say that for sure."

"Oh?"

Alice checked Jon's sleeping face again, "I was dying to break some good news tonight, too." Looking to Ellie, she tapped her fingers on her stomach.

Ellie's face lit up. "You're not?"

"Looks like it." Suddenly Alice felt tears welling up.

They hugged each other, then Alice's eyes strayed back to Jon as he started to snore. "I've been bursting to tell him, but this investigation he's on . . . I'll just have to wait for a better time."

"I won't say a thing," whispered Ellie.

Later, as the film credits rolled, Ellie yawned and got to her feet. "Right, I'd better get back." She started reaching for her jacket.

"You're not walking home now."

Ellie laughed. "It's only five minutes away."

"Ellie," Alice said more sternly, cursing the fact she'd never passed her driving test. "I'll wake Jon up — he can take you in the car."

"No, leave him."

"Crash in the spare room, then," Alice insisted. "I've got a clean T-shirt and knickers you can borrow."

Ellie hovered at the door. "You sure? I don't want to be —"

"You're not," Alice interrupted. "Anyway, you can't leave me to sort those two out on my own."

As they looked at Jon and Punch, both dead to the world, a mobile started to ring.

"Who's taking care of . . ." Jon started saying, the fractured remains of a dream dying on his lips. He blinked at the two women, realizing where he was. "That my phone?"

Alice fetched it from his jacket and tossed it over.

"Jon Spicer here," he said, rubbing at the back of his neck. He remained silent for a few seconds before interrupting the flow of words. "Hold it, hold it. I'm not on the case any more." He listened again. "Well, the list should have been updated. A memo went out yesterday. No, don't worry, it's not your fault. Yeah, any of the other officers." He was about to hang up when he said, "By the way, what type of car was it?" He gave the sort of nod that indicated he wasn't surprised and pressed the red button.

Looking at Alice and Ellie's questioning faces, he explained, "It was the duty officer at Altrincham police station. He still had me down as being on the team for Operation Fisherman. Some guy just heard a car revving on his front drive, looked out the window to see his Porsche roaring off up the street."

Hating the fact he was no longer involved, Jon sat back in the armchair. One hand returned to the top of Punch's head as a memory of Tom in his Porsche Boxter resurfaced.

CHAPTER
THIRTEEN

July 2002

Jon stood next to the officer brushing powder over the handle of Tom's garage door. Hearing a car slow down on the road behind him, he turned to see a bright yellow Porsche Boxter coming to a halt at the mouth of the drive, its way blocked by the police van. The car reversed back on to the street and Tom got out.

"How are you?" called Jon, striding across the small lawn, one hand held out.

His friend looked up and Jon was shocked at how washed out he looked.

As they shook hands Tom said, "I didn't expect plain clothes to come out for a garage break in."

"Well, anything for a mate, you know? How's tricks anyway?"

Tom sighed. "I'm just about hanging in there — praying for these bloody Games to be over. It's been absolutely crazy at work."

"You and me both. We've had to pull in extra officers from all the forces bordering Greater Manchester. Someone's worked out that the Commonwealth Games operation is equivalent to policing three premiership football matches every day for ten days."

Tom nodded. "I can believe that. Still," he spoke out of the side of his mouth, as if sharing a secret, "not long now until I pack the whole thing in. Then it's Cornwall here I come."

"I must admit, it looks like all that corporate entertaining is finally taking its toll on you," said Jon with a good-natured grin. "Can you not delegate a bit of the wining and dining?"

Tom rolled his eyes. "I wish. These marketing types, they feel like it's an affront to their status if it's not the MD personally taking them out. I never thought I'd say it, but I'm absolutely sick of restaurant meals. Unfortunately, I have another tonight." He shrugged. "Anyway, enough about me. What brings you out to something like this?" He nodded towards his garage. "I didn't miss a dead body in there, did I?"

Jon smiled. "No, you're fine there. Actually, the reason why I'm involved is this." He placed a hand on the bonnet of Tom's Porsche. "Was it parked in your garage last night?"

"No. I was entertaining clients, so I left it in town. I rang a cab to take me back in this morning and when I came out of the house I saw the garage door was open. I couldn't remember if I'd locked it or not, so I glanced inside and could see someone had been in."

"Anything taken?"

"No, but I thought I'd better report it for insurance purposes at least."

"Which is how I got to hear about it," said Jon, leading Tom towards the officer who was now kneeling at the garage door's lock. "Anything that looks like it could be the work of the gang stealing high-performance cars is referred to us."

"But I don't understand. Why my garage?"

"Well." Jon lowered his voice. "I didn't mention it to Charlotte, but a car was taken off a driveway on the next street, so it appears they were in this area last night. They've obviously cased out your house before. Perhaps they saw your Porsche wasn't on the drive and thought it might be in the garage, with the keys."

"Jesus Christ, Jon, you're saying that they're actively targeting my house?"

Jon weighed up how to play things. "You live in an area they regularly drive around, that's all. But they're getting nastier with their tactics. One has gone into a couple of houses recently and threatened the owners. Single women so far. The last time he went up the stairs and into the victim's bedroom because she'd taken her handbag and car keys upstairs with her. Just be careful with your keys at night. You keep them on a hook now, don't you?"

Tom nodded. "Ever since the Audi went."

"Good. Keep them there. If they're on a hook, you prevent the fishing trick. But if they burst in anyway, at least your keys are there for them to grab."

"What? You're saying if they kick in my front door I should just let them take the Porsche?"

"It would be the best way to resolve the situation without anyone getting injured."

"Bollocks! The best way to resolve it would be to keep a baseball bat in my bedroom and brain the fuckers with it."

Jon shook his head. "Tom, it's just a car. What if you run down the stairs, trip in the dark, go arse over tit, drop your bat and end up with some very angry car thieves standing over you?"

Tom considered this and snorted in reluctant agreement. "It's tempting to get a bloody gun."

Jon looked at him. "Don't even think about it. We're not the States. Not yet, anyway. Don't do anything stupid, OK?"

Tom was silent for a bit and then said, "Remember that time in the Bull's Head? You said these people live in a different world from you and me. You said I didn't want them coming anywhere near my world. Well Jon, it looks like they're in it, doesn't it? It looks like they're wandering around just as they please. And it seems you can't do a thing about it, and I'm not allowed to."

His words stung, and not just because they were pointing out how ineffective the police were. In Jon's mind they were also a statement of how he was failing to protect a friend. "We'll catch these guys soon; they're getting far too cocky. You can make my job easier by not getting involved. OK?"

"OK."

Suspecting that his capitulation wasn't genuine, Jon looked down at the officer. "Anything?"

The other man got back to his feet. "A couple of partials."

Jon looked at Tom. "We'll keep those prints on file. When we catch this lot we'll be able to link them to here and dozens of other places."

As the uniformed officer loaded his kit into the back of the van, Jon said, "Hey, talking of the Commonwealth Games, I put my name down for tickets to the rugby sevens and got allocated a couple for the quarter-finals. Fancy it?"

Tom thought for a few seconds. "What day's it on?"

"Saturday the third of August."

"Yeah, I'm up for it, cheers."

"Nice one," said Jon, walking round to the passenger seat of the van. "I'll give you a bell nearer the time."

As the van pulled out on to the road, Jon looked over his shoulder and saw Tom standing on his front lawn, one hand held in the air.

Once the vehicle had disappeared round the corner, Tom dropped his hand and looked at the garage door. The thought of people prowling round his property at night, lifting his letterbox and testing his doors, created a strange mix of fear and anger. And now he'd learned they were bursting in to people's bedrooms. He took his mobile from his pocket and dialled a number. "Brain, it's Tom here."

They went through the usual formalities before Brain said he had plenty of shopping in.

"Great," said Tom, thinking how fast the bag of powder seemed to be disappearing. "I'm also after something a little more unusual. It's to do with self-protection, if you know what I mean."

Brain said he'd better call round to discuss it.

Tom arrived at his house a short while later. Stepping into the dimly lit front room, he saw three student types slouched on beanbags and felt totally incongruous in his suit. He took the armchair in the corner and declined the joint offered to him by the dreadlocked white guy to his right.

"Last blasts anyway," the other man replied, taking the final puffs for himself. He flicked the roach into the upturned metal bin lid that served as a gigantic ashtray in the middle of the room. "Cheers Brain. See you around."

All three of them rose to their feet and shuffled from the room. As the smoke haze began to thin, Brain tied his mop of straggly black hair back in a ponytail and turned his attention to the electronic scales and small mound of cannabis resin before him. "So Tom, what are you after?" His voice sounded even closer to total disintegration.

Deciding it was appropriate to purchase some drugs first, Tom replied, "Any more of that special powder you blended yourself?"

Brain looked surprised. "You've nearly got through the last lot already?"

"Well, me and a few friends," Tom lied. "It's such a nice rush."

Brain nodded in agreement. "You're not wrong. You mentioned something about self-protection, too."

Tom sat forward in his seat. "I've got these bastards trying to get into my house. The price of driving a Porsche, it seems."

"And you want to get hold of?"

"A gun."

"What?"

"Just a pistol. Something I could wave at them so they never come near my house again."

Brain lit a cigarette. "I'm not a frigging arms dealer. I've got a degree in chemistry and I deal in chemicals."

"I know," said Tom. "But you must know . . . people."

Brain loosed a plume of smoke at the ceiling. "I'll give your number to this guy I know. If he calls you, he calls you. I'm not getting any more involved than that."

"Cheers, Brain, I appreciate it."

CHAPTER
FOURTEEN

July 2002

As he slowed to a stop in front of the traffic lights, Tom looked anxiously up at the number glowing from the screen on the side of Portland Tower. Nine days to go before the Games started. As if he needed reminding. He sipped latte with an extra shot through the lid of the cup before replacing it in the holder on the Porsche Boxter's dashboard.

Ahead of him the coloured banners billowed out slightly as a gentle summer breeze sighed down the wide street. He thought of the chaos waiting for him in the office and took another long sip, feeling the caffeine surging through the veins in his temples as his heart beat a little faster.

Carrying on towards Piccadilly station, trees now shrouded in a thick layer of leaves, he examined the scaffolding outside the Rossetti hotel, praying the printers had finished the Nastro Azzurro job by now. Erection date was in two days' time.

The traffic thinned out after the junction for the cab rank at the back of Piccadilly station and soon he swept up to Ardwick Green, taking the sharp left-hand turn and pulling up outside his office. He sat for a moment to steel himself then, feeling for the little bag of powder in the breast pocket of his suit jacket, he jumped out of the car and walked into reception.

"Morning," said Sarah brightly.

Tom took the pieces of notepaper she held out and went straight into Ian's old office. First was from Jim Morrell in the IT department down in London. Something about needing access to the system in order to trace some missing files. More of Ian's fucking handiwork no doubt, thought Tom. Next was from Austen Rogers, asking for the exact dates for their promotion of X-treme chewing gum in Piccadilly station. Tom placed the piece of paper on his desk and slid his appointments book over it. Out of sight, out of mind. Next was from a rep from Motorola. He was arriving at lunchtime and wanted to visit the printer where their building wrap was being produced. Tom couldn't remember offhand which printer was handling it. Since Lorzo's went bust, they had jobs scattered all over the place.

Feeling slightly sick at the prospect of the coming day, Tom slipped the sachet from his pocket, opened the airtight seal and dabbed a forefinger inside. Licking the dust from his fingertip, he felt his mood lift with just the anticipation of the drug hitting his bloodstream.

He turned on the computer and typed in "WINNER". The drug had just started to kick in and he tried to convince himself that the word applied just as much to him. Opening the file for Motorola, he saw, with relief, that the giant poster was being produced at a printer on the Trafford Park industrial estate. He rang to warn them he would be turning up with the client later that afternoon.

By twelve thirty he was waiting on the platform at Piccadilly station. When the train finally pulled in forty-five minutes late, he found himself shaking hands with a belligerent-looking middle-aged man called Graham Lock who obviously resented any commercial event that didn't take place in London.

"This is a bloody mess," he said, looking around the station at the boarded-up shop fronts with their "Opening Soon" signs.

"All ready in time for the Games," Tom assured him as workmen furiously thumped tiles into place with rubber-headed mallets.

Sitting in Tom's Porsche, the man scanned each billboard they passed. "Lust, envy, jealousy. The dangers of Volvo," he read out in a dramatic voice, before continuing with the body copy. "Beauty, charm and strength of character are enough to drive anyone mad. Prices start at £24,860 on the road, so watch your back and discover more at blah, blah, blah, blah. Bit menacing, don't you think?"

Without waiting for an answer, his attention turned to the council-paid building wraps covering the derelict building at the end of Ancoats Street. "New East Manchester. The New Town in the City," he read out, scepticism filling his voice.

Tom felt a pang of irritation. "Millions have been invested in this part of the city."

They emerged from the other side of the tunnel, Tom careful to follow the designated route to Sportcity because the carefully arranged screens and building wraps hid the boarded-up houses and empty mill buildings, their windows smashed years ago.

After a few minutes they turned a corner and the futuristic structure of the main stadium loomed into view, angular struts poking up into the clear blue sky.

On the street around them posters and banners hung from every available surface: a yellow and black Boddington's cow standing outside the houses of parliament with a hitchhiking sign saying, "Manchester", a young female gymnast in a Microsoft leotard midway through a flip, a ninety-six-sheet poster for the BBC reading, "Commonwealth Games. Bring on the Superhumans. 72 nations, 17 sports." Below the headline was an image of a sprinter leading a pack of greyhounds, sharp canines bared behind the dogs' wire muzzles.

Tom got onto the A57 and followed it to the Mancunian Way, whipping past various red brick University of Manchester buildings on their right before taking the A56 as it curled alongside the Manchester Ship Canal.

Soon they were on the A5801, Manchester United Football Club's stadium rearing up on their left, heading into Salford's bleak landscape of industrial buildings, depots and docks.

Coming to a halt in front of what looked like a small aircraft hangar, Tom announced, "Here we are, Vision Printers. Proud owners of one of just a handful of Vutek 5300s in Britain today."

Tom led the way into a cramped reception area and waved to a thin man with a loosely knotted tie. "Hi Simon, this is Graham Lock. We were hoping to catch a glimpse of their building wrap as it's rolling off the Vutek."

Simon and Graham shook hands. "Follow me."

They proceeded through to the shop floor, stepping off the beige nylon carpet onto a smooth concrete floor coated in a thick layer of pale blue industrial paint. The air was sharp with the smell of paints and solvent. Covering most of the grey breezeblock walls were a variety of supersize posters. Several printers were dotted around, but they headed straight for the massive one in the corner.

When Simon spoke, his voice echoed slightly. "Here she is: the Vutek Ultravu 5300."

Long and thin, the machine stood about eight feet high and thirty feet wide. A huge roll of material was loaded into its top. Below it a printer head the size of a TV ran backwards and forwards along a highly polished rail, a wide ribbon of computer cable trailing along behind it.

"Essentially, it's just an enormous version of a desktop printer. Except it costs tens of thousands of pounds more," Simon explained, opening a door at its base. Inside was a row of three-litre plastic drums, a pipe leading out of the top of each. "Four colour — CMYK — printing process. The ink is pumped up from here into a secondary tank in the printer head. The computer takes care of the mixing and the ink is applied by means of a Piezo chamber."

Graham peered at the printer head as it toiled to and fro. "Meaning?"

"There's an electrostatic charge as it goes one way, a vacuum the other. That way the ink is bonded like glue to the substrate we're using. In the case of your job — and most building wraps — we use a PVC mesh. It allows the builders working on the scaffolding behind to see out. Obvious safety benefits."

Graham looked at the roll. Each time the printer head returned to the far end of the rail, the length of PVC moved round a few centimetres. On the small area of exposed material he could make out a fraction of the mobile phone's image. Each button was the size of his head. The model's unique selling point was a facia that could swivel right round. Graham was convinced it would prove a massive seller. Tom thought it was crap.

As soon as the train door shut behind his client, Tom turned away and started walking quickly towards the station's toilets. His jaw muscles ached from maintaining a smile for so long. Finding his way barred by pristine new turnstiles, he scrabbled around to find a twenty-pence piece, cursing the fact you now had to pay in order to piss.

When he had locked the cubicle door behind him, he lowered the toilet seat lid, sat down and extracted the sachet from his pocket. After taking a dab of the powder, he sat back and shut his eyes, waiting for the drug's reassuring grip. A few minutes later he stepped back out into the real world, feeling charged up once more.

"Sarah? Anything I should know?" he asked, marching back towards his car, mobile phone pressed to his ear.

"A Mr Austen Rogers from X-treme called regarding their . . ."

"Next," interrupted Tom.

"Giles Peters and Sarah Palmer from Cussons will be here at six o'clock."

"For what?"

"Rhodes and Co? Your table is booked for 7.45."

Shit, thought Tom, only now remembering the dinner date. When, he wondered, would he have any time to spend with Charlotte?

CHAPTER
FIFTEEN

July 2002

Once Ges reached the bottom of the stairs, Creepy George emerged from behind his bank of computer monitors and walked over to the window. He watched as the large figure emerged on to the street and walked slowly off to his parked car.

Satisfied he wasn't coming back, George relaxed — he had the office to himself at last. Back at his computer, he loaded up the path-shredder programme to destroy the trail of his internet wanderings. Then he keyed in the address for his favourite portal and scrolled down the screen to see which girls had been posting up entries that day. There were a few promising images but nothing that really got him excited. That was the problem with having to rely on other people's images; he could spend hours trawling the internet and still not find anything ideal.

Lifting up the black briefcase on to his desk, he entered the combination for the lock and opened it up. Next to the digital camera with its collection of lenses was a small stack of adult contact magazines. Picking up the top one, he turned to the section he wanted and traced a finger over the small boxed ads, selecting the section for the north-west. There she was; height, build and even hair colour very similar to Julie's.

The phone was answered after the second ring. Female voice, accent a little too strong for his liking — but what she sounded like hardly mattered.

"Are you posing tonight?" he asked in a low voice.

"Yes. For a half an hour, starting at eight o'clock. It'll be forty quid."

George decided to go for it, but couldn't be bothered to speak with her any more. Instead he just hung up and then closed down his workstation. After doing up the top button of his shirt, he pulled out a tie from the bottom drawer of his desk and retrieved his suit jacket from the cabinet. He liked to look smart for any photo session — not like some of the drooling scum that shuffled up to events.

By seven fifty he was parking on a small estate of new houses just outside Leigh. Looking around he saw a basketball hoop mounted above a garage door. A tricycle lying on its side on a tiny patch of front lawn. Curtains drawn, tellies on — just average people completely unaware of what went on just around the corner.

After retrieving the briefcase and his suit jacket from the boot of his car, he walked the short distance to the house, arriving at the same time as another man. Each glanced at the other's briefcase and they didn't need to speak. The door was answered by a tall, thin bloke in his late thirties — perhaps her husband, perhaps not. He showed them through into what was obviously the spare room. A double bed occupied the top part of the room, stripped down to the undersheet, the obligatory little photo album placed on the bed like some sort of menu. Three other men were already there. Cameras mounted on tripods, they fiddled around with lenses and light meters while avoiding each other's eyes.

"Forty pounds please, gents," the man said. George and the other man produced the cash. "I'll give you a few minutes to set up. She's keen to get going at eight on the dot. Now she's got a few uniforms. Photos are on the bed over there," he said, pointing towards the booklet. "If you want her in anything, just shout."

The other newcomer stepped over to the bed and picked up the album, eagerly flicking through the images. George stayed where he was, knowing the chances of his particular tastes being met were unlikely in the extreme.

The room stayed completely silent until the door opened again five minutes later and a woman in her early twenties stepped inside. Five pairs of eyes greedily appraised her. "Anyone want me to dress up?" she asked.

The men remained as silent as an audience being addressed from the stage. She shrugged, then without hesitation strode over to the bed and threw off her dressing gown. Announcing to no one in particular, she said, "If you want any particular pose, just say. Otherwise I'll do my own selection."

She lay down and the men's faces were sucked towards their viewfinders. As the half hour went by, marked by the steady click of cameras, the odd request came from the men around him. But George was hardly interested in the performance. He took a few snaps for appearance's sake, but quickly decided to save the memory in his digital camera for a more promising scenario.

At 8.30 exactly the man who had answered the front door said, "Time!"

The woman climbed from the bed and put her dressing gown back on. As the others packed up their equipment, George approached the man. He coughed lightly to get his attention. "Would the lady be interested in posing for a few more pictures?"

"Private session?" the man asked matter of factly.

George nodded.

"What sort of stuff?"

"Nothing other than she's just done, really," answered George. "It's just that I'd like to use my own background cloth. She would merely have to recline with her eyes shut."

The man shrugged. "I shouldn't think she'll mind. Hang on."

He went over and spoke quietly in her ear. Adopting a bowed and shy posture, George pretended to fiddle with his camera, aware of her eyes glancing over him. Her harlot's eyes, assessing and judging. He wanted them shut, wanted their crawling appraisal to stop. He clamped his face in a neutral expression, afraid his features would betray the loathing he felt at her power.

The man came back over. "Forty quid for ten minutes."

"That's fine," George replied, handing over the cash, keeping his eyes down.

220

As the man showed the other photographers out, she spoke to him. "So how do you want me?" Her hands were straying to the waistband of her dressing gown.

"No, no. Please stay robed. If you could simply recline on the bed and close your eyes."

She looked at him for a moment longer, then uncertainly lay back and lowered her eyelids. "Like this?"

Her posture was far too rigid, but George whispered, "Yes," and the camera began to click. After a couple of minutes shooting from various angles he said, "That's good. And just let your head fall to the side." More photographs. "Lovely. Now, um . . ."

Her eyes opened.

From his briefcase he got the background drape for Julie's staff shot. He spread it out on the floor by the side of the bed. "Would you lie on the blue cloth, please?"

"The floor?"

"Yes. Perhaps you've got a bad back and the floor is a natural resting place. You see?"

A little warily she lay down on the square of cloth, arms crossed defensively over her chest, ankles tight together. Her eyes shut once more.

"You need to relax," George cooed, standing over her. "Arms lying outwards to the side. Good." He began taking more shots. "Perhaps your head back a bit, legs slightly akimbo?" The camera began clicking again, his heart now racing. "And could you open your mouth a tiny bit?"

Barely moving her lips so her pose didn't change, she whispered in a toneless voice, "What, like I'm dead?"

Lost in the moment and unable to hear the sarcasm in her voice, George said, "Yes."

"Barry!"

The door flew open and the man almost leaped into the room. George shied backwards as the girl stood up.

"What happened? Did he touch you?" The man looked from her to George and back again.

"No, he just . . ."

"Why were you on the floor?"

"He wanted me to stretch my arms out and pretend I was . . ." She sounded scared, but when she glanced at George her eyes were full of contempt. "He's just weird. I want him out."

The man turned towards George, but he was already sliding along the wall, mumbling how he was so sorry to have offended the lady, imagining how she'd look on his computer once he had whitened her skin to that of a corpse.

As he let himself in through the back door, a voice called out, "Is that you, George?"

As he had done since he was a boy, he replied, "Yes, mother."

Suit jacket and tie now removed, he stopped to put his briefcase on the bottom stair, then poked his head into the front room. She sat in her usual seat, knitting something for the charity shop, radio on in the corner. The scene hadn't changed in thirty years: the same lacework antimacassars over the backs of the chairs, the same sheepskin rug in front of the clumsy-looking gas fire, chunky brown tiles round the hearth. "There's a package for you in the hall. It's got Mexican stamps on."

George felt a jolt of excitement.

"Who's it from?" she asked.

"Just work stuff," he replied, stepping over to the table and picking it up. The wrapping hadn't been tampered with by customs. He turned around and hurried up the stairs to his bedroom.

She emerged on spindly legs behind him, repeating the same question she'd been asking for years. "When can I hoover your room? It hasn't been done for weeks."

He would never let her in. "I'll do it this weekend, Mum."

She flapped a hand in disgust and went back into the front room. George took the key from his pocket and undid the padlock securing his bedroom door. Inside, he bolted it behind him, sat down at his desk and turned the anglepoise lamp on. The light spilled out, pushing the shadows back a little but not enough to properly illuminate the photos of women that plastered his walls. Taking a scalpel from his mini toolbox, he slit open the package and pulled the sheet of pills out. He really didn't believe they would ever show up. The website was American but it warned that, due to US narcotic laws, the pills would be sent from Mexico where regulations concerning that particular sedative were far more lax.

He looked at them as if they were sacred things. Which, in a sense, they were: they had the power to make his dreams come true.

Sly gazed down at the motionless spider crouched in the corner of its glass home. The way its legs were bunched up — knee joints higher than its body — reminded Sly of the eight roof struts encircling the newly completed Commonwealth Games stadium, Manchester City's new ground once the Games were over and the stupid running track had been ripped out so another tier of seats could be added. He clenched a fist in triumph — finally the Blues would have a stadium to match their status in the city. Something newer and better than those bastard Reds at Old Trafford.

Slamming his front door shut behind him, he looked around the courtyard. The snotty couple were sitting in the sun on one of the benches at the side of the Zen garden, Sunday papers spread out across their laps. Next to the bench were two cups and a pot of fresh coffee, curls of steam catching in the sunlight.

He yawned loudly to intrude on the peaceful atmosphere, snorted and then trudged over to them. They tried to ignore his presence, but once he was behind them he leaned over the girl's shoulder and remarked, "Dirty slag." Manchester accent deliberately made heavier.

Her head whipped round. "I beg your pa —"

"That bird." He pointed to the photo of the reality gameshow hostess in the paper on her knee. "You can just tell she is." He looked at the man sitting on the bench. "Bet you'd give her one, though you can't admit it. Not with your missus sat here, right?" He laughed loudly and carried on his way, imagining the couple shaking with suppressed anger.

He slid into his car, put on a pair of sunglasses, lowered the windows and pressed play on the CD player. The Stone Roses started booming out and he smiled at memories of nights spent in the Hacienda, so out of his tree he could hardly speak.

The drive to his grandma's little terraced house didn't take long. As he got out of his car he could see her in the front window waiting for him, coat already on. He walked her round to the passenger seat and helped her in, then they drove back into the centre of town, parking in the NCP near Affleck's Palace.

With her arm linked through his, they walked to the top of Market Street, the old lady pausing to look across into Piccadilly Gardens.

"It's all changed so much," she said, with more wonder than regret in her voice. "Lewis's has gone." She stared across the street at the art deco front of the old family-run department store. Now bright red TK Maxx signs were above the doors. "Used to take you there as a little boy. Me and your grandad would go to the dances on the top floor."

"What dances were those?"

"Ballroom dances. There's a sprung wooden floor up there, you know."

He shook his head, "No Gran, I didn't."

225

"What's that bloody great thing?" she asked, pointing across the gardens to the grey concrete wall.

"Some designer's idea, I think," he said chirpily. "It's meant to be Chinese style — they put it there to screen off the noise and stuff from the bus depot behind."

"Looks bloody awful to me," she said. "More like the Berlin Wall than a Chinese one."

He grinned, leading her down the pedestrianized street towards the new Marks & Spencer.

"Oh, they've done a grand job with those hanging baskets," she said, gazing appreciatively at the masses of flowers dotting the way ahead. "And those banners add a nice splash of colour, too. Why can't they keep it this pretty all the time? Even the litter has disappeared," she added, looking at the street in front. "And these cobbles, when did they put them in?" she asked, nodding at the rustic brickettes at her feet.

"Not long ago."

"The trams used to run up this street, you know. Right where we're walking."

"Well, things move on, don't they?"

"They certainly do," she replied, looking at the lines of mobile phone shops, leisure clothing stores and coffee bars.

At the other end of the street they were confronted by the towering new Marks & Spencer with its overhead Perspex walkway leading into the Arndale Centre.

"We'll have lunch at a place over here, Gran." He led her along the smooth pavement, then across the plaza towards the upmarket Triangle shopping centre. As they passed the giant TV screen set up for the Commonwealth Games it blared a loud commentary down at them. Athletes were profiled, sporting venues reviewed. She hunched her shoulders slightly at the noise and they carried on to the tables arranged on the pavement in front of Zinc.

"What's that thing?" She was looking at the Urbis museum as it reared straight up out of the concrete like some submarine surfacing in a future ocean.

"Don't know." He lit a cigarette. "Some art gallery, probably."

Choosing a table where they could watch — and be seen by — everyone passing, he handed a menu to the old lady. She examined the list, mouthing the names of unfamiliar dishes: bruschetta, pappardelle, antipasto, arancini.

When a waitress appeared Sly raised a hand, then watched her closely as she approached their table. He was keen for her to notice that he was taking his grandma out, wanting her to think he was a decent guy. Caring. Perhaps attractive. "Coffee, Gran?"

"Yes please."

The waitress looked down at her. "Espresso, latte, cappuccino, mocha?"

"Just normal, dear. And a glass of water please."

"Sparkling or still?"

"Whatever comes out of your taps, thank you."

The waitress gave a tight smile and looked at Sly.

"Tea with two sugars, cheers."

"And to eat?"

"Gran?"

"Oh, I don't know. You choose for me." She shifted the shiny aluminium seat so the sun didn't shine in her eyes.

Knowing he wouldn't be able to say the names of the foreign dishes properly, Sly ordered two smoked salmons with scrambled eggs, then sat back to look at the Sunday shoppers milling past.

"One of your friends rang when I was round at your mum's the other day," said his gran. "I don't like it when they call you Sly. Why do they do it? Your name is Ashley."

Believing it referred to his cleverness when it came to blagging things, he smiled as he stubbed out his cigarette. "It's just a nickname. Like you get at school."

"Yes, but it isn't even part of your name, is it? Sly. It makes you sound all shifty. Anyway, your mum gave him your new number. Told him you'd moved into a flat of your own."

"Thanks."

"So how's your job?"

It didn't exist, but Sly had his lie ready prepared. "It's going great. I got this as part of a bonus." He ran a hand along the sleeve of his Dolce and Gabbana jacket. "My boss said I'm one of the best performers he's ever had."

She smiled back. "And are you courting?"

He almost laughed at her old-fashioned language. "You mean seeing anyone?" Again he lied. "There are a couple of girls I'm friendly with. But nothing too serious."

228

"A couple," she tutted. "What's wrong with one? It would give you a chance of getting to know her properly. All this flitting between people."

Sly picked a bit of tobacco off his slightly protruding upper teeth. "Plenty of time for that later, Gran."

She did her best to eat the food when it arrived. But she found the eggs too runny and the fish seemed almost raw. Plus the bread was too crusty for her liking.

Finally Sly asked, "Do you want to get going?" He noticed how she was leaning to one side, trying to keep out of the sun's creeping rays.

"Yes please," she said without hesitation.

Seeing the waitress standing nearby, he said loudly, "Let's go to Marks & Spencer. I'll get you a new coat."

"Why? Is there something wrong with this one?" she demanded, looking down at her beige raincoat, lapels and pocket flaps straight out of the Seventies.

"No, it's just you've had it for years."

She leaned forward. "Then why change it if there's nothing wrong with it? You lot today, you buy something and throw it out after a few weeks."

"OK, you win," he said, holding up his hands. "Shall we go to the cafe at your local Co-op? A nice bit of cake and a brew?"

"Lovely!"

He beckoned to the waitress and flipped out a large wad of notes. Peeling off the top one he said casually, "Keep the change." He searched her face for any sign that his nonchalant use of money impressed her. But all he got was a bright and emotionless thank you.

229

CHAPTER
SIXTEEN

July 2002

"Morning Sarah," said Tom, trying to put a bounce in his step as he crossed reception, sunglasses on.

"Good morning, Tom. Popular as ever," she said, holding up the pile of letters and phone messages.

Tom took it with a forced smile, went through to Ian's office, dropped them on the table and retreated straight to the single toilet on the ground floor. He locked the door behind him, then took the sunglasses off. Staring grimly at his ravaged face in the mirror, he reached into his pocket for the eye drops he'd just bought. He tipped his head back and, pulling his eyelids down, administered a drip of liquid into each. It was cold and tingled, making him blink rapidly. But the liquid closed up the spider's web of tiny veins, making his eyes look whiter and less hungover.

Next he took out the tube of concealer he'd taken from Charlotte's enormous make-up bag and applied a smear to the dark smudges of skin below each eye. Checking the mirror again, he saw that he looked a whole lot better — not like someone who had been to bed the wrong side of midnight for weeks on end.

Lastly he took the little bag of powder from his suit jacket. Holding it up, he noted that there was barely enough left to fill up its bottom corner and thought it was lucky he'd got the fresh bag from Brain. The moistened tip of his forefinger poked inside. He took a deep breath and dipped his finger in again: the drug seemed to be having less of an effect. Perhaps it lost its potency after a little while.

Ready to face the day, he went back through to Ian's office and started trying to prioritize his tasks for that morning. But the sheer number of things to do prevented him from starting anything. Half the letters were marked "urgent" and the phone on his desk was already flashing with unanswered messages. Rubbing a hand over his chin, he turned on the computer and went to his Cornwall link.

Just a few days more to go, he told himself. The thought gave him enough strength to answer his ringing phone. "Tom, hi. It's Sarah. There's a van here. A delivery of X-treme chewing gum, display cart and leaflets. Shall I get one of the boys in the studio to take it all upstairs?"

Tom knew that he couldn't afford to have the items hanging around in the office for long. He would have to get rid of it all. "No, don't worry about it. It's going straight back out. I'll help him take it through to the store room at the back."

He took his jacket off and walked through to reception. A man wearing green trousers, white polo shirt and a green baseball cap was placing several more boxes on to the stack piling up in front of Sarah's desk. Each one was labelled "X-treme. Contents — 36 packets."

"Cheers, mate. Could you give me a hand humping it through to the back?" asked Tom.

"Sorry pal," he replied without a hint of apology in his voice. "I'm a van driver, not a labourer. I just deliver the stuff to your premises."

There wasn't time to argue. Tom crouched down and picked up the outermost column of boxes. By the time he got back to reception Creepy George was standing there. "Sarah said you needed a hand."

"Yeah, thanks," said Tom, masking his irritation that someone else now knew about the delivery.

"Right," announced the driver, carrying in some large cardboard tubes. "The promotional panels for the cart are in these. They fit on to your standard Cooper's Barrow."

"Right. We've got a couple out back," Tom replied.

"And these," the driver tapped two boxes that were slightly smaller than the rest, "are your competition entry forms."

Tom signed for everything and, with George's help, began ferrying them through to the back storage room.

Later that night, once everyone else had left, George went back to the storage room. He had a whole pile of merchandise samples he'd skimmed from previous deliveries hidden in his bedroom. After picking up a box of chewing gum from the top of the pile, he examined it, in two minds whether to steal it or not. Citrus flavour with energy-giving guarana. It sounded a bit weird to him.

But it always gave him a kick to put one over on the company, so through force of habit he put the box under his arm and set off for home.

A few days later one of the directors from London called. Putting aside the delivery schedules for the printer in Dublin and praying he wasn't going to be asked for any status reports, Tom waited for Sarah to put him through. "Hi, Andrew." He was careful to sound upbeat. "How can I help you?"

"Hi there, Tom. Listen, Jim Morrell has finished his search of the computer system. There's some good news and some bad news."

There was silence as Tom sat back in his chair and shut his eyes. "OK — perhaps the good news first?"

"Good news is, he's found nothing amiss with the files on the main server. Tracking back through all the activity on Ian's computer, it's apparent he'd been accessing a lot of files and printing them off. But nothing more."

It was all too little too late — they'd had to struggle along with misfiled documents for the last month. If that was the good news, Tom wondered, what was the bad?

"Now, the other news isn't so welcome. He found quite a few locked files — ones needing a password for access. Apart from the ones in finance, they shouldn't have been there."

"So who had created them?"

"They were all on the computer of a George Norris."

"Creepy George?"

"I'm sorry?"

"Creepy George — it's what we call him up here."

"To his face?"

"No, we're too childish for that."

"Well, the name isn't too far off the mark. Perhaps add on perverted and sick."

"What do you mean?"

"It took Jim a while to get into them — he treated it as a bit of a challenge eventually. And he thinks he's only found a fraction of the offending material. He suspects a lot more has been transferred on to a laptop to keep it clear of the main server."

"What offending material?"

"You've heard of snuff movies?"

"Oh God, you're not serious?"

"Not movies. Photos. Lots of them. They're of women and they don't look asleep. More collapsed. Maybe dead, maybe unconscious. Clothed, semi-clothed, some naked. Indoors, outdoors. He's been downloading a lot from a US site called — you're not going to believe this — comatosex.com. It has information on date-rape drugs too — benefits and disadvantages of each type. Where you can order them from."

"Jesus Christ, how do these sites get away with it?"

"God knows, but it gets worse. You know the staff photo gallery on our company web site?"

"Yes."

"Was there a photo taken recently of Julie Bowers? Her one on the Manchester site is different from our one down here."

"Yes — George insisted on taking it a few weeks ago."

"Well, he's been using a shot of her face, eyes shut, and mounting it on the corpse of another female."

"Corpse?"

"Well, you know, a torso. Someone sprawled out on the floor in a dressing gown against the same blue background cloth as the company mugshots. He's used Photoshop to comp the two images together. At first we actually thought it was Julie."

"Oh, Christ. So he's actually taking these shots himself?"

"He appears to be. Tom, this isn't just a sackable offence. It's highly bloody illegal."

Tom thought for a few seconds. "So what are we going to do?"

"Get rid of him, fast as possible. Look at it this way: what if he's planning to attack Julie Bowers? Does he seem the sort?"

"Seem the sort? How do I bloody know?" Tom felt himself getting angry. "Did the Yorkshire Ripper's bloody wife think that he seemed the sort? Surely that's the point with these people — you can never really tell them apart from the rest of us."

"All right, Tom. This is how we'll play it. Jim's wiped all the offending material from the computer system. Under no circumstances can we afford for this to get out. You just have a quiet word with this George character, tell him that if he goes without a fuss, we won't create one either."

"So it's OK for us to sack him, but not for us to tell the police?"

"Tom, we've got a company to look after here. What he gets up to in his own time isn't our concern."

"And what about Julie Bowers? Just because George no longer works here, doesn't mean he's not a threat to her."

"We'll move her back down to London; I assume you can do without her?"

Tom wanted to laugh. "Oh yeah, we've never been quieter. She's just twiddling her thumbs most days. Just like the rest of us."

"She can carry on helping you from down here. It's the only way to play it."

Just a few more days of this shit and I'm out, thought Tom. He suppressed the urge to giggle because he knew if he did, he might not be able to stop. He imagined the reaction if waves of hysterical laughter suddenly started flooding out of the director's earpiece. "OK, but you have the conversation with Julie. I'm not dealing with them both."

"Done. I'll call her now." Tom hung up, reached for his powder and headed straight for the toilets again.

He emerged a couple of minutes later, got a cup of water from the cooler and as he slowly sipped it, worked out what to say to George. Feeling slightly better, he rang upstairs to George's desk.

"Hello," came the reply, sounding faintly hostile, as if no one was meant to know his extension number.

"George, it's Tom. Could you pop down to Ian's old office? I need a word."

236

As he waited for George to appear he imagined how the conversation would go, picturing George's abject embarrassment. He guessed hardly any eye contact would be made — certainly not after he revealed what he knew.

There was a knock at the door, the top of George's bushy haircut appearing first as he looked round the door.

"Come in, George. Sit down," said Tom, now adding a note of formality to his voice.

George did as he was asked, dead eyes staring across the desk dividing them. "George, I've just had a call from the London office about some material the IT department has found on the system up here."

"Material?"

"Certain locked files on your system. You know what I'm talking about?"

George leaned back and folded his arms. "No," he said warily.

"George, the IT guy has gained access to them. You've got a . . ." he searched for the right word, ". . . glut of offensive images stored on your computer. Or you did; the lot has been deleted."

He waited for George to start squirming, eyes fixed to the floor, but to Tom's astonishment he sat up in his seat, genuine fury in his face.

"Someone's destroyed my personal files? Without my permission?" He glared directly at Tom. "That's bloody outrageous! An invasion of my human rights."

Thinking about the human rights of the women in the photos, Tom raised himself up slightly too. "George, the only outrageous things in all of this are the images on your computer." He had to bolster his argument, turn the emphasis back on George. He resorted to a lie. "I've seen them. I've seen the images you've created of Julie upstairs."

Still George was indignant. "You . . . you bloody snipe! You've got no right, no right at all."

His anger was beginning to antagonize Tom, who pointed a finger across the desk. "Listen. You've been using company property to access sites of a sadistic nature. If we turned that stuff over to the police, what do you think would happen?"

He paused to let the comment sink in.

Finally George broke eye contact, looking to the side and quietly saying, "Sadistic, am I?"

Tom didn't know how to answer that comment, so he carried on in a more conciliatory tone. "Look, George, we're not going to pass it on to the police. But I'm going to have to let you go."

George stared at him, hatred in his face. "You've destroyed my personal property and now you're sacking me?" He brooded for a second. "What if I'm not prepared to go?"

Tom stood up. "I'm not discussing this. Go upstairs and clear your desk or the police are getting involved."

George didn't move.

Tom knew he couldn't break eye contact, but the intensity of suppressed emotion emanating from the other man was unsettling him.

Suddenly George looked down and pressed a fist to his lips. Registering the anguish in the gesture, Tom knew he had won. "Come on, I'll help you."

Still avoiding eye contact, George got up. Silently they climbed the stairs. The solemn way they entered the room caused everyone to look up and watch. Tom stood awkwardly to one side as George unlocked his cabinet and removed his briefcase, jacket and tie. Next he pulled a plastic bag from his bottom drawer and began emptying the contents of his drawers into it.

Finally Ges stood up. "George, Tom, what's happening?"

George kept his head down and Tom waved a silencing hand at Ges. "If there's any other stuff we can come in at the weekend and sort it out," said Tom quietly. He walked George back down the stairs and through to reception. As George went to leave, Tom steeled himself for the last thing he had to do. "George, I'll need your key to the office."

George stopped and remained still as if contemplating the comment. Tom could see tears in the corner of the other man's eyes as he slid a keyring from his pocket, extricated a key from the metal loop, then hurled it to the floor.

Tom was trawling through overhead variances on the monthly Purchase and Ledger analysis when he heard multiple footsteps coming down the stairs. Guessing what was going on, he kept the files open on his desk.

Julie knocked on the door a second later. Ges, Ed and Gemma were visible behind her.

"Tom," Julie began hesitantly. "We're going for a drink at The Church. A leaving drink actually . . ."

"Yes, I heard," Tom interrupted. "Sorry I didn't have time to pop upstairs earlier."

"Oh," she replied, sounding disappointed. "Some new account they've won down in London." She looked at him to confirm the story.

"They didn't give me any details," said Tom. "Just said we're going to lose you. When is it that you . . ."

"Straight away. Well, tomorrow. My last night in that soulless hotel, thank God."

Tom smiled. "We'll miss you. Look." He stood up and went over to her. "I'll try and make it over, but I've got loads on, so if I don't . . ."

He gave her a big hug and she used the opportunity to whisper in his ear, "No job is worth your health, Tom. You take care of yourself."

The comment left him at a loss for words. Was it that obvious he was under so much strain? Self-conscious now, he searched for an answer but she saved him the trouble. "You know what? I enjoyed it here — the North isn't quite so grim as everyone makes out."

Tom laughed. "You take care."

There was an awkward silence and Tom knew they were all waiting for him to explain what had happened earlier.

"By the way, George has left the company."

Everyone stared at him, waiting for more information.

240

"He had been using work computers for his own business. Head office found some files and that was it, they wanted him out. Immediately."

Ges let out a low whistle. "What sort of files?"

"I don't know, to be honest," Tom answered, making sure his glance missed Julie.

After they had all trooped out Tom waited for five minutes, then checked Sarah in reception had gone, too. Grabbing the keys to the works van from the cabinet behind her desk, he opened up the back door of the office and loaded the boxes of X-treme gum into the rear of the van. He had just opened the gates to the courtyard when he heard a footstep in the alleyway behind him. Turning round he saw George fixing him with a malevolent stare.

"You've got rid of Julie," he announced flatly, all his plans ruined.

Needing time to think, Tom walked back to the storage room and wheeled a Cooper's Barrow into the back of the van. "George, it doesn't concern you, but I haven't got rid of her. She's been called back down to London. They need her there."

"Really?" he sneered. "That's not just a ploy?"

A ploy. By using that word George was indicating he knew they were removing Julie from the equation before anything happened. Unable to believe the man's audacity, Tom said, "I hate to think what you're getting at with that comment." He shut the rear of the van and started walking round to the driver's door. "Now, if you could step out of the way."

"Why? Where are you taking that lot?"

"To the promotions company," Tom answered impatiently, hoping his tone would deter any further questions.

"At six forty in the evening?" George's eyes narrowed.

"Yes," said Tom, unlocking the driver's door.

He had started the engine and put it into first gear when George knocked on the van's window. He wound it down halfway and George spoke quickly, barely audible over the chug of the diesel engine. "Tell your wife she should draw the curtains when she's ironing at night. I can see straight in."

Tom replayed the sinister implications of the comment in his head. By the time he'd got the van in neutral and jumped out, the man had vanished. "You sick bastard," he announced weakly to the empty alleyway.

By the time Tom had stacked all the boxes at the end of his garage and covered them with a large tarpaulin, it was after eight o'clock. Charlotte was out with some friends from her gym, not due back until late. He let himself into the house, opened a bottle of wine and went through to the living room.

Slumped on the sofa, he kicked off his shoes and put his feet up on the coffee table, a glass of wine resting on his stomach. He had gone beyond exhausted to a state where he just felt hollowed out and zombie-like. He so desperately wanted to sleep but there was too much going round his head, too much going round his bloodstream.

Draining the glass, he poured another and then remembered that the work van was parked on the driveway and his Porsche was outside the office. Bollocks to it, he thought, deciding that he would return it early the next morning and no one apart from that twisted bastard George would be any the wiser. Creepy George. What was going on in that man's head? He'd seemed genuinely devastated by the news that Julie was going, as if he'd developed a real crush on her. He snorted. A crush was something teenagers or giddy adults experienced. Men like George didn't have crushes: they had obsessions. Dark and frightening ones.

Gulping down the second glass of wine, his thoughts turned to George's last comment. The bastard had been outside his house at some stage. He must have got his address from a computer file at work. Tom climbed the stairs and slid the shoebox out from under the bed. The man who delivered the gun didn't say a lot, other than to ask for his four hundred quid then show him how the safety catch worked. It looked like a small air pistol, almost toy-like in size.

George lurked in the shadows of the car park at The Church. He couldn't stand pubs. The smoke, the music, and worst of all, the women. Obscene in their make-up and short skirts, laughing loudly as they got more drunk. More confident. Looking at men, chatting with them, playing their flirtatious games. But never with him. Never with him.

Hands thrust deep into his anorak pockets, he crossed the car park and peered in through the window, fingers turning the packet of pills round and round. Julie was there, at a table with the rest of them. Red lips smiling, she got to her feet, circled a finger above everyone's glass, then set off for the bar.

He willed himself to go inside, knowing that it was his last chance. Maybe the others would get too drunk and go home. He constructed the scenario in his head; him and Julie the last to leave. Slipping the pill into her final bottle of beer, then — because he didn't drink — offering to drive her to the Ibis hotel. Her speech getting awkward, clever comments no longer on the tip of her tongue. Her losing control as she got out of the car. His car, with the briefcase in the boot. Helping her into the lift and up to her room. Getting her on to the bed and then waiting for her to pass out completely. The hours of fun he'd have with her.

Mere photographic images were leaving him less and less satisfied. And now he had the pills that would allow his fantasies to take place. But he couldn't go inside. A pub wasn't the place to put his plans into action. He would have to find another situation.

He thought about the women who allowed him to photograph them in their houses. In their bedrooms. It would be easy to drug the ones who posed on their own.

But even as the thought occurred to him, the image of Tom's wife teased him. Curtains open as she did the ironing in those tight vest tops. Urgently now, his fingers probed at the pills. She was a far more attractive prospect than the little strumpets who posed for cash.

Shivering with outrage at the ordeal he'd suffered at the hands of her husband, he knew something in his mind had altered for ever.

CHAPTER
SEVENTEEN

July 2002

As soon as the alarm started beeping Tom hauled himself to a sitting position, legs over the side of the bed.

"Turn it off," moaned Charlotte, pulling the duvet up around her head. He had no idea when she'd got in. Head all over the place, he blinked stupidly a few times before reaching over and pressing the off button.

Peeling his tongue from the roof of his mouth, he trudged like a sleepwalker through the archway and into their en-suite bathroom. He needed water. After gulping at the tap for a while, he filled the sink with cold water and plunged his head in, letting the iciness cut through the warm fog clogging his brain. Feeling slightly more awake, he rubbed a towel through his hair and went downstairs.

Two bottles of wine stood on the sideboard in the kitchen; one empty, one with a few inches left in the bottom. He stared at them, barely able to remember opening the second. Then he shuffled across the room and swigged the last of it down, to take the edge off his headache.

Forty minutes later he'd showered, scrubbed his teeth and forced a bowl of cornflakes down. At his front door he reached up to take his Porsche keys off the hook and saw an unfamiliar set hanging there. It took him a couple of seconds to remember that he'd driven home in the work van. With Charlotte still asleep, he let himself out of the front door without saying goodbye.

Immediately he noticed that his garage door was slightly open. "I don't believe it," he whispered, walking over and lifting it up.

"Thieving little bastards," he cursed, staring at the tarpaulin. It had been half pulled off the stack of chewing gum boxes and he could see several were missing. After rearranging it, he went back into the house and called up the stairs. "Charlotte! Those little shits have broken into the garage again. I'll phone the police from the office."

There was no reply, so he said to himself, "OK, well done Tom. See you later. I love you."

At the end of the afternoon he checked with Sarah that his evening meal with the marketing people from Manchester airport was still on. "OK, I'll need to pop home and change. Can you phone them and say I'll meet them at The Living Room at seven forty-five?"

"Fine," answered Sarah. Before Tom got out of the door she added, "Austen Rogers from X-treme called again, sounding very pissed off. He wants to know which promotions company is going to be handing out the X-treme gum at Piccadilly station. Shall I call him back?"

"No," said Tom more forcefully than he meant to. "I'll take care of it."

★   ★   ★

The digital display on the side of Portland Tower had changed again. Now the countdown was complete, the lettering above the screen read, "Bruntwood Welcomes All." The number on the screen had changed to "72" and the lettering below it read "Commonwealth Nations."

The pavement was alive with colour and activity as hundreds of people mingled through the city, many with plastic squares around their necks identifying them as Games officials. Sitting in his Porsche and taking long sips from a double espresso, Tom watched the crowds from behind his dark glasses. He took in the strange fashions and unfamiliar clothes: African men in loose-fitting shirts with green and gold patterns like the ones favoured by Nelson Mandela, women with elaborate headdresses and long, flowing shawls. Young white women, hair tied back in sensible ponytails, red Maple leaf badges sewn onto their Jansport backpacks. Squarely built South Sea Islanders ambling along in American T-shirts. Men in yellow and green rugby tops, hair looking like it had been bleached by the sun.

Tom examined their happy, excited expressions and thought about the days he had to drag himself through.

Passing the official Commonwealth Games shop, he looked at the queue of people waiting for customers to come out so they could get in, and he thought about the sales projections the taxi driver had mentioned all those weeks ago. It looked like they would be comfortably met.

Once he had got past Sarah, he shut the door to Ian's old office behind him, gulped down the last of his coffee, then took a pinch of powder. Staring at his computer screen, he cursed the cleaner for fiddling with the monitor's brightness control. Turning the knob had little effect and it was only when he went to rub a hand over his face in frustration did he realize that his sunglasses were still on. Shaking his head, he took them off and the room suddenly brightened.

By late morning he was feeling a lot better. The last of the building wraps had gone up the day before and he'd even received a couple of emails from clients thanking him for all his work.

He was turning his attention to lunch when his phone went. It was Sarah. Although she was trying to sound cheery, he could detect a slightly strained note in her voice. "Hi there, Tom. I have Austen Rogers from X-treme chewing gum in reception. He's just arrived at Piccadilly station but can't find the promotion there."

Tom looked fearfully towards the door. "He's in reception right now?"

"That's right."

"OK, just give me two minutes. Get him a coffee or something."

He hung up, waves of trepidation suddenly making him feel queasy. Darting through to the toilets, he fumbled for his little bag of powder while checking his reflection in the mirror. Not too bad — eyes still looked wrecked but the rest of his face was all right. He sucked powder from the tip of his forefinger, then straightened his tie and wandered casually through to reception.

Sarah flashed him a wide-eyed look of warning. The client was standing on the other side of the room examining photos of previous building wraps on the walls. His posture looked far from relaxed.

"Austen, this is a welcome surprise," said Tom, stepping across the room with his hand out.

The other man turned around. He had wispy brown hair and a slightly pudgy face, red at the cheeks. His kept his hands clasped behind his back. "Tom," he answered with a fractional dip of his head. "I've been trying to contact you for weeks."

"I'm so sorry. We've been having an awful time of it. Poor Sarah here is only just back from sick leave." He turned to the reception desk. "How long were you off sick for, Sarah?"

"Almost three weeks," she replied woodenly.

"You know how temps are," Tom continued. "Messages have been going everywhere but to the correct person."

Austen eyed him suspiciously. "I assume you received all the merchandise? I couldn't find any sign of the promotion in Piccadilly station just now."

"Yes, it's all been taken care of," said Tom, attempting a smile. "Can we not offer you a coffee?"

"No thank you. I'm keen to see the promotion, actually."

"Right," said Tom, clapping his hands together. "I can understand that." He turned to Sarah, trying to look relaxed. "Sarah, could you order us a cab, please? Just down to Piccadilly." He turned to Austen. "There's no point in even trying to park in town at the moment."

"That's fine. In fact, I'd prefer to walk."

"Why not? In fact, I could take you on a little tour of the city centre if you'd like."

"That should be interesting."

Tom knew the other man suspected there had been some sort of balls-up. He fetched his jacket, put his sunglasses on and they set off towards the centre of town.

"What's Key 103?" asked Austen, pointing up at the airship circling lazily in the clear blue sky above them.

"It's the main commercial radio station in Manchester," replied Tom, looking up at the zeppelin-shaped balloon. "They've got a reporter up there delivering traffic and travel information along with Games bulletins."

"Nice idea." Austen seemed to relax a little.

As they carried on past the BT office and towards the back of Piccadilly station, Tom was glad to be able to point out the building wrap that had been hung the week before. "It's one of over thirty we've arranged to be on display throughout the Games."

"Quite an achievement," answered Austen, looking up at the giant image of a sprinter handing over a baton that was marked with the logo of a courier company. "We'll get it to you first", the headline announced.

"Thanks," said Tom, wondering what to do once they got into the station. "So, are you booked on any particular train home?"

"Yes, the 3.50. A tour of the city centre would be a nice way to use up the afternoon."

"Absolutely!" Tom wondered how to stall the other man for the next few hours.

Standing below the live billboard for the *Manchester Evening News* with its ever changing headline display, they waited for the lights to change before crossing Fairfield Street and walking round the queue of taxis swallowing up passengers in ones, twos and threes.

"All this was derelict about a year ago," said Tom, waving a hand at the sandblasted brick archways and spotless sheet glass windows. "The entrances were all blocked up, except for some grubby little tunnels leading to the tram platforms below the station. Not the type of route you'd use after dark."

They walked through the giant sliding doors into an airy lobby area where a gleaming escalator took them up through the bowels of the station and into the main terminal area.

The final few days before the Games' official start date had consisted of twenty-four-hour shifts as the contractors fought desperately to have the station ready. Somehow they had almost succeeded. Full-size palm trees had been wheeled in across the newly laid tile floor as the last retail units had been cleared for the staff of various shops to swarm in. Displays, shelves and stands had appeared with miraculous speed and in hours each shop was crammed with merchandise, tills manned and ready. Only the odd corner or section of the station remained screened off behind building boards that had been draped in colourful banners welcoming visitors from around the world to Manchester and the XVII Commonwealth Games.

The two men looked around the station area, taking in the throng of people, most clutching bright yellow

Commonwealth Games guides. Positioned around were clusters of Games volunteers, eager to give advice and information on where to get free shuttle buses out to Sportcity.

Tom felt his heart begin to flutter. "Well, it's all go in here," he said. "Let's see where our team have positioned themselves."

"Yes, let's," Austen replied. "I certainly couldn't find them."

They walked towards a stall loaded with umbrellas, toys, pens, keyrings, T-shirts, baseball caps, mugs, plates and ties. Most items featured a vaguely cat-like creature. "That's Kit, the official Games mascot," Tom explained. "His cheeky smile is sure to be a winner with both children and adults alike — to quote the PR release," he added.

Austen didn't look amused as they wandered round to the front part of the station.

All they could see were other stalls selling official Games merchandise, a stand promoting designer sunglasses and a cart manned by a red and white suited promotions team thrusting free cereal bars into the hands of the many people walking past. Tom faked a frown at the absence of the X-treme cart.

"Strange — I thought they were booked into Piccadilly this morning." Suddenly he clicked his fingers, as if remembering something. "Ah — unless this is one of the mornings they've been given a slot at Victoria station."

Austen raised an eyebrow.

"You see, we have a different catchment of people at Victoria — passengers arriving from the west and north of the country."

"But I understood Piccadilly is the city's main terminal." Austen pointed to a banner masking an unfinished set of side exit doors. "Piccadilly: Gateway to the Games," he read out.

Tom's stomach twisted into a tight knot and his mouth dried up. Knowing that his grin was imbecilic, he said, "True — but I think you'll be impressed by Victoria station. As the name implies, it's all very grandiose — elaborate brickwork and wrought iron pillars." He thought about its leaking roofs, moss-stained walls and padlocked doors. "In fact, it will be a great opportunity for a stroll through the city centre. Shall we?" He held a hand towards the main doors and Austen reluctantly walked towards them. Pointing to a line of Rovers with the three figures painted on their sides, Tom said, "That's the official Games transport for VIPs — the rest of us can walk or get the tram though."

His attempts at light-hearted humour were drawing no response from Austen.

"I'll take you through Piccadilly Gardens, then down King Street. It's where the likes of DKNY, Armani and the rest are located. If we're lucky we could spot a celebrity shopper. David Beckham and Posh Spice perhaps."

"Or Rio Ferdinand, now he's signed for United," said Austen, with some enthusiasm.

"A United supporter then?" asked Tom, keen to open up some line of conversation.

"That's right."

"Do you see them play much?"

Now he looked uncomfortable. "Just their away games, really. It's hard to see them play at home when you live down in Surrey. How about you? Red or Blue?"

"I prefer rugby, to be honest," answered Tom. "But I suppose my sympathies are with Manchester City. The British thing about supporting the underdog, I suppose."

They joined the crowds walking down the concourse and into the city centre, Tom struggling for another topic of conversation. "It's a shame you won't have time to see the Olympic village, an entire purpose-built community. It's got the UK's largest temporary restaurant. They're producing almost fifteen hundred meals a day in it." Tom realized he was beginning to witter, but his nerves were dancing at the prospect of how he would explain the absence of the chewing gum promotion at Victoria station. "They anticipate the athletes will get through about ten thousand kilos of bananas and pasta in the next few days. And that's not to mention the hundred and fifty thousand condoms provided in their rooms. They should be describing them as bed athletes, I reckon!"

Austen glanced briefly at his sweating companion. "Tom, that's all very interesting. But the purpose of my visit is to see how our promotion is going. We've paid you sixteen thousand to arrange it after all." He held up a small leather pouch hanging from one wrist. "I need to get some photos for our marketing department, too. The sporting details of this event really aren't of much interest."

"Right . . . of course," said Tom, feeling his skin start to itch as the effects of Brain's powder began to subside. The cacophony of noise started to reach them halfway up the road, and as they reached Piccadilly Gardens they entered a riot of activity. Giant TV screens mounted on platforms displayed reports of the coming events to the masses of people below. At the far end of the gardens, red and blue inflatable figures swayed and danced as air from a mobile generator was blasted up through them. To their side an urgent tattoo was being beaten out by a Samba band as young kids capered and whirled before them. Above it all towered the seventy-metre-tall banner of Ashia Hansen, caught in mid air during a triple jump.

"This is all part of the Spirit of Friendship festival," Tom almost had to shout as two stilt walkers dressed as robots stalked past them, metal costume plates clanging as they went.

"Could we move on?" asked Austen, unmoved by the fun being had all around.

Tom peered through his sunglasses at Austen's impatient face. "Of course." He walked uncertainly onwards, unable to delay their approach towards Victoria station.

Turning right at York Street, they were soon passing the Athenaeum, a glorious building constructed in the Venetian Gothic style at the height of Manchester's domination of the cotton industry. Tom slowed down, pointing out the Ionic columns supporting a cathedral-like dome. "I especially like the brickwork; the red colouring has led to the term 'Slaughterhouse Gothic'. Manchester has got some of the best examples you'll find anywhere."

Austen looked at his watch. "Fascinating. And now it's a pub."

His dismissive tone picked at Tom's frayed nerves. "Not any old pub. It's increasingly the pre-match choice of Manchester City's firm. Go in there on a Saturday with a red shirt on and you'll probably come back out with a broken glass stuck in your face."

"I beg your pardon?"

"Not you personally." Tom smiled. "I mean Man U fans in general. Though a southern accent wouldn't do you any favours either."

Austen's eyes narrowed but he couldn't tell if it was a genuine piece of advice or a piss-take.

"Anyway," said Tom, emotions alternating between a fluttery elation at having got away with a jibe at his client and heart-sinking dread at the prospect of reaching Victoria station. "Here we are at the top of King Street."

They looked down the long, straight road lined with designer stores. In front of each plate glass window were stone blocks and posts. Designed to look like seats, they were actually placed there to stop ram raiders.

"So where's Victoria from here? It's almost lunchtime," said Austen.

"You're right," said Tom quickly. "Why don't we grab a bite now before everywhere fills up?"

Austen looked around uncertainly. "Well . . ."

"It's on me. What do you prefer? Traditional pub or contemporary bar?"

"Traditional, I suppose."

"Do you drink bitter?" asked Tom, stepping into Mr Thomas's Chop House. Austen nodded.

"Two pints of Landlord, please."

After walking the length of the narrow bar, they entered the seating area at the back of the pub, dark wood tables glowing faintly in the light shining through ancient-looking panes of frosted glass. A young man in a shirt and bow tie showed them across the black and white tiled floor to a table.

After turning his mobile off, Tom opened his menu and looked down the list of dishes. "I don't know why I even look — I always go for their home-made corned beef hash."

Austen continued looking at his menu. "Well, given the name of this place, I had better go for the pork chops."

After ordering their meals, Tom excused himself and headed downstairs for the toilets. Looking at his watch he saw, to his dismay, that it was only midday. Even if he stretched lunch out to a couple of hours they'd still have over an hour to get to Victoria station, and it was now only a five-minute walk away. He stood just inside the door, wondering what to do. The sound of water trickling into a cistern made him want to urinate, so he stood in front of the urinal. But his stomach muscles felt too tight and, apart from a few measly drips, his bladder refused to empty.

Looking down, he saw the usual lumps of discarded chewing gum in the bowl and his gag reaction hit him without warning. Walking backwards and zipping himself up at the same time, he retreated into the only cubicle, sat down and felt inside the pocket of his jacket for the powder. Unable to find it, he stood up and ferreted through the rest of his pockets before realizing that he'd left it in the top drawer of his desk.

He crumpled back down on to the toilet, pressing the tips of his fingers against the back of his neck and rotating them round and round. Erratic surges of panicky emotion were playing with him — acute nervousness, crippling fear and the odd spark of inexplicable elation.

Suddenly he became convinced he was being watched. Fearfully, he looked up at the top of the cubicle. But no one was there. He took several deep breaths and began to follow the advice of the therapist from when he'd become ill a few years before.

One, two, three, four, five, six . . . his heartbeat began to slow a bit and the feelings of panic eased . . . seven, eight, nine, ten.

Back in the pub a crush of office workers had appeared and Austen was sitting at the table, looking uncomfortable at being alone.

"Cheers!" said Tom, sitting down and clinking his glass against Austen's. He sucked down over half his pint in one go, abruptly aware of how thirsty he was. Austen was staring at him oddly, and Tom began to feel uncomfortable. Was there a scrap of toilet roll stuck to his forehead? A bogey hanging from his nose? Casually, he brushed the back of his fingers across his nostrils. Now Austen was actually smirking at him. "Er, Tom — is it a bit too bright in here for you?"

Tom looked up, lips vacillating between an uncertain smile and a trembling grimace. It was a dim pub. What did he mean? "Sorry?"

Austen tapped the bridge of his nose. "Your sunglasses. You haven't taken them off yet."

Relief flooded him and he let out a burst of laughter shrill enough to cause several other diners to look around. "Totally forgot they were on!" He slipped them into the breast pocket of his jacket.

Austen sat there with an expectant look on his face, happy to play the client's role and wait to be entertained.

Needing something to do, Tom fished his cigarettes out. "Smoke?"

Austen shook his head disapprovingly.

"I'll just squeeze one in before the food arrives."

He was barely two drags in when the waiter reappeared with their plates. "Isn't that always the way?" observed Tom, stubbing his cigarette out. Smoke swirled across Austen's food and Tom tried to fan it away with his other hand. Next he unwrapped his knife and fork, knowing his appetite wouldn't stretch further than a few mouthfuls. Gingerly scooping up some mashed potato, he popped it into his mouth and looked at Austen as he sawed through a pork chop with his knife. The layer of white fat between the rind and meat quivered and bulged as the knife pressed down. Tom felt the muscles in his throat start to spasm.

He gulped some beer as Austen put it into his mouth and began to grind with his molars, a frown slowly coming over his face. Eventually he picked up his napkin and said, "Sorry, can't get my teeth through the rind — too rubbery." He hooked a forefinger and thumb into his mouth and pulled out a long strip of mangled gristle.

Tom had to look away, the press of conversation at his back getting closer and closer. He kept his eyes averted until he heard Austen place his knife and fork on the plate.

"Very good," he remarked, unwrapping a stick of X-treme gum and popping it into his mouth. Tom could feel the pinpricks of sweat breaking out on his upper lip as he tried to control his feelings of nausea.

The waiter stepped over. "Dessert? We have bread and butter pudding on the specials board."

"Oh, go on then," said Austen, with a conspiratorial smile. "You've tempted me."

Horror struck, Tom watched as Austen plucked the lump of gum from his mouth and dropped it in the ashtray.

He vomited all over the table, gouts of still-foaming beer that flooded Austen's plate, then bounced up, spattering his chest and arms. Even before the spew finished, Tom had lost it. His heart was racing uncontrollably and an overwhelming sense of disaster bore down on him. Gasping for breath, he staggered to his feet. At the other end of the narrow pub sunshine shone through the open door with the promise of fresh air and open space. The source of light became the sole focus of his vision: he had to be out in it at all costs. He began a headlong charge for the door, shouldering other drinkers, knocking drinks from hands. A waiter loomed up in front of him, plates of food balanced in each hand, his silhouette obstructing Tom's view of the door. The heel of Tom's hand connected squarely with the man's chest, and he flew backwards in a shower of chips, peas and gravy-covered slices of meat.

Tom fell out onto the pavement, looked down and saw grey spots on the paving stones under his hands. Gum. He stood up, realizing it dotted the pavement in both directions. Terror now gripping him completely, he ran up King Street, jumping from side to side, taking small steps, then great bounds, desperate to avoid treading on the gum — white fresh blobs, older blackened ones, clusters of it peppering the areas around bins. He veered towards the road but it was there too, embedded in the bumpy surface, a plague from the mouths of the masses.

He kept going, careering round the top of King Street, back past the Athenaeum, sprinting towards Piccadilly Gardens, images of wide lawns filling his head. Bursting out onto the pavement by the Bradford and Bingley, he knocked over a woman and staggered across the tram tracks. An enormous sonic blast cut through him and hydraulic brakes hissed in anger as the approaching tram was forced into an emergency stop.

Two men dressed as giant kangaroos jumped out of his way, one shouting, "Easy mate!" Tom raced past, the safety of the lawns now less than fifty metres away. Swerving to avoid a bench he finally lost his footing, shoulder connecting heavily with the pavement, rolling over, knees and elbows bouncing off the paving stones.

The stilt walkers had stopped and were looking down at him. The giant inflatable figures nodded and swayed as Tom, regaining his feet, saw the smear of fresh gum stuck to his knee. As the Samba drums continued in the background, he started to tear off his trousers, a hoarse scream coming from his throat. He had kicked one leg free when the first neon-jacketed police officer arrived. Grabbing Tom in a bear hug he began to repeat, "Calm down sir, calm down sir, calm down sir," like some religious mantra as his female colleague radioed for a police car.

Stepping out of the Athenaeum, Sly thought there was something familiar about the forlorn-looking figure across the road. Not just the thin build and beaten up clothes that many *Big Issue* sellers seemed to have, but something about his stoop and the way he shifted his weight shyly from foot to foot. As he got nearer the man turned round and finally Sly recognized him: one of the beggars who used to hang around Piccadilly station.

Sly's approach to life was simple — you got ahead by keeping other people down. He'd learned it at an extremely early age. The years of bullying and piss-taking he'd suffered through having ginger hair and goofy teeth only ended when he'd picked out a weaker boy amongst his tormentors and jammed a sharpened pencil into his upper arm.

The action didn't gain him acceptance or friendship, just the respect people gave to the school nutter. It taught him the power of extreme and sudden violence and it was why he still carried a Stanley knife to this day.

So now, as he got closer to the man whose beggings he used to tax, the thought of walking past simply didn't occur. A display of his superiority was needed — something to prove to himself that he was above the other person.

The man had fully turned round now, and seeing someone in smart designer clothes approaching, had immediately begun to say, "Help the homeless sir, copy of the *Big Issue?*"

Sly stopped and with a sneering smile said, "Moved up in the world, then?"

His voice made the *Big Issue* seller freeze and, on recognizing Sly, his stoop seemed to become more exaggerated, the posture of someone used to being victimized. Knowing that wasn't the end of the encounter, he said nervously, "Sly." No trace of a smile.

"I need some cigarettes; knock us some change, mate." Sly held out a cupped hand and clamped his jaw on the lump of gum in his mouth. Its flavour was sharp and lemony, like every other packet he'd taken the other week from the garage in Didsbury. Although the taste was novel to begin with, he'd got tired of its sourness and had flogged most of it to a stallholder in the Arndale market. "Here, I'll swap you for some chuddy." He spat the lump out onto the other man's disintegrating trainers.

The *Big Issue* seller cast his eyes downwards and said miserably, "You don't control the pitches around here. Leave me alone."

Sly got his face up close to the other man's and cocked his head to one side. "Do you want me to cut you?"

The man stepped back. He was still avoiding eye contact, but defeat was written all over him. "No."

"Then give me some money," Sly hissed.

Resignedly the man reached into an inner pocket and produced three pound coins.

"Is that fucking it?"

"I've only sold three copies. It's everything I've got."

Sly wrinkled his nose in disgust. "Three copies? With these crowds? I know you're lying, but I'm not going through your stinking coat. I'd probably get fucking lice."

He plucked the three coins from the man's palm, then produced a thick bundle of twenty-pound notes from his pocket.

The man looked at the money, face devoid of any expression.

Slightly irked by the other man's failure to react to his cash, Sly said, "I'll get the smokes after I've picked up my suit." With a mocking smile, he sauntered on down King Street and entered the Armani shop. When the assistant asked if he needed any help, Sly pointed straight to the pale green suit in the window.

CHAPTER
EIGHTEEN

July 2002

The sense of terror only began to subside once they'd fought through the traffic and made it onto the slightly less busy Oxford Road. Sitting in the back seat of the car, Tom shrugged the blanket off his shoulders and whispered, "Could you turn the fan on, please? It's so hot in here."

The female officer in the passenger seat immediately did as he asked, then turned round in her seat. "What's your name, sir?"

The official note in her voice set his nerves off again and the muscles in his throat clamped up. A few minutes later they turned off into the grounds of the Manchester Royal Infirmary, the patrol car driving round to the Accident & Emergency entrance and parking in a bay marked "Ambulances Only".

Again the female officer turned round. "Sir, you're being detained under section 13B of the Mental Health Act. As police officers we're required to take you to a place of safety — which is here. We're going to find a psychiatric nurse to check you over and make sure you're OK. Is all of that clear?"

His whole body trembling, Tom was only able to nod.

"Good," she continued. "I'll go in first and my colleague, PC Garrett, will stay with you."

She got out of the car and walked through the sliding doors. A short while later she reappeared, walking back over to address her colleague first. "Surprise surprise, no one is available."

As the driver shook his head, she turned to Tom. "Sir, we're going to have to sit tight for a while. Are you OK back there?"

Tom nodded, his heart still fluttering.

After what seemed like an age, a nurse emerged through the doors and beckoned to the officers.

"Right," said the male officer, getting out of the car and opening up the rear door. "Let's put that blanket around you again, shall we? We don't want the nurses getting all excited." He grinned at Tom.

Tom looked down at his bare legs and boxer shorts as the officer draped the blanket around him. Shakily, he got out of the car and allowed himself to be guided into the foyer. Acutely aware of the entire crowded waiting room watching, Tom felt himself growing embarrassed and knew it was a sure sign he was returning to normal.

He was led quickly across into a room at the top of a corridor. Inside was a table and a few soft chairs. A children's mobile hung in the corner, garishly coloured tigers, giraffes and parrots stirred by the commotion as they entered the room. Sitting in one of the chairs was an overweight man in a white tunic, long hair tied back in a ponytail. He smiled at Tom and waved him to a seat. Turning his body so he wasn't directly facing Tom, he said, "Hello, my name's Keith Pilkington. I'm the psychiatric nurse on duty this afternoon. PC Hines tells me they picked you up in Piccadilly Gardens. Can you tell me what was upsetting you so much?"

Tom breathed deeply and when he spoke his voice quivered only slightly. "I'm sorry to have caused such a fuss."

Apologetically, he glanced at each officer. PC Garrett smiled and said, "Don't worry about it. By the way, these are your trousers." He placed them on the shelf near the door.

The psychiatric nurse had been watching Tom carefully and now he said to the officers, "I don't need to keep you two any longer, thanks."

The officers nodded in reply and quietly left the room. Once the door had shut, he looked at Tom. "So what was it all about?"

Tom could still feel the sheen of sweat coating his face. But he knew how to put that right. The remedy lay in the top drawer of his desk at work. Looking at his bare knees, he said, "I've had them in the past. But that's the first for years."

The nurse was looking at his notepad. "The first what?" he gently coaxed.

"Panic attack." He raised a hand to show how his fingertips trembled. "It suddenly hit me. I just had to run."

"Why did you feel the need to remove your trousers?"

Tom shook his head. "They had chewing gum on them."

268

"Had chewing gum on them?"

Tom took another deep breath. "I think I've developed a bit of a phobia. It's a long story, but it started with rubbery things. The mouthpiece of a diving mask, in fact." He let out a short and cheerless laugh. "Then it somehow got to be anything rubbery that's been in someone's mouth. It makes me want to be sick — I get flooded with a kind of revulsion." He stopped and looked up. "I sound mad, don't I?"

The nurse's features were full of understanding. "I've dealt with far worse. Could I ask your name?"

"Tom. Tom Benwell."

"Are you using drugs, Tom? You look like you haven't been getting much sleep. And the sort of state the officers described . . . I assumed you were heavily under the influence of something."

Tom shook his head. "I've just got so much on at work. I was having lunch with a client. God!" He turned his head, and looked at the door. "I left him in Mr Thomas's Chop House. Just sprinted out of there."

"Well, your health is far more important than any contract," said the nurse. "Just think of it as a lunch he'll always remember."

Tom appreciated his attempt at making light of the situation and, taking advantage of the softening in the atmosphere, asked, "So what happens now? I'm not under arrest, am I?"

"No, not at all. Do you have any history of mental illness, Tom?"

Now Tom wanted to get the interview over with as quickly as possible. "No," he lied, not mentioning his episode of a few years before. "Apart from the panic attacks, of course."

"And this attitude you have towards," he glanced at his notes and quoted, " 'anything rubbery that's been in someone's mouth'. You called it a phobia. We'd refer to it as a neurosis. Are you familiar with the word?"

"Like a weird habit?"

"Compulsive or obsessive behaviour, usually provoked by an irrational fear or belief. It's amazingly common, so don't worry. Have you mentioned your concerns about rubbery things to your GP?"

"No; I'm so busy at work. But I should do. I mean, will do." Eager to please, eager to get out.

"Yes, you should. Who is your GP?"

Tom gave him the doctor's name and practice address.

The nurse noted it down and said, "Dr Goldspink can arrange for you to be referred to a counsellor; there are very effective forms of therapy available. You needn't let it have such a detrimental effect on your life and job."

Tom nodded. "Fair enough. I will."

"Right. I'll let your doctor know what happened and recommend that he book you in to see a therapist. In the meantime, you'll need some trousers. Now, I can get you a pair of these." He pointed to the thin green cotton pair he was wearing. "Or there's a little trick I know about for removing chewing gum. We can freeze it off — there's a gas here that can do it."

Tom looked bemused.

"Freezing chewing gum turns it brittle, then we can scrape it off with a scalpel."

"Option number two, please."

He had a ten-pound note ready for the taxi driver. As soon as the car pulled up outside his office he said, "Here mate, keep the change."

The driver said, "Cheers! You want a receipt with that?"

But Tom was already half out of the car, keys to the office in his hand. "No, you're all right," he called over his shoulder.

Reception was deserted and the door locked, but when the alarm didn't start buzzing as he opened up, he knew someone else was still in the building.

Quickly he walked through to his office, shut the door and made straight for his desk. Two large dabs of powder later and he was sitting in his chair staring at the screensaver of the Cornish beach. Though it no longer gave him the same sense of exhilaration, the drug was working its way through his system, easing his nerves and smoothing the ruffles of his mind. He was just contemplating pulling out the bottom drawer and putting his feet up when there was a knock on the door.

"Yeah?" he said, surprised at the dreamy way the word came out.

The door opened halfway and Ges poked his head into the room. "Where've you been? All hell's been breaking out here."

"Go on," said Tom. For the moment, nothing really mattered but the relief coursing through him.

"The guy from the chewing gum company called. Then his boss called from London. Then our bosses called from London. No one can get hold of you, so suddenly everyone's after you. Was there some sort of problem with the chewing gum promotion?"

"Ges, I'll fill you in tomorrow."

Ges frowned, but didn't say anything. Without a word he stepped back out of the office and disappeared up the stairs.

Tom went on the internet and checked that the cafe in Cornwall was still for sale. Seeing that it was, he gathered up his jacket and set off home. He hadn't even put his briefcase down in the hall when Charlotte called from the sitting room. "Tom, your bloody mobile can't be turned on. One of the directors down in London has called here three times. He's left his home number for you."

Tom went up to their bedroom, climbed out of his suit and dumped it in the wardrobe. Pulling on jeans and a T-shirt, he went back down the stairs, preparing his speech to Charlotte. He'd use the beach location to persuade her — emphasize the prospect of fresh air and opportunities for exercise. He'd already enquired about membership at the best gym in the area.

As he walked into the sitting room, he saw the TV was tuned into the build-up for the Opening Ceremony in the Commonwealth Games stadium. The place was already packed, every seat sold out. But his wife was sitting on the edge of the sofa, looking tense and uncomfortable.

"Charlotte," he began, "don't worry about that knob down in London. What has he said, anyway?"

"Nothing," she said, biting on the edge of a thumbnail. "Just for you to call him immediately."

Tom moved to the sofa and sat down. He put his arm around her. "Charlotte, it's all going to be fine. I've got this plan —"

She cut him off. "I'm not bothered by some rude prick down in London. I'm bothered about this."

She held up a white plastic object the shape of an ice-lolly stick. Halfway up was a little window with a blue cross in it.

"What's that?"

"A pregnancy test. The cross means it's positive."

"You're pregnant?"

She nodded.

Tom stared at the top of her down-turned head, found himself focusing on the individual strands of hair poking through her scalp. He felt like he was looking through a microscope. "But that's . . . that's perfect. It'll all work out brilliantly. I've got this plan, you see. We'll pack everything in and move to Cornwall. There's this cafe for sale. It's so beautiful — it's wooden, painted a pale blue. It's got this great big veranda. We can live by the beach, raise our child there, away from all this filth and pressure."

Charlotte looked up. "Cornwall? What the hell are you on about Cornwall for? Cafe? I'm only a few weeks late for my period. What if this stupid test is wrong?"

Tom realized he'd got ahead of himself. "No there's more to it than that. I've had a disaster at work. Something serious. Resignation serious."

"Is that why that director has been ringing?"

"Yeah, but it doesn't matter," Tom replied, brightening his voice. "Charlotte, I'm desperate to pack it in. You know that. I'll work a settlement out with them and we can use the cash from it along with the money from selling this place to get out. Downsize. I've worked it all out."

Very slowly Charlotte began to shake her head. "I knew you were desperate to get through the run-up to the Commonwealth Games. And you've done it — look." She waved a hand at the dancers on the TV. "The Games are starting in ten minutes. What's all this stuff about Cornwall? You never mentioned about packing the job in completely."

"Well, I thought it was obvious. Sorry. It's been intense lately. But they've already begun to work out our next set of targets. It doesn't stop, Charlotte, it just goes on and on and fucking on. I feel so trapped." He thought about the sensation of the spider's web around his head.

Looking agitated, she reached for a cigarette.

Tom placed his hand over the pack. "Charlotte, do you think you should?"

Angrily she sat back and took a deep breath.

"Don't look so sad." He placed a reassuring hand on her stomach. "This is such perfect timing. We can start a new life . . . a family. Everything."

She grabbed his hand and threw it back on his lap. "I'm not having this thing!" she said, tears filling her eyes. "How dare you presume that? I'm twenty-two for God's sake. I've got my life to live. Babies?" She let out a snort of disgust. "You're bloody joking!" She leaned forwards, grabbed a cigarette and lit up.

Tom stared at her. "What do you mean? It's our child. Ours." Bizarrely, an image of the diving instructor from the Seychelles flashed through his mind.

She stood up and snarled, "It's not a child. It's a blip, a few cells . . . a cross on this thing." She waved the pregnancy tester in his face. "One pill and it's gone."

"Charlotte," he moaned, hands thrust anxiously between his knees. "You can't destroy it. It's our future."

She held up both palms to him. "Slow the fuck down. What the hell were you thinking?" Her cheeks grew red as anger began to take hold. "You plan all this without telling me a thing?"

"I meant to. I was waiting for the right time, that was all. Charlotte, please — it could be so perfect."

"My future's here, in Manchester. Not in some windswept wooden shack serving cups of bloody tea."

Tom looked down at the carpet. "What's this city got that's so great?"

She put a finger on her lower lip and began counting with her other hand. "Well, let me see. Restaurants, bars, delis, coffee shops, beauty salons." She ran out of fingers and carried on anyway. "Nightclubs, nightlife,

275

life full stop! Selfridges has just opened and there's a Harvey Nichols opening next year."

Tom said very quietly, "You'd destroy our baby because a Harvey fucking Nichols is opening next year?"

"Don't call it a baby! It barely exists yet!"

"You'll kill our baby because it might ruin your shopping? You selfish, self-centred, self-important bitch."

"I'm not listening to this." She began walking from the room.

He pursued her, weeks of tension suddenly finding an outlet. "Do you realize how shallow you sound? How shallow you are? We've got a chance to build a meaningful life — not one based around what you purchased in town today — and you can't be arsed because you don't want to miss out on lounging around in the sports centre, going shopping, eating in nice restaurants and taking expensive drugs!"

She changed her mind about going upstairs and grabbed her jacket and handbag, heading for the front door instead.

"Where are you going?" he yelled. Bounding forwards, he grabbed her arm.

She spun round and said mockingly, "Late night shopping."

Without thinking he slapped her.

"Don't you fucking touch me!" she screamed, tears spilling down her face. "You go to bloody Cornwall. Don't expect me to come."

She stormed out of the house, slamming the door shut behind her.

Tom stood, fists clenching and unclenching, nostrils flaring as breath shot in and out of his nose. He turned round and climbed the stairs two at a time. Rummaging around in his wardrobe, he found the packet of powder and tapped a large pinch of it into the palm of his hand. Greedily he licked it up.

Back downstairs he'd just got the stopper out of a bottle of single malt when the phone rang. Grabbing it, he breathlessly demanded, "Charlotte?"

"Tom?"

"Who's this?"

"Andrew Soloman. I've been trying to get hold of you all afternoon. What the bloody hell happened in Manchester today? I've had the top guy at X-treme UK on to me. They've pulled the business. They've been on to Centri-Media and there's no promotion for their chewing gum booked into Piccadilly station. They say we've invoiced them sixteen grand for that job, and they sent the cheque weeks ago. Where's the money, Tom?"

"I have it — it's just that the slot at the station wasn't booked. They can have a refund."

"A refund? They had an entire promotion arranged, luxury holiday to Malaysia, boxes of a special limited edition flavour made. We're liable for all those costs. Too right they'll get a refund — and if the cheque hasn't been touched, you might just avoid being prosecuted for fraud."

Tom was staring at the TV, but not seeing a thing. "Listen, they can have their money back. Every penny of it. Just tell them there was a mix-up. Shit happens, you know?"

"*Shit happens?* Are you drunk?"

"What do you mean?"

"This is it, you realize that, don't you Tom? They want blood, so you're out of here. We're taking the Porsche back and you get three months' money as a senior account handler."

"Actually, I'm the managing director, in case you've forgotten. That's six months' money and my profit-related bonus."

"You think there'll be any profits after this fuck-up? And check your contract, Tom — it's another thing you forgot to sign. As far as we're concerned, you're still a senior account handler."

Realizing he'd lost it all, Tom started laughing down the phone, the hysterical whooping of a hyena. The handset fell from his hand and he staggered through the French windows onto the patio. Swigging directly from the bottle, he was just able to make out The Plough above him before fireworks from the opening ceremony filled the sky with showers of bronze, silver and gold.

CHAPTER
NINETEEN

2 November 2002

Jon's car pulled to a halt by the incident van positioned at the top of forty-six Lea Road. It had started drizzling a couple of hours earlier and, leaning forwards for a better view of the sky, Jon could see the motionless layer of cloud stretching away like an expanse of concrete in all directions. "Great," he muttered to himself. He opened the car door and jogged over to the van, noticing the Lexus tucked in beside it.

Stepping in to what was really a mobile home made into an office, Jon used one hand to wipe the droplets of rain coating his cropped hair. He said to the crime scene manager inside, "Nice motor parked alongside. What are they paying you guys again?"

A middle-aged man with a thick head of grey hair smiled. "The Lexus? I should be so lucky. It's the couple's in the flat above the victim's. They don't like leaving it on the road — it's been keyed too many times."

Jon nodded. "Are they in? I need to question them about Mary Walters' death."

"I haven't seen them go out," the CSM replied.

Jon ran to the front door of the house and pressed the intercom for flat two. After he'd told them who he was, he was buzzed in. A smooth-looking man in his mid-to-late twenties showed him into the flat and through to the front room. Inside were cream leather sofas and stripped floorboards, palms stretching almost up to the roof, Rothko prints on the walls. He sat in the chair opposite the man and his wife and pulled his notebook out.

"You've done this flat out nicely. Is it housing-association owned?"

"Was," replied the husband. "We bought this flat off them last year. They said they'll be selling off the others, too."

Jon understood the process taking place: prices had shot up and the housing association was cashing in by selling its properties in the area, probably to buy more in the cheaper Moss Side. The wealthy couple he was looking at were at the vanguard of a wave that would soon sweep the older residents of Whalley Range clean away.

Their statement had little of potential interest — both husband and wife worked long hours for a law firm in Manchester. The only conversation they'd had with Mary was when she had asked if they had any objection to her pinning the CCTV notice up.

"Ah yes," said Jon. "One of her friends mentioned she had problems with prostitutes and their clients parking in the back yard."

The couple nodded knowingly. "I think it bothered her more than us," said the husband. "We come and go by the front hallway."

"Excuse me," interrupted the wife. "We usually park round the back and driving over used condoms most mornings wasn't exactly pleasant."

"The Lexus?"

They nodded, looking proud.

"Nice car, that," Jon said, looking at his notebook. "So did the notice work?"

"Like that," replied the wife with a snap of her fingers.

Back in the incident van he asked the crime scene manager if any photographic albums had been found lying around Mary's flat. Nothing so far, came the reply. Jon asked if he could go back in for another look around. The man signed his name in the log book and tossed him a crime scene suit, overshoes and gloves.

Jon nodded to the uniformed officer at the back steps and then let himself into the flat. He wandered into the front room and stared at the carpet where the body had been lying. Then he glanced round the walls, taking in the immaculately arranged books lining the shelves. His eye was caught by a set of drawers; the uppermost one was fractionally open, as if it had been pushed hurriedly back in. He wedged a pen into the slight gap and pulled the drawer out. Bills and documents were arranged in neat piles. TV licence, gas, electricity, telephone.

Crouching down he opened the cupboard door to the side, grunting with satisfaction when he saw the stack of photo albums. Slipping on the gloves, he began flicking through. The front page was labelled, "Oberammergau, 1999." An alpine setting — some sort of a play about the crucifixion. He recognized the friend, Emma, amongst the beaming members of the coach party.

He went through the other albums and wasn't surprised to find only harmless photos of churches. Frowning, he walked through into her bedroom, feeling slightly guilty as he opened up her bedside cupboard and peered inside. A little rush of excitement played up his spine when he saw a stack of small magazines. He lifted the top few out and read the titles with disappointment. *The Everlasting Life. Our Creator Cares About You. The Search for God.* Religious magazines delivered by women who turn up on your doorstep and stare a little too intensely as they hand them over. Jon nodded in grim acceptance: try as he might, he couldn't imagine that any of the type of snaps found in Polly Mather's flat would turn up here.

In the kitchen he started idly looking through the cupboards, amazed to see that she even had a system of labels on each door to denote which items should be eaten first. Examining what was stored on each shelf, he noted there were quite a few promotional packs of merchandise — no doubt part of the same economical approach that led her to collect the coupons and tokens on the hallway table.

He looked in the top drawer and saw knives, forks and spoons neatly lined up. The drawer below was labelled "Miscellaneous" and was full of odds and ends — spare batteries, rolls of sellotape, a box of plasters, bags of foreign coins, a pack of chewing gum, tubes of indigestion tablets. The bottom drawer was full of tea towels, mostly souvenirs from places like Scarborough, Cromer and St Ives.

Jon straightened his legs and, sighing deeply, began to mentally sift through what the investigation had uncovered so far. The pairs of cups that had been recently washed up in Polly Mather's and Mary Walter's houses had yielded nothing to forensic examination. The CCTV lead had turned out to be nonexistent. No usable fingerprints had been lifted from Mary's doorbell. Phil Wainwright had a solid alibi for the night of Mary's death — he was staying at his mum's over in Burnley. He thought about Polly Mather's flat. The contacts magazines seemed the most promising lead, but tracing the three pay-as-you-go numbers was impossible.

Absolutely nothing seemed to link the victims and he was painfully aware that, due to the lack of solid leads, the investigation was stalling in its very earliest stages. Hoping that someone else might have made a significant discovery, he set off back to the station.

The top floor of Longsight police station made a city trading room seem sedate. Officers were scurrying between desks, others were on the telephone or furiously entering their reports onto HOLMES. Messages were being shouted from all directions.

Making his way between the tables, Jon headed for DCI McCloughlin's room. He saw him inside, surrounded by other senior officers. Jon knocked and was immediately beckoned in.

"Gentlemen, this is DI Spicer," McCloughlin announced. "He was taking care of the investigation while it stood at one victim and was first in with me at Mary Walters' flat." He turned to Jon. "The autopsy on the third victim, Heather Rayne, has just come back. She had been dead for over a day, which actually makes her the second one to be killed."

"One a day for the past three days," Jon said, staying by the door.

"Precisely. And every time my bloody phone rings — which is almost non-stop — I'm expecting it to be news of number four."

He pointed through the windows of his office at the white boards that stood at the top of the main room. The usual smattering of victims' photos adorned each one with various other names and addresses dotted around below. What was missing were the crucial interconnecting lines between each victim. Jon had never seen such a lack of them.

"As you can see, we're still thrashing around in the dark here. Any progress on your part? What was the score with the CCTV at Mary Walters' place?"

Jon shook his head. "Afraid it was just that — a notice. Mary Walters pinned it up to put off curb crawlers bringing their pickups round into the back yard. I've just had a talk with the owners of the flat above. They spend their lives in the office so had very little to say."

McCloughlin shook his head. "Well, there were two recently washed up cups on Heather Rayne's draining board. This bastard knows the victims, I'm certain."

"What's the profile so far of the latest one to be found?" Jon asked.

McCloughlin spoke from memory. "Heather Rayne. Single, aged thirty-two. A high flyer at Kellogg's where she worked as a training manager in the IT department. An upstanding member of the community, helping to raise money for various local projects through sponsored runs and the like. Also active in the local branch of the Conservative party. No familial or obvious social connections to the other two victims."

The room was silent for a few moments before McCloughlin continued. "Jon — you've had a fairly good look around two of the victims' flats. Go and view the crime scene video from Heather Rayne's property and check the white boards. See if any angles show up."

Taking that as his cue to get going, Jon replied, "Yes sir," and went to find the video room. Other officers had obviously been watching the tapes late into the night — a full ashtray and a box of matches had been left on the corner table. Opening the window slightly, Jon looked hungrily at a half-smoked cigarette. Rothman's. His favourite brand before giving up. He loaded the tape marked with Heather Rayne's name into the cassette recorder.

The footage opened on a leafy street, the sound of starlings arguing in the background. The video panned towards the victim's property, the picture moving across a fir tree in the front garden, the edge of a Jaguar coming into the other side of the screen as the officer started walking up the short path leading to the front door. A hand extended into the frame and pushed the front door open. The picture dimmed out and then objects slowly took shape. As the camera made a slow sweep of the hallway area, something began nagging at the back of Jon's mind.

He rewound the tape, unsure of what he was looking for. The footage started again, birds twittering, fir tree, edge of the Jaguar, front path, door. Glancing at the ashtray, he jabbed the pause button, unable to quite work out what had caught his attention. It was as frustrating as having a word on the tip of his tongue. He rewound the tape again. Still it wouldn't come. Angrily he reached over and lifted the half-smoked Rothman's out of the ashtray. He sniffed the charred end, aware that most of the tar, nicotine and various poisons would be concentrated in the cigarette's last third. Hating himself, he lit it up and took a deep drag. As the harsh smoke started his brain dancing, he thought back to the first victim, Polly Mather.

He remembered the Subaru Impreza belonging to the neighbour jutting across on to Polly's half of the shared drive. He remembered that a Lexus was usually parked in the third victim's backyard, near to Mary Walters' door. Staring at the TV, he saw the front corner of the Jaguar intruding into the screen. Pulling another lungful of smoke from the cigarette, he stubbed it out and got up. Feeling like he was walking on cotton wool, he entered the main incident room and went over to the allocator. "Charlie, can you tell me who's compiling the vehicle index for Heather Rayne?"

The officer checked on his computer. "Sergeant N Darcourt — over there." He pointed to a bald man with the frame of an overweight bulldog, hunched over a PC.

Jon walked over. "Nobby, how's it going? You still playing scrum half for Wilmslow?"

The man looked up, one cauliflower ear sprouting from the side of his skull. "Prop nowadays, mate. Don't know why," he joked, sitting back and patting his paunch. "And yourself?"

"Still open side flanker for Cheadle Ironsides. When I get the chance."

The man gave an understanding grimace. "What can I do you for?"

Jon sat down on the edge of his desk. "Just a quick question about Heather Rayne if you have a second."

"Fire away."

"Has the inventory been completed for all the vehicles on her street? I'm wondering about a Jag parked outside the front of her house. It shows up on the video footage."

Sergeant Darcourt flicked through the form he had been filling out. "No Jag registered to her — the Kellogg's training sessions she held usually took place in a hotel in the city centre. She'd go in on the train. Her registered vehicle is a Golf." He then leafed through some other notes, "Here you go. Jaguar XJ7. Registered to D Armstrong, number twenty-five Ivy Green Road. That's her neighbour."

But Jon was already hurrying back to the video room. "Cheers mate!" he called out over his shoulder.

Once back in his seat, he let the video roll again. The cameraman stepped into the flat, everything dark while the camera automatically readjusted to the drop in light. Next he turned right into the main room. It looked like an interior designer had been let loose on the place: huge terracotta pots with curly willow jutting out, recessed lighting and white curtains. The room was lit by several arc lamps that bathed the body in a harsh glare. Once again she was lying on her back, arms out to her sides, clothes slightly crumpled, the fringe of her raven hair messed up. But Jon had seen enough. All the victims so far lived in the immediate vicinity of someone who owned a high performance car.

He tried to think objectively, asking himself if his theory could have been unduly influenced by the fact that the case to occupy most of his time over the last few months was the theft of similar cars in the south Manchester area. His mind went back to the car chase in May. How he was almost close enough to smell the panic coming from the dark figure before he had jumped off the bridge and plunged into the black water below. There was no doubt that the bastard escaping him was a serious source of irritation. Biting his lip, he wondered whether to go out on a limb and air his theory to McCloughlin.

The man walked confidently up the short driveway. Glancing over the Mercedes SLK, he rang the doorbell and waited, the fingers of both hands curled round the handle of his briefcase.

The door opened and an elderly man holding a bottle of Guinness looked out. "Yes?" he asked, taking in the suit and tie.

The caller looked confused. "I'm sorry, I was looking for . . ."

"Liz?" the man interrupted. "I didn't know she was expecting anyone else. Come in. Are you a friend?"

The person on the doorstep hesitated, clearly wrong-footed by the presence of the elderly man. "No, it's all right."

"Please," he insisted. "She's only popped out for two minutes. She'll be most annoyed if I tell her she had a caller who didn't stay on account of me."

"You live here as well?"

"No no no," the old man smiled. "I'm her dad. She picks me up every other Saturday. She's seen the stuff they serve in the retirement home, so she treats me to a roast lunch every fortnight. She's just getting some parsnips now."

The visitor had made up his mind and was backing off down the drive.

"Who should I say called?" asked the old man.

"No one," said the man, retreating towards the road. "I'll call another time."

Reluctantly, the man shut the door, afraid his presence had somehow caused offence or — worse — scared off a potential suitor for his permanently single daughter.

Jon was sitting in the video room, resignedly finishing off another half-smoked cigarette. In the main room, he heard the office manager announce that everyone was to gather for a briefing in five minutes' time.

Work was put on hold and the enquiry team gathered in the open area at the top of the room. DCI McCloughlin emerged from his office, clutching a sheet of paper and accompanied by a thin man in wire-framed glasses. Feeling the gaze of so many people upon him, the man nervously pushed the glasses up his nose and ran a hand through his thinning hair.

"OK people," announced McCloughlin. "The forensics lab at Chepstow have got back to us."

Jon sat at the back of the listening crowd, feeling a pang of jealousy that, two days ago, the call would have been directed through to him.

"Toxicology analysis of all three victims' blood shows traces of the same drug. Problem is, it's one they've never come across before. The technician said two of them have spent 'quite some time' analysing the ions on the mass spectrometer. God knows what that involves exactly but take it from me: it was expensive. All they can say is that the drug is acid-based and broadly similar in structural terms to gamma hydroxybutyrate. GHB or — as it's known in the clubs — GBH or liquid ecstasy."

"A date rape drug," someone muttered at the front.

"Yes," confirmed McCloughlin. Looking back at the report, he continued to read, "Colourless, odourless, can be easily made in home-based labs using solvents and caustic soda. Sold in either liquid or powder form, it's a powerful anaesthetic that can render someone unconscious in under twenty minutes. Initial effects are feelings of euphoria — hence the popularity amongst clubbers. But larger doses can lead to unconsciousness, convulsions and coma. When mixed with alcohol results can be fatal. Long-term use has been poorly researched, but studies show it leads to massive mood swings, paranoia and irritability. Can also lead to psychotic episodes, especially if the user has a prior history of mental illness."

McCloughlin looked up. "In other words the usual druggy shit: it all ends in tears. So from what I was told on the phone just now, what we appear to have is a very similar substance to GHB but with certain structures altered to produce — and I use the technician's words — massively enhanced biological activity. GHB is hard enough to detect in the bloodstream anyway, but the guy said this stuff showed up as just a shadow of a trace on the gas chromatograph. As you know, drugs affect different people in different ways, but he thinks in each case the amount ingested is minute — we're talking a tiny pinch.

"On the basis of that information and the post-mortems, what appears to be happening is this: our victims are being knocked out first — probably in minutes by this stuff — and then this white gunk is being injected down their throats. The gunk, as it turns out, is simple silicon gel. Several people have commented that its smell was familiar — that's because it's the stuff you use around windows, sinks and the like to make them watertight. Tubes of it can be bought in any DIY store nationwide." He waited for the buzz of comments to die down. "Now, I'd like to introduce Dr Neville Heath. He's a criminal psychologist and hopefully can shed some light on why the killer is choosing this particular modus operandi." McCloughlin turned to the man and gestured towards the waiting room. "It's all yours."

With a nervous cough the man stepped forwards. "Unlike the forensics laboratory technician, I'll try and keep my analysis simple." Several officers laughed and, looking more confident, the doctor continued. "Three victims, all relatively young females. None showing evidence of sexual assault, yet all subdued with a powerful derivative of a known date rape drug. Killed in a very particular manner and then laid out on the floor with their arms out at their sides. It all suggests considerable planning, the acting out of a long-held fantasy, perhaps. It's a confusing scenario and one that, I believe, results from one of two possible motivations."

He paused and glanced around the room before continuing. "Let's start with the sexual one. The first victim had been posing for glamour photographs and advertising her services in adult contact magazines. It is my opinion that this will turn out to be what links all three victims. The second victim had fetish clothing in her wardrobe. On the face of it, the third victim seems very unlikely to share this . . . hobby. Churchgoer, very religious, straight-laced. But don't let that fool you. Often these types have very surprising sides to them, just very well hidden. Take, for instance, this fact. To which part of Britain does the Post Office deliver the most mail order sex toys? The God-fearing, outer-lying Scottish islands. This may well be the result of there being no sex shops closer than Aberdeen. But it also reveals a side to the island's population you don't read about in any tourist literature.

"Now our perpetrator — and let's assume it's a man for probability's sake — obtains sexual gratification in a very unusual way. It not only excludes any willing, or even conscious, participation from the female — it also seems not to include any physical contact on his part. He's a watcher, an observer. And he probably doesn't like to be seen by anyone other than himself when seeking his own sexual gratification — hence he subdues his victims first."

"Like that American guy, the heir to some cosmetics fortune. Wasn't he sent down for raping women he had drugged?" asked a female officer.

"You pre-empt me," answered the doctor with a quick smile. "Although that person did seek physical contact: he's currently serving out a one hundred and twenty year sentence having filmed himself having sex with his victims and even saying to camera, 'That's exactly what I like in my room — a passed-out beautiful girl.' In contrast, our perpetrator doesn't actually touch his victims. But I do believe he's making films or photographs of them for later use."

He paused again and took a sip from a glass of water on the table beside him. "Therefore we're looking for someone with an interest in cameras or camcorders. When it comes to a property search, the first thing you should look for is some sort of darkroom facility if he's shooting on film, or a computer with the appropriate software if he's shooting on digital. I'd guess the images he's already taken have been made into some sort of display — perhaps on the walls or in albums. Somewhere readily accessible for when he needs to look at them. Another factor to bear in mind is how he's getting to his victim's houses. He's carrying photographic equipment. So at the least he has a briefcase or bag. Is he driving to the houses? Is he getting the train? All three victims lived within walking distance of train stations. Next thing to consider is why he's adopted this pattern of behaviour. My guess is that he's impotent."

"So we start staking out all the clinics round town?" someone asked teasingly.

"Or people ordering Viagra?" asked another.

McCloughlin cut in, "Our job is working out how to find this man. Dr Heath's here to give us pointers as to what to look for. Carry on, Doctor."

The doctor continued a little more slowly. "I'll produce a profile soon. But with most serial killers, a white middle-class male aged between twenty-five and fifty-five years are the usual parameters. I think he's likely to still have a close relationship with a significant female relative — probably his mother, but could be an aunt or grandmother. He may well live with her, and the relationship is likely to have become strained ever since he reached sexual maturity. This man craves his privacy after all."

Jon noticed several officers discreetly roll their eyes at one another. He heard someone whisper, "Well that narrows things down a bit."

"Normally I'd be happy to just develop this profile," the doctor continued. "But there's one aspect to the

294

killings that doesn't seem to fit with it. Why is he killing his victims by closing up their airways with silicon gel? Perhaps our man is trying to still his victims' tongues, or more accurately their voice boxes. It's a symbolic way of ensuring their silence. Again, this could be for a number of reasons — perhaps they have discovered something about him, or have already revealed to other people something about him. It appears all the victims felt comfortable enough with the attacker to let him into their house, so it's reasonable to expect some degree of familiarity. I know this hypothesis appears more tenuous." The authority was now ebbing slightly from his voice. "I need more time to look at the information we have on the victims so far. But please bear it in mind during your investigations."

Jon didn't know if it was the rush from the cigarette that made him do it, but he cleared his throat and stood up. "I might have something that fits with your second theory."

The doctor looked at Jon, who looked at McCloughlin, who gave him the nod.

"I've just noticed all the victims so far lived in the immediate vicinity of owners of high-performance cars. Victim one, Polly Mather, shared her driveway with her neighbour who owns a Subaru Impreza. Victim two, Heather Rayne, lived on a road with no off-road parking. Her neighbour had left his Jag directly in front of her house. Third victim, Mary Walters, shared the back yard of her building with a couple that own a Lexus. I hope I'm not letting the car gang case I've been working on cloud my judgement here, but take this scenario. The thief is casing out expensive cars and making the mistaken assumption that our victims are the owners — basically because the cars are parked directly outside the victims' properties. He's opening up their letterboxes and snagging what he thinks are the car keys. Problem is, they're not. So when he can't get the car open, he's using the keys to let himself into the house: and we end up with a dead body."

The room was silent for a few seconds before someone asked, "Why the bizarre way of killing them?"

"I don't know," shrugged Jon. "But it fits with this ensuring their silence business. They've seen him and he can't afford to leave any witnesses?"

"So the fact that he's only killed females so far," said the female officer who had spoken earlier, "that's just coincidence? If a flashy car is parked outside a bloke's house, he could be next?"

The room began murmuring as Jon replied, "I suppose so. That drug will knock you out if you're male or female."

"This spate of car thefts you've been investigating," said McCloughlin. "The method they're using relies on the cover of darkness I presume?"

Jon nodded.

McCloughlin frowned. "Heather Rayne had lain undiscovered for a day in a centrally heated flat — time of death somewhere between five and ten in the morning the day before. The other two victims were discovered first thing in the morning. Could they have been killed at night? What are their estimated times of death?"

A couple of officers darted off to their desks. "Polly Mather — early morning. Probably between six and nine."

"She was found in her dressing gown," added Jon.

The other officer spoke up. "Mary Walters — same. Probably between six and nine. But she was fully clothed."

"So," Jon started, aware he was trying to make the facts fit as he went along, beginning to regret that he'd spoken out without fully considering his theory from all angles. "Maybe he's going into the house during the last few minutes of darkness. It could explain the absence of any witnesses so far. Perhaps he's dressed Mary Walters and Heather Rayne afterwards — their clothes showed some signs of disturbance."

From the high and low tones in everyone's voices, Jon could tell his hypothesis had provoked a mixture of excitement and doubt.

McCloughlin looked at him for a moment before addressing the room in general. "I want that theory checked against all three victims so far. For a start let's see whether any keys are missing from their flats. See if you can disprove Jon's line of reasoning. Now, while we're at it, anyone else got any thoughts they'd like to air?"

The female officer who, earlier in the investigation, had wondered if Polly was planning to travel with anyone, said, "Polly Mather was about to embark on a round-the-world trip — as far as we know, on her own. I've checked her property inventory and there's no sign of a passport, which seems strange. Is it worth checking to see if the other victims' passports are missing too?"

"With which line of enquiry in mind?" McCloughlin demanded.

"I don't know," she shrugged. "It was just a thought."

He nodded at her. "Go for it. Let me know what you find. What we have to establish is the link between our three victims — and there has to be one. So we'll be widening the circle of enquiry; in addition to friends and family, we'll be getting statements from all colleagues and other associates. I also want their exact movements over the last seven days mapped out — where they've been, how they got there, who they went with. I want everywhere they visited covered: shops, pubs, cinemas, even toilets. I can't emphasize how important more haste, less speed is on this one. Work quickly everyone, but with total concentration. We've got to find the thread that links them together before another body shows up. Oh and one other thing." Self-consciously he began adjusting his tie. "I'm doing a TV interview tonight, some details to stop the press piranhas going into a total frenzy. I'll use it to appeal for information from anyone who has had someone suspicious or unusual knock on their door, trying to gain entry to their house. It might throw up something interesting."

As the outside enquiry team queued up at the allocator's desk to receive their next action, Jon lingered at the white boards, staring at the photographs once again.

"Not bad, not bad at all."

The voice took him by surprise and he was smiling before he'd turned his head. "Hi, Nikki." He looked down at her. "You don't think I just made a total twat of myself?"

She didn't patronize him with a blank denial. "OK, there were a few holes in your theory. But at least you're thinking around the problem. Who else had the balls to air any sort of a theory?"

"You mean who else was thick enough to spout off with a half-baked hunch? Still, what brings you to the incident room?"

She looked around. "Central heating. Do you realize how crap my fan heater is at warming up that draughty bloody caravan they've given me?"

Jon grinned, feeling the familiar urge to give her a hug. "So, apart from thawing out, what else are you up to?"

Nikki continued in a more businesslike tone. "Actually, I'm just dropping off the plan-drawer's pictures. Then I'm back over to my office to look at getting the crime scene painted with ninhydrin."

Jon knew that, although ninhydrin showed up fingerprints, it also destroyed more fragile forms of evidence. As a result, it was usually the very final stage in the forensic examination. "Are we calling it a day, then?"

"Well, unless you've got any other particular tests in mind. But there's not much for us to go on. No blood splatters, no broken locks, windows or wrecked furniture that could have caught on clothing or scratched skin. In fact, the only promising thing we've removed are a few fibres from the upholstery. I'm talking to the other CSMs in the hope they might find more of the same in the property of the other victims."

"What are they like? These fibres."

"I'd say they were pure wool. A sort of pale green. Perhaps from a suit; it's hard to say."

"Fair enough. Well, I'd better go over and see what my next task is. I'll see you around."

"All right," answered Nikki brightly. "But remember, if you want a cup of lukewarm instant coffee, don't hang around. I'll not be in my caravan for much longer."

DCI McCloughlin's interview was the lead story for Granada News and not far behind in the national bulletins. He gave the usual limited information about the three victims, then aired his concern that the killer, or killers, appeared to be gaining access to his victims' homes without any sign of a struggle.

"Therefore, I would like to hear from anyone who has had someone call at their house, probably first thing in the morning, with an unusual or unconvincing reason for doing so. Perhaps you've turned such a person away because they were unable to show you a proper ID card, or they were offering a product or service that seemed bogus. If you've had such a call we urge you to phone us immediately."

In his daughter Liz's flat the old man sat directly in front of the TV screen, several empty bottles of

Guinness now on the table beside the armchair. She was upstairs, completing some designs for a presentation on Monday morning. As DCI McCloughlin finished his appeal, holding the camera with an earnest gaze, Liz's father let out a slow, rasping snore.

CHAPTER
TWENTY

August 2002

Tom came to with a start, unsure if it was the sound of his own snores or the rain battering down on his head that had awoken him.

He didn't know if it was something to do with air being blown in off the Irish Sea, then rising and cooling on reaching the Peak District, but downpours in Manchester were a way of life.

Normally the rain was consistent in its intensity — a never-ending sheet of fine drops that managed to soak their way through outer layers of clothing in no time. But occasionally the skies really opened up, releasing a barrage of droplets that bordered on tropical in their heaviness.

This was such a downpour.

Slumped in a chair on the patio, Tom focused on the TV through the French windows, drips catching in his eyebrows, falling in a steady stream from his nose, running down his legs and into his shoes. The dancers in the closing ceremony at the Commonwealth Games stadium tried to keep their movements synchronized as they splashed and slipped through the puddles of water.

Despite the rain, the temperature was pleasantly warm. With a movement so deliberate he could only be exceptionally drunk, Tom held the whisky bottle up. He considered whether to replace the top: he didn't want any rain watering it down.

He'd given up trying to ring Charlotte's mobile. For the first few days after their argument it went onto answerphone every time he called. Then the number went dead and he realized she must have moved to another one.

Slowly he raised the bottle to his lips, sucked down a great mouthful and decided the drink wasn't suffering. Turning his eyes back to the screen, he watched as the Queen was escorted to her place, attendants struggling to keep umbrellas over her. After another hour or so, the firework display began. Tom watched the screen, seeing the rockets taking off in a Mexican wave around the rim of the stadium. Then, tilting his head to the night sky, he watched the flickering lights bouncing off the low-lying cloud, water coursing down his chin, snaking in rivulets across his bare chest and wildly racing heart.

The next day he remembered that Charlotte's parents, Martin and Sheila, had moved to the Cotswolds in the weeks after he had married their daughter. He and Charlotte had met up with them in a restaurant with the surprise news that they had got married. It was an announcement that provoked only tight smiles and forced words of congratulation. He sensed the distance between the couple and their daughter, as if they'd resigned themselves to the fact that their little girl had chosen a path in life of which they didn't approve but dared not criticize.

On the internet he went to the directory enquiries web site, typed in their details and geographic location. The search threw up five possibilities and Tom found them on his fourth call.

"Hello, it's Tom Benwell here." A pause followed, long enough to force him into saying, "Your daughter's husband?"

The information finally clicked and Sheila exclaimed, "Tom! Oh how silly of me to get mixed up. How are you and Charlotte? Everything OK I hope?"

"Well . . ." He knew then that his wife wasn't with them. "As a matter of fact, we've had a bit of a bust up — a few days ago now. She wanted some space, so we're spending some time apart. I was kind of hoping she may have gone to you."

Sheila didn't seem at all concerned that her daughter had apparently vanished. "No, she hasn't rung us. How odd. I hope it turns out to be nothing you can't resolve."

"I'm sure we will." He paused and when he carried on, there were tears running down his cheeks. "I was silly, Sheila. Made plans about moving house and jobs without telling her. I think it all took her by surprise. Listen, if she calls can you tell her to please phone me?"

"Of course."

"Thank you. And I was wondering, do you have the numbers for any school friends she might have gone to at a time like this?"

"Tom," she said, "you struck me as a very nice man, if a touch naïve. I'll be honest with you, though it seems very strange to be telling my daughter's husband this. Charlotte has always been very single-minded, to the point of not really having any close friends. She always preferred the company of men. Wealthy men, to be frank." A wistful note had crept into her voice. "I don't know why."

"The numbers of any friends, male or female, will do."

"That's what I'm trying to get to. I don't have any numbers. I'm ashamed to say that her life isn't that familiar to us."

Tom was only half taking it in. "OK, well thanks Mrs Davenport."

"Hang on!" she suddenly exclaimed. "She got a postcard the other day. It was redirected from our old address to here. Sent from Olivia, her old flat mate."

Tom had no idea who she was.

"Anyway, Olivia gives her new address; she's still near Manchester. A place called Disley, I think. Hang on, I'll just get it." She came back on the line a minute later and read out the address. "Oh and Tom? Please ring me when she does turn up. She's done this sort of disappearing act before, but it's always nice to know that she's safe and sound."

Tom felt his guts tightening and anxiety beginning to build at the back of his head. It was time. He reached for the new bag he'd got from Brain, so plump and soft and comforting.

★ ★ ★

The video had finished long ago, rewound itself and was waiting for something else to happen. Tom was slumped in his seat, a bottle of brandy, the powder and the gun on the coffee table before him. He drifted in and out of sleep, stirring every now and again to take another sip or pinch.

Where had she gone? What about their baby? He'd tried everything he could think of. The staff at the David Lloyd Club wouldn't help. Details of their members' training classes were confidential. When he had lost his temper two assistants from the gym had almost carried him out the door. That was another thing: his temper. It would flare up so easily, then die down to be replaced with stifling despair. The swings in emotion were exhausting him, making it hard to sleep. The only thing that seemed able to straighten out his emotions and make him feel better was the powder.

The sole evidence that Charlotte still existed was the withdrawals from their joint bank account. A few hundred here, a few hundred there. But always from cashpoints — never transactions at a hotel or somewhere that would give him a clue as to where she was staying.

Staring at the blank screen in the darkness, he was vaguely aware of a car driving slowly past. A couple of minutes later he heard a tiny creaking noise. Groggily he looked towards the doorway.

A shaft of light shone in the hall, flickering around, catching on the mirror at the end of the corridor. He got to his feet, having to grab the back of the sofa before he fell over. He picked the gun off the table and staggered to the door. Peering round, he could see a thin ray of light shining through the letterbox. Caught in the bright beam was a piece of wood with a hook on the end. Raising up the gun, he stepped out of the front room. The torch beam jumped to his legs and started travelling upwards as he tried to squeeze the trigger. The thing wouldn't budge and he realized the safety was on.

The light suddenly cut as the letterbox snapped shut.

Tom lurched down the corridor. As he snatched the keys off the hook he could hear someone scrabbling to their feet beyond the door. Pushing the key in the lock, he flung his front door open. A dark figure was running from the end of his driveway.

"You fucker!" Tom screamed, trying to go after him but tripping on the doormat. He fell down the steps, the gun clattering across the tarmac and under the Porsche.

A car started up further down the street but, by the time he'd got back to his feet, the vehicle had accelerated away.

He paced to the end of his drive and watched the red lights as the vehicle sped round the corner and out of sight. Hyperventilating, he marched back to his car, reached underneath and retrieved the gun.

Back inside he turned the hallway light on and examined the weapon. A couple of new scratches had been added to the scarred black metal, merging with the file marks that obliterated where some writing and numbers used to be.

He flicked the safety catch off, stepped into the dining room and placed it in the second drawer of the sideboard under some napkins.

He decided that Charlotte would see sense once she had accepted the fact they were starting a family. Every parent yearned for a safe environment to bring their children up in. She would too; she just needed time to come around to the fact she was going to be a mother.

What he had to do, he decided, was have everything ready for when she came home. He went on to the businesses for sale section of the Cornwall Tourist Board web site, then scrolled through to the cafe.

A red band across the screen read "under offer".

Tom stared at the screen, heart suddenly thumping. It couldn't be right. He'd wanted that cafe for so long, it had to be his. Switching to directory enquiries he typed the name into the box and a number sprang up a nanosecond later.

The phone cut straight to an answer phone message. "Hi, Meg's Cafe is now closed, but we're open again at seven tomorrow morning doing hot drinks and bacon rolls for you early-morning surfers. If you need to leave a message, speak now."

He left his message and mobile number, knowing there was no time to lose. He had to find Charlotte and let her know everything was all right, make her see that he had worked out a happy and safe future for all of them. He slipped the Porsche's keys off the hook and drove out of Didsbury, taking the M60 for a couple of junctions then cutting across to the A6 and following it away from Manchester, through Stockport and out towards the Peak District National Park. At the crossroads in Disley he turned up the hill, keeping an eye out for the lane on his right-hand side that would take him out on to the moors and the farm where Charlotte's old friend, Olivia, had moved to.

Soon the countryside around him was almost black, lit only by the dim glow from an occasional cottage or farm and the unnaturally bright road markings in front. After several minutes of slowly following the narrow road as it veered left and right, dipping down and rising up with the contours of the National Park, he saw the tiny sign for Higgleswade Farm. The drive was potholed and bumpy, the bottom of the Porsche scraping several times as he drove up to a farmhouse whose porch was suddenly illuminated by a small security light. The white beam shone down over the rough-hewn chunks of stone forming the farmhouse walls, emphasizing the dark shadows filling the deeply recessed windows. Parking next to a Toyota Land Cruiser, he walked across to the sturdy-looking wooden door and shook a bell mounted on the wall. Immediately several dogs started to bark and whine in the low-roofed buildings to his left. Soon after, footsteps approached the other side of the door. It opened to reveal a woman in her mid-twenties, blonde hair carefully tousled.

"Hello," she said uncertainly, keeping the door half open.

"My name's Tom Benwell and I'm looking for my wife. Is she here?"

"Tom Benwell . . . who Charlotte married?"

"Yes, I must speak with her." He stepped forward, trying to see into the kitchen beyond.

She remained where she was. "She's not here. I haven't seen Charlotte in years."

Tom shook his head. "It's very important. Charlotte!" he called into the house.

The dogs started barking again. More footsteps and a heavyset man appeared. A large hand with dirt ingrained around the nails was placed against the doorframe. He leaned round the woman. "Who's this?"

"It's the husband of someone I used to share a flat with. He thinks his wife is here."

Tom raised a hand as if to push his way into the house. The door opened fully and the man stepped out. "She said she's not here. So she's not here."

Tom stayed where he was, weighing up his options. He looked at the outbuildings to his left, as if she could be hiding there.

The man followed his glance and said, "If you walk over to the sheds and get the dogs any more excited, I'll let them out on you."

Tom faltered and he turned back to the couple. "She's really not here?" he pleaded.

"Really," said the man impatiently as the woman's expression softened with concern.

Tom walked slowly back to his car, looking up at the dark windows of the first floor as he did so. With one last glance at the couple in the doorway, he climbed into his car and drove back down the drive.

He had been going for less than three minutes when his mobile phone rang. Yanking the steering wheel over,

310

he came to a stop on the grassy verge and grabbed it. The signal was weak, so he climbed out of the car and stood up in the vain hope it would help the reception.

"Hello, this is Megan here," said a quiet female voice. Even though it wasn't a question, her inflection went up at the end of the sentence.

"Your cafe," said Tom. "It's under offer."

"Yes," she said. "Who is this?"

"My name's Tom. I've been planning to buy it for months. You haven't signed a contract, have you?"

"No," she replied. "You know it's ten forty-five at night. You must be very keen."

"I really must have it. I'll offer you more money."

She laughed. "The offer I have is already for the asking price. You can't say fairer than that."

"You don't understand," Tom cut across her. "We're starting a family; we need somewhere nice for the kids to grow up." A thought suddenly occurred to him. "There isn't any chewing gum, is there? On the pavements and roads around you?"

She laughed again, but more warily. "Where are you calling from?"

"Manchester."

"You've been to Newquay? Seen my posters in the windows, right?"

"No. What do you mean?"

"I've been putting petitions together for the last two years. The place is covered with the stuff and it's getting worse every summer. We're trying to get a ban put on it, but the council say they can't do a thing. Listen —

you're a reporter, right? From the local paper? I've told you already — the chewing gum is why I'm moving."

"To where?" Tom whispered.

"Back to New Zealand. We've got a bit more respect for our surroundings over there. I'm sticking with the offer I have; I don't believe in this gazumping business you have over here. If you're not a reporter, thanks for your interest."

She hung up and Tom dropped the handset through the car window onto the driver's seat. In his mind's eye he could see the resort swarming with grey spots. Nowhere was free of it. Nowhere. Miserably, he took the sachet of powder from his pocket, licked his finger and dabbed it in. He looked around him. Just visible in the darkness was a footpath sign. He climbed over the stile and trudged across the fields, the occasional bleating of a sheep the only noise to interrupt the utter silence. The sky above was clear, a slither of moon providing just enough light to follow what was little more than a sheep trail. Scrambling to the top of a rocky outcrop, he leaned back against a smooth slab and looked up.

Out here there were no streetlights or massed homes polluting the night and turning the sky a hazy orange. His view upwards was unbroken and the stars shimmered in the heavens with almost the same intensity as in the Seychelles.

His plans for Charlotte and the baby were ruined. He could never take them to a place that had been desecrated with gum. Pulling the sachet out, he took another dab and sat back, waiting for the sense of despair to subside. The drug was just beginning to deaden his emotions when his eyes settled on The Plough. As usual, it hung in the same spot, low in the sky. He was staring directly at it, taking a strange comfort in its unchanging presence above, when the chorus of voices spoke.

They didn't just come from all around him, they filled the very air and surged up from the ground, resonating in his chest. Tom froze until they stopped, then scrabbled on to all fours, eyes blindly searching the rocks he had been sitting against.

Again they spoke, words enveloping him like a TV surround sound system. Jumping to his feet, he twirled about, but in every direction were empty fields.

Terror of the incomprehensible took over and he slid back down the rocks, ran towards the road. He got to his car, jumped in and locked the doors. There was no credible explanation — the only possible way a group of voices could suddenly sound in the middle of nowhere was if there were loudspeakers hidden all around the rocks.

Yet there could be no doubt it was him they were addressing. Because the voices he'd heard were repeating the same word over and over again. "Tom, Tom, Tom."

They came for the car a week later.

He found that his sleep pattern was coinciding less and less with the night. Now he tended to stay up until the small hours, watching videos, surfing the internet, waiting for the phone to ring. Always suppressing the memory of that awful collection of disembodied voices. Mornings were becoming a thing of the past; his days usually started after lunch.

So when the doorbell went at ten thirty in the morning, he struggled from a shallow and listless sleep to shuffle down the stairs in his dressing gown. Hoping it might be Charlotte, he pulled open the door to find Ges and Ed outside.

Ges spoke first, awkward and uncomfortable. "Hello Tom."

Tom scratched his fingers through his hair. "Ges."

"Late night, then?" said Ges. "The joys of being in between jobs, hey?"

Ed simply stared at him, shock registering on his face.

Hesitantly Ges announced, "Sorry mate, we've come for the Porsche. London office has been hassling us. You haven't been answering the phone and I couldn't put them off any longer."

Tom thought about how he'd ignored all his calls. "No, I understand," he murmured. As he unclipped the Porsche key he said almost absent-mindedly, "Seen anything of Creepy George?"

Ges looked confused. "Erm, no. You sacked him."

Tom was about to answer, then saw Ed standing there. He handed the key to him and beckoned Ges down the corridor.

In the front room Tom let out an exasperated sigh. "He's evil. Keep him away from your house. Have you ever seen him hanging around? Has your wife ever seen him hanging around?"

"Sally? No, she's never met him."

"Good, that's good. But if she does ever see him, get her to call the police. I think he has all of our addresses." He ran a hand through his tangled curls.

"I don't understand. Is this to do with why he was sacked? What happened, Tom?"

Tapping his nose, Tom replied. "Confidential." His eyes shifted to the window, filling with regret as Ed circled the Porsche. He turned back to Ges. "He's evil. Just keep him away from your house. And tell Ed too. I've taken precautions." He gave a secretive smile.

Ges hesitated. "You all right, Tom? I'm sorry I haven't called round before. You can imagine how it's been."

Tom waved the comment away. "Yeah, yeah. I'm fine." He looked back out of the window. The silence stretched out as he kept his eyes on Ed unlocking the Porsche and climbing in.

"Well, I'd better get back too . . ." Ges suggested. He walked slowly back to the front door and hovered at the top step. "Give us a call. We could go for lunch one day. How about it?"

Tom nodded. "Yeah." He glanced around Ges to have one last look at the car, then shut the door in the face of one of his few remaining friends.

CHAPTER
TWENTY-ONE

3 November 2002

The investigation was going nowhere. More than fifty officers were now assigned to the case. Despite dozens of statements from anyone who had been in contact with the three victims, an obvious thread linking them together refused to emerge.

In desperation they had begun to retread old ground, including raking through the contents of each victim's home again.

Jon was en route to the facility at Trafford Park police station to help go through the refuse recovered from Polly Mather's flat when the call came through on his mobile.

"Bad news, Jon. Another body has just been discovered. A Gabrielle Harnett, same MO as all the rest," said the officer back at Longsight.

Jaw set tight, he speeded up, anxious to get to Trafford Park and start making phone calls. He pulled into the car park about a quarter of an hour later. Without bothering to get out of the car, he called back the incident room at Longsight.

"DI Spicer here. The victim who's just been discovered — what type of property did she live in?"

"Some sort of flat complex."

"Can you give me the phone number of any officer attending the scene?"

He jotted the number down and immediately called it. "DS Moffatt? DI Spicer here. Where are you exactly?"

"Outside the victim's flat."

"What's the parking situation like?"

"Bloody nightmare. Half of Manchester's newspaper reporters are already here. I don't know who's got more vehicles in the vicinity — us or them."

"I mean for the residents. Is there private parking for them?"

"Oh, hang on." There was a pause. "Yeah, I'm standing in a kind of courtyard. It's all little one or two bedroom flats, residents-only parking. Each slot is allocated to a flat."

"And what's parked in the slot for the victim's flat?"

"Hang on," he said again. "Flat six, here you go. It's a Mini — one of those new BMW ones."

"Registration?"

Jon noted it down, then called the incident room at Longsight again. "Hi, DI Spicer. Can you run me a vehicle check?" He read out the registration and waited with his crossed fingers resting on the steering wheel. "Please don't let it be Gabrielle Harnett's," he whispered to himself.

"Here we go," said the operator, "Gabrielle Harnett, flat six, Richmond Court . . ."

"Fuck!" He thumped the back of his skull against the headrest.

"You just crashed?" came the alarmed voice.

"No. My fucking theory has, though." He hung up, got out and walked over to the prefabricated hut in which the rubbish had been laid out on long trestle tables. Standing outside the doors were a couple of uniformed officers getting a last cigarette in before having to don rubber gloves and start sifting.

"Morning," said one, seeing Jon approaching.

"Morning," Jon grunted. A couple of seconds' silence followed before the officer produced a packet of cigarettes and held one out.

Jon realized his eyes had been fixed hungrily on the man's lit cigarette. He hesitated for a second, then sagged a little and took it. "Cheers. This case is doing my head in." He leaned forward to take a light as Nikki Kingston stepped out of the hut. Her face had brightened on seeing Jon but, on spotting the cigarette in his mouth, her smile died. Their eyes met and with a sigh Jon pulled the cigarette from his lips. "Bad day, all right?"

"Here," she said and gestured him inside. They walked along the side of a table scattered with a layer of mouldering food scraps, old tea bags and crumpled packaging. "What's up?"

"Another body has just been found."

"Oh, Jesus." She picked up her handbag and took out a pack of chewing gum. "Try one of these. I'm not sure about the flavour, but it's got to be better than going back to smoking."

He conceded with a half smile and slid a stick from the pack. After popping it into his mouth, he said, "What is it? Lemon flavour?"

Nikki looked at the pack and with a lofty tone said, "Actually, it's citrus flavour with extracts of energy-giving guarana. Limited edition too, so count yourself lucky."

Jon was shaking his head. "What is it with these limited edition sweets? They were doing mint-flavoured Kit Kats the other day. Meddling with a classic. Go on, let's have a look."

She handed him the pack and he looked at it with a cynical expression. Alongside the spiky yellow lettering spelling "X-treme" was a yellow lightning bolt that zig-zagged down the ice-blue wrapper, its point entering a cartoon-style lemon sitting on a bed of what he guessed were guarana leaves. His eyes narrowed and he looked at the rubbish on the trestle tables.

"What?" said Nikki, watching him closely.

"I've seen a pack of this stuff before. Where did you get it from?"

"Some freebie handout," she said, putting her handbag back on the chair.

"No, I've seen it somewhere else. Not in a shop, either." He searched for the memory and started seeing all sorts of images. A white-painted room, crushed packets of cigarettes, cups stacked up in a dirty sink, rows of tins in a cupboard, empty beer cans piled high in a waste-paper basket, a drawer slightly open with the contents neatly arranged inside.

He knew that he had two strands of memory twisted together: one suggested cleanliness and carefully controlled behaviour, the other disorder and abandonment. He squeezed his eyes shut and pressed against them with a forefinger and thumb, trying to make sense of the opposing images. Polly Mather's kitchen? No, her place was a tip. Must have been Mary Walters' kitchen. Then the memory of the discarded chewing gum wrapper sprang up in his mind and he saw the distinctive diamond pattern of the carpet surrounding it. "Polly Mather's floor. In her front room," he said, certainty filling his voice. With that strand of memory established, he was able to concentrate on the one suggesting a well-ordered living space. He clicked his fingers and opened his eyes. "And in Mary Walters' kitchen drawer."

Nikki looked at him in silence with her eyebrows raised.

"Have you got any gloves?"

She handed him a pair.

Jon walked round the tables, stopping at the one marked "front room". The waste-paper basket was lying on its side and next to it crumpled beer cans, cigarette butts and torn-up packets of Rizla covered the surface. With a forefinger, he poked around, suddenly stopping and holding up a loosely folded rectangle of paper. Straightening it out, he said, "Bingo." It was the outer wrapping from a stick of X-treme gum.

Nikki was standing next to him. "Yes?"

"I'm sure there's also an unopened pack of this stuff in Mary Walters' kitchen drawer."

She turned her hands outwards. "So? There's probably tins of baked beans in both their flats, too."

"Yes, but this is unusual isn't it? A limited edition — part of a relatively small batch."

Picking up on Jon's line of thought, she clapped her hands together in excitement. "I saw it for sale just the other day!"

"Where?"

"One of those dodgy stalls in the Arndale Market that sells end-of-line and out-of-date stuff."

He put the gum wrapper in an evidence bag, then yanked his gloves off. "Come on. I'd like to know how the stallholder came by it."

He parked next to the incident van outside forty-six Lea Road and got out. Nikki stayed where she was. "You coming or what?" he asked, leaning in through the open door.

"I can't enter another crime scene that's part of an investigation I'm involved with — it's regulations."

Jon nodded. "OK. I won't be long."

The crime scene manager was inside the vehicle drinking a cup of tea. Jon signed his name in the log book and slipped on a crime scene suit. Squeezing past a couple of forensics guys in the hallway, he followed the footplates into the kitchen, going straight over to the second drawer down. There amongst the other odds and ends was the pack of X-treme chewing gum.

He dropped it into an evidence bag and returned to the incident van. Placing it on the table in front of the crime scene manager, he peeled off his suit. "Could you catalogue that, please? Recovered from the second drawer down in her kitchen."

Back in his car he said with a grin, "Next stop, the Arndale."

The shopping centre was crowded with the usual array of people. Young mums wheeled their pushchairs aimlessly around. Clusters of teenagers shuffled into the computer games shops, their nylon shell suits swishing as they went. Jon and Nikki headed straight for the escalator, taking it down to the lower level and walking past rows of shop fronts. At the end of the corridor they turned left, the tiled floor sloping down into a tunnel, cramped shopping units on each side. The air was coppery with the aroma from a butcher's stall selling cleaved-up chunks of meat, slabs of tripe and anaemic-looking sausages. They had entered the centre's economy shopping zone.

Emerging into the main hall, Nikki led Jon past a stall piled high with baby clothes and another almost buried under rolls of material. Next they passed one selling jokes and adult novelty toys. "Fake dog turd?" asked Nikki with a grin, before stopping at a stall crammed with assorted items of food — bags of slightly damaged jaffa cakes for ninety-nine pence, dented cans of fizzy drinks for twenty pence, bottles of ketchup with German labels for seventy-five pence.

Nikki scanned the front of the stall. "There," she said, pointing to a tray of X-treme gum.

Jon nodded then looked at the stallholder. "Excuse me?"

322

The man looked up from his newspaper to find a warrant card inches from his face.

"DI Spicer, Greater Manchester Police. This chewing gum you're selling — where did you get it?"

The man closed one eye, as if trying to recall. "Probably from the cash'n'carry on the Oldham Road. That or a wholesaler's." He waved a hand to signal that was the best he could do.

Jon knew the man was being deliberately vague. "Listen mate, I'm investigating a murder. Do you think it will jog your memory if you close up for the day and come down to the cop shop with me? Bring all your books as well. We'll go through everything and make sure all your accounts tally up."

The man folded his paper. "OK. It was a one-off. This guy, he's always coming round with stuff."

"So if it was a one-off, what's he usually selling?"

The man looked uneasy. "This and that."

Jon leaned forward, "Fuck me around any more and you're coming to the station. What does he usually sell?"

The man raised a hand to run it along his top lip as if in thought. From behind his fingers he mumbled, "Car stereos."

"Selling to you?"

"No! What would I want with them?" He gave the slightest of nods in the direction of the stall behind. "Ed's Electrical Emporium. Behind you. Just this one time though, he had a few boxes of that chewing gum. I took the lot off him, ten quid cash I think."

"What does this person look like?"

"I don't know. Always kitted out in designer stuff. Wiry ginger hair, top teeth stick out a bit. Thin." His eyes shifted to the side of Jon's head and his words dried up.

Jon glanced over his shoulder, saw the Ferret sauntering across the hall. He looked back at the stallholder. "That's him, isn't it?"

Reluctantly, the man nodded. Nikki started to turn around but Jon hissed at her to keep looking at the stallholder.

"He's coming in this direction?" asked Jon.

The stallholder watched from the corner of his eye. "Yes . . . no . . . he's going over to Ed's. Looks like he's got some more stuff to sell."

Jon took another glance over his shoulder. The Ferret was approaching the electrical stall, a sports bag in one hand.

"Who is it? Do you know him?" asked Nikki.

Jon nodded his head in reply, slipping his mobile out of his pocket, but the market was below ground and his mobile was flashing red. "No bloody reception." He thought for a moment. "Right Nikki, I'm going to lift him. I want you to stand behind him and put on your stern face."

Nikki took a deep breath. "Oh, Jesus."

"Don't worry," Jon whispered. "I'll do everything."

Jon walked over to Ed's Electrical Emporium. The Ferret was talking to the stallholder with quick snatches of speech, shifting his weight from foot to foot.

Jon stepped up behind him and raised his warrant card. "Excuse me."

The stallholder's eyes went wide, his expression saying it all. Without even turning his head, the Ferret dropped the bag and bolted to his right, slamming directly into Nikki. Their bodies were in contact for an instant before she flew backwards to the tiled floor, head cracking against it. He stumbled into the corner of the stall, toppling a couple of CD players to the floor before regaining his balance and starting to run.

Jon took some stuttering steps after him, looking down at Nikki and shouting, "You OK?"

Keeping her eyes closed, she yelled, "Go!"

Jon was off. The Ferret had about twenty metres on him as he ran towards the steps leading up to Cannon Street. Jon kept his head bowed and pumped his legs, taking smaller steps to get his momentum going, only lengthening his stride and looking up when he hit sprinting speed.

By the time the Ferret reached the bottom step Jon was less than ten metres behind him. Halfway up, the man's toe caught and he half fell, scrabbling up to the top. But Jon had closed the distance and, after taking the first four steps in one bound, he dived upwards, shoulder connecting with the back of his quarry's knees. Jon's arms then wrapped around his legs, bringing him crashing down in a classic rugby tackle.

Keeping his arms locked, Jon yanked him halfway back down the steps. As soon as he released his legs and reached for his collar, the Ferret whipped an elbow up at Jon's face. He saw it coming and, rather than lean back and expose the underside of his chin, Jon dipped his head into the blow so it glanced harmlessly off his forehead. He replied with a powerful jab to the man's right temple that sent his molars clacking together and the side of his head bouncing off the edge of a step.

Jon's vision had narrowed right down: his sight was completely filled by the man beneath him, the man he had been chasing for so long. He was so pumped, everything happened a fraction slower than normal. His right hand shot out and closed around the Ferret's elbow as it rose up again, fingers crushing the soft flesh on the inside of the joint. As he let out a howl of pain, Jon's left fist cracked into the back of his head. The man's mouth was wide open as it connected with the top of the step and a fragment of tooth flew out followed by a spray of blood. Jon let go of his elbow, grabbed two handfuls of lank gingery hair and got ready to smash his face back down again.

"Jon, stop!"

The scream brought him out of his rage and he looked down the steps, eyes blazing.

Nikki shrank backwards and said more quietly, "You've got him."

Suddenly Jon became aware of other shoppers. They hovered behind Nikki, looking shocked.

"He was resisting arrest," Jon growled. Yanking the Ferret to his feet, he whispered in his ear, "That was for knocking my friend over back there."

"I've done nothing," the man gasped, blood dribbling down his chin. "I'll fucking sue you for this. It's assault." He began to struggle again.

"And this," said Jon, putting him in a thumb lock, "is for nicking my girlfriend's handbag." The Ferret cried out as his knuckle was bent back.

"Shut it," said Jon, forcing his arm upwards so he had to bend double to avoid more pain.

Marching him back to the main hall he said, "Let's see what's in your sports bag. My guess is that, by the end of today, I'll be charging you with a fuck of a lot more than petty theft."

As soon as the Ferret was safely locked up in a cell at Longsight, Jon raced upstairs to the incident room. He'd phoned ahead from the Arndale centre, requesting that the third and fourth victims' houses and bins be searched for any evidence of X-treme chewing gum.

Walking into the incident room, he was immediately waved over by the office manager.

"I hear you've got someone in the traps downstairs."

"Yeah," replied Jon, suddenly loving every second of his job. "Could be significant; we'll know more once his house has been turned over."

"Well, I've just received a call from the crime scene manager at Gabrielle Harnett's place. A wrapper of something called X-treme chewing gum with energy-giving guarana has been recovered from the waste-paper bin in her front room."

Jon raised a clenched fist and shut his eyes for a second. "Fucking win! Can I take that?" he asked, looking at the memo.

"Be my guest. The gum wrapper is being driven over now."

Jon walked into McCloughlin's office, gathering quizzical looks from everyone in the room as he went.

"Come in and close the door," said McCloughlin as soon as Jon appeared in his doorway. "Who've you got downstairs?"

"A nasty little shit," replied Jon, taking a seat. "He's a general scrote — snatching handbags, taxing the city beggars for their pitches. He's also peddling car stereos and other bits and bobs, including a few boxes of a particular brand of chewing gum. X-treme citrus flavour with guarana."

"Never heard of it," said McCloughlin.

"It's one of those limited editions they do. However, wrappers and packs of it have now turned up in three of the victims' properties."

McCloughlin blew out a thin stream of breath. "Carry on."

"I arrested him in the Arndale Centre, where he was trying to sell on a couple of car stereos. The serial numbers are being checked as we speak, but I'd bet a month's salary they're stolen."

"Very interesting," said McCloughlin. He got up and reached for his coat. "Have you got his name and address?"

"Right here, along with his front door key," said Jon, holding up a plastic bag with a smile. "His name's Ashley Charlton, but he goes by the name of Sly."

★ ★ ★

McCloughlin looked up at the Urban Living flats and said, "A bit upmarket for our little toe-rag don't you think?"

They buzzed the manager of the complex to be let in and less than thirty seconds later eight plain-clothes officers were standing in Ashley Charlton's flat.

Surveying the room, McCloughlin's eyes settled on the tarantula's vivarium. "Never mind bringing in national ID cards, if we could keep tabs on every misfit who keeps snakes and spiders, there'd be a lot less crime committed. Right, specifically, we're looking for packs of X-treme chewing gum, but shout if you see anything else."

Seven of them began rummaging through the flat while the last officer started sweeping all the electrical items and ornaments with a UV light. At the same instant he announced, "Boss", another officer in the kitchen said, "Got something here."

McCloughlin called towards the kitchen, "What's in there?"

"One box of X-treme chewing gum. Limited edition citrus with energy-giving guarana. Thirty-six packs originally inside, now about a dozen left."

"Bag it," said McCloughlin, turning to the officer with the UV torch. "You?"

He turned the art deco lamp to the side so McCloughlin could see its base. Shining purple in the invisible glow of the torch was a series of numbers and letters. "Postcode. Looks like Altrincham, sir."

"Excellent. Get the address so we can phone the house owner immediately."

As the officer got his mobile phone out to make the call, another officer standing at the coat pegs by the door spoke up. "Boss, take a look at this." He was holding up a garden cane with a hook on the end.

McCloughlin rubbed his hands. "This guy is so screwed. Anything else, people?"

Jon turned round. "Interesting stash here."

McCloughlin looked down into the wooden box Jon had opened up.

Inside was a couple of packets of cigarette papers, a lump of cannabis resin and a small plastic bag containing a couple of teaspoons of white powder.

"What do you reckon that is? Speed?" asked McCloughlin.

Jon turned it over with the end of a gloved finger. "Probably, but I'm not volunteering to taste it."

McCloughlin laughed. "You know what, Jon? When you blurted out your theory that these killings were being carried out by some rogue member of a car-theft gang, I had serious doubts. Now I think you might be right."

Jon smiled, but he didn't feel the same certainty as his senior officer.

An hour later they were all back at Longsight station and Sly had been hauled out of his cell and into an interview room. Having been told which investigation his client was a suspect in, a very nervous member from the local twenty-four-hour solicitor's was sitting next to Sly.

"So, you've been a very busy man," opened McCloughlin.

"That bastard chipped my tooth," said Sly, jabbing a finger at Jon.

Across the table McCloughlin shrugged. "You were resisting arrest. We have several witnesses who will attest to that."

Sly lit a cigarette and stared back with narrowed eyes. Wisps of smoke carried across the table into Jon's face.

"The car stereos. Where did you get them?" McCloughlin continued.

Sly looked away. "No comment."

McCloughlin nodded, like he'd been expecting that response. "Your bad-boy mates been telling you how to play it in an interview? Well, I'll tell you something. They came from two Mercedes, both reported as stolen last week. One from a house in Alderley Edge, one from a house in Altrincham. The owners believe the keys were hooked out of their house through the letterbox. Probably by an implement very similar to the one we found in your flat. Nice pad, by the way. Were you left an inheritance? It's just that I can't work out how you could afford it. You being out of work at the moment."

Sly shot a glance to his solicitor, who gave an almost imperceptible shake of his head. "No comment," came the answer again.

"We'll move on," said McCloughlin with a smile. "We also found a rather nice art deco lamp in your flat."

The same uninterested look remained on Sly's face and he blew out a stream of smoke. Jon breathed some of it in, noting that it was weaker after being filtered by the other man's lungs.

"Where did you find that? A car boot sale?" McCloughlin asked.

"No comment."

McCloughlin nodded. "Of course. However, the lamp had a postcode written on it with a special pen that fluoresces under UV light. The owner of the lamp is en route to this police station as we speak. But before setting off, she informed us that the person who took it also took her BMW A5, stating that he would kill her if she didn't provide him with the keys."

The room was silent as McCloughlin and Jon stared at Sly who, apart from jiggling one knee up and down, remained slouched in his seat.

McCloughlin whispered, "Do you think, Ashley — or should we call you Sly? It suits you — when she hears your voice on this interview tape, she'll remember it as the one from her hallway that night?"

Sly kept his eyes on the floor. "No comment," he mumbled again.

The sense of calm that had descended on the room was suddenly shattered by Jon slamming his fist on to the table. The solicitor nearly fell off his chair in fright and Sly flinched away.

"Do you think," Jon roared, "that saying 'no comment' will get you out of this? We haven't even started on the fact we've recovered the same type of chewing gum from your flat and the flats of three murder victims. All had nice flashy cars parked right outside their properties. The type of car, in fact, you like to steal."

Finally the look of boredom was wiped from Sly's face. Sitting up, he began to say, "No, no, no, no man. You're not pinning that on me."

"We'll not be doing any pinning, my friend," answered Jon. "I noticed there were some expensive suits in your flat. One was an Armani. Pure wool, pale green colour? Just like some fibres we've lifted from the victims' properties."

Sly looked at his solicitor again, who just stared back at him like a frightened rabbit.

A knock sounded on the door and an officer poked his head into the room. "Boss, the lady from Altrincham is here."

McCloughlin nodded. "OK, interview suspended at," he glanced at the clock on the wall, "seventeen forty-eight." He turned the cassette recorder off.

Jon stood up, leaned across the table and brought his face to within butting distance of Sly's nose. Quietly, he said, "All it takes is for the threads we've picked up from those crime scenes to match your suit and you're going down. High profile case like this? Someone always goes down, and you're our best bet. By a long way." He then looked at the wide-eyed solicitor. "Maybe you should explain to your buck-toothed scum of a client here how plenty of people are currently serving life sentences for far less evidence than we've got on him already."

★　★　★

Anxious to catch up with McCloughlin, Jon stepped quickly out of the interview room. His senior officer was waiting for him, face bright with anger.

"In here," he said, opening a spare interview room.

Surprised, Jon stepped through the door and heard it shut behind him.

"I can't believe the state of that guy's face," McCloughlin spat.

"Sir?"

"You started smacking him around in front of members of the public. Half a bloody tooth was left on the steps in the Arndale. What the fuck were you playing at?"

Jon was caught completely by surprise. "He was resisting arrest, sir, like you said."

"He was struggling a bit," McCloughlin corrected him. "I've got more members of the public complaining about your rough methods than I have agreeing that he was resisting arrest. I just hope that solicitor is as incompetent as he looks."

McCloughlin rubbed the palms of his hands up and down his cheeks, the skin around his eyes bunching up and stretching out as he did so. He let out a big breath. "Jon, when I recommended you for promotion, I did so with one reservation in mind. And that's your propensity for getting so obsessed with a case you lose control. It's one thing to dish it out a bit in the cells or the back of a police van, but you never do it in front of the public. They'll start up about human rights quick as a flash, no matter what sort of a pondlife it is. Your aggression must be controlled. And what do you do next? Nearly smash the interview table in half with your fist."

Jon was silent as McCloughlin looked at his watch. "Nearly six o'clock. Why don't you call it a day? Go to the gym and blow off some steam. I'll finish the interview in a bit."

Jon stood, but he couldn't go without saying something. "I caught him, sir. You can't cut me out of the investigation like this."

McCloughlin kept his eyes on the wall to Jon's side. "You'll be back on the case tomorrow, once you've cooled down. In your present state, you're of no use to me."

Jon slammed the door shut, marched from the building and kept going straight down the road. He walked without purpose, anger blinkering his view. He needed a pub, somewhere dimly lit and deserted where he could sit and drink.

Looking around, he saw a soulless-looking place on the opposite side of the road. He crossed over and went inside. As he started to ask for a pint of bitter, he stopped and said instead, "A pint of Stella, and a double Talisker, cheers."

No one else was at the bar, so he took a corner stool, hung his jacket over his knee and rolled up his sleeves.

The whisky came first and he rolled the liquid around in his mouth before swallowing it in a single gulp. Immediately he breathed in through his lips, the fiery fumes in his mouth mixing with the air and causing his gums to contract. The barman placed a pint of Stella before him and Jon pushed the whisky tumbler across the bar in return. "Another double in there. Can you run me a tab?"

"Bad day at the office?"

"You guessed it." He loosened his tie and picked up the lager, studying the streams of tiny bubbles as they spiralled magically from the bottom of the glass. The first gulp washed away the heat of the Talisker, seeming to return his throat to normal. The second gulp was uncomfortably cold, and by the third and fourth his throat was completely numb.

Later he jammed a cigarette out in the ashtray before him, coins spread across the bar from when he'd changed a tenner for the vending machine. His head was thick with alcohol, his chest tight from smoking. Slowly he rotated his pint through quarter turns, brushing off the condensation clinging to the glass as he did so. He replayed McCloughlin's words in his head again and again: ". . . your propensity for getting so obsessed with a case you lose control."

He thought back to their earlier conversation. "You're not a Mountie, always getting your man."

Then he thought of the comment Tom had made after they had visited the compound for stolen cars. Something about his role on the rugby pitch being to hunt down and take out members from the opposite team.

Even as he tried to dismiss the comment, the words of the old guy in the blazer at the Cheshire Sevens rang in his mind. "Saw this man taking apart more than a few players when he ran out for Stockport."

Spicer the Slicer. That was what they called him at the rugby club.

Jon stared at his knuckles, reasoning that he always played within the rules. And in his role as a police officer, he only used the required level of force. He lit another cigarette and wondered how true that was. Did he get away with using violence in his job just because he was a police officer? What if he had failed the entry exam? Would he still be dealing out his form of justice to whoever crossed his path?

The air in the pub was making his eyes sore. After draining his pint, he tried to catch the barman's attention by waving a finger and watched with confusion as his entire hand flapped to and fro. He settled his bill and stood up, feet wide apart as he shrugged his jacket back on. Out on the street, car lights floated past, leaving trails in the air before him. He started walking, hand out at his side, hoping for a cab. But the thrill of catching Sly couldn't be ignored, and neither could the burst of sheer pleasure he felt when his fist connected with the man's head.

Finally he faced up to the thought he'd been hiding from all night. He'd wanted to carry on at that point. The man's hair was grasped in both of his hands and it was only Nikki crying out that had stopped him from . . .

He stumbled into a doorway and fumbled for his phone, needing contact with someone not connected with violence.

"Hi there," he said, confident he'd got the words out clearly.

"Bloody hell, how many have you had?" Alice replied.

"A few. I mean, a few too many," he corrected himself.

"Where are you?"

Unsure, Jon looked around. "Near the nick."

"You sound tired as well as pissed."

"I feel like shit, but I think we're close to cracking it."

"I hope so. It's in all the news, Jon. It sounds horrible."

Jon's head hung a bit lower. "Don't believe all the details, Ali. Half of it's made up."

"Is it true they were all posing for nude photographs? The paper said one victim had got an advert in some seedy contact magazine."

Jon couldn't believe how details like that got out; some bastard on the investigation had sold that snippet of information for the price of a family holiday. Now the families of all the victims were suffering.

"No. We think one of them was. Anyway, how are you?"

"So so," Alice answered. "To be honest, I can't get away from the case. It's all everyone wants to talk about — the salon, my tae kwon do class, everywhere I go."

"Well, let's hope something more worthwhile crops up and takes the pressure off."

"You're right," said Alice. "Oh, I forgot to ask. What happened at Tom's office? Did you speak to that guy who works late?"

Jon closed his eyes, "No, it was shut. Boarded up like it had gone out of business."

"So he has lost his job."

He couldn't face getting in to the Tom thing again. "Not necessarily. Who knows what happened? Listen Ali, I'm sure everything is fine with Tom. In fact, I bet I'll get a postcard from him one of these days. It'll say he's got his cafe in Cornwall and he's given up on phones, mobiles and e-mail."

CHAPTER
TWENTY-TWO

September 2002

The mirrors in Tom's house weren't working properly. As he passed in front of them, he could only make out a blurred figure, details indistinct and hazy. He dropped the remains of the Chinese takeaway onto the other cartons filling the sink and shuffled through to his front room. Sitting in his tracksuit bottoms, he logged on to their joint internet bank account for the third time that day. Her last withdrawal was still from yesterday — another £500 counter transaction.

He brought up the account's summary for the past few weeks, going over the numerous withdrawals that she'd made. It was the only evidence he had that she still existed. His last remaining form of contact.

Then he heard a key in the lock. He fell onto all fours, crawled quickly across the floor and peeped over the windowsill. It was her! He could see her through the net curtains, struggling to get the door open, several empty boxes at her feet. She tried the door again, looking exasperated that it wouldn't open.

He remembered he'd left his key in the lock. Afraid she would give up and go away, he jumped to his feet and hurried out of the room. Eagerly he turned the key,

340

then was hit by a sudden wave of anxiety as he yanked the door open.

"Tom," she said, looking him up and down.

"Charlotte." He tried to smile. She was staring at his chin. His hand went up and he scratched at the thick stubble. "You've come back."

"Yeah — I need some things, that's all."

Tom chose to ignore her comment. She was back; that was all that mattered. They would be a family soon. She turned round, gave a quick wave to the large silver vehicle parked on the road outside, then picked up the empty boxes and stepped inside. He saw her looking around with a disgusted expression. He supposed the place did look a bit of a tip. As he hovered at her side, his hand repeatedly went up to his mouth, then veered nervously off to tug at an earlobe.

"I need a few bits and bobs, personal items," she announced.

"Why? Are we going somewhere?"

"No, we're not. They are my things, for where I'm going."

He stepped backwards, searching for what to say.

"It smells in here," she said, not looking at him. "Hasn't Mrs Hanson been?"

"I sent her away. I didn't want her poking around with the vacuum while I was at home."

She nodded. Climbing the stairs, she walked briskly along to the bedroom where she began taking clothes out of the wardrobe and laying them on the bed. Tom watched from the doorway in silence. Finally he stalked back downstairs, found the little bag and took a pinch of powder. Standing in the kitchen, he waited for the drug to make him feel stronger. By the time he could feel its effects, she was coming down the stairs, a pile of dresses, shirts and skirts over one arm.

"Where are you going with those?" he called as she walked out of the house.

"A friend's," she answered, not breaking her step.

He brooded in the kitchen, working up the courage to ask exactly what she was planning.

Next she came down the stairs with a box full of shoes and carried them out to the car.

He slid through into the front room and peered out the window. But whoever was waiting in the driving seat of what looked like a Land Cruiser was obscured by the trunk of a tree. All he could see was a pair of large hands on the steering wheel.

Back in the house she walked quickly through to the kitchen, took the keys for the garage and walked back out.

Tom lingered in the front room, listening as the garage door was unlocked and raised up. A minute later she came back into the house, her tennis rackets cradled in the crook of an arm, a pile of chewing gum packets balanced on the face of the uppermost racket. Pausing in the hallway, she called, "Tom? Where are you? Can you hear me?"

Behind the door, he stood absolutely still, watching her through the tiny crack.

"Fuck him," she whispered nervously to herself, and walked into the front room.

342

He stepped out from behind her. "What are you doing?"

Letting out a yelp of terror, she nearly jumped over the sofa, packs of gum flying everywhere.

"Jesus!" she said, one hand reaching into the pocket of her body warmer. He stood still, staring directly at her. When he made no attempt to move closer, she took her hand back out. "You made me jump," she said warily, backing away.

"What are you doing with that chewing gum?"

A momentary look of guilt, followed by an irritated expression. "I was just taking a few packs. You've got a bloody mountain of the stuff in the garage."

"You opened one of the boxes?"

"No, it was open already. Jesus, keep them if they're that precious." She walked over to the corner of the room and picked up a sculpture of a dolphin she'd made at art college. Tom stood where he was, one hand fiddling with the drawstring of his tracksuit bottoms, a frown on his face. Keeping her eyes on him, she skirted round to the door and back out of the house.

Next foray she came back down the stairs with all her bottles of perfume and toiletries. He stood in the hallway. "I don't understand. Where are you going with that stuff? You're coming home soon, aren't you?"

She tried to get past him without replying, but he blocked her exit.

Charlotte said nothing. Instead she headed back into the front room, crouched at the video cabinet and flicked through the cassettes and DVDs inside. She dropped *It's a Wonderful Life, The Wizard of Oz* and *Pretty Woman* into the box.

"I've also made enquiries about nurseries," Tom continued. "There are some very good ones in the area."

Suddenly she swept Tom's collection of videos onto the carpet. The violence of her action caused him to sit down suddenly on the sofa. "Tom!" she yelled, her voice quickly dying down to a whisper. "There is no bloody baby."

A slither of Tom's brain understood the words, but it was outweighed by the far larger part of his mind that was in total denial. "Where've you been, anyway? I've been so worried about you."

"You what?" She looked at him uncertainly.

"Where've you been?"

"Tom, are you hearing me? There is no bloody baby."

"I was worried about you."

Confused, she raked strands of blonde hair from her face. "Well, don't be," she replied, getting to her feet and walking through to the dining room. She placed the box on the dining table, opened up the dresser's top drawer and started dropping her silver napkin rings into the box. Next she pulled open the second drawer, lifted the napkins out and froze. "There's a gun in this drawer."

"Yes," Tom replied.

"What's it doing there? Is it real?"

"Yes. It's to protect us. There are dangerous people out there, Charlotte. We have to be more careful,

344

especially with the little one on the way. I've been thinking about babies' names."

Very slowly Charlotte slid the drawer shut, then moved round towards the door, reaching into her pocket again as she did so. "There is no baby," she repeated.

"Oh, but there is. You're pregnant, Charlotte."

"It was terminated. Last month."

Tom's head dropped forwards, as if the muscles in his neck had suddenly dissolved. He looked towards his hand and began picking at the seam on the backrest of the dining chair. "No baby?" he whimpered. His thumbnail began to go white as he dug it with ever growing force into the leather. "No baby?" His breathing was deepening and picking up in speed, his mind shrinking from her words, desperate to find some way to make them manageable. Suddenly he had it. He looked up at her with tears in his eyes. "Get out. You're not Charlotte. You've been sent to impersonate her. You're not Charlotte. Get out!"

"Charlotte?" came a voice from the doorway. Tom heard an Australian accent.

Leaving her box on the table, she edged round the wall and ran from the room.

Across the road Creepy George placed his camera on his lap, tilting it forward so he could see the viewfinder. He'd got several good shots of her as she ferried the boxes into the back of the jeep and many at the point when she had leaned forwards to slide them inside the vehicle, bottom poking outwards as she did so. He reached over to the glove compartment and removed a packet of gum from the box he'd stolen from It's A Wrap a couple of months before. Folding a stick into his mouth, he began to ruminate on what was going on.

Inside the house Tom couldn't move. Her words bounced around his head like a pinball, lighting up every part of his brain so there was nowhere dark and comforting for him to crawl. The only way he could make everything all right was to remind himself her words were fake, spoken by something that looked exactly like his wife. Perhaps a robot.

He needed some sort of sense in his world. He could feel the threads of reality unravelling in his fingers, everything becoming disjointed. He looked towards the door, saw his feet moving beneath him. Was he awake? He looked at the clock on the kitchen wall. Tick tock, tick tock. He turned on the taps. Water flooded the takeaway cartons. Soon he saw steam. He held a hand under each jet of water, felt sweet and sour. No, hot and cold. He held up his hands, looked at their backs. Both were bright red. Holding them against his cheeks, one was hot and one was cold. Had Charlotte just been? He wasn't sure. He turned off the taps and went into the front room. An ornament was gone. There was mess on the floor — chewing gum and videos. He thought she had been, but he was so confused.

His mind needed something to latch on to. Something he could reason with. He looked at the video at his feet. *Seven*. With Brad Pitt and Morgan

Freeman. He looked at the packet of chewing gum lying next to it.

Chewing gum. Everything had gone wrong because of chewing gum. Those dots on the streets, making it impossible for him to walk through the city centre. The blobs ejected from people's mouths, coated in saliva, dropping into ashtrays, urinals, the pavement itself. Squashed flat by feet. Clinging to the soles of shoes. Cementing itself to paving stones. Swarming at the bases of bins. Massing by the bus stops. Gradually drying, losing its whiteness. Turning grey, then black, but never dissolving, stubbornly existing like some ancient lichen, surviving the rain and frost and sun. Chewing gum. It was why he had fled the city centre, why he had lost his job.

He focused on the packet, noticed the words "seven sticks".

His eyes shifted back to the video. *Seven*. That number again.

Why seven? he wondered, mind scrabbling desperately to mesh something solid out of his fragmenting reality. One for each deadly sin, he knew that. But why seven sticks of gum? One for each day of the week?

Other collections of seven occurred to him. The seven colours of the rainbow. Snow White and the Seven Dwarves. His mind flitted about, coming up with the seven wonders of the ancient world. What was it about that number? he wondered, fingertips pressed to his temples.

Tentatively, he edged over to his computer and turned it on. Sitting down, he typed into Google "the significance of seven". Results one to ten of more than 1,280,000 hits came up. He started scrolling down the screen.

He read about how often the number features in western culture. Seven days of the week. Seven ages of man. Seven planets in the heavens of old. He browsed through a document that outlined how alchemy was based on seven metals: gold, silver, lead, tin, iron, copper and mercury. Each metal corresponds with one of the seven wandering bodies on which astrology was originally based: the sun, moon, Mercury, Venus, Mars, Jupiter and Saturn.

Tom scanned on down, skimming articles that spoke of other collections of seven — the seven seas, seven league boots, *The Magnificent Seven*.

Tom turned the packet of gum over and over in his hand, his mind seizing on the various occurrences of the number, knitting together some sort of framework, trying to create some stability. As a sense of excitement began coursing through him, he got up and went over to the drinks cabinet. All his whisky was gone, so he pulled out a bottle of tequila.

Back at the computer, he swigged some down, doubling over in a fit of coughing. After wiping the tears from his eyes he found that he'd clicked on a new document. Its title was "The prevalence of seven in the religions of the world".

Tom leaned forward, his face now inches from the screen.

★ ★ ★

By the time dawn broke he knew he had to get out. To the side of the computer was a pile of printouts almost two inches thick, each sheet of paper featuring aspects of his new-found knowledge.

He thought about changing out of his tracksuit bottoms, but couldn't be bothered. Rummaging around in his room, he found a pair of white towelling socks, black work shoes and a beige jumper. Finally he put his Timberland jacket on, slipped the gun into the pocket, picked up the nearly empty bottle of tequila and set off for the city centre.

Specks of gum made walking on the pavement difficult. He stepped carefully round them, walking along the grass verges or in the road where the asphalt was newly laid and relatively clean. Cars beeped him and he ignored them.

During his walk in, Manchester had been bathed in a light shower. The rain had made the streets damp, darkening the colour of the paving stones and making the white lumps of gum stand out. He looked at the dots all around, tip-toeing into Piccadilly Gardens like he was walking through a minefield. Sitting down on a bench, he watched the people pass by; office workers walking along with phones to their ears, cups of coffee or carry-out bags from McDonald's in their spare hand.

After nine thirty the shoppers started to appear, heading at a more leisurely pace for the big department stores and expensive boutiques.

Tom crept along, ever careful to watch where he placed his feet. The colourful Commonwealth Games banners and hanging baskets of flowers had long been removed from the lampposts. The building wraps were gone too, derelict structures that had previously been hidden now plain for everyone to see. Craning his neck back, he stared up, saw tiny saplings growing in their gutters, pigeons coming and going through glassless windows.

The special litter-busting teams in their red jackets had also ceased to exist, so the sweet wrappers, discarded free newspapers, polystyrene cups and cigarette ends had begun to accumulate, forming a layer of rubbish that was pushed to and fro by the wind, shifting restlessly over the immovable spots peppering the paving slabs. Tom stalked through the debris, looking around him as the people emerged from shops, full bags hanging from their arms. Their lifestyle was, he realized, the one that had beguiled Charlotte, clouded her judgement as to what really mattered in life. He watched them as they took a break from their shopping to sit at pavement cafes and drink coffee, eat pastries or muffins and browse through glossy in-store magazines, always contemplating their next purchase.

Then they would get up, leaving dirty cups and crumb-covered saucers. A light wind blew crinkled napkins and empty sugar sachets on to the street as they strode off, credit cards ready, futilely trying to stave off their feelings of emptiness by purchasing more and more useless things.

CHAPTER
TWENTY-THREE

4 November 2002

Head still pounding from last night's booze, Jon watched Sly through the interview room's one-way mirror. His posture of boredom had long been replaced by one of tense agitation. He leaned forward on the plastic chair, arms wrapped tightly round his stomach, rocking backwards and forwards. Half turning to the mirrored window, he repeated yet again, "You're not fitting me up with those murders. You're fucking not!"

"What do you think?" McCloughlin asked Jon and the other officers gathered in the shadows beyond.

Bodies shifted in the narrow room. "Guilty as sin," said a voice that curled with disgust. "Look at him; he's sweating like a pig in an abattoir."

"There's certainly enough to charge him," observed someone else. "Especially with the fibres at two of the murder scenes matching the suit from his flat."

"DI Spicer?" McCloughlin demanded.

Turning the extra strong mint over in his mouth, Jon hesitated, aware that the men around him were of senior rank. Despite all the evidence, there were doubts in his head that he couldn't ignore. "I agree that we've got enough to charge him, but I'm not totally convinced yet."

"You bloody arrested him," McCloughlin growled.

Jon suppressed the urge to apologise. "I think we've got a member — possibly the leader — of the car theft gang. His prints match partials we've lifted from the letterboxes of sixteen properties where car keys have been hooked out of the hallway. But why has he suddenly started killing people?"

There was silence all around.

"OK," McCloughlin said. "We've had him for almost twenty-four hours. I've already requested an extension of another twelve. Then I'll apply for a warrant of further detention — so we have him for another three and a half days if we need. In the meantime, let's keep turning things over. Something's got to give soon. DI Spicer, you can return him to the cells."

Leaving Jon, they all filed back up the stairs. Walking into the incident room, McCloughlin called over to the office manager. "Any progress on where our suspect got all those packs of chewing gum?"

"The manufacturers confirm it was a limited edition that was produced specifically for a Commonwealth Games promotion. However the agency that was handling the promotion — a place called It's A Wrap — closed their Manchester branch down last month. We've been on to their head office in London and they're getting back to us with more details as soon as possible."

CHAPTER
TWENTY-FOUR

October 2002

Tom now spent the majority of his waking hours at his computer, the bag of powder next to the mouse. Though his sense of reality was becoming increasingly blurred, one part of his mind remained clearly focused: the part concerned with researching the number seven.

The obsession was taking him throughout history, bouncing him between cultures, religions and faiths. He had noted down how the Lord's Prayer is divided into seven lines, how there were seven days of creation and seven days for Noah to load the ark. Bezalel made a lampstand with seven lamps for the tabernacle, Joshua's army marched around Jericho on seven successive days with seven priests blowing seven trumpets. In the book of Revelation he counted no less than fifty-four occurrences of the number, including seven churches, seven candlesticks, seven spirits, seven thunders, a seven-headed dragon, a seven-headed beast and seven vials of wrath.

And his scouring of the subject didn't focus solely on Christianity. He found mentions of the number in Judaism when it spoke of the seven supreme angels and seven continents; and Islam, which mentions seven heavens, seven hells and seven seas. He read about how

353

devotees walk around Kaaba at Mecca seven times. The tantric system holds that humans have seven chakras, Buddhism analyses human life as an evolution through seven cycles. He found the number repeatedly cropped up in the Rig Veda, the first Hindu sacred book thought to be three thousand years old.

There could be no doubt the number played a huge part in man's ordering of the world. What Tom couldn't work out was why such massive importance had been attached to it. Something must have happened long ago which had led people to regard the number as so significant. What had occurred?

After a fortnight of surfing, he stumbled across a document that provided an explanation. The writer of the document believed that, far back in the mists of time, seven Masters descended from the heavens and imparted their wisdom to select groups of people across the earth. Their visit explained why so many early societies boasted such an astonishingly advanced knowledge of things like astronomy and maths. He stated that structures such as Stonehenge, the pyramids and Easter Island are all lunar observatories, their construction and planning requiring levels of calculation and engineering far beyond anything else the people of those societies possessed.

The writer went on to say that, because this knowledge was passed on only in part, and usually by word of mouth, it slowly fragmented, pieces of it emerging at various points in history. He pointed out how many major western thinkers believed their insights were the result of picking up on these fragments of long-lost philosophy. Even Isaac Newton stated that he was only "rediscovering what the sages of antiquity knew".

This is it, thought Tom. This is why seven is so important. The Masters numbered seven: that's why seven has come to be treated with such enormous importance.

One night he had taken a pinch of the powder and was resting from his research. The street lamp outside his house flickered and winked, sending brief bursts of light across his windowsill. Tom stared, intrigued by the flashes. At first they'd seemed totally random but the more he looked, the more he suspected there was a pattern, a code being directed at him. He rose to his feet and wearing nothing but his boxer shorts, walked out of his front door and down his driveway. He stood beneath the lamppost listening to the phosphorescent tube buzz and plink as the light went on and off. In the brief moments of darkness Tom could see the sky above; it was the colour of a bruised apricot, ruined by the light emanating from the city.

Then, as he stood looking up at it, the lamp went out completely. Though Tom's eyes remained fixed on the lamp above him, he sensed something closing in on him, something surrounding him. He looked down and realized what had enveloped him from all sides: darkness. He turned towards his house and saw that the entire street was plunged in blackness. Wandering to the end of the road, bare feet connecting with the cool pavement, he couldn't see a light in any direction. Standing there, he became aware of the natural light shining down from above and he looked up at a sky that sparkled with the same intensity as in the Seychelles.

Arching his head back in wonder, his eyes settled once again on The Plough. And as he counted all seven stars making up the constellation, the collection of voices boomed down from the sky above.

Tom! Tom! Tom!

He fell to his knees, hands clamped over his ears. But the voices carried on with undiminished clarity, repeating his name again and again. He ran back down the street and into his house, slamming the door shut. The voices followed him, and he crumpled on to the sofa, pulling a pillow up to his face and squeezing his eyes tightly shut in fear.

When Tom awoke the next day, he was still cowering under the cushion. He crept back to his computer. The power was now working again so he turned it on and altered his search to "the significance of the plough". Another twenty-nine thousand hits came up.

Ignoring the sites that spoke about the plough as a tool of cultivation, Tom focused on the quasi-religious, pagan sites. On these he read about how the constellation of seven stars has been called many things by many societies throughout history.

The Wagon, The Dipper, Arthur's Wain. Greek mythology described it as Ursa Major or the great bear. For the Egyptians it was the astral shape of their god, Seth. The Mexicans believed it to be the foot of Tezcatlipoca. To the Lapps it is the bow of a hunter, to the Sioux a bier. The Siberian Kirghiz legend calls it the seven watchmen. In Hinduism it is known as Saptarshi, or the seven rishis — semi divine sages and sources of all sublunary wisdom.

Tom knew they were all wrong. The Plough was the seven Masters, hanging in the night sky, keeping a watch on Earth. And now they had chosen him as their prophet. They had told him how, for centuries, they had looked down as man had strayed further and further from their teachings. The wisdom they had imparted had evolved along false lines and greed had corrupted the people of Earth, tricking them into living lives of decadence and excess. His own wife and baby had been lost for ever to it.

Now, they had announced, was the time to act. Through him their words would be relayed and people would see the error of their ways. Through his teachings the evils of wanton consumption would be cast aside. A new Golden Age would be ushered in — one where people lived simple, happy lives. Their obsession with shopping would be cured. Superstores, hypermarkets, arcades and shopping centres — those temples built to pursue the activity would be razed to the ground.

With the realization that they had chosen him to spread their word, Tom began to weep. And his tears were born of fear: fear at what they would ask him to do.

In the front room he found his Sennheiser headphones, the type that clamped right over the ears. In the kitchen he searched through the drawers for foil, eventually finding the roll and tearing off great squares.

Then he proceeded to wrap layer upon layer over each earpiece. By wearing the headphones at all times he intended to stop the Masters beaming their voices into his head.

Now that he had no job, Creepy George spent a lot of time parked outside Sixteen Moorfield Road. At night he could see the flicker of the computer monitor in the front room, but it was only ever Tom in the house. She had disappeared.

In frustration he started scouring the city centre. Guessing the types of places she'd visit, he wandered up and down King Street, glancing in the windows of Diesel, Tommy Hilfiger, DKNY and Armani.

At lunchtime he'd switch his search to nice restaurants: Zinc, Stock, Lime, Croma. Then, one day, he glimpsed her going into Selfridges. He broke into an ungainly trot, making it through the doors thirty metres behind her.

She took the escalator down to the food hall and went across to the sushi bar in the corner. A man was already there and she took the seat next to him. As they kissed the bile rose in George's throat.

They ordered fresh fruit juices, then, for the next half an hour, plucked morsels from the conveyor belt. Eventually the man flicked his credit card on to the counter.

At the top of the escalator they kissed again and parted company. George followed her around Harvey Nichols for an hour, then trailed her across to Quay Street where she slipped into an expensive-looking health centre. Hesitating at the doors, George began to read the notices in the window.

State-of-the-art, fully air-conditioned gymnasium, swimming pool and spa, aerobics studio with classes in yoga, pilates and boxercise, spinning studio, beauty salon and relaxation room.

George stared at the photos of women in their leotards, determined expressions on their faces. He liked best the picture of the lady lying on a bed in the beauty salon. Her hair was tied up in a towel and her eyes were closed. Then he saw the notice inviting anyone in for a free tour and day pass. He walked into the reception area, its shiny wooden floors and halogen spotlights dazzling him. "Hello, I would like a look around, if I may."

The young lady kept her face bright and welcoming. "Of course, sir. I'll just give one of our assistants a call."

When the man appeared he had a glow of vitality that George knew contrasted all too obviously with his own pale face. As he was led around, George scanned each room for her. The pool was virtually empty, the aerobics studio deserted. At the gym he saw her, wearing a crop top and shorts, lifting a pair of pink plastic dumb-bells up and down. He wanted to stand and drink in the sight of her, wanted the man's irritating prattle to stop. But after a cursory look at the remaining facilities, he was shown back down to reception.

"I'd like to apply for membership, please," he said to the receptionist.

Taking the form and a brochure, he sat down in the cafe area and grudgingly ordered a cup of coffee. He took as long as he could to read the brochure, then pored over the small print about membership terms and conditions. Eventually he heard footsteps and she came down the stairs, blonde ponytail bouncing with each step. George looked down and, out of the corner of his eye, watched as she went over to the notice board and trailed a finger over the group exercise timetables.

"Jules," she called over to the receptionist. "Could you book me in for your pilates class?"

"Sure, which one?"

"Oh, at seven o'clock on Thursday nights, please."

George scrawled the information down on the back of his brochure.

Tom heard nothing for three days. In that time he struggled with his newfound understanding. Rather than freeing him, the knowledge he now possessed was crushing him. He was unable to raise himself to his feet. Keeping the headphones on at all times, he dragged himself around the house, the powder his only source of comfort.

He was lying at the bottom of the stairs when they began to say his name again. Immediately he reached his hands up, assuming the headphones had slipped off, only to find they were in place. One by one, they took turns to speak.

Do not deny your destiny.

You are the one.

We have chosen you.

Chosen you to spread our word.

It is time to be strong.

Time for the Golden Age to dawn.

Stand up, Tom.

The enormous power in their voices couldn't be denied. The Masters had selected him. Tentatively he tried to get up. He found that he could stand without problem, so he removed the headphones and climbed the stairs two at a time.

Poking through the pile of clothes on his bedroom floor, he located a top and trousers that didn't seem too dirty. Downstairs he pulled on his coat and a pair of shoes. Pausing in the doorway to the dining room, he decided to leave the gun in its drawer. Instead he packed a spare pair of trainers and a towel into a small rucksack, then set off into Manchester.

Walking along Portland Street he looked again at the message on the tower: "Bruntwood welcomes all 72 Commonwealth Nations". He was certain that the Games had finished a few months before, and he couldn't understand why the message was still there.

The city's few days of glory were long gone, and unemployment had crept back up as the hundreds of jobs created by the event had vanished with the end of the closing ceremony. The fountain in Piccadilly Gardens had been turned off several weeks ago for routine maintenance and had still not started working again. Tom walked slowly through the bare trees dotted around the gardens, carefully placing his steps until he made it on to the grass.

He walked quickly across it, slowing down at the gum-marred pavement on the other side. The stuff had multiplied, like bacteria in a petri dish, spreading slowly across the stones, becoming ever more concentrated. With trepidation, he made his way to the top of Market Street, looking at the mass of humans crowding the area ahead. He told himself he was there to help them.

He pulled the towel out of his rucksack and spread it out across the pavement so he didn't risk treading on any gum. Then he took the speech he'd prepared earlier and surveyed the shoppers passing by.

He held up the piece of paper, but his hand was trembling so much he couldn't actually read the words. His mouth was dry and his legs felt weak as he watched the flow of people pass by, bags of shopping hanging from curled fingers. He lowered the sheet of paper and was accepting the fact that he could not address the crowd, when the voices took it in turns to speak to him again.

Be strong!

You must spread our message!

Speak!

Wildly he looked about, but everyone was carrying on as they had before and he realized that only he, The Chosen One, could hear their words.

"People of Manchester," he tried to announce, but his voice came out as a croak. He looked up to the sky, prayed for strength and felt better that, somewhere above the clouds, the Masters were watching him. He walked to the edge of his towel, looked directly at the shoppers who stared curiously at him, and said,

"People of Manchester! You must end the errors of your ways. You must discard the bags that weigh you down, shake off the shackles of your consumerist ways. Only then will the Golden Age dawn and our happiness be ensured."

He paused to check his words were being registered. Numerous half-smiles and whispered comments told him that they were. The beginnings of the crowd were causing more people to stop.

"I come to you with a message from the Masters. Through me they have chosen to speak; through me can their message be heard. You must change the way you live. No longer can we allow their sacred teachings to go unheeded."

"Shut up you weirdy-beard!" shouted a teenager, instantly ducking behind his giggling mates.

Tom paused to look around him, taking in the expressions of mild amusement and smirking interest. "Today we must show that we are ready for the Masters to return," he continued, holding up his hands to the sky. "Cast aside your purchases." He reached out towards a young woman who, with a squeal of fright, shrank away. "Can you not see how this desire to accumulate possessions is corrupting you? Rid yourselves of the baggage you carry so the Masters may return!"

"That's a novel way for someone to get some free shopping," a man with a Debenhams bag said, addressing the crowd more than Tom. Laughter broke out and heads were shaking at him. Women held fingers up to their temples and whirled them round in circular motions.

"Do not walk away. You must hear my message. I have been chosen!"

But more backs were turning. The crowd began to disperse, some tutting sadly.

Soon only the group of teenagers remained. "Who the fuck are you, anyway?" demanded the lad who had spoken earlier.

"I am the Chosen One," repeated Tom. "Through me the Masters, who have circled in the sky since time immemorial, have chosen to act. You," he pointed to a girl, "do not allow the temptations of this materialistic world to sway you from your sacred ability."

"What ability? Shoplifting?" said another lad.

"Shut up," she said, pretending to be outraged at the accusation. "I never nicked anything. It was you who went into Boots and —"

Tom's voice rose above her. "I mean your ability to reproduce. That which you were placed on Earth for."

"You what, you dirty bastard?" she said, aggressively placing her hands on her hips.

"To be a mother is to fulfil the most sacred of roles. Do not reject that blessing."

"Is he wanting to shag you?" said another in the group, looking at her with a grin.

The girl balled up the gum in her mouth and spat it towards Tom. It rolled across the paving stones, stopping abruptly when it came into contact with the edge of his towel. Immediately he retched loudly. He heard laughter.

"What was that about?" said a voice. "Hey, weirdy-beardy, what was that about?"

But Tom was staring with horror at the wet lump.

Another plucked the gum from his mouth and threw it in Tom's direction. He started backing away towards the other end of the towel. Another lump flew. Turning round, he ran, hopping from paving stone to paving stone, laughter ringing in his ears.

He was afraid after he fled the city centre, afraid the Masters would be angry with him for failing to spread their message. He stayed in his house and awaited their judgement.

He heard nothing for five days and was beginning to imagine that they had chosen someone else. Someone more able than him. One evening he was watching television with the sound turned down low. He sat through a news bulletin about climate change — the hurricanes ravaging the American Midwest with increasing frequency, the floods hitting Europe throughout the year. Switching channels, he looked at a documentary detailing the plight of Indonesia's Orang-utans, explaining how their habitat was being felled to meet the West's insatiable demands for timber. Turning over again, he watched a scientist standing on a rocky shoreline that, a few years before, was covered by a glacier.

Tom! Tom! Tom!

He fell to the floor and crawled under the coffee table whispering, "I'm sorry, I'm sorry."

Once again, they took it in turns to speak.

Do not be afraid, we are not angry with you.

It is the gum chewers who have angered us.

Of all the acts we see, theirs cannot be forgiven.

It symbolizes the frenzy consuming the planet.

They aren't satisfied collecting more and more goods.

Instead they work their jaws in a gross parody of consumption.

They disgust us.

"Yes," Tom agreed, relieved not to be the focus of their wrath. "And what do they do with the lumps?" he dared to ask. "They spit them on to the streets, ruining the world."

He said that he hated all gum chewers, too. Thinking of the youngsters who had driven him from his preaching, he looked towards the window and told the Masters that he wished they could all be destroyed.

The chorus of approval stopped, and a wheedling voice asked if he was sincere.

"Yes," he whispered, meaning it with all his heart.

So they told him how to fulfil his destiny. By following their instructions to the letter, the Golden Age would be allowed to dawn.

The next day he looked out of his French windows, across the garden at the smouldering remains of his armchair. On it sat the television, its screen blackened and cracked from the smoke and heat, the plastic casing melted along the bottom.

The sofa had burned itself out earlier. The telephone, answer machine, hi-fi system, computer, keyboard, food blender, DVD player, coffee percolator, alarm-clock radio, camcorder, video, toaster, personal stereo, cameras and golf clubs, forming a charred sculpture that had partially sunk into the exposed frame and springs. Next to the remains was a pile of ash that had once been his jackets, coats, jeans, T-shirts and most of his trainers. Only a few items of clothing in his wardrobe upstairs.

He had faithfully followed their commands and rid himself of his worldly possessions in preparation for his mission. Now they spoke to him again. Tom listened calmly to the words, nodding in understanding.

He went to his garage and assembled the Cooper's Barrow, pinning the X-treme panel banners to its frame, bolts of lightning striking the lemons and infusing them with electricity.

Next he found the box with all the entry forms for the competition to win a year's supply of X-treme gum and a luxury holiday for two in Malaysia. He opened it up and surveyed the form. The whole competition was really a data-capturing exercise for the chewing gum manufacturer; a way of collecting demographical information about the type of people who purchased their gum.

Examining the glossy front of the form, Tom saw questions asking for the person's name, address, home phone number, mobile phone number, email address, age, marital status and, finally, a convenient time to call to inform them if they were the lucky winner. The wording was carefully couched so the person would think it was necessary to complete all the boxes in order to stand a chance of winning.

Tom looked at the pile of boxes. It appeared that he had enough packets of gum to hand out to half the population of Manchester.

George tried the number again but the line was now dead. He'd been ringing Tom's house quite a lot over the last few weeks but Charlotte never answered. Listening to Tom's tortured breathing made him feel good. But the fact she was never there presented a problem. He needed to know where she lived if he was to carry out his plans for her.

He tried the number again but there was still no tone. Strange, he thought, wondering if it had anything to do with the fire he could see burning in the back garden the other evening.

Glancing at his watch, he saw that her pilates class was in an hour. He set off towards the health centre so he could watch from across the road as she arrived. This time he'd keep track of her all night, right the way back to her front door.

She emerged from the health centre at ten past eight and walked up to Albert Square, where she met another man. They went into some trendy-looking cafe bar and George sat on the benches in front of the town hall for another two hours. Finally they emerged and walked down to Deansgate. A few hundred yards on they disappeared into a place called The Living Room.

George approached the doors but the bouncer waved him on before he could get near. "Not tonight mate; we're full."

He crossed the road, stood in a dark side street and waited. A group of glamorous people arrived minutes later and walked straight in. Charlotte finally appeared at two o'clock in the morning, arms around the man she had arrived with. She seemed full of energy, laughing raucously and grabbing at the man's buttocks. George's eyes widened in alarm as they flagged down a passing cab. He was on the wrong side of the road. As they jumped in he emerged into the light, furiously waving at a cab as it approached on his side of the road. The driver pulled over and he jumped in the back. "Turn around! Follow that taxi over there!"

"You what, mate?" said the driver, twisting round in his seat to look at his passenger.

George was staring out the back window as Charlotte's cab turned up a side street and disappeared from view. "Do a U-turn, you imbecile! Hurry up!"

The driver turned the keys and the diesel engine rattled to a halt. "Get out, you fat prick."

George roared with frustration.

CHAPTER
TWENTY-FIVE

October 2002

Carefully Tom raised the nail scissors to his face. As he started cutting away clumps of beard, he felt better and better. Now he had accepted that he was merely an instrument of the Masters, courage and confidence flooded through him. His life had purpose once again.

When the stubble was short enough, he filled the sink with water, then shaved off the remains with a razor that had lain unused for over a month. In his bedroom he kicked aside the pile of musty-smelling clothes that he had been wearing for weeks. He turned to the X-treme branded tracksuit and baseball cap laid out on the bed and put them on.

In his garage he stocked the cart with boxes of gum and competition entry forms. The minivan he'd hired was parked on the drive and he wheeled the cart up the ramps and into the rear of the vehicle.

Next he drove into Manchester, parking by the Student Union on Oxford Road. He hung about on the flight of steps leading up to the main entrance, waiting for a group of three students. Soon he spotted two lads and a girl. He walked over to them and asked if they'd each like to earn thirty pounds cash for an hour's work.

Within seconds all three were in the van and he was heading towards the city centre.

En route he explained to them that, because of a mix-up, he hadn't received a permit to distribute goods. If any officials approached them, he said, be prepared to pack up fast.

By 2.50p.m. he had wheeled the cart on to the end of the concourse leading up to Piccadilly station. Two of the students — now wearing the ice-blue tracksuits with bags full of gum packets over their shoulders — positioned themselves on the pavement. The girl manned the cart to supervise the filling-in of the competition entry forms. Tom watched as clusters of shoppers approached from the city centre, hauling their purchases towards the trains, heading back to houses already crowded with junk.

He watched them ambling closer, many idly chewing gum, arms pulled straight by the weight of the bags hanging from their hands. Boots, River Island, Next, Sainsbury's, JJB Sports, Primark, HMV, Tesco.

The Masters' voices pointed out how similar they were to cows, chewing the cud and plodding back to their sheds, shopping bags swaying like swollen udders. And looking at them Tom realized the voices were right: they were nothing more than beasts.

"Hello there," he said brightly as two women approached the cart. "I see you like gum. Care for a free promotional pack?"

"Citrus flavour? Sounds interesting," one said, plucking the gum from her mouth and dropping it on the pavement.

Tom's stomach turned over. Swallowing hard, he said, "How about the chance for a luxury holiday to Malaysia? Just fill out this form — it only takes two seconds."

Tom knelt in front of the coffee table in his front room as if he was at an altar. After selecting the Swiss army knife's most slender blade, he lifted the first pack of X-treme chewing gum. He stood it upright and pushed the thin point of the blade under the triangular shaped flap of foil at its end. By wiggling the blade from side to side, he got its point underneath, then prised the flap upwards with a tiny crackling sound. The smell of lemons entered his nostrils. He turned the pack around and prised the other triangle of foil up as well. Now he was able to fold open the end wrapping, pushing it back with the blade until the ends of the seven sticks inside were exposed to view. Pushing the sealed end of the packet with his thumb, he eased the sticks upwards until the top of one stood clear. Grasping it with the penknife's tweezer attachment, he dragged the stick out of the pack and laid it on the table.

Good, the voices coaxed, good.

Gently he slid the foil-coated stick clear of the paper jacket it was encased in. Next he turned the fold of foil at each end of the stick backwards and used the blade of the knife to ease apart the serrated edge of the wrapper, revealing the stick of gum itself.

Picking it up with the tweezers, he dusted each side of it with the special powder then relaid it in its foil wrapping. After that he followed the process in reverse

— refolding the foil wrapping, sliding it back into the paper jacket, easing it into the pack alongside the other six sticks. Once they were all pushed properly back into the foil outer packaging, he folded the triangular flaps back down and sealed them with a spot of glue.

Turning it over in his hands, he noted with satisfaction that there was no way anyone could tell that the pack had been tampered with.

Pausing at the end of Berrybridge Road, Tom placed the briefcase at his feet, took the bag of powder from his pocket and allowed himself a pinch. As he continued along the street, he looked at the dozens of other commuters walking with bowed heads for work that morning. He smoothed the arm of his suit, glad he looked exactly the same.

He turned up the driveway of number fifteen, stopped at the front door and knocked twice. A few moments later, the door was opened by a young woman with spiky blonde hair, wearing a dressing gown. She looked at him and placed her hand back on the door in readiness to close it again. "I'm sorry, I'm not interested in whatever you're selling."

Tom held up the competition entry form she had completed several weeks before. "Miss Polly Mather?"

She peered at the piece of paper, recognizing her handwriting and signature, still unsure of what she'd filled in.

"You recently entered our prize draw for a year's supply of X-treme chewing gum and a luxury holiday for two in Malaysia."

Her eyes widened as the memory came back. "Don't tell me I've won."

Tom gave her his widest smile. "You most certainly have."

"Oh my God, I'm going to Malaysia? I always thought no one actually won those things. I can't believe this!"

"Well, we're legally obliged to check you have a valid passport before the prize can be officially awarded . . ."

She stepped aside and waved him inside the house.

"I don't want to stop you from going anywhere."

"No, that's fine, I have Wednesdays off." She clapped her hands in excitement. "I can't believe this," she repeated, directing him into the front room, one hand fluttering at her throat.

"OK," said Tom, sitting down and placing the briefcase on the floor to the side of the armchair.

Polly sat down on the sofa, elbows on her knees, leaning forwards expectantly. Without saying anything, Tom removed a pack of X-treme gum from his jacket, grasped the little tab on its side and opened it up. He slid out the uppermost stick of the seven inside the pack and said to her with an official note in his voice, "On behalf of X-treme Incorporated, may I offer our congratulations?"

Leaning forward on the sofa, she gratefully accepted the stick of gum, unwrapped it and then folded it into her mouth. "Thanks," she said breathlessly, looking expectantly at her visitor and eagerly chewing.

"My pleasure," Tom replied. They continued looking at each other for a moment longer. "Now, if you could just get . . ."

"Oh God, yes, sorry! It's upstairs." She jumped to her feet. "I'm all excited. Sorry."

He smiled. "No problem."

She almost skipped across the room, then ran up the stairs. While she was gone Tom stood up, walked over to her living room window and checked the street outside. By the time she returned he was sitting down once again.

"Here," she said, handing him her passport.

"Great," he replied. Although her neck was beginning to show up slight patches of red, Tom knew he needed more time before the drug took full control. As he reached for his pen he paused, then looked up with a slightly embarrassed expression. Coughing as if his throat was dry, he said, "Do you mind if I have a cup of tea before we get started?"

"Oh!" She jumped up again, pale pink dressing gown falling slightly open to reveal a flash of upper thigh. "I'm so rude. Sorry. Milk? Sugar?"

"Milk and two sugars, thanks."

Flustered, she paced quickly down the short corridor to the kitchen. He listened to the sound of her bare feet slapping against the lino then heard crockery being shifted around in a sink. A tap was turned on followed by the sound of a kettle heating up.

He sat back in his seat and closed his eyes. The voices whispered reassuring encouragement. He felt so proud — for himself and Polly. Of course she didn't know it, but her life had been given a far higher purpose. She was helping to usher in the Golden Age. It was a sacrifice anyone should be glad to make.

When she walked back into the room a few minutes later a red flush covered her throat and cheeks.

"Here you go." She placed a mug decorated with a cartoon style snail on the coffee table before him.

Tom could see she was now chewing furiously on the gum. She went to sit down again but, on impulse, veered towards the hi-fi system in the corner and turned up the music.

"God, I feel like I could dance," she said urgently, blowing her breath out and running her fingers through her hair. "Is it hot in here? Are you hot?" He could hear a mixture of euphoria and confusion in her voice.

Tom looked around the room as if heat was a visible thing. "No," he replied with a little shake of his head.

"I feel hot," she said, placing her mug on the table. She started waving one hand a little too energetically at her cheek and pulling distractedly at the neck of her dressing gown. Tom kept his head lowered, pretending to search for a pen in his jacket pocket.

She went to sit down, stumbling against the leg of the coffee table. "Whoops!" she said with a strange giggle, though panic was beginning to show in her eyes. "I . . . I'm dizzy."

Now visibly distressed, she attempted a half turn to sit down, but her coordination was going and she missed the sofa, crashing onto the carpet. As she lay on her back, her eyes rolled up into her head and then closed completely.

Tom lifted up the briefcase and placed it on the coffee table. He dialled the combination for the lock and opened it up. From inside he took out the large stainless steel pincers and a plastic bag. He opened the bag up on the floor in case he was sick, then pulled Polly's lower jaw down. There at the back of her mouth was the lump of chewing gum. Seeing the little bubbles of saliva clinging to it, Tom experienced his first retch.

Carefully, he inserted the pincers into her mouth and picked the lump out. Keeping his head turned away, he dropped it into the bag, twisted the neck and knotted it. As he replaced the pincers, the voices began to speak.

Put her in position so she can welcome in the Golden Age.

Dutifully, Tom stretched her arms out at her sides, then tilted her head back to ensure her airways were fully open.

Turning round, he then lifted the silicon gun out of his briefcase. Seeing the workmen applying the white gel round the edges of his bath those months before had made him retreat back down the corridor in disgust. The stuff had dried into something rubbery, and though it hadn't actually been in anyone's mouth, its presence in the corner of the bathroom was a continual source of discomfort to him.

Now he lifted the gun up, the tube of silicon gel mounted in the heavy metal frame. The thought of the tube's contents sent waves of nausea through him but, knowing how important his actions were, he inserted the tapered end of the tube deep into her open mouth.

Grasping the solid metal plunger piece in one hand, he then pushed half a pint of thick white gel down the back of her throat.

Even though she was heavily sedated, her chest heaved and the tendons at the side of her throat flexed as she started to choke. But he pressed the plunger harder, sending a snake of it coiling into her windpipe where it quickly formed an immovable plug.

Her torso jerked and rocked as her lungs fought to drag in air. But the substance was too stubborn to be shifted and after a few more seconds her movements slowed and then stopped.

Tom got up and dropped the gun back into his briefcase. He looked around him and picked her passport off the table. After locking up his briefcase he carried their cups through to the kitchen and tipped the tea down the sink. Once he had sluiced them out with water, he placed them on the draining board and walked out of the flat.

CHAPTER
TWENTY-SIX

5 November 2002

The incident room was silent as everyone waited for the two search teams to report back. Jon sat at his desk, furious that McCloughlin had excluded him from both.

The leader of the team sent to the house of Sly's grandma phoned at ten past eleven. The call was quickly patched through to McCloughlin and people tried not to watch as he listened to the message.

"Fuck!" The phone was slammed down and McCloughlin stepped out of his office. "They've been through the whole house. Nothing that links him to any of the victims."

"How about the attic? Did they search the roof cavity?" someone asked.

"Of course they fucking searched the roof cavity! They ripped her whole house apart!" His door slammed shut.

Half an hour later the team sent to the house of Sly's mum called. Again McCloughlin's face darkened with every second he was on the phone. This time he carefully replaced the handset and opened his office door with a bowed head. "Nothing again." He looked up and searched out Jon with an accusatory stare. "Not a fucking scrap."

In the silence a phone started to ring. Eventually someone picked it up. "Yes. When?"

Something in the officer's voice set off an alarm in Jon's head. He glanced across as the officer cupped his hand over the mouthpiece and said to McCloughlin, "Boss? Another body's turned up. Emily Sanderson. Looks like she's been dead for more than a day."

Tom paced around his front room. The wall above the fireplace was covered with seven rows of seven competition entry forms. He stepped closer to the uppermost row. The entry forms of Polly Mather, Heather Rayne and Mary Walters all had red lines drawn through them. The fourth — Liz Wilson — didn't. He would have to go back to claim her when the old man wasn't there. The next two forms — those of Gabrielle Harnett and Emily Sanderson — were both scored through. Emily's name had been crossed out only yesterday. Tom reached up and removed the seventh form from the wall.

Now was time to call, the voices whispered. Now was the time for her sacrifice.

Two minutes after receiving the call, McCloughlin and three other senior officers set off for the crime scene.

As soon as their cars left the station's car park, the smokers in the incident room poured down the stairs, heading for the rear of the building. In the murmur of voices, Jon heard someone say, "If she was killed yesterday, Sly couldn't have done it."

Jon watched them go, resisting the urge to follow. He popped a stick of gum in his mouth. Balling up the wrapper, he trotted down the stairs and asked the custody officer to let him into Sly's cell.

"No need." He nodded to a side room with an officer standing outside. "He's in there with his solicitor."

Jon knocked on the door and stepped into the room. "Can I have a word?"

Sly just stared back, but his solicitor nodded.

"We've found another body, same circumstances as all the others." He paused to let the information sink in, then took his gamble. "Now this isn't the viewpoint of my senior officers but, as far as I'm concerned, this puts you clear of the murders."

"Too fucking right." Sly sat forward and jabbed a finger at Jon. "I said you're not fitting me up."

The solicitor held up a hand. "So what exactly will you be charging my client with?"

Jon looked at him. "He's still up to his neck in other shit, but that's open to negotiation. I believe he's somehow linked to the murders. So he can help us now and save himself a load of hassle." He looked Sly directly in the eyes. "Where did you get that chewing gum from?"

Sly looked at his solicitor, who nodded at him.

"Some bloke's garage over in Didsbury."

"Address?"

"I don't know. I could drive to it, but I don't know what the name of the road is."

"So if I took you in a car, you could point it out?"

Sly nodded.

Jon left the room and went over to the custody officer's desk. As he phoned the top floor, he placed a pair of handcuffs in his pocket. "Can you put me through to Sergeant Darcourt? It's Jon Spicer. I'm down in the cells."

The phone clicked. "Jon, what's up?"

"Nobby, I need a hand driving a suspect over to a property in Didsbury. Are you up for it?"

"If it gets me out of this miserable room, yes."

George watched as Tom, dressed in a suit and carrying a briefcase, left the house and walked off down the road. Where was he going each day? As he reached the end of the street and disappeared round the corner, the door of a car parked further along opened and Charlotte got out. George's breath caught in his throat as she hurried up the driveway.

She had unlocked the front door and almost closed it behind her when he began to knock. Looking terrified, she peeped through the crack. Seeing him, her features relaxed slightly. "Not today, thanks."

"Charlotte Benwell?" he asked almost apologetically.

"Yes."

"Could I come in, please? I really need to discuss something with you."

"Who are you?"

"My name is Austen Rogers," George replied. "I work for X-treme chewing gum. We're a client of It's A Wrap."

"You just missed my husband. He's gone out."

"I need to speak with you."

"I'm sorry, but now really isn't a good time. I've only popped in to get a few things —"

Interrupting her, George said, "I've been trying to get hold of you. I believe your husband is defrauding our company."

"You mean all that chewing gum? It's in the garage. Take it."

"No, no," George answered, hiding his surprise. "There's more to it than that. I think he's preparing to defraud you, too." George looked down. "It's to do with your separation."

"Defraud me? How? You mean over the house, don't you?"

"This is really very awkward. Could I at least explain inside?"

Nervously, Charlotte glanced down the street. "It's got to be quick, all right?" She opened the door and turned round. "We can talk in the kitchen."

She stepped past the living room without looking in. As soon as the door clicked shut behind him the blood surged in George's head and he found himself lunging at her, mouth open in an ugly, silent grimace.

His thick arms began to close around her head and she ducked instinctively. Twisting free of his grip, she ran into the kitchen and raced around the other side of the table, heading for the rack of knives in the corner.

The worktop was bare. No kettle, no toaster, nothing. She whirled around; only the kitchen table was between them. A glistening sheen was breaking out over his face and he was breathing hard. Placing something on the table, he whispered, "Now be a good girl and take one of these."

As soon as her eyes flicked down to the strip of pills he hurled the table aside with a roar. She screamed with terror, dodged around him and sprinted for the front door.

He was right behind her, too close for her to get it open. At the last instant she jumped to the side and ran in to the dining room. His body slammed against the door and he steadied himself, knowing she was trapped.

He could hear her sobbing, then a drawer being pulled out and clattering to the floor. He stepped through the door, saw her crouching down, scrabbling for something among the napkins strewn on the floor. She started raising her arms up, a gun gripped in both hands.

As he landed on top of her, the pistol went off with a muffled crack.

Sly and the solicitor sat in the back seat of the unmarked police car. Jon drove onto the long, straight Kingsway Road and they followed it for a mile or so before turning right towards Didsbury. When they reached the junction with Wilmslow Road, Sly got his bearings. "You need to turn right here," he said.

Jon took the turning and Sly directed him through the rows of residential streets. When they reached Moorfield Road, Sly said, "Down this one."

They had driven another fifty metres when Sly said, "That one on the left. Number sixteen."

Jon stopped the car. It couldn't be. "Are you sure?" He swivelled round.

Sly rolled his eyes. "Yeah, I'm sure. He had a Porsche Boxter. I got into his garage a couple of times. Nothing inside except for a pile of that chewing gum. I took three or four boxes, to get something for my trouble, you know?"

Jon turned to Sergeant Darcourt. "I know this guy. Used to play rugby with him for Stockport. Tom Benwell? Played fly half."

Darcourt frowned. "Name rings a bell. Can't picture him, though."

"I'll give him a knock. You stay here, OK?"

Darcourt nodded. Jon climbed out of the car and walked up Tom's drive, not holding out much hope that he was going to answer his door. He waited for a few seconds after ringing the bell, then walked across the lawn and tried to peer through the net curtains into the living room. It still appeared to be stripped bare.

He walked round the house for a look through the French windows. In the back garden he saw piles of charred furniture and electrical equipment. He began to get a bad feeling about his old team mate. The French doors were slightly ajar. Easing them open with the toe of a shoe, he looked into the room. Sheets of paper were pinned to all the walls. Jon started reading the first.

And it came to pass at the seventh time, when the seven priests blew with the seven trumpets, Joshua said unto the people, shout; for the Lord hath given you the city. And they utterly destroyed all that was in the city, both men and women, young and old.

Joshua.

Jon walked quickly round the house and back to the waiting car. "Nobby, there's something very strange going on here. Can you take these two back to the station? And get a SOCO sent round here, too."

Sergeant Darcourt slid his chubby frame across into the driver's seat. "How do you mean, strange?"

"Drop them off and you can come back for a look yourself," Jon called out, heading off round the side of the house. Slipping through the French windows, he looked at the next sheet of paper. Titled "Shakespeare", it read,

Touch. Faith, we met, and found the quarrel was upon the seventh cause.
As You Like It.

Jon carried on staring at the sheet of paper for long after he'd finished reading it. Like someone in an art gallery, he began walking slowly along. Each sheet of paper he read added to his sense of trepidation. He reached the end of the wall, looked to the next one, saw more pieces of paper stretching away. Quotes from the Koran and something called Rig Veda.

From somewhere inside the house he heard a sniff. Jon remained absolutely still until he heard it again. It was coming from across the corridor.

386

He stepped into the dining room.

The man he remembered as Creepy George was kneeling on the floor. His shirt was off and he was trying to unbuckle his belt. Before him, stretched out on her back, was Charlotte. A rosette of blood showed on her chest and a pool of it was spreading out from below her right shoulder. On the carpet next to her was an empty drawer, a scattering of napkins and a gun.

Quickly, Jon bent down and grabbed it by the barrel. He flicked the safety on and then said with as much force as he could muster, "Police. Move away from the woman."

A string of drool began to drip from George's chin.

Seeing his words were having no effect, Jon stepped forwards and kicked George hard in the stomach. He keeled over onto his back, the breath driven from his lungs. Jon grabbed a wrist, snapped a cuff on it, dragged George across the room and locked him to the radiator pipe. Then he stepped over to Charlotte and felt for a pulse. It was faint, but there.

As Jon started to pack napkins beneath the exit wound, George began to cough and cry behind him. He pulled out his mobile, walked into the front room and called for an ambulance and support.

Hanging up, he let out a long and shuddering sigh. Now being careful where he stepped, he looked at the pile of boxes. The lid of the first one was open and he could see stacks of X-treme gum inside. Next to them was a larger box. He lifted the flap up with the end of the gun and saw the tubes of silicon gel inside.

He looked round the rest of the room and noticed the wall above the fireplace for the first time. Row after row of much smaller pieces of paper. He stepped across for a closer look, the red lines drawn through the top row of competition entry forms catching his eye. He read the names: Polly Mather, Heather Rayne, Mary Walters, Liz Wilson, Gabrielle Harnett, Emily Sanderson.

Oh, Jesus.

Striding back into the dining room, he grabbed George by the hair. "You sick fuck. Where's Tom?"

George's eyes were tightly shut. "I didn't mean to hurt her."

Jon yanked his head back. "What have you done with Tom Benwell?"

George started crying again.

"When did you put all that stuff in there?"

"What stuff?"

"Those entry forms. The chewing gum. How long have you been living here?"

"I don't know what you mean. Tom lives here."

Jon stood up and went back into the living room. On the small mantelpiece above the fireplace was a stack of passports. Using the barrel of the gun, he opened the uppermost one and saw the name Emily Sanderson.

He ran back into the dining room, grabbed George by his throat and rammed the end of the gun into his fat cheek. "What the fuck is going on?"

George tried to shrink backwards, eyes still shut.

"Open your eyes!"

George did as he was told.

"Who's been living here?"

"Tom. He's always been here."

Jon could see he was telling the truth. He returned to the front room, placed the gun on the mantelpiece and scrutinized the entry forms. They were all in rows of seven. Except the uppermost one, which had only six. The killings had started six days ago, with no body turning up on the fourth day. There was no line through the fourth entry form — Liz Wilson's. And there was no seventh form, just a tiny hole in the paint where a drawing pin had been.

"Oh my fucking God, what have you done?" he whispered, reaching for his phone to ring the station. It went off.

Transferring the call to answerphone, he punched in the number for Longsight, barking out that he needed the works sent out to Sixteen Moorfield Road, Didsbury. "Also, send a car immediately to . . ." he looked at Liz Wilson's entry form and read out her address. "Also, put out a general alert on a Tom Benwell. White, mid-thirties, blond curly hair, five foot eleven, medium build. He's probably wearing a light green Armani suit and carrying a briefcase. I think he's currently en route to his next victim's house."

As he said "next victim's house", the words of Nikki Kingston rang in his head. She had told him that she'd got her pack of gum in some sort of a freebie promotion a while ago. The forms he was looking at were headed "Win a year's supply of X-treme gum and an all expenses paid luxury holiday for two in Malaysia."

Frantically he started scrolling through his phone book, knowing that, after being knocked over by Sly in the Arndale, she'd been signed off work with a stiff neck.

Her phone began to ring.

"Nikki, it's Jon!" He realized he was shouting.

"OK — I hear you. Christ, Jon —"

He cut her off. "Nikki, do not open the door to anyone, do you understand?"

"What do you mean?"

"Just say you'll keep it shut!"

"OK, OK! What's going on?"

Jon breathed out. "That pack of X-treme gum you gave me. When you picked it up, did you fill out a competition entry form?"

"Yeah, how did you know?"

"Just lock the door, will you?"

"OK, I'm locking it now. What's all this about?"

Jon was able to speak a little more calmly. "Where did you get it again?"

"One of those promotional giveaways, at Piccadilly station."

Suddenly everything made sense. All of the victims lived around the south and east of Manchester, by rail lines that led into Piccadilly station. "It's how he's selecting his victims. He's got all the entry forms to that competition in his house. He must have been picking the ones filled in by single females. There's just a chance your entry form is in there too." He didn't mention that one was missing from the kill list on the wall. "Just keep your door locked, OK?"

"Don't worry. Shall I call the police?"

"I'll have a car sent round. What's your address?"

He repeated it back to her to make sure he'd heard it correctly, then hung up, called Longsight and ordered a patrol car to be sent round immediately.

Back in the front room, he checked Charlotte's pulse once more. He could only just feel it. He grasped her hand and began to rub it vigorously. "Charlotte, stay with me. Do you hear? Stay with me!"

A siren was growing louder.

"Can you hear that, Charlotte?"

George's sobbing filled the room. Jon turned on him and snarled, "Shut the fuck up!"

George bit on his lip, snot and tears making his face glisten.

Jon heard the siren come to a halt on the road outside. He jumped up and opened the front door. Two paramedics were hurrying up the driveway, cases in their hands. "Gunshot wound. Her name's Charlotte. She's lost a lot of blood!"

They ran in and knelt down beside her. As one ripped open compression bandages the other hastily prepared an oxygen mask.

"Will she survive?" Jon asked, leaning over their shoulders.

"Yeah, if we stop the flow of blood immediately. Just give us some space."

Jon backed out of the room and began to anxiously pace up and down the corridor, overwhelmed by an urge to do something. Seeing the answerphone icon on his screen, he called it up and heard his sister's voice.

"Hi Jon, little sis here. Just on the off chance, seeing as I didn't take you up on your offer to get me that Violet Crumble the other day . . . Alice gave me a pack of this really nice gum the other night. I can't find it for sale in any of the shops around here. She said she got it in some promotion at Piccadilly station. I'm hoping it might be for sale in the newsagent's there — it's called X-treme and it's citrus flavoured. I just thought if you were passing. See ya soon, bye!"

"Oh no, oh please God no," prayed Jon, calling his home number, suddenly remembering that Alice got the train into Manchester, too.

After five rings it clicked on to the answerphone, but Jon was sprinting out of the front door before the message even started.

The weak November sun had now sunk from sight and fireworks screeched and screamed up into the darkening sky. He raced along Fog Lane, shouting pedestrians out of his way. In the recreation ground kids whooped and cheered as they let off strings of bangers. He careered on to Kingsway knowing that, from there, his house was only minutes away. A solid line of slow-moving cars stretched off in both directions and he leaped into the path of the nearest vehicle, arms raised up. As it went into an emergency stop he clearly heard the driver yell, "You fucking dickhead!"

He darted into the next lane, barely registering the crunch of shunting cars behind him. On to Lane End and he raced along, knowing that as soon as he saw Heaton Moor Golf Course on his left, his own road was just ahead.

★ ★ ★

Tom checked the entry form and saw that he was on the correct street. He placed the briefcase at his feet, removed the bag of powder from his pocket and took a large pinch. Then he flexed his shoulders, took a breath in and looked at the number on the nearest house. He carried on along the road, then turned up a driveway. As he stood on the front doorstep, he looked down at the entry form again, thinking that the surname was vaguely familiar. But with all the whispering in his head, he couldn't concentrate on trying to dredge up where he'd seen or heard it before. He rang the bell.

There was a burning in his throat and he could feel his knees going numb as the heels of his shoes pounded on the pavement. He got to the end of his road and charged up to his house. The front door was shut and the sitting room light was on. He slowed to a halt, trying to catch his breath and calm himself. His hands were shaking as he pulled the keys from his pocket and they jingled slightly before he found the lock. The door opened. Silence. He needed to take in air, but didn't dare breathe because of the sound it would make. In a couple of strides he was at the living room door.

Alice lay on the floor, stretched out in front of the gas fire, Punch shivering on the rug next to her.

Wide-eyed and now able to gasp for breath, Jon said, "Are you all right?"

Alice looked at him like he was mad. "Yes. Why shouldn't I be?"

"What are you doing?" He stepped fully into the room and looked around.

"Trying to calm your dog. Firework night, remember? Bangs, whistles, explosions. What the hell are you doing?"

Jon swallowed hard and took in a lungful of air. "You wouldn't believe it." He let out a sudden nervous laugh and then went back to the front door to push it shut, saying over his shoulder as he did so, "I honestly thought you were in serious trouble. I mean serious trouble."

Tom watched as a wavery figure approached the frosted glass. A female's form. The door opened up.

"Good evening," Tom smiled. "Miss Ellie Spicer?"

He hung his jacket on the banister and paused in the living room doorway to wipe the sweat off his forehead and check again that she really was OK. Shaking his head in relief, he said, "Oh God, that was horrible," before carrying along the corridor to the kitchen.

With Punch slinking miserably along behind her, Alice followed him. "Jon Spicer, will you just tell me what the hell you are on about?"

Jon yanked his shirt off and wiped himself down with it. "I'll explain later. I've got to get back to Tom's house."

"Tom's house? What's going on?"

Jon reached into the laundry basket and pulled out a rugby shirt. "These murders. I hate to say this, but it looks like it was Tom Benwell."

"Tom? The guy you used to play rugby with? But why? Why would he be killing people?"

Not wanting to give Alice a glimpse of the insanity he'd just witnessed, Jon could only shake his head in reply. "I don't know, but I've just come from his house. There's stuff there that . . . stuff there which is pretty conclusive."

"What stuff?"

"Things. Things he used to select his victims. Listen, I've got to get back. I'll phone to get a car sent over here. Don't open the door to anyone who isn't in a uniform." He pulled the rugby shirt on as a crackle of fireworks went off.

"Jon!" Alice said sharply, causing Punch to cower at his feet. "You're not bursting in here with eyes popping out of your head, telling me a friend of yours could be killing people, then buggering off again. What do you mean by things to select his victims? Am I in danger?"

Jon looked towards the front door. "OK, you picked up some gum in a promotion at Piccadilly station a few weeks back?"

She nodded in reply.

"And you filled out one of the competition entry forms?"

"Yes," Alice whispered, eyes going wide.

"That's what he's using to select his victims — everything he needs is on the bloody entry . . ." Alice was looking sick. Jon stepped towards her. "Hey, don't worry. You're not in any danger now."

The fingertips of one hand had gone up to her trembling lips. "Oh my God. I'm so sorry. I didn't put my name on the form." She grabbed him by the arm, started pushing him down the hall. "Your sister. I thought she deserved the chance of a nice holiday."

Jon was trying to turn around. "Ellie's name and address are on the form?"

Tears were in Alice's eyes.

Jon shouted, "Phone her!" He grabbed the keys to the spare car and roared off down the street.

The pops and crackles came thick and fast, sending flashes of multicoloured lights through the curtains.

"You sure I can't ring my friend, Alice?" asked Ellie, happily chewing away on the stick of gum. "It's her writing on the entry form. She'll be so chuffed to find out. In fact, I'll take her with me. God, this is so exciting!"

Tom smiled. "It would be better if we confirm everything is in order first."

"Oh right, my passport. Hang on, it's in here somewhere."

As she started rummaging around in a set of drawers in the corner of the room, the phone started ringing outside in the hallway. Ellie stopped searching and straightened up, raising a hand to her forehead. "Wow! I've come over all dizzy! I'll just get —"

Tom interrupted her. "Please — if we could just confirm everything's in order first. I wouldn't want you to spill the good news to anyone before we're sure you can claim the prize."

Ellie looked at him, then shrugged. "OK." She turned back to the open drawer as the answerphone took the call. "Here you go," she said, handing him the passport.

"That's great," said Tom, clearing his throat. "Could I ask for a cup of tea before we get started?"

"Good idea!" said Ellie. "I'd like one too; I feel a bit wobbly. How do you take it?"

"Milk and two sugars, thanks."

She disappeared down the corridor to the kitchen.

Tom sat quite still, whispering replies to the voices.

Jon skidded to a halt and jumped from the car, leaving its door hanging open as he charged up his sister's path. It had started raining and drops bounced off his head as he moaned, "Keys." He realized Ellie's spare set was still in the kitchen drawer back at his place. He hammered with his fist, then crouched down and shouted her name through the letterbox.

There was no reply, but he could see her coat and handbag in the hallway. Taking a step back, he flexed his knees once then, fixing his eyes on the section of wood immediately below the key hole, he brought the heel of his shoe crashing against the door. Wood splintered and, slamming his shoulder against it, he fell through into her house. Forgetting all his training, Jon blundered onwards, down the corridor and in to the front room.

Ellie lay on the floor, arms out at her sides, eyes rolled up into her head. His momentum had carried him several steps across the carpet, and Jon began to turn, knowing he had exposed himself to an attack from behind. Something crashed onto the back of his neck.

Purple flooded his vision and he dropped to his knees, the jarring impact snapping his head to the side and sending a wave of pins and needles shooting up his spine. He felt himself falling to the side, but was unable to raise his hands to cushion the fall.

Tom turned the glue gun round in his hands so the solid metal plunger faced outwards. The voices screamed their encouragement and he raised the implement high in to the air, ready to smash it down onto the man's skull with all his strength. But then he saw the large number seven on his back. Slowly, his eyes moved up to the man's face.

Kill him!

Tom remained still, his lips barely moving. "But it's Jon. I know this man. He's wearing your number. What should I do? He's wearing your number."

The colour began to melt away from Jon's vision and he found himself kneeling with his upper body half slumped forward on the sofa. Looking down, Ellie's face was inches from his. He watched as she breathed slowly out. Then he heard Tom plead behind him, "But he's wearing your number. I cannot."

Footsteps suddenly ran from the room and out of the house. Using the arm of the sofa, Jon got unsteadily to his feet. There was barely any feeling in his legs and, as he took his first tottering steps, he wasn't sure if his knees would buckle. But his legs held firm, growing stronger each time he felt a foot connect with the floor. By the time he reached the front door, he could feel the adrenaline pumping right down to his toes. He jogged down Ellie's path. A rocket exploded in the sky above him and, through the sheets of rain, he was just able to see a figure running round the corner at the end of the street. Jon exploded on to the pavement, sprinting the first sixty metres without taking a breath. He reached the end of the road and looked up to see the silhouette cutting towards the A6.

"Tom!" he yelled at the top of his voice.

Tom glanced over his shoulder and saw Jon closing on him fast. He cried out for guidance and was told to run for the main road. Reaching the pavement, he looked to his side. Down the road an eighteen-ton Argos lorry trundled towards him. He knew that its thirty-foot-long container would be packed with every type of household item imaginable. Enough merchandise to meet demand at the Manchester store for less than a week.

Tom strode purposefully across the lanes and into the vehicle's path. Raising the palms of his hands outwards, he closed his eyes and commanded the vehicle to halt. He felt the power of the Masters coursing down his arms and imagined the light that must be crackling from his fingertips.

At the kerb, Jon could only watch as the driver stamped on his brakes. Rain pouring off the vehicle's mudflaps suddenly flew forward on a diagonal trajectory under the vehicle's huge tyres. The lorry began to slide over the wet road surface. The first thing to connect with

Tom's outstretched hands was the grille below the cab. As both arms were driven out of his shoulder sockets, a moving wall of metal slammed into his face and chest. Like some grotesque mascot pinioned to the vehicle, he was carried back for over forty feet, straight past Jon, before the vehicle slowed enough to let him slip down.

As his head slammed against the tarmac, Tom's right eye opened a fraction, allowing him to see an infinite galaxy of brilliant stars. An instant later, the first tyre rolled directly over his head.

"Oh my God!" someone screamed.

A couple of people were jogging uncertainly to the motionless lorry, the driver already on his mobile phone.

Jon bent over his knees for a moment, breathing heavily after his sprint. Ellie. He must get back to her. He straightened up, turned and began walking back to her house, his pace quickening as a desire to distance himself from Tom's mangled corpse combined with concern for his sister. As he neared her house, he could see a woman approaching in the opposite direction. Alice. He held up an arm and she stopped running. "Jon! What's happened? Where's Ellie?"

"In here. We'll need an ambulance. She's been drugged." He took her hand and led her towards the open front door.

"Is it safe? Where's Tom?"

"Tom's gone."

The sight of Ellie on the carpet caused Jon to fall to his knees. He slid a hand under her head, lifted it up and pressed his cheek against hers. In the hallway he could hear Alice on the phone, demanding an ambulance. He hugged her close, rocking back and forth as if he was comforting a baby. After a few moments he felt Alice's arms curling round his head and the tears suddenly came.

Author's note

To chart Tom's descent into madness, I described symptoms that accompany various types of mental illness. The most notorious of these is probably the auditory hallucinations that many schizophrenics experience.

However, I wouldn't like any reader to make the mistake of believing schizophrenics are likely to be driven to murder by the voices they hear. (Sadly, they're far more likely to hurt themselves.) If any readers are wondering who is most likely to murder them, look to your family. Statistically, you're far, far more likely to be killed by a relative than a stranger suffering from schizophrenia.

For a very readable and illuminating description of schizophrenia, I recommend, *Schizophrenia: A very short introduction*, by Christopher Frith and Eve Johnstone.

The significance of seven obviously plays a pivotal part in the story. There is enough material about its repeated and mysterious occurrences throughout history to fill several books (and swathes of my references were wisely cut by my editor for the sake of pace!). Although the internet does provide a rich source of material on seven, much of my information, including Tom's belief in The Masters, is based unashamedly on a theory put forward by Geoffrey Ashe in *The Ancient Wisdom*.

Also available in ISIS Large Print:

Strange Blood

Lindsay Ashford

A worthy new talent **Guardian**

Women are dying with pentagrams carved on their faces. Satanic ritual or cunning deception?

Forensic psychologist Megan Rhys is called in to help police investigate what they believe is a ritual killing. She feels that prejudice is taking the inquiry in the wrong direction and she is suspicious of the media-obsessed police chief in charge of the case.

As more women die — and as the press, the police, her boss and her own family turn on her — Megan stakes everything on finding the killer.

ISBN 0-7531-7477-4 (hb)
ISBN 0-7531-7478-2 (pb)

The Forest of Souls

Carla Banks

Gripping, vivid and moving — an excellent mystery which combines the resonance and drama of the Second World War with page-turning suspense
Laura Wilson

A passion for history had already cost Helen Kovacs her marriage. Now she's paid with her life. Helen had told no one of her research into the Nazi occupation of Eastern Europe. Even her closest friend, Faith Lange, had no idea — until she began retracing the dead woman's steps. Though the police have a suspect in custody, Faith is convinced that the murderer is still at large. She is troubled, too, by the presence of Jake Denbigh, a journalist who appears to be investigating Faith's grandfather, a refugee from the Eastern front.

Jake and Faith undertake terrifying journeys through their investigations: from the mass graves of the Kurapaty Forest to the heart of Faith's own family, where a tragic secret lies hidden.

ISBN 0-7531-7487-1 (hb)
ISBN 0-7531-7488-X (pb)